Eye of the Magpie

JAN PIERS

MAP SHOWING POINTS OF INTEREST WEST OF
THE CITY OF EDMONTON

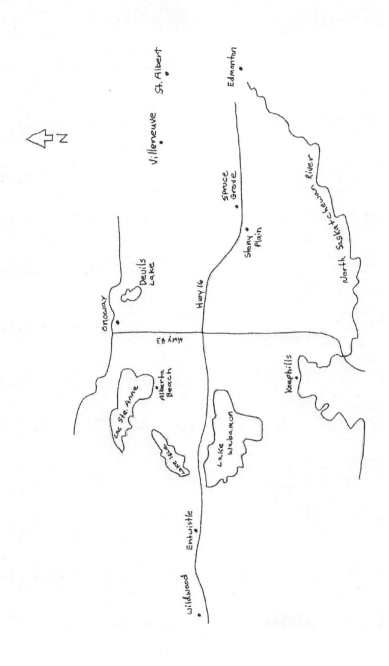

For Dad, who taught me the magic and the power of words and for Mom
who taught me to believe in myself

Copyright © 2018 Jan Piers

ISBN-13:978-1721834013

Front cover image by Joelle Johnson

Map and author photograph by Adrian Pearce

ACKNOWLEDGMENTS

This book would never have been written without the support and encouragement of a village: Can Lit teachers of high school days, the many, many Creative Writing teachers I have met over a lifetime, NaNoWriMo Edmonton, family members close by and far away and my many wonderful friends. You are all part of the rich fabric of my life, some providing golden threads, others, multi-hued.

Particularly, a big thank Danielle Metcalfe-Chenail for her quiet, unwavering encouragement and my husband, Adrian Pearce, for his unflagging belief in me and undaunted support. You believed even when I faltered.

Without Cathy (C J) Johnston's repeated questioning of 'is it finished yet? When can I read it?" I might still be procrastinating over writing this novel. Thank you, C J for your boundless enthusiasm and many suggestions to improve the story. Nancy Milakovic gave me excellent feedback on characters, timelines and nitty details. Thank you for your encouragement, insights and discerning eye. Kathy Friederichsen and I discussed research into psychopaths during the writing of the manuscript. She has an eye for detail and grammar, improving the flow of the story and she asked pointed questions on characters and motivations that had me strengthening the storyline. Hats off to you, Kathy, for your help.

Thanks also to Janet Ruffell for her excitement and feedback. You were an invaluable spell checker. Finally, I would like to thank my two editing sisters, Kathy York and Susan Hall, for their help in making the storyline flow more smoothly and their technical prowess.

In closing, thank you, Dear Reader, for choosing my book. I hope you find it enjoyable and a worthwhile read. The book entwines three themes: you may cry out at the horrors inflicted by a psychopath intent only on feeding his demented appetites, then chuckle over the light-heartedness of a contented rural life, then rail against the injustices of society. I guess that is the quintessence of life as I view it.

Love to All,

Jan Piers

1 PITCH-BLACK

It is very late, almost midnight. Standing at the kitchen sink, hands plunged into hot soapy water filled with her greasy frying pan, Glenda McTavish can hear a few coyotes calling back and forth in the moonless night. Her husband, Dave Ellis, is working out of town and their baby, Connor, has finally fallen asleep. Where she desperately wants to be, instead of here, standing with her hands in dishwater.

Suddenly chills run down her spine, she peers out into the blackness. Of course, she can't see anything. Shivering, feeling that she is being watched in a malicious way, she quickly steps away from the window. Glenda checks all the doors and windows to assure herself they are locked. Before re-entering the kitchen, she turns out the light. There is no curtain here to pull shut and she scans the darkness in vain. The fear leaves her, she shakes her head at her foolishness as she turns on the dishwasher. She quickly goes to bed, sure the baby will have her up in a few hours.

Her next day is quiet. As is the next. Life on maternity leave has not turned out to be as exciting as she had expected. Her days are filled with only herself and her baby, Connor. She muses over the baby's name. The Ellis pregnancy had been a high-risk one. They had not followed all the usual rituals of most young couples expecting their first child. If it had not been for their friends, family and co-workers, even her loyal fans from the television station, then they might not have had a blanket to wrap around their newborn. And they certainly had not discussed baby names. Glenda was still sleeping in the recovery room when the nurses pressured Dave to register the birth. How he came up with Connor, Glenda had no idea. Happily, little Connor is growing into his name.

Glenda gave herself a project to keep herself busy while on leave; she loved to cook and had always wanted to write a cookbook. She was already a chapter behind according to her pre-birth schedule and resented the news

1

stories that took Dave out of town, leaving her to fend with the newborn on her own.

Finally, the weekend arrives and Dave returns home. They visit with their neighbours, Aimee and Kyle Brace, for a Friday night barbecue. Both couples live in the same acreage development, just off Highway 43, not far from Onoway. Both families have newborns. The women have been friends since high school. Dave and Kyle have become close pals since being introduced to each other by their sweethearts. Dave is a videographer at the same television station where Glenda works. Kyle, a webmaster, is a super technical person. They both enjoy photography, camping and cycling and often spend their spare time together on one of those passions.

The men are settled on the warm back deck with beers and babies as the women chat in the kitchen. Aimee has gone quiet, she seems lost in some thought. Glenda tries small-talk to get her back to her bubbly self.

"So, how's your Mom?" she asks.

"Oh, she's fine. She and Dad have taken the RV. They're headed to the Grand Canyon. They were going to go in the fall but with Dad just retired they decided to go early."

"Oh? So, are you looking after their place while they're gone?"

"Yep. Someone broke into Dad's shop. Looks like they slept there. Another weird thing is that there's an old dead tree behind his shop up a way back in the woods. Someone's used it for target practice."

"You mean with a gun?" asked Glenda, her eyes going wide.

"Hmm, maybe a rifle. You heard about the couple that were shot at in their home? Over on the other side of Onoway. Just this past week?"

"No, I didn't."

"Honestly, Glenda! For someone who is a television anchor, delivering the news to the city and us humble country folk every weekday morning, you'd think you'd keep up."

Glenda giggled, then said haughtily, "I am on maternity leave I'll have you know; I don't technically have to keep up. And I am working on my cookbook. And I am a new mother." Aimee chortled at her. Glenda added, "was anything stolen from your Dad, is the couple okay?"

"No, Dad's stuff is fine. It's just weird that someone was there. The couple were watching TV late at night. They're on their own farm. The house is fairly close to the road and I guess anyone going by could see they were there as they had not drawn the curtains. Someone was in the woods across from it on a slight hill and they had a direct shot into their living room. The bullet sliced through the picture window, which by the way smashed everywhere and then the bullet lodged into the wall a few inches away from their heads. It was on all the local radio stations and picked up by the TV stations in the city. Your eyes have gone big as saucers, Glenda. The RCMP put it down to a drive-by shooting and they were not interested in my tree that was shot at behind my folks' place."

Glenda's eyebrows shot up, "well, your folks' place is south of here and that's north so there wouldn't be much of a connection," she answered, on autopilot, visualizing an imaginary line that had their acreage development dead in its centre.

A few days later Aimee phoned Glenda.

"Can you come with me to my folks' place? I just need to check on it and I'm nervous about going out there on my own."

With both babies in carseats, the friends drove south in Aimee's truck.

"Aimee Brace, I have never known you to be afraid of anything. What gives?"

Aimee shot her a sharp glance.

"You haven't been listening to the news, have you?" Glenda shook her head. "Well, last week they found the body of an Aboriginal woman in a gravel pit by Spruce Grove. She was half-naked, had been beaten and raped and strangled to death."

"Wow, no, I had not heard. That's terrible. Did they identify her? Is she a local person?"

Despite the seriousness of the conversation, Aimee laughed. "You are in reporter-mode, Glenda. Yes, she is from one of the bands around here. Her name was Alice Grant. She was known to the police, which means she probably worked in the sex trade at some point. She was a mother. And someone's sister. She had two small children."

Glenda stayed quiet to give Aimee her moment. She knew there would not be much of an investigation into this death. There was no one to call the authorities to task. As far as news would go, it would be a flash in the pan.

"You know, Aimee," she started, "I don't know what to say. I'm sorry to hear it happened. Did you know her family?"

"No, but that's not the point. Glenda, about a year ago, a woman over by Carvel was killed."

They were pulling into the familiar gravel driveway of the Cardinal's acreage. Aimee's parents, Josie and Winston had accepted Aimee's new high school friend and treated her as a second daughter. Glenda had spent a lot of time at the Cardinal house and enjoyed their relaxed home life. While she knew her own parents loved her, they were more reserved and liked things kept quieter than their boisterous teenage daughter would have liked. She enjoyed escaping to the Cardinals place.

Both baby boys were fast asleep. Aimee drove right up to the shade at the back door and they left the truck windows open. Aimee locked the doors with the key fob as the women left the truck, walking the few steps to the door.

Glenda picked up the conversation, "was the Carvel victim First Nations as well?"

"No, she wasn't. A rifle shot was fired through her kitchen window as she was washing dishes, about eight at night on a February evening."

The goosebumps that ran up Glenda's back and arms could not be explained by standing in the cool shadow of the back porch. A faint breeze fanned the pair while Aimee fumbled to find the key to her folks' door and open it. Glenda was glumly thinking that eight o'clock on a February evening in Alberta would be just as dark as midnight in the middle of the June.

Aimee shot a glance over to her friend, "well, you're whiter than ever," she said, pushing the door open and ushering them in. "You stay here and keep an eye on the babies. I'll do a walk around and water Mom's plants."

Glenda found herself standing at the kitchen sink, looking out at the huge backyard beyond Aimee's truck. She was not really focusing on anything she could see. She had spent a lot of time at the Cardinals' place since befriending Aimee and had always felt it was a safe, protected place. Her mind was spinning. Aimee came by and shooed her from the sink to fill a watering can.

"You did say that the drive-by north of Onoway was committed with a rifle as well?" Glenda asked.

"Yep," she said, setting the watering can on the counter, "let's get the boys and go to Dad's shop."

One of the boys had awoken and begun to cry. The women picked up their babies and crossed the sunny backyard. The scene was idyllic. The grass glistened with last night's rain, the vegetable and flower gardens looked fresh and cool. Two beautiful women, one dark, the other light, bounded across the verdant lawn, their hair glistening in the sunlight.

"Aimee, have there been more signs of someone sleeping in the shed?" Glenda asked.

"Maybe," she answered, "I'm not sure. That's why there are two of us checking."

Glenda stopped dead. They were halfway across the yard heading towards the shop. "And what would two buxom women, carrying babies, do to an intruder?" she asked her friend.

From a few steps ahead of her, Aimee answered, "well, I haven't seen anyone here in the daytime, and I don't think there's someone here all the time, so we'll just go take a quick, little look-see."

The shed's door was unlocked. The women hesitated, looking at each other, Aimee pushed the door open for them to go in, "Trevor's cries will have scared anyone away by now," she shrugged.

Aimee said she thought someone had been in the shop although nothing seemed amiss. She was sure she had locked the door, as always, yet once again she was mystified to find it unlocked. Nothing was missing or even seemed to have been moved. They carefully locked the door and double-checked it. Glenda headed back to the truck.

"Wait a sec, Glenda. Come look at the tree."

About six feet into the woods stood a dead pine. It was tall, with a good girth. A lightning strike had killed it. Now besides the twisted black upper branches, its lower trunk was pitted on either side from repeated rifle blasts.

"Did you look around for casings?" Glenda asked her friend.

"Yes, I even used Dad's metal detector. But I didn't find anything."

The two women walked around a bit then looked at each other. A magpie suddenly scolded them from somewhere overhead, startling both of them.

"Let's get out of here," Glenda said, looking about, then chuckling. They began walking towards the truck. Glenda felt goosebumps on her arms. She began walking with more purpose and both of them were practically running by the time they got to the pickup. Giggling, they strapped the babies into their carseats and Aimee spun gravel on their sharp turn out of there.

Glenda knew Aimee was driving just a tad faster than normal. They went past their turn and headed into Stony Plain and ordered brewed teas at Tim Horton's.

"Okay, since I noticed that tree, I've never headed straight home after leaving Mom and Dad's place," confessed Aimee. "I don't think I'm being followed but I have to think of Trevor and not just myself," she added. She looked up at Glenda with pleading brown eyes.

"You know, Dave could hook up one of his wildlife cameras to a motion-detector and we could set it up in the shop and see anyone that may go there," suggested Glenda. "And I'm not so sure if it's such a good idea for you to go to your folk's place alone, or even with me along. We need a big guy, with a big stick, to go with you to check it out."

"I could ask my cousin next time," Aimee suggested.

"So, if I'm following the crumb trail that you have been dropping over the past week, Aimee, you are nervous because you think the Carvel murder, the drive-by shooting out past Onoway, and the gravel pit murder are all connected?" Glenda asked, as she patted baby Connor's back.

"Yep," she acknowledged, "and I bet that if we got Roger Lafontaine to check his files, there'll be more."

"Well I can see the drive-by shooting and Carvel murder connected. How do you think the gravel pit murder fits in?"

Aimee shrugged, "I don't know. It's just a gut feeling. That's why I'm curious about the newspaper files."

Roger Lafontaine was the owner and editor of the only independent local newspaper in their rural part of Alberta. Well into his seventies, he sat on a gold mine of local information and gossip. He was a cantankerous old man full of conspiracy theories who also happened not to like Aboriginal people. Aimee's Mom was full-blood Native American, her Dad was Métis. Glenda spoke the unspoken request aloud.

"So, you want me to contact him and start digging?"

"Yep, I'll babysit," she offered with a smile.

"It's a deal if you help me make one of your willow arbours," responded Glenda.

"I'll even throw in a willow chair," Aimee promised, locking the agreement.

2 COUNTY BLUE

It took three days before Roger answered Glenda's calls. He had been away on a fishing trip and offered her whitefish when they finally connected.

"Huh, no thanks Roger. Say, I'm working on a story to do with drive-by shootings out here in the country and I wondered if you'd let me poke through your files to see if I can find out how long this has been going on."

"Yup," acknowledged Roger, "Least ways as long as people had pickups, I'd say. Remember when the year I got married, old man Mathews had his eye shot out standing on his front porch. Never wore a patch. Ugliest scar I ever seen. When you want to come over?"

"How about tomorrow afternoon?"

"'Okay, got that catch filleted and frozen. Give you a couple then. See you at one."

Glenda reported her appointment to Aimee, adding, "and you'll have to take the fish. Dave won't eat it. Will Kyle?"

"Yum, yum," said Aimee chuckling. "Kyle will eat whatever is put in front of him. You and I can have a supper of it sometime when they're both working out of town. Winter whitefish is better'n summer but free whitefish is free whitefish!"

On her way into Stony Plain to visit Roger, Glenda kept reminding herself to pick up some teething gel for Connor before going home. The little guy had a front tooth trying to come in that was making him cranky.

Once Glenda had the file room to herself, she began poking around in earnest. Roger, out of stubbornness, had nothing on the computer and eschewed microfiche. In some ways, doing research at his place was easier though, as he made multiple copies of notes and articles and filed them by various topics, with sometimes the same article in five or six places.

There were several homicide folders. Glenda paged through them quickly. She noticed that for the majority of them no one had been charged.

There was no closure.

"Hey, Roger," she called, looking out her door across the hallway to his office, "can you take a look at this?"

Roger came bounding into the room, trailing nylon fishing line. He had been wrapping a hand-made fly.

"What's up? Find a spider?" he grinned.

"No," said Glenda casting her eyes about, just in case. "I've found a bunch of folders on homicides and most were never solved. Or is there another file, maybe under court house?" she asked.

Holding the fly in one hand and pliers in the other, Roger came loping across to the desk and looked over Glenda's shoulder at the opened folders.

"Naw, most of those were not solved. Some really grisly ones too. Like Ed Boyko, the poor bastard. That one there, the Doherty's, their own son killed them and torched their house. Took a long time for the RCMP to figure it out and catch him. Personally, I think some of those were committed by truckers passing through."

Glenda gave him a searching look.

"What? You ever hear of a psychopath? Truckers can be psychopaths too, you know." Roger used the flat part of his palm to spread the files out a bit. "This one here, twin Native girls. Too weird to have been a human. I know, I know, 'ya don't believe in UFOs but I'm telling you this one was aliens for sure."

Glenda managed a small smile. "Thanks Roger. Can I make photocopies? I'll pay you for them."

"Yeah, sure, a nickel a page," he said, just now realizing the nylon line had strung along with him down the hall from his office and across to the file room. Trailing a wake of swears, he straightened up, made an about face and tried to wind the monofilament with the hand that held the pliers as he left the office.

There wasn't a file on drive-by shootings. After much digging she found a file labelled "Conspiracy Theories" and there, amongst pranks, crop circles and reports of UFO sightings, is where she hit pay-dirt. Glenda photocopied over three dozen articles that went back about thirty years. Later she would weed out the chaff.

She searched for Roger before leaving; he was still at his desk working on his fly-tying. "Roger, I lost count on the photocopies but it was a lot. I had to load in more paper. How does twenty dollars sound?"

Roger's head popped up to look at her, "sure, that'll be fine. And I'll toast one of the beers I buy with it to you and yours," he said laughing. "Just make sure the door closes behind you, I'll lock up once I'm done this."

Glenda waved goodbye and popped into the nearby drug store for Connor's teething gel. She mused that this was her favorite drugstore ever.

It still had an old country charm to it, having never lost its small-town appeal, yet it offered just about anything the big chain stores had and there were people willing to help you find things. She went home feeling happy with her time spent in town.

3 TIGER EYE

Jim Drucker, owner of Drucker's Drug Store, noticed Glenda as she came in. He smiled upon seeing her. Glenda was tall at almost six feet, with beautiful long copper hair that waved in a perfect frame around her beautiful face then fell to her ample bosom. She had large green eyes that shone with intelligence and full ruby red lips. He thought she had perfect legs, long, sleek and muscular. Glenda had not approached the pharmacy area and they did not speak.

The last time Jim had seen Glenda was through the scope of his rifle. She seemed to sense something and had left the kitchen. He had mused about that, how some people seem to have a sixth sense and know he was out there, watching them while most were oblivious. He knew he wouldn't shoot, she was a lady like his late Aunt Doris. Respectable. Jim had decided then and there to give her a wide berth.

Hell, she was a looker, thought Jim. He no longer kept regular hours at the store and felt it was a treat to have caught a glimpse of her while working.

Jim wondered how he had missed her growing up. He had only one memory of an encounter with her: she was about fourteen and she was walking her bike on the shoulder of highway 43. It had a flat and she was miles away from home. He had stopped and chatted with her and even offered her a ride. She had refused and determinately set off on foot. Jim had chuckled when he drove away. He stopped at Alberta Beach, a summer village that had the nearest convenience store, and he bought a bicycle pump, then drove back and gave it to her with a wink, before driving off.

4 ECRU

The next morning Glenda went to Aimee's house with her copies. Kyle and Aimee lived in a large, two-storey. Inside the front door was a landing with a large closet for coats and two short sets of stairs, one going up to the main level and one down to the basement. Aimee set them up in the basement's family room. The land fell away behind the house. The family room had sliding glass doors that opened onto the patio and it was shaded most of the summer, when the sun was high in the Alberta sky, by the deck above off the dining room. Even in the worst heat wave, this room remained cool. Glenda noticed that Aimee had pulled out the big blackboard they had used together for school projects, and mats were laid on the floor by the outside glass sliding doors and that there were two huge boxes in front of the couch.

Aimee set down the tray with tea, fruit and cookies on the coffee table while Glenda lay the boys down on their tummies on the mats, facing the outdoors. They could get some exercise holding up their heads and trying to roll over.

"Good idea, pulling out the mats for the boys, Aimee," Glenda said.

"Oh, they can use them for now, I pulled them out for us. C'mere, I got you a gift."

Glenda walked over to the couch. "Pour moi? What's the occasion?" she asked.

"You and I need to get back into shape. It's a jogging stroller. I called Miss Malik over at the high school and we can jog around the track with our new strollers any weekday from seven thirty to nine in the morning. If we're going to chase down bad guys, then it's a good idea that we can actually run."

Glenda sighed. "I thought those laps around the acreage development while pregnant would be it for a while," she complained.

"Well you stopped at seven and a half months, yes, I know, because the doctor insisted on it. I jogged the full nine months, through a freezing winter," Aimee said accusingly. "And besides, you'll need your svelte figure back once your maternity leave is over and I get to have both boys to myself," she added.

The two best friends had a pre-pregnancy agreement: once Glenda returned to work she would pay her friend handsomely to watch the baby and cook a few meals a week for her and Dave. Aimee had no plans to return as a paralegal to the firm in Stony Plain, where she had been employed since graduating college.

"And I think we should practice our Tai Kwan Do too, it may come in handy."

"Huh, with babies in tow, what exactly do you think you and I are going to get up to, Miss Nancy Drew?" asked Glenda.

"Let's just be prepared. Have a cookie for now. I raided them from Mom's freezer."

"Okay, thanks. You know I love Mama Josie's baking. Let's get through these newspaper files. Good idea to pull out the blackboard," said Glenda, happy for the change of subject.

With time needed to care for their young babies and some difficulty with reading the photocopied handwritten notes, it took them three days to look at all the papers. On the third day, breaking for lunch outside on the patio, Glenda was reminded of the many times they crammed together for exams. They came back indoors and Aimee took her place at the blackboard. Glenda scanned each of the piles of notes and clippings they had made. "I think we can discount this pile," she said, "it mostly deals with shootouts of signs, lights, mailboxes, that sort of thing. We can ignore it for now."

"Now this pile is interesting. It's the H.M. pile, for Helen Majeau's bylines on the clipped articles. She kept a list of her news stories that dealt with drive-by shootings and another list of murders They span the time she worked for Roger at the Parkland Examiner. She recorded the dates of the event, then the weather, then The Examiner publishing date and page number... Let's put them up and see if we can find anything that correlates. I'll read them out to you ... hmm, this is interesting. I'm seeing a lot of notes saying 'dark night, dry weather.' I wonder if she is referring to the new moon, that is when the night sky is at its darkest. What phase was the moon in for our recent events, I wonder?" Aimee moved her hand holding the chalk to the top left-hand corner and notated 'check on moon phase for recent events.'

Once all the dates were up with pertinent information from the newspaper clippings, both of them stood facing the board to see if any patterns were emerging.

"Other than the new moon thing, I got nothing," Glenda finally said.

She pulled out her cellphone and took a picture of their work on the blackboard.

"'K, me neither. Let's do other things and let it percolate in the grey matter," agreed Aimee, as she picked up both babies and handed them to Glenda. "I'll go first. You watch and see if you can keep up when it's your turn."

Glenda griped, "Aimee you know well enough I won't be able to," she said with a chuckle. "You're the natural athlete, not me. Okay, okay, don't worry. I'll give it a try." Aimee came off the trampoline, grabbed the babies and waved Glenda on. Glenda did her best to mimic her friend.

"I'll pick you up tomorrow at eight and we'll try out the strollers then. Let's have another turn each and call it quits for today," she said, skipping past a breathless Glenda to the floor mats.

The next day, once they figured out the strollers and began their stroll/jog, Glenda said, "you know, I think there is a sort of pattern in those dates. But it's not precise. There's a rash of drive-by shootings, then a murder, then nothing. Sometimes there's no shootings and yet a murder, and then a rash of drive-by shootings. I'm not sure what it all means."

"If it's the work of one person …," began Aimee, "I think the classic serial criminal tends to up the ante; crimes become closer and closer together as time goes on. They're like addicts, they need their rush but we aren't seeing that pattern."

"Hmm, serial killers are psychopaths, Aimee, and I'm not sure that they are like junkies. I think that's just Hollywood's take on them."

"Could be."

"I tell you what, I'll get some books and do some research," said Glenda

"And Glenda, lots of people take pot-shots at road signs. I don't really think we can include them into our data."

"Right. I'm going to check with Roger when we get back and see if Helen Majeau is still around. I have a lot of questions for her about her data."

5 PERIWINKLE

After a few phone calls, Glenda connected with Helen Majeau in a retirement home in St. Albert. She made an appointment to go see her the next day.

The apartment was small yet made bright by a large window behind the dining table and with a sliding glass door that led to a small balcony next to it in the living room. The rooms were decorated in a modern style with lots of glass and chrome and in bright colours. The balcony sported plastic rattan chairs and a small table. Walking in, Glenda noticed a magpie at a bird feeder in the corner of the balcony. Suddenly a small flock of sparrows appeared and noisily dispatched the intruder.

Helen, a small, fit woman in her seventies who could easily pass for someone ten years younger, had curly, steely grey hair and brown eyes that took in everything, reflecting back her reactions. She laughed at the birds and explained to Glenda that she thought the magpie was old and too weak to hunt for itself, so it looked for easy meals. It had visited more than once and was often chased away by the tiny sparrows.

She ushered Glenda and Connor into her living room where she had set out a pitcher of lemonade and oatmeal cookies. She cooed and rocked Connor while Glenda sipped her lemonade.

"Miss Majeau," began Glenda, getting down to business. She was immediately interrupted and told to use 'Helen' with a smile from the former reporter.

"Okay, well, Helen, this may sound really silly to you, but my friend Aimee Brace and myself are looking at old newspaper records to see if there's any kind of pattern or connection. This is to do with drive-by shootings out in the counties of Parkland and the southern part of Lac Ste. Anne." Glenda paused and smiled, gauging Helen Majeau's reaction. Deadpan, except for her eyes that looked inquisitive. Taking a deep breath,

14

she continued, "we came across some articles you wrote for the Parkland Examiner to do with murders and drive-by shootings," she said, handing over some photocopies.

"Oh, my," Helen said softly, looking them over, then in a normal tone, she asked, "whatever got you involved in all of this?" looking Glenda straight in the eye.

"Well, we live on an acreage close to Onoway," Glenda paused before continuing.

"My husband was out of town and Connor had been fussy all day. It was late at night and I was finally doing the day's dishes. While on Mat Leave I am trying out new recipes for a cookbook I am hoping to publish. My kitchen sink looks out onto the road, it's a good three hundred feet away and I just had goosebumps all of a sudden. I felt like I was in the cross-hairs of someone's rifle." Glenda stopped again, gauging Helen's reaction. Helen smiled but her eyes looked anxious.

"What did you do then?" she asked.

"I looked straight out the window. I backed away from it and went and checked that the doors were locked and I closed and locked the windows. I checked on Connor then went back to the kitchen. I turned the light out before going to the sink. I was no longer spooked but I closed and locked the window by the sink anyways. There's no curtain on it to pull shut. Then I left the pan to soak and went to bed. Later that night there was a drive-by shooting at a farm on the other side of Onoway, and the next week a woman's body was found in a gravel pit. She was raped and strangled to death."

Helen still bore a non-committal expression on her face. Her eyes had widened. Glenda continued, "I thought I was just being hormonal. I'm not usually the jumpy type. The feeling was so strong, like when someone is staring at you in public. I've been wondering about it for a while now."

"Have you told anyone about it? A friend or your husband?"

"No. I'm a very self-reliant person. I like to think that I am an objectional person. I can't see how anyone could believe that because I felt something happened, that it actually did happen. Then my friend, Aimee, told me about the two incidents I just mentioned, that she heard about on the news. I really haven't listened to the news or public affairs since Connor was born," she added, with a small smile. "I'll pick that up again soon. Anyways, Aimee was watching over her folks' place while they were away and had me come with her. She thought someone was using her dad's shop and she found a tree, blasted by rifle fire behind it. This caused her alarm and she is not easily intimidated. She has had someone go with her whenever she checks on the place ever since."

"Do you think someone was there?"

"Yes, for a while anyways. I went with her once and the shop door was unlocked. Aimee would never leave it unlocked while her parents were away. When we went inside she thought someone had been there although I couldn't tell either way. Our husbands went out on the weekend and set up a wildlife camera on a motion detector for her. The next time she went, there was nothing recorded on the camera. She does not think there has been any activity at her Dad's shop since our visit. However, she now has someone with her whenever she goes and rather than return straight home, she always goes into Stony Plain or Spruce Grove first. She lives in the same acreage development where I live, just off Highway 43."

"So that's how you know each other?"

"No," replied Glenda with a smile. "We've been best friends for a long time, ever since high school. We were each other's maid of honour. We're very close, we're like sisters," she smiled at Helen.

Helen returned her smile and took a moment to digest it all.

"Well, if I can judge you by your work on television and this fine young fellow, then I'd say you are a respectable citizen that I can trust. I too wondered if there was some kind of connection between these random shootings, at signs or people's houses and the murders that were never solved," Helen looked up from the baby in her lap and caught Glenda's eye.

"I noticed a pattern emerging over years while I worked for Roger. I retired many years ago. I had been reporting about twenty years of shenanigans that had been going on in the community. There were even more murders in the last ten years since then." Helen looked Glenda straight in the eye.

"I noted three categories of victims. Those of women, and a high proportion were Aboriginal, anywhere in age from teenagers to forty or fifty years old: poor, unknown, perhaps unemployed. Usually these victims were beaten and raped and left bound and partially naked. Some were not tied up, though. All were strangled with an item of their own clothing. The grizzliest murders were ones of both men and women, horribly tortured, often knifed, or strangled. The bodies sometimes were burnt. The clean murders all appeared to be drive-by types, a clean shot through a kitchen or a living room window.

Out in the country there are always random shootings at signs or barns. I kept a tally of shootings at people's houses. There were quite a few, some even in the coldest months. They mostly happened at night, under the cover of darkness. Eight or nine o'clock in the winter, eleven or midnight in the summer. Very few happened later than those times if I remember correctly. Most were non-fatal. The fatal ones, ..., well, ... it seemed to me that most were either middle-aged housewives, forty-five or so, innocently sitting watching TV or standing up at a window. Or they were older men, usually known to be difficult or cantankerous."

Glenda shivered noticeably. "The couple that were shot at were watching TV. They're in their late forties or early fifties. Ms. Majeau, did you ever take your data to the authorities? Were they investigating it?"

"It's Helen and you're making me laugh. You sound just like a news reporter right now. Yes, I've shown it to the authorities. No one is interested. The fatal shootings never happened in clusters, close together in time or in place. The RCMP officers that I talked to didn't feel there was a pattern or that it was the same person committing the crime.

"They said things to me like, go play detective somewhere else and don't come back here bugging us about dead Indians. Don't look so outraged; police forces today are under-funded and under-manned and will shoo away whatever they can, just to keep their heads above water," retorted Helen to Glenda's look of disbelief.

"We found this in Roger's file," Glenda handed Helen the list of events that had four columns: the event, its date, the corresponding weather conditions and the Parkland Examiner edition information. "Did you make this list?"

Helen took the paper and peered at it, her hand moving to cover her mouth. She had that anxious look in her eyes again.

"Goodness, I thought I had taken all my notes out of Roger's files," she said. Glenda took back the photocopy of the handwritten page.

"So, this is yours. Do you have more data? Can I see it?" asked Glenda.

Helen did not answer. After a moment of silence, she said, "now this little guy, I think he needs a change. It's time to give him back to his mama."

Helen handed Connor back to Glenda. Glenda changed the baby and took her leave noting Helen's reticence to continue the conversation. As she said goodbye, she asked if Helen would agree to a follow-up phone call later if she had new questions. After a beat, Helen nodded yes. Her eyes had a faraway look in them.

6 CANARY

The next day, Aimee's parents came home early. Josie, Aimee's mom, had fallen and broke her wrist while on vacation. Aimee went daily to help out; an infection had set in and Josie was in a lot of pain. A few times Glenda went with her friend to help out as well. Josie was on antibiotics and painkillers and could not use the arm at all.

On a Tuesday, both women headed over to the Cardinal's place after their rounds at the track. Aimee could now jog five miles, or twenty times around the track. Glenda could easily jog a few miles and doggedly kept going, albeit at a much slower pace, until Aimee had finished her five miles. The friends planned to weed the Cardinal's huge garden before heading home to their own chores.

Josie sat with the boys on a blanket and was chatting with the weeding women when her husband, Winston, arrived back from town with a prescription refill for her. He hollered a hello from his pickup and walked over to the garden.

"You girls look hot. What say we take a break? I'll make us some grilled cheese sandwiches and lemonade for lunch. Josie, you still got some gingersnap cookies in the freezer?"

Both 'girls' started giggling. Josie shot them a look as she struggled to her feet.

"Yep, if they haven't already been raided that is," she said, following her husband into the house.

"Oh, you hot thing, you!" teased Glenda to Aimee as they walked towards the blanket. Aimee struck a sexy pose. "Yep. And we'll have gingersnaps too. I only raided the peanut butter and the chocolate macadamia nut cookies while they were gone." Both women collapsed on the blanket with hoots of laughter. The babies, unsure of what was going on, joined in with grins and chuckles of their own.

They finally settled down and scooping up the boys, headed indoors.

"Smells good Dad," said Aimee as they stepped in.

"Yep. Be ready soon. I'm just explaining to your mom that the pharmacist says she should take the painkillers round the clock, and not wait until she feels she needs them because they won't be very effective if she lets the pain build up too long."

"How is Mr. Drucker anyways? He's a real character, isn't he? Aimee, remember last New Year's? He must have propositioned every woman at that party, including you and me, you never even really looked pregnant but I looked like a whale."

"He is a bachelor," said Josie, "so I guess that's alright if he chases the gals."

"He brought a hot date. Remember, Glenda? The red dress, the perfect long black hair and the shoes!"

"Oh, I remember those shoes. Six-inch black spikes all done up in red glitter. I don't think I could walk across the room in a pair of shoes like that. But did they have a fight? Did she leave? I don't remember her later on and wow, he was after every female in the room."

"Aw, he's okay," said Winston. "He supports the little league and stuff. And I spoke to the other pharmacist. He wasn't there."

"Yeah Dad, but he sure gets around. That girl was from Maskwacis. I think her name is Charlize or something like that. She was home for Christmas from New York, where she is a model. And she's only about seventeen. And he's what, fifty something? And she ditched him. I heard him call her a squaw and she told him where …"

"Now that is enough!" said Josie, cutting her daughter off. You two girls just stop your gossiping right now."

"Yes Mama," both girls chorused, with Glenda adding a 'Josie' to her mama. Then they both burst out laughing.

Winston cut into the conversation before Josie could show more of her ire.

"Sandwiches are ready. Josie, do you have any pickles? Girls grab me some plates and stop cutting the poor guy up."

"Okay Dad, but only if you cut me one of those sandwiches," said Aimee.

That afternoon, Connor woke up early from his nap. Glenda turned her mind to more fun things as she cuddled, changed then fed the little guy.

In a few weeks' time, it would be Dave's birthday. She had a party to plan and shopping to do. She packed up her baby bag, grabbed Connor and his regular stroller, packed up the car and drove into the city. She thought she would pick up groceries then go to MEC – Mountain Equipment Co-op, Dave's favourite store, and maybe even grab a bite to eat somewhere chic.

Driving into Edmonton, she played classical music; Glenda was a music junkie and loved just about anything. She thought it wise to play the classics for Connor. She had selected "Carmen" and was excitedly anticipating Connor's reaction to its more dramatic moments. As he was in his carseat, in the backseat facing backwards, she had no idea what the effect of the music or her antics were having; she went with it anyways. The ride into Edmonton was uneventful although she did notice the RCMP had set up radar on the west side of Spruce Grove. She, happily, was travelling east.

Glenda stopped at Costco on the edge of the city and filled her coolers with her shopping. She then headed further into Edmonton. At MEC, Glenda soon gave up looking over camping and bike paraphernalia and drifted in and out of the shoe and women's clothing area. Still not having completely lost her baby bump, despite Aimee's fitness plan, she began feeling depressed, cut the visit short and just picked up a gift card for Dave. She decided to push baby Connor up the road for a while until she made up her mind on where to go for dinner. Really, she should have planned this trip to the city and called up some friends to join her. Oh well. Connor was happy in his stroller, watching the cars and pedestrians that they passed. Before long Glenda was at Stony Plain Road and she decided to go to The Manor for her meal. It was situated behind some businesses on the corner of 124th Street and Stony Plain Road in an old house and it had a superb dining patio.

It was early and the place was quiet. Glenda was seated outdoors, with lots of room for Connor's stroller. She ordered green tea and the pear pecan salad, a very chic and grownup dinner. Halfway through her meal the place began to fill up. A couple off to her right kept waving at Connor and she turned his stroller slightly to improve their line of vision. As she straightened back up, she heard her name being called out, "Glenda, what are you doing here?"

Walking onto the restaurant's patio was her Assignment Editor, Dianna with her husband, Joe. She smiled and waved them over.

"Oh, just some shopping in town," she answered, quickly wiping her mouth with her napkin, "for Dave's birthday party. Are you guys coming?"

"Wouldn't miss it. You look great. Can't wait to have you back!" said Dianna as she squeezed Glenda's arm and followed the waiter to their table.

Glenda enjoyed every bite of her dinner and paused over the pecans, which had been oven roasted. Perhaps she should experiment with that for her cookbook. She finished her tea and signalled for the bill. Soon Connor would be wanting his own dinner, it was time to go. She paid quickly, stood, looking around for Dianna. They were sitting at the back of the patio, with glasses raised in a toast. She waved and headed out.

Connor began fussing as soon as he was placed in his carseat. Glenda hollered, "hang on little fella," as she grimly drove homeward. She pulled over at the first rest stop outside of the city limits to nurse him in relative privacy.

Sitting in the front seat of the car, Glenda looked all about her in the almost deserted rest stop. There was a huge truck parked parallel to the highway and a white pickup a little further ahead of it. After a while it registered on her brain that in Alberta white pickups were ubiquitous – you saw them everywhere. She wondered if that could be a featurette topic that she could pursue once she went back to work. She'd mention it to Dianna at the party.

Leaving the rest area Glenda noted that the white pickup was gone. On the drive home, she played a compilation Kyle had made for her, a '90s rock band medley and wondered at Connor's reaction. She hoped it was keeping him awake.

Glenda pulled up her long driveway. Half-way to the house, she noticed someone was sitting on her front deck. She soon recognized her friend Aimee and shouted a hello to her as she got out of the vehicle. Rescuing Connor from his carseat, she walked over to her friend.

"I just went for a run and stopped in. Your peonies are looking fantastic," Aimee gave her a hug and grabbed the baby from her.

"It's so nice to see you. Here are my keys. Can you open the door? I've got a cooler full of groceries to unload."

Aimee stayed and helped her friend unload and put away her groceries. Glenda updated Aimee on her research: there was a full moon when Alice Grant was killed.

Aimee then filled Glenda in on what she found out about Alice Grant. Alice had told friends she had a new boyfriend. That he was a local guy and he did not want her to talk about him to anyone. She had been dating him for almost two months. Apparently, they fought because she wanted him to come and meet some of her friends at the 02s Tap House and Grill in Stony and he kept putting her off, saying their friendship was private and she was not to tell anyone about it. Her friends thought he was a married man. Yet Alice kept saying he wasn't and that they'd be surprised when they found out who he was, like he was a big shot or something. All they knew about him was that he had gone to school in Stony Plain and that he drove a white pickup.

"Hmm, I was just thinking about Alberta men and their pickups – especially white ones. Well that could be a lot of guys, married or bachelors. It doesn't really narrow things down for us, does it?" said Glenda.

"It does tell us it is most likely someone local that, at least in Alice Grant's case, is the perpetrator."

"Yes, you are right Aimee."

"Well, get some sleep, I'm going to head home. See you early tomorrow."

Glenda walked Aimee out of doors. Just then, Dave pulled into the driveway and waved to the women. As he walked towards them he shouted, "Aimee, be safe walking home. Or better yet, let me give you a ride. This guy in a pickup just about ran me off the road on my way in, he was going so fast."

Aimee and Glenda looked at each other. "Wow, this afternoon, I was just contemplating about doing a featurette on pickups in Alberta," Glenda told Dave.

"Don't worry, I'll be okay, Dave. I'm going to cut through the bush anyways so the crazies on the road won't bother me," said Aimee. She smiled at both of them and waved them a good night.

7 PAYNES GREY

"Well, looksee here, there goes that gorgeous TV woman with her baby," thought Jim as he passed Glenda pushing Connor's stroller along 124 Street. "Wonder what she's up to in the city."

Jim drove to his appointment in Edmonton. He was meeting with other pharmacists to discuss their latest grievance with the provincial government. Jim hoped they would agree to the hiring of a lobbyist. He was also hoping the meeting would conclude with an invitation to go for beers. He'd love a night of cutting loose in the big city.

Jim's appointment did not go as he wished. It had gone long, and whenever Jim pushed for a lobbyist, Raymond Denton, that old wind-bag, would cut him off and argue against it. To show his displeasure, he left very quickly at its conclusion. He stopped at the first rest stop out of town to relieve himself. Jim was shocked to see Glenda pull in. She parked just within the entrance. His pickup was in plain sight but far enough away from where she was that he doubted if she would recognize him. For some reason, he hesitated moving back to it while she could see him.

After quite a while Glenda left the front of the car to put Connor into his carseat. While her back was turned, Jim sprinted to his pickup from the far side of the building where he had been waiting. A magpie scolded as it flew horizontally along his path. Jim wanted to strangle it. Once at his truck's door, he looked back to see if Glenda had heard it and was looking his way. She was still busy tethering her young into the backseat. He quickly started the vehicle and quietly drove out of the rest area. Jim pulled off at the nearest country road, turned his truck around and waited for Glenda to go by. For no good reason, he had decided to follow her.

Glenda pulled up her long driveway. Half-way along, she noticed someone was sitting on her front deck and honked her horn. She drove the rest of the way and parked, she began talking with the person right away while untangling her son from the carseat, then turned towards the person.

Jim watched all of this from the road, in his truck, through scraggly bushes. He could see that the person was female and Native. "So," Jim thought, "a classy lady like Glenda McTavish is friends with a low-life. And I thought she was a real lady. Christ, what is this world coming to? Look at that squaw. Betcha she's a foster kid who put out for all the older kids."

Jim's quick anger annoyed him and he grabbed his binoculars for a better look. "oh, sweet Jesus," he exclaimed aloud. It was the busy-body Cardinal daughter who almost cornered him in Winston's toolshed. "Jesus Christ," he thought, "I can't believe it, these two are connected. Who knew?" A smile spread across the bottom half of his face, his eyes remained steely grey. Suddenly Jim wanted to be home, his bow in his hands, doing some target practice.

Jim pulled a U-turn to leave the subdivision; he almost hit a van as he was going around a curve a little too fast as he left. He sped away, raising a huge cloud of dust. He drove to Aunt Doris's farm, now his own home. After eating a quick supper and feeding his dog, Jim wandered out the back way to where his archery practice area was set up. He strung his bow and reached for an arrow. The dog had followed him and was nosing around in the bush behind him.

Jim could not shake Glenda from his thoughts. He wondered if she would be a good mother to her son. Jim remembered only one of his many mothers half-favourably. Most were only interested in the money they got from taking in foster children. They would order him around, get him to do all the chores and never feed him enough. As a little boy, he had learned how to steal money for school field trips and how to steal warm coats from unwary school mates. As an adult, he tried to forget all his childhood. He had even changed his name from Gene Dzuik to Jim Drucker.

Mary was really the only 'good' mother. And even she failed him. She was a Métis woman, middle aged and, except for the fact that she was a holy-roller, she was the best mother he'd ever known. He had really applied himself in her home and really hoped this one would be it. He was probably about nine when he moved to Mary's house and about twelve when he was forced out. Her mother, who lived in Winnipeg, was sick and she had to go there to take care of her. He was shunted off to some other forsaken foster home. If she ever tried to get him back, like she promised, and Gene doubted that fact, but if she did, well, he might have been AWOL. He had spent a miserable winter on the poorest farm he ever had seen and left as soon as nighttime temperatures warmed. Camping in the wilds around Alberta Beach, Gene had scrounged for everything he had: the pup tent that was missing a pole, the ripped tarp, a cooking grill and a long-handled fork, various dishes, a folding chair, a sleeping bag and some clothes. His prized possessions were his fishing rod, his slingshot and several knives. He fed himself from what he managed to catch in the woods or the lake and from what he could mooch or steal. He did earn honest money, mowing lawns for cottagers too lazy to do it themselves. Often, he'd manage to be around at mealtimes and would get a hotdog or a sandwich as an extra bonus.

Towards the end of August, Gene sat down late one afternoon by his campfire to think. His future was bleak and he knew it. Alberta Beach was a summer village and not very many people stayed over the winter. Its lake, Lac Ste. Anne, was huge and already the breeze coming from it was cooler. The nights were colder, there were fewer campers and cottagers and how was he supposed to get by? At thirteen, he was too small to get a real job and he would never make enough money cutting grass or shovelling snow to afford a place for himself. Besides, some do-gooder would squeal on him to the authorities. He knew he had to turn himself into Child Services. He decided he'd do it on the Friday afternoon before Labour Day weekend. Chances were, there'd be nowhere for them to place him and he'd end up in a hotel with a case worker. He'd have long showers and restaurant food and could even go swimming if they had a pool. Tomorrow he'd hitch-hike to Mary's house. Maybe she was back. If she was, maybe he could go there instead.

When Gene went by Mary's place he discovered that a new family was living there. He had a tantrum in front of the house, right there on the street, swearing at Mary for deserting him. Finally, he settled down. That Friday he would go to Child and Family Services; the decision was made. Back at his camp, he found a place to stash all his gear in case he would ever need it again.

His Labour Day weekend went even better than Gene had planned. His case worker took him to a motel just outside the city. Gene had the longest shower of his life and sat wrapped in hotel towels watching TV, while his case worker laundered his clothes. Saturday, he was taken to West Edmonton Mall, given a haircut and taken shopping for new clothes, shoes and school supplies. They went bowling and ate dinner at a restaurant. Sunday, he was taken to church then to a big church barbecue. He played baseball and joined in a potato sack race. Monday, he slept in. He spent the rest of the morning using a black marker to write his name on all his new clothing and school supplies, while sitting in the warm motel room. His case worker took him to a matinee movie and then to dinner at a nice restaurant. Tuesday, he was taken to a school in Stony Plain and registered in grade eight. He wondered if he'd be there for the whole year.

After school, the case worker met him and took him to the Child and Family Services office. There he met his new family, or part of it anyways; Mr. and Mrs. Doherty, the loathsome Anthony and the lovely and compliant Eliza. There were more children at home, some theirs, some foster kids like him. They lived on an acreage just outside of Stony Plain and yes, he would remain at the same school and in actual fact, he eventually graduated high school in Stony Plain.

The Doherty parents thought Anthony, their son, was a saint. Huh, they were they dead wrong. Eventually they were dead because they were so wrong. Ha! Ha! Years later, Anthony was convicted of multiple murders. In a court of law, he was found guilty of tying his half-naked mother to the bed with bungee cords and strangling her with her own stockings, and beating, knifing and hanging his father from the basement rafters, then starting a gasoline fire in a garbage can that he kicked over, setting it up to look like his father did it. There were also three small children killed in the fire, all were foster kids. As far as Gene knew, none of the kids ever came back once they left that miserable home, except Anthony.

On Gene's first night, his new jacket went missing. He believed Anthony had stolen it yet had nothing to go on except his gut feeling. The next morning, Gene took all his new things to school and locked them in his locker. He'd change in the morning at school and eventually he figured out that he could wash his clothes in Stony Plain at the laundromat. The following summer, Gene found the remains of his jacket in an old campfire in the woods, confirming that someone in the house had obviously stolen it, carried it away and tried to burn it. His suspicions fell heavily on Anthony. He would never forget that slight.

Mr. and Mrs. Doherty were sure he did not come with a jacket and gave him one of Anthony's old jackets to wear. Anthony pointed it out as his hand-me-down to everyone. Once it was colder, he also pointed out the ski jacket and boots, gloves and tuque Gene wore, as his hand-me-downs to all the kids on the bus and to anyone who would listen at school and at every possible opportunity. It wasn't just for this that Gene hated Anthony. Anthony had it all, parents who thought he was great, he was tall, muscular, blond, good looking, and popular at school. He had everything Gene coveted.

Anthony was a pervert and committed all kinds of atrocities on the younger kids. Hell, Eliza moved into Gene's bed just to get away from her older brother. Many a time Gene stepped in between Anthony and a younger boy or girl and fought him so that the kid could have peace for the night. If they were caught fighting by Mr. or Mrs. Doherty, Anthony always accused Gene of bullying the younger kids while he, Anthony was defending them. Mr. and Mrs. Doherty believed him. Gene would get a licking from Mr. Doherty's belt, double chores for a week and no meals for twenty-four hours as punishment. Gene could care less about the troubles of the younger kids, he battled Anthony to vent his anger and frustrations. Mr. Doherty's beatings meant nothing to him, the extra chores ate up idle daytime hours and he always managed to scrounge enough food to never go hungry.

Monroe Doherty was a mean and cruel man, the only saving grace about him was that he was not home much. Years later, Gene learned the man had a gambling addiction. Although he had a good paying job with TransAlta, the electrical company, money was scarce in the household. It was Mrs. Doherty who actually kept everything afloat. Gene never knew her given name; she took abuse from her husband yet remained loyal to him. He either called her Mrs. Doherty, Woman or Squaw.

The woman could make a supper from nothing, stretching a pound of hamburger to feed a household of eight to ten people. Besides cooking and laundry, she kept a garden and canned a majority of their food. She gave everyone chores, from chopping vegetables to chopping wood, or mopping floors and weeding gardens, or darning socks and mending busted knees in pants, or clearing away the snow in winter and mowing the lawn in summer. She was a thin, bony woman who never rested, never gave a child a hug or a smile, yet managed to keep them all fed, dressed and sheltered. Gene realized years later this was where he learned basic cooking skills and how to mend his clothes. Grudgingly he gave thanks for having a Mrs. Doherty in his life. That small thanks was all he could give her, he never spared a good word for the woman, nor could he remember a fond memory of her.

Gene coped with the chaotic home life and focussed on his school work. He kept mostly to himself. He excelled in shop and was an overall good student. Gene spent his lunch hours either in shop or the library. It was the librarian who helped him with his homework, fed him extra sandwiches and apples and told him about the laundromat. Old Mrs. Reeds, a chubby, freckled, spectacled, curly-haired, smiling lady with twinkly blue eyes. She must have been ready for retirement when Gene knew her. In the spring of his ninth grade, she suggested Gene look for a part-time job after school. She helped him fill out the application forms and prepared him for the interview questions.

Mid-June Gene did get a part-time job at one of the gas stations in Stony Plain. Mr. and Mrs. Doherty told the other kids how proud they were of him. Gene was almost fifteen and tall for his age, he told the owner he was sixteen. School ended during his second week on the job and he then worked there every day. On Friday, Mr. Doherty took him to the bank to 'cash his paycheck.' This involved depositing the money in Mr. Doherty's account and leaving the bank together. When Gene began to complain, Mr. Doherty grabbed him by the arm and pulled him outside to the sidewalk.

Lifting Gene by his shirt collar, Mr. Doherty pulled his face close to his own and glared down at him, "boy, we feed you, give you clothes, a roof over your head. It is mighty fine of you to finally contribute to the household. From now on we'll give you an allowance of twenty dollars a week. And I don't want any back-chat, you hear?" he snarled into Gene's face, and with a final shake, he let go of his shirt and walked quickly to his truck, not even looking back to see if Gene followed.

'Back chat' was a key word in the Doherty household. Two kids could be playing checkers and giggle over some joke. "Quiet there! And I don't want to hear no back chat," Mr. Doherty would bellow. If, after a while, the kids began laughing or talking quietly again, he would get up and whack both over the back of the head.

"Did I not say," shouted Mr. Doherty, "that I didn't want any back chat? Now stop your yammering or it's off to bed right now for the two of you."

If they were smaller children, unable to stop their hiccupping tears, he would drag them by the arm upstairs to their bedroom, take his belt to them and lock them in the room.

One such small boy of about six, another foster child, was a bed-wetter. Mr. Doherty made him sleep in the old barn, on straw, in an old dilapidated sleeping bag. One morning the boy did not come in for breakfast. They found him dead, curled up in his frozen sleeping bag on a pile of wet straw. Mr. Doherty called the police.

"Must have slept-walked in the night and ended up in the old barn," he told the cops. Everyone held their breaths. Would they drag his sorry-ass off to jail or would he get away with his bold-faced lie? "Well," Gene thought, "there was no justice on this earth." There was not even an inquiry into the 'accident.'

Gene took it all; the beatings, the stealing, the bullying, the chores. He wanted to finish high school and he was in love with the lovely Eliza Doherty. Many a night they plotted how they would escape and how they would live together, happily ever after.

Over the summer, Gene slacked off at the gas station a few times; which resulted in his hours being cut. He was still grudgingly given the twenty dollars a week allowance, was called a dead-beat and harassed by Mr. Doherty at every opportunity, and was no longer given rides to work when they left at the same time. No matter, Gene either used one of the busted-up bicycles from the house or he hitch-hiked.

When not at work or doing chores, Gene was busy protecting his possessions from Anthony. He had to keep moving his stash: his clothes, school supplies and now his cash as Anthony was forever hunting for them.

That was also the summer he was into birds. Gene could not count the number of birds he had caught that summer. There was a path in the woods behind the acreage and he spent many an hour following it. Sometimes he'd meet other hikers on the path. Gene pretended he was a Boy Scout working on his birding badge. He'd tag along with those he met, pestering them with bird questions, trying to find out as much as he could about wild birds.

'Wouldn't they laugh if they knew what I did with the birds I caught!' he remembered thinking.

He mostly caught small birds, like chickadees. However, one day he caught a magpie. He stabbed out an eye and let it go. He saw it from time to time, shrieking at him ceaselessly from high in a tall tree. Gene was quite disappointed to see that it healed well enough and learned to adapt – it had not starved to death and it hardly seemed to suffer. Worse, it remembered him and haunted him. It would fly down from behind, dive bombing him while cawing and as he turned to look, it would either use its beak or its feet to peck or claw at him. Gene threw rocks at it yet never quite managed to hit it. This was the beginning of his deep-seated hatred of magpies. Whenever it was around the trail and spotted by hikers, they would point it out to Gene, saying things like it probably lost its eye in a fight with another bird.

He could never get over how stupid the hikers were. They were almost as gullible as the chickadees. You just had to stand still for a minute with an open hand and a chickadee or two would land on it, thinking you'll feed them. Gene never did; unless it was something 'special' he had cooked up, to see how they would react to it. Like oatmeal and Warfarin. Now that was a nasty mixture. That was what the Alberta Rat Patrol used on any Saskatchewan rats found crossing the provincial border, or so his schoolbooks taught him.

He had captured four little chickadees and hung them in a cage in a tree where no one ever went, so it was unlikely that anyone would find them. All he fed them was Warfarin-laced oats. He checked on them three or four times a day, his excitement mounting as they dehydrated and died. In the evening, the lovely Eliza would ask what he had been up to that day to put him in such a good mood.

"Never you mind, Miss Eliza, never you mind, lovely Eliza," was all that he would answer her.

The trouble was Eliza was lovely. Too lovely. She had long straight dark brown hair with auburn highlights, an upturned nose in her heart shaped face, a clear complexion with rosy cheeks and grey eyes like Gene's. She turned fourteen that fall and the older boys on the school bus started noticing her and she noticed that they were noticing. It wasn't long before she was dating sixteen and seventeen-year old boys with trucks or cars. She could now stand up to her brother. She no longer needed Gene to protect her and she stopped visiting his bed. Gene stuck it out at the Doherty's until the school year ended. That summer, he went back to his old haunts around Alberta Beach.

Mosquitoes were buzzing in Jim's ears. His reverie broken, he looked around himself. He had only let fly a few arrows and yet it was already getting dark. He wondered how Glenda McTavish had gotten under his skin to the point that he had made that trip back in memory to his childhood.

Jim whistled for his dog and went into the house to watch the news.

8 ELECTRIC BLUE

Helen Majeau, the retired reporter, gave Glenda a call the next day. She told Glenda that several years ago, a rifle shot blew tore a hole in the backyard playhouse where her granddaughter was, in broad daylight. The police were called in and put it down to pranksters. They were not willing to listen to her serial shooter maniac theories. Her family took a very different view. They saw it as a warning for her to back off and begged her to leave things alone. She gave them her word that she would. This was over ten years ago. Helen said that if Glenda could keep her involvement quiet, then her conscience would be at peace and she would give several files on floppies to Glenda. Glenda agreed on behalf of herself and her friend and made arrangements to go and collect the floppies right away.

She texted Aimee before she left.

"Aimee, Helen Majeau is giving me some floppy discs that she" says holds information on the drive-by shootings."

Aimee texted back, "floppy discs? I haven't seen them in years. How are we going to open it?"

Glenda responded, "I was hoping Kyle might be able to help us with that."

"Okay, I'll ask him. Why don't you guys come over after supper with the floppies and we'll see what we can do."

Aimee called Kyle to let him know the plan for the evening. Kyle borrowed a gadget from work that he said was a floppy disc reader. Once Glenda and Dave came over, he plugged it into Aimee's laptop. She put in the first disc, labelled 'Drive-by Shootings'. Bingo! The files came up on the screen.

Once the first file opened, Kyle was satisfied his gadget had worked. He invited Dave to join him on the patio. The two men grabbed the babies and headed out of doors. They sat down to enjoy the sunset with their sons and a cold beer in hand.

All the files were in Excel. The first floppy contained three files that dealt with drive-by shootings of people. The first one showed a cluster bar graph correlating Helen's list of dates and weather patterns. This list was expanded from the handwritten paper Glenda had found over at Roger's newspaper office. The different colours in the cluster graphs arranged the data by types of shootings: green for objects, blue for residences, and red for victims. If you hovered over a cluster point, a comment box would appear with the date and victim or the object and its location and date.

The second file, again in Excel showed a similarly coloured cluster graph spanning the years. This time it was arranged by location. There were incidents located west of the city as far as Entwhistle. Again, if you hovered, a comment box appeared with the particulars of the incident.

Glenda did not believe in coincidences. Yet she realized how tenuous this information would seem to the authorities. For one, the incidents occurred in towns, industrial areas, wooded areas, farms and acreages. Within each small community there wasn't much of a pattern. This was proved in the next file, when she opened Helen's third Excel spreadsheet to find the information laid out by area. The patterns within the graphs were haphazard at best, even if all three criteria were inputted on a single line graph in each county.

The second floppy disc, labelled 'Murders,' held similar files with graphs of the dates of murders going back about thirty years. The first file contained all the murders that had occurred in the counties of Lac Ste. Anne and Parkland. Helen used blue for murders that had been solved and red for murders that had not been solved. The second file combined the drive-by shootings with all the murders by location and time. Again, those in red were unsolved murders. Helen had coloured the drive-by shootings black except for those that had occurred near where murders had occurred, these were green for solved murders (in blue) or pink for unsolved murders (in red.) There were very few green dots preceding blue dots. However, there were quite a few pink dots preceding red dots. Glenda exchanged a look with Aimee. Shivers ran up Glenda's spine.

The third file held similar information with two new colours included: yellow and orange. They puzzled over it then Aimee said, "this first graph is colour coded the same way as on the other file. She used green for drive-by shootings preceding blue for solved murders, and pink for drive-by murders preceding red for unsolved murders. The new colours are for rapes and strangulations; yellow for drive-by shootings that occurred before a murder by rape and strangulation close in location to where the victim was found. Those crimes are coloured orange," explained Aimee, who was sitting at the keyboard and had looked at a few of the comment boxes.

"Oh!" said Glenda, excitedly, "Helen Majeau and I did not talk about the rapes. She told me she no longer had a computer that could read a floppy. She probably is not aware that she gave us this."

"She came to the same conclusion we did. She thought it was a serial killer," Aimee said, looking over her shoulder to her friend.

There were three more floppies. The first contained copies of newspaper articles on the reports of the extremely gory murders. Besides the 'Parkland Examiner' there were copies of other newspaper reporting the events from Edmonton and St. Albert. The second floppy held reportage on local murders by drive-by shootings. The third file had newspaper copies of stories about rape and murders by strangulation. These victims were anywhere in age from teenagers to their fifties. They mostly appeared to be Aboriginal. These last two floppies did not have any reportage other than from the 'Parkland Examiner.'

After reviewing the data, Aimee and Glenda looked at each other. Aimee finally broke their wild, stunned thoughts.

"Well, this is much bigger than we thought," acknowledged Aimee. "We'll have to double-check all her information. She has newspaper citations on her data pages."

"I wonder if she brought this to anyone's attention outside of the counties of Parkland and Lac Ste. Anne," said Glenda.

Aimee was making notes. "What else do we need to do?" she asked.

"Obviously stay out of this guy's way," answered Glenda. "You, in particular, fall into his victim profile."

"Thanks for that," Aimee sighed. "Of course, you're right. Okay, so we proceed very slowly and cautiously. It seems he isn't very active in the dead of winter. Did you notice that? And the raped bodies have been found close to Edmonton and as far west as Wildwood?"

"Let's look at that. He moves all around Spruce Grove and Stony Plain, westward past Wabamun Lake and northward past Onoway according to this. We may only have a part of his territory, the part that Helen concentrated on. It could be bigger, branch out somewhere, who knows? He could be a local guy."

"Hmm," said Aimee. "Glenda, there's very little action in the winter months. Look. No murders, just the drive-by shootings. For murders, the latest dates are in November and the earliest are in May."

"Well, think about it, you can't go tracking through snow in the winter, anyone could follow your footsteps," said Glenda.

"Or you just don't know about the cold, where you live you don't get snow," mused Aimee out loud.

"So, who would visit this part of the world on a regular basis, avoiding the coldest weather?" asked Glenda.

"Dunno," said Aimee, "maybe it could have something to do with drugs. I could always ask my cousin, he's involved in that world."

"Hmm, … You'll have to be very careful. 'We proceed very slowly and cautiously' remember?"

"Yep. You check out the citations in the data and the weather and moon phases. And see if Helen will talk to you. Ask her if she went to anyone besides the local RCMP detachment on this. I'll find out what I can about drugs moving into the area and see if there's a fit."

"Carefully," warned Glenda.

"Yep, carefully," responded Aimee. "See you tomorrow morning at eight. We're going jogging," she laughed, linking her arm with her friend's and directing her outside to the patio. Glenda rolled her eyes at her.

9 OCHRE

The next afternoon Aimee drove into Onoway to visit her cousin. As she drove up, she could see Brock in the garage, pressing weights on a bench. Brock was older than Aimee, he was tough looking with close-cropped hair, an earring, a torn undershirt and tight jeans tucked into boots. Aimee loved and trusted her cousin, he had given her a lot of advice when she moved south from her grandparents' home to her parents' acreage, on how to deal with the kids at school and how to fit in. She smiled as she remembered in particular his dance lessons and how light he was on his feet doing the two-step.

"Hey, cousin," she waved, stepping out of the car. She reached back in and unhooked Trevor from his baby carseat. Brock stood up, wiped his hands on a rag which he threw behind himself onto the bench and walked across the lawn to meet them. He grabbed the baby and settled him into the crook of one arm. With the other hand, he made a mock fist and lightly feigned a pass to Trevor's chin.

"How's my little Terror?" he asked looking up and giving his cousin a peck on the cheek.

"C'mon in, you have time for a coffee?" he called over his shoulder, as he headed towards the front door. They walked through the house to the kitchen. Brock handed her the baby and grabbed two coffee mugs from the cupboard and poured them each a coffee. Once milk and sugar were added they headed out to the backyard where they sat at the picnic table. Aimee took a sip of her coffee.

"Man, that's nice," she said, unfolding a blanket and laying Trevor on the ground. Brock laughed. "You're probably not drinking much coffee with the baby. No, I respect that. A mama has to take care of her brood," he said, lifting his coffee cup to clink hers. Aimee took another small sip.

"Yep, there's a lot of responsibility," she acknowledged. "I was in the

35

bush as a kid so I wasn't exposed to a lot of stuff. I'm not sure how to keep him safe as he grows up," she said, looking her cousin straight in the eye.

Brock laughed and broke her gaze, moving his eyes over to Trevor.

"Well, you came to the right place. I've been in and out of juvie and jail until I was thirty-two and finally smartened up. You gotta teach him values and that he's better n what's all around us," he continued.

"Oomph, that's a tall order. There was a kid in grade five busted for dealing on school grounds. It was on the news as I drove here," she said.

"Yep," said Brock, "the trick is to keep him away from drugs altogether. You stayed away from them."

"I had track. I went to the provincials, remember. I thought I could go on from there. It got me a partial college scholarship."

"Yep. Something that you love that keeps you busy might work. But some athletes still use," he said.

"How does it all work?" she asked, taking another small sip of her coffee.

Brock got up and headed to the kitchen. "Want a refill?" he called.

"No. I'm good."

When Brock came back he looked at her very seriously. He shook his head, then said, "This has got to do with you and your friend Glenda, the TV reporter, right?" He wagged a finger at her. "You asking me about this. Is it just to get a story for her?"

"Naw," she laughed. Then after a beat, she added, "although the two of us do like to play detective. We'd love to know who was around Mom and Dad's place, for example."

Brock looked at her with a puzzled expression, then to Trevor, then back to her. His face impassive, he said, "shit! I dunno what you two broads are getting up to but drugs is serious business with serious players. It's really just big business that operates underground. Yes, they are always looking for a market for their product but really what makes it work is that they find the loopholes in the law and use them. That's why they recruit grade schoolers to deal. If they come from a good family, they can try for three strikes with the authorities with the same kid before they'll leave him alone. They know the parents will spring for lawyers and the kid won't go to juvie. Other kids, they'll coach a bit more 'cause they'll end up in juvie faster. See? They want to keep their asset for as long as they can. Today they're moving into senior's homes."

"What?"

"Yep." They both laughed a bit incredulously.

"Think about it. They are starting to fill up with the Baby Boomers, the love generation! Half of them have prescriptions to smoke pot. The stuff you get from the government is safer than what's on the street but some don't like it. There's a market there."

They laughed and sipped their coffee. Trevor had worked his way to the edge of the blanket and Aimee scooted him back to the center. He smiled up at her, rolled over then looked back to the grass and began his slow trek anew, pulling his body forward with his two chubby arms.

"Who are the guys running everything? Do people grow it locally and set up networks to distribute it?" she asked, turning back to the picnic table.

"Some comes in from British Columbia but really, most of it is from the drug cartels in Mexico. You don't fool around with those folks. One, they just don't care about you and me. Two, you don't know what cops they've paid off. You're on your own. It's like old England with the lords doing whatever they liked and the commoners just trying to stay out of their way. Your best bet for Trevor is to get him focused like you were. Teach him as you were taught by Kookum and Mooshoom," he said, patting her knee. "The old ways. Hell, I'll take him into the bush, fishing and tracking once he's bigger myself," he said, going to the blanket and picking up Trevor who was at its edge again. He tousled the baby's head.

"Thanks Brock. I'll do that. He'll grow up to love his Uncle Brock," she scratched her head.

"What? he said, "you want to ask something? I wouldn't drink around him, you know I don't do drugs or drink anymore."

"No, no," she said. "I just had a picture of a Mexican coming up to Onoway and getting a school kid hooked on MJ then getting him to push on the schoolyard."

"It doesn't happen like that. I'd be shocked to ever hear of someone from a drug cartel coming this far north. They have a whole crew that distributes for them. It's not likely they cross their own border very often and when they do, we see the aftermath on the six o'clock news," he said, finishing his coffee and lighting a cigarette.

"So, no Mexicans in Canada then?" Aimee said, taking Trevor from his arms.

"I have only ever heard of one guy, maybe. It's all very mysterious. No one ever sees him. They call him the Ghost. He's like a whisper and no one talks about him but you hear a little bit here and a little bit there. Usually someone bragging so who knows how true it is. He's supposed to be from the south and only comes when it's warm. I first heard about it in juvie from a tough guy trying to impress me. I don't know if it's true. Once, we were out at Devil's Lake, six big guys riding bikes at night, escorting a van with a shit-load of cash that we just left there. The next day another guy and I went back on my bike. He picked up the van, now full of weed and we came back to town. I was told I saw nothing and was never to talk about it."

"Wow, the stories you can tell! One day you'll have to write a book."

"The only way I could ever write about it would be if everyone else involved was dead," he said solemnly, flicking his cigarette butt into a can.

"Well, on that cheerful note, I'm going to head out. Hey, I found some smokes at home and I don't want them. Here," Aimee rummaged through her bag and tossed her cousin a pack of cigarettes.

"A gift of tobacco? And I thought you just came by for a visit," Brock said, wagging his eyebrows at her.

She laughed. "I'm going to take you up on your offer to help teach Trevor the old ways and help me to keep him out of drugs as he grows up."

Aimee packed up her bag. Brock folded up the blanket and walked his cousin to her car, holding everything while she put Trevor into his carseat. As Aimee drove away, she could see him back in his garage, lifting weights.

The next morning, jogging around the track, the sun already hot in the sky, Aimee filled Glenda in on what she had found out from her cousin. They could now both do over three miles quite briskly around the track while talking, so Aimee had upped their laps quota. She knew Glenda was thinking about what she had reported but that her friend would save her breath and try not to carry on a conversation. As it was, Glenda cut out after the seventeenth lap, finishing it quite slowly. Aimee continued on her own. She joined Glenda on the bench after going six miles.

"Well, I wonder if this mystery ghost is our guy?" said Glenda, handing Aimee a bottle of water.

"Who knows? He'd be pretty tough to find, let alone to follow. We're stabbing in the dark, anyways. We're making an assumption that our guy could be a drug runner but we really don't know anything about him."

"We know a few things," said Glenda, her face serious. "The incidents happen between the early spring and late fall, the murder victims are mostly women, with a high proportion being First Nations. He's got to be one cool customer if he can hide in the bush by folks' houses, waiting to take pot-shots at their windows. He uses a 22 rifle for the drive-by shootings and he beats and then strangles the women that he rapes, usually with their own clothing. Nothing ties the strangulations and the rifle murders together nor with those murders that feature torture. Except for the fact that they are all unsolved. No bullet casings have been found at any of the murders or drive-by shootings. Actually, no clues to the perpetrator have been reported. And it seems, in our neck of the woods anyways, that this has been going on for thirty years or so."

"Then he's an old guy now," Aimee added, "And, if he is the same guy that murdered Alice Grant then he probably isn't into drugs. We believe he is a local guy, the person she was dating."

Glenda shrugged. "What if he started in his late teens or around twenty? He'd be in his fifties now. Lots of fifty-year-old men are quite fit and they still date."

They sipped their drinks and fussed with their babies in their strollers.

Trevor was sleeping, Connor was wide awake. Glenda turned his stroller around so that he faced them.

"Did you do any work on the citations? she asked her friend.

"Yes. I'm not done but everything I've checked so far is good. I created a new column on the spreadsheets and put in URLs for corroborating sources. I'll call Helen this morning and do more research later. Hopefully Connor will sleep most of the afternoon."

"Both of our husbands are out of town tonight. Come over for supper. I'll cook up the whitefish for us."

"Okay, I'll come early with my Notepad and write all your steps down. I can add it to my cookbook, if you agree."

Aimee shook her head and smiled at her friend, "tell me again why you're writing a cookbook?"

"Oh, you know. My fans," replied Glenda with a bow, "every now and then I mention a meal on air, especially if we are interviewing a chef from a local restaurant, and I get a flurry of emails asking for recipes. I have a list I'll never get through," she laughed as they packed up their things and headed to Aimee's truck.

Glenda fed Connor and had an early lunch at home. Once the baby was sleeping, she called Helen Majeau. They only spoke for a short while, Helen obviously was not very comfortable with any follow-up questions. In the afternoon, Glenda began checking on the weather and moon phases for the dates of events on the Excel spreadsheet. Her research corroborated their theory of dark, relatively warm, spring to fall nights. There would be no snow or there would be old, crusty snow on the ground so that boot prints would not be left behind. Glenda was thinking less and less of a traveller to the area and more and more that the serial killer was a local person.

That evening, sitting around Aimee's fire in the copper firepit in her backyard, both friends wearing hoodies, the babies nestled in a playpen with mosquito netting over it, they pulled their fish and roasted vegetables out of the fire and began their dinner.

"It's nice having a girl's night together while both our guys are out of town working," Aimee said.

"Yep," agreed Glenda, "It's interesting how the two of them, working for very different companies, ended up on out of town trips to Calgary at the same time. I wonder where they're dining tonight?"

"Well Kyle's at a convention so they probably have evening things planned or he's deep in software-land with some other computer dude," Aimee answered.

"Unh huh," said Glenda. "If I know Dave, he's pulled Kyle out of there and they're enjoying a great dinner or some beers with live music somewhere." The women laughed.

"Helen pish-poshed the idea of a drug runner," Glenda reported. "She does not think someone is travelling here with goods. She thinks it is a local guy."

"And the other thing, Aimee, our data is spotty for the last ten years when Helen no longer worked at the Examiner."

"I was thinking about that, too. We have a few unsolved murders from the last ten years and a few rapes that were reported in The Examiner. However, the number of horrendous crimes really dropped off." Aimee shook her head, "maybe Roger just didn't run any stories or there just weren't any more murders and rapes."

"I'll tell you what," said Glenda, "I'll do some research on the web and with my contacts. Can you ask around about Alice and see if anyone knows of any other similar crimes?"

Aimee nodded her assent.

"I have tea and bannock for dessert," she smiled, "and you guys may as well sleep over. I made up the spare room. Then we can do some tai kwon do in the morning before we go jogging."

"That'll be nice, Aimee, except for the jogging," Glenda said as she smiled back at her friend.

The boys woke them up quite early in the morning. Once everyone was fed, the women sat on the back deck with a morning coffee.

Glenda returned to their conversation of last night.

"So, if Alice's killer is the same guy from Helen's news stories, how do we flush him out?"

"That's going to be really hard," said Aimee, "it's not like in high school where we knew who the bullies were and started our counter-attack."

Glenda had been a new girl at Onoway High. Her childhood in Scotland left its mark with an accent most rural Albertans found snobbish. That and her much more self-assured composure than any of the other local students had the bullies set on her as an easy target. Late on a fall afternoon, Aimee placed herself in front of a downed Glenda and fended off her two assailants. The friendship was rocky at first. Aimee did not trust Glenda, they were two opposites. Aimee had grown up in the bush with her grandparents. Only recently, had she returned south to her parents care in the Onoway area. She had intervened because the fight had been unfair, two against one, not out of friendship. Aimee helped Glenda up and called her a sissy. They walked into the school together and Aimee helped Glenda clean her cuts and scrapes. The next day, they kept noticing each other; they had many classes in common. Aimee had aspirations to go to business college however her grades were poor. Glenda got straight A's. After school, Glenda passed by Aimee's locker. Aimee had had trouble in their math class. Glenda offered to help her with her homework. The girls went to the library and studied together, Glenda tutoring Aimee. The way that Glenda explained the math problems was easy for Aimee to understand.

She offered a deal; Aimee would teach Glenda how to defend herself and Glenda would help Aimee get better marks. They became the best of friends ever since that fateful day.

"We need bait," Aimee finally concluded.

"But what bait? Sometimes it's a sign that is shot at, sometimes it's a mailbox and sometimes it is murder."

"You're right," said Aimee, scratching her head, "we need more research. There has to be a pattern, some kind of clue that we are missing. Why one time is it the one thing and another time the other? We need to figure it out. ... and also, things like signs and mailboxes, that could just be kids or someone blowing off steam."

"Okay. I'll go through the data again to try and filter out those things, Aimee."

"And Glenda, the other thing that bothers me is the spacing between murders and rapes. It sounds cold but hear me out; most psychopaths get a rush from hurting people, it is a well-documented fact. Serial killers usually ramp up their activities, not commit crimes sporadically, attacking people only when the weather is warm; they are driven by their impulses and, like junkies, the rush they get after a hit doesn't last as long as time goes on. They need more and more."

"Yeah, I'm not up on my psychology. I don't know if they still think psychopaths do it for the adrenalin rush. I've picked up a few books. Want to help me go through them?" asked Glenda. "You are right though; the victims do seem disconnected. I keep hoping to find a link between them. Yes, I see he goes after Aboriginal women but they are from all over and of a wide range in age. A racial prejudice does not explain the gruesome murders, most of which involve white men. ... Maybe he is really egotistical and somehow they crossed him?"

Aimee added, "I'd like to know who the fellow was that Alice Grant was dating before this happened to her."

"For all we know he was her killer," Glenda replied softly.

"Yep, that is true. Glenda, where's all this leading? What would we do if we did find this guy?"

"We get Dave involved to do some shooting of his own and then we go to the cops."

"First things first, let's go do some exercising," said Aimee, getting up and reaching for Glenda's empty mug.

10 ANTHRACITE

Jim sat in his study, in front of his computer. He was looking over some stock options and was growing weary of staring at the numbers. He could not concentrate. For some reason, his mind kept flashing back to that warm and familiar greeting he had witnessed between Glenda McTavish and the Carpenter girl. She dressed mostly in athletic wear. Her long dark hair was caught up in a pony tail and although she wore no makeup, she was cute, he mused. Short, dark, with big brown eyes and a sexy, athletic body. Jim worked out daily and always admired that discipline in women who kept in shape.

Jim connected her with some past memory. He let his mind wander back to his old life, to the summer he met his Aunt Doris, to long before he changed his name.

Gene was sixteen years old. He was facing his summer of hell. He had left the Doherty house, found his way to Alberta Beach and his cache with his tent and knives. A lot of it had been ruined over the time he was gone. He salvaged and cleaned what he could and scrounged around for replacements and upgrades.

Soon after arriving he met a couple, Marvin and Tonya. Marvin was a big guy with longish blond hair and a constant blond five o'clock shadow on his face. He had a huge smile and always wore a ball cap. Tonya had dyed blond hair that belied her Aboriginal origins. She was short and thin, with an athlete's body, she wore high heels everywhere, and dressed sexily, flashing her ample bosom to the whole world. She was the one that the Carpenter girl looked like.

Gene guessed they were in their late twenties or maybe early thirties. At first everything was great. They would have Gene over to their cottage and feed him and even give him the odd beer. Their place was small and unkept. It sat at the end of a road and it was filled inside and out with second-hand furniture. Tonya brightened it up with many multi-colored blankets and scarves, strewn everywhere. Music always played, day and night. They always had beer and were always drinking beer, even having a beer first thing in the morning.

Gene had practically moved in. He spent many nights sleeping on their couch, and only cleared out when they locked their door, on their way out to somewhere in their old dilapidated truck. This all came to an end, abruptly, in just a few short weeks.

One day Tonya kept flirting with him, sidling up and feeling the muscles on his arms and gushing about how strong and handsome he was. Gene had grown even taller over the last year, he excelled in gym class and at most sports, he had well developed broad shoulders and a sleek physique. Tonya would walk away, then pause, look back, flicking her long-bleached hair at him and wink one of her lovely brown eyes at him. After a while Gene noticed that Marvin was watching all of this, sitting in a lawn chair on the deck, with a smile on his face.

"Well, go on, boy," he said to Gene. "I think she's sweet on you." This went on all afternoon. Gene could not figure out what was happening. But Marvin kept egging him on. Finally, he confronted him, "Marvin, your wife keeps teasing me. I'm helpless here. Why don't you take her off to bed and do what you two do? I'm going to go fishing."

"No sir, you are not!" said Marvin, standing up. "That aint my wife and that young lady wants your services. You, young man, march right into that house and fuck her till her eyes go crossed, you hear?"

Gene could not believe his ears. At that moment, Tonya came by and grabbed his hands and dragged him in the house and into the bedroom. She pushed him down onto the bed and undressed him. Handing him an opened beer, she swayed to the music as she undressed herself in front of him. Then she literally threw herself on top of him. Gene could not believe his good fortune. They were going at it great guns. At one point, Gene happened to open his eyes and he spied Marvin sitting across from them on the dresser. Marvin smiled and waved his beer can at him. Tonya rolled him over, telling him not to pay Marvin any attention, just to pay attention to her. That it was her turn now.

Once they were done, Tonya laughed and went off for a shower. Gene lay on the bed, half-asleep. Suddenly, Marvin shook Gene by the ankles and angrily shouted at him, "boy, who do you think you are? Coming in here, drinking my beer and fucking my girl? Why I ought to kill you." He grabbed Gene's half-drunk beer can and tossed the beer into his face. Gene was clearing out his eyes, sputtering at Marvin. Marvin slapped him across the head, grabbed his ankles again and flipped him over. "Why, I'm a going to teach you a lesson boy, that you won't surely forget." Marvin forced himself onto Gene. Gene yelled. He had not seen this coming and yet he should have.

Marvin was not the first man to force himself on Gene; in foster homes there had been older boys who had done the same before this. He was a big, heavy man and Gene could not wrestle himself free. He knew to go limp, the more he fought the worse it would go for him. He looked wildly around the room. Somewhere in Gene's head it registered that Tonya was now sitting on the dresser, drinking a beer and smiling at them. As he lay there, thumping up and down on the filthy mattress, it occurred to him that he was not only being raped by Marvin but had in effect also been raped by Tonya when it had been 'her turn.'

When it was over, Marvin finally got up from on top of him, slapped him across the ass and said, "whew! boy that was some ride. We're gonna love partying with you." Then he and Tonya left the cottage, laughing, and he heard the put-putting to life of their rusted old truck as they headed out.

Gene took a shower and gathered up all his stuff that was at their place. He went to his camp, busted it up and moved a good five miles further afield. He'd have gone even further but it was now late, beginning to get dark, and harder to move through the bush. He stopped at a ravine in a lonely part of the woods. he knew that it was hard to find and tomorrow he planned to set up some string and tin cans on his perimeter just in case Marvin and Tonya came looking for him.

Someday he'd make them pay. The anger scorched inside his head, his body. He was mad at himself for believing in their friendship and for having trusted them, frustrated with his rotten luck, furious at himself for not seeing the trap being set. He howled his rage out to the night sky, heard it echoed back by coyotes. Why had he trusted them? He was alone in the world and it was bloody well time he grew up and figured out what he was going to do about it. Gene had no sleep that night, he entertained visions of hog-tying Tonya and Marvin in their bedroom, then setting their cabin on fire and listening to their screams as it burned to the ground. He kept revising the scenario, to hog-tying Marvin and forcing him to watch as he raped and strangled Tonya or hanging the son of a bitch and setting his cabin on fire. Finally, his hunger made him close down those thoughts and bury them in an icy, dark cavern deep in his psyche. It was almost mid-day, he had no money and no food.

Gene could still get lawn mowing jobs. However, at sixteen, tall and gawky, he was very seldom asked to stay for a sandwich or hot dog. He was sullen and found it hard to look adults in the eyes. He did not trust any of them. His hunger nevertheless drove him back to the cottages, looking for work. He was constantly on the look-out for Marvin and Tonya as he knocked on door after door, asking anyone who answered if they would like their lawn cut.

In the next week, Gene found a small rotted boat stowed halfway around the lake and decided to fix it up. A hobo he knew showed him how to cut out the rot and add in new boards, which they salvaged mostly from dumpsters, and how to waterproof her. He carved out a paddle from a plank and taped up its handle to prevent splinters. With this boat, he could go further out onto the lake and fish on his own. He grudgingly brought along his hobo friend on a few trips and actually enjoyed himself on the water and later around a campfire, cooking his fish with him.

Using the guts and heads from his fish as bait, Gene fashioned traps. He was after birds, and mostly caught magpies, the odd crow and many gulls. They were a prey big enough and wily enough to be a challenge and provided an outlet for his anger. They would put up a good fight and even get in a few good licks of their own. Gene soon learned how to grab them and cut off a part of a wing, so they were unsteady on their feet and could not fly away and thus be more easily controlled. He would tether them around his camp, usually on a low tree branch about waist high. Sometimes he would blindfold them. He did offer them food and water but mostly he played with them. He'd pull out feathers just to hear them squawk. When he was really angry, he'd go at them with heated knives or nails. He'd bad-mouth every foster home he had ever been in, yell obscenities at the women he trusted, Eliza Doherty, Tonya and Mary, the foster mother who ran off to Winnipeg. He vowed he would get even with Marvin and Tonya and cursed whoever his parents were for bringing him into this miserable existence.

He'd heard that crows will peck out the eyes of a wounded prey, eating them while standing on the live body where they had just been stolen. He decided to try this and pierced a crow's eyeballs with a hot nail then gouged them out. Only once a bird was so spent that it no longer fought back did he kill it, usually by wringing its neck while shouting swears at everyone he could remember to name. Once, a nasty magpie had ripped a huge gash in his hand. He slowly slit the magpie open, starting at the neckline, each hour or so getting his knife and sticking it in it and carving the gouge longer by another half-inch or so. It took that sucker over a day to die and once it did, he stomped on its body, cursing, until nothing of it was recognizable. Gene hated all magpies with a passion. He'd love to shoot every damned one of them.

In the late summer, towards evening, the homeless camping out in the woods came together and shared a large campfire. Gene sometimes wandered closer to the town limits to join them. What food was available was shared fairly decently, what drink on hand was not, often resulting in a fracas or two. Gene was not interested in liquor and often passed up the offers of green hotdogs or warmed up beans cooked in their own cans. He liked to bring along a bag of marshmallows to these get-togethers and watch the full-grown men become boys again as they toasted theirs on the end of a green stick they'd invariably cut down and whittle for themselves.

Talk gravitated to winter plans. Gene kept quiet and listened to what the others had to say, hoping to glean a plan for himself.

One night one of the older guys sidled over and sat next to him.

"Yore name is Zook, right?"

"How do you know that? What's it to you?" Gene replied.

"I'd heard someone say it once, it's no matter, ..., Well now, in Keephills, there's an old lady named Zook, only it's spelt with a 'D.' Something like D-Z-U-K. I wasn't ever good at spellin. Anyways, she's probably related to ya an she's a real lady. Betcha if ya met her, cleaned up, mind, she might take ya in for a spell. Do some chores an' make yaself helpful, I betcha she'd keep ya for the winter," he said, his wild blue eyes boring into Gene.

"Anyhow, it's an idea. Young fella like you should have no cause ta be on the road. You don't wanna go ta any shelters or soup kitchens. Take it from old Dog, no sirree, that's not for ya. Think about it. You know where ta find me if'n yore interested. I've done chores for her and can introduce ya like."

Then he got up and left Gene with a, "ya know where ta find me," and joined his buddies on the far side of the fire.

Over the next week, the more Gene thought about it, the more he realized he had two choices, go back to Child Services, who would probably only take him in for one more year anyways or try his luck with the Lady Dzuk. Finally, he searched out Dog and arranged an introduction.

"Fine boy. I'm supposed ta go there next Monday, not Sunday mind, as that's the Lord's Day, an cut some firewood. Ya can come along. The money's all mine, ya hear, but she'll feed us a good lunch. She always does."

"You didn't mention she was a holy-roller. I've had enough of them. Maybe this isn't such a good idea," Gene replied.

"If'n ya got a better plan then do it. If'n not then Sunday mornin' ya and me are gonna hitch a ride out ta Keephills an camp there for the night so's we can start cuttin' wood early Monday mornin. We'll meet by the cantina. See ya then."

The canteen, a small shack with a huge cut-out window that sported a narrow counter, was a central meeting place on the beach of Lac Ste. Anne, in the village of Alberta Beach. It opened early and closed late. It served beach food, hot dogs, hamburgers, fries and sold potato chips and pop and ice cream. Its staff never shooed any homeless away as sometimes the homeless looked cleaner and better dressed than the cottagers. Gene and Dog would need to hitch-hike or walk out to Highway 43, then beg a ride south to Highway 16 and take that west to Keephills. They most likely would split up; it was unlikely anyone would invite both of them into their vehicle.

On Monday morning, when Dog introduced Gene to Ms. Dziuk, she peered closely at the boy, to the point that he began to squirm. She then asked him where he was from and who his folks were. Except for his name, Gene had no answers for her. Then she grabbed him by the hand and sat him down in an Adirondack chair, close to the back door. She told him to stay put and that she would be right back. She went into the house and after quite a bit of time she came out with a pile of old photo albums.

Sitting close to Gene, she opened one and started telling him the names of the people in the pictures. The pictures were in black and white, from the thirties or forties or thereabouts, Gene thought. It was uncanny how much he looked like so many of them. He felt weird about it at first then he felt a small spark of hope at the pit of his being. Gene began to wonder if maybe he had found something of his biological family. Then the thought occurred to him, "Why should he care?" they had obviously dropped him off on someone's doorstep years ago and forgot all about him. Gene felt angry and fiercely questioned the old lady.

"These people look like me. Are they my family? Why should I care about them? They are all dead anyways. Why did they just drop me off on someone's doorstep? What's wrong with these people?"

This took Doris Dziuk aback for a moment. Then, smiling at Gene, she said, "well now, let's move on to this here album."

Doris pulled out the second album from the bottom of her pile. She opened it and the pictures were in colour and of a more recent Dziuk family.

"See this little blonde, here? That's Nattie. Short for Natalie. Natalie Ann Dziuk. Born in April with the baby lambs. Oh, what a sweet child she was, always smiling and busy as a minute. Of course, she grew up and was too busy with her friends to come visit anymore. She was my oldest brother's middle child. See here, her brother Boyce and little sister MJ, for Mary-Jean. Well, anyways, she was the one that left home early. There was a rumour that she had a baby. She died young. Your grand-parents looked and looked for you. I think you are her child! She had a lot of friends and none of them would talk to your grandparents. I bet you one of them raised you. Don't you remember anything from when you were little?"

Gene shook his head no, "I try not to. I don't remember much from before I went to school. I was in foster care by then. Some families tried to get me to take their names but I knew my name was Gene Dziuk and I stuck with it. If I had the same name, wouldn't you think those people could have found me? Or did they just give up?"

Doris grabbed the album and turned the pages towards the middle. Gene realized each of the kids in the family had their own section. The middle of the album had pages without pictures, just a frame that outlined where they should go. Some of these were for a baby, with little blocks and teddy bears on their edges.

Doris was talking, something about access and parental rights. Gene could make no sense of it. He had a huge lump in his throat and his eyes were burning. Abruptly, he got up, said, "excuse me," and ran off.

Gene ran out of her yard, across the road and into the bush, he ran and ran, letting the branches whack him in the face, catching himself and running on when his feet snagged on a root or bramble. Gene ran for his life. He imagined all kinds of monsters, fierce wolves, people like Tonya and Marvin and Mr. Doherty, all chasing him with baseball bats studded with nails, huge magpies with steel claws ready to rip into his back. Suddenly he was on the edge of a cliff overlooking the Saskatchewan River; had he kept running straight, he'd have gone over it, he veered to his left and stopped in time. Bending over, hands on his knees, he let his heart rate slow as he caught his breath. He wandered around all day through the bush, using a stout stick to whack back at the bush and cursing to the skies. Eventually he found his way back to the camp he and Dog had set up the night before.

Dog was waiting for him. He handed him a large brown paper bag, "lunch, as promised," was all he said, handing it to him then turning his back as he walked back to his seat.

Gene muttered thanks to Dog, turned his back on him, squatted down on the ground and opened the brown bag. He ate the lunch mechanically. It was good. Damn good. Finally, he turned around and asked Dog if he wanted any. "No thanks I a ready ate ma share," Dog answered.

Dog left Gene to his thoughts as they sat around their campfire and he prepared for bed early.

"The Lady sent me back ta camp early. See, there's still lots of work ta do. We'll go back same time tomorra mornin'," he said, before turning in for the night.

The next morning, Gene woke early and felt giddy. He was quite nervous about what to expect this day. Part of him just wanted to take off, get out of there, run away. He was smart enough to know he had few options and weird as it made him feel, this was his best one.

He breakfasted over the campfire with Dog and they headed off to work.

Doris Dziuk met them as they came up the lane. She must have been looking out for them. She invited them in for coffee. The two males looked at each other, a bit perplexed. They were not used to being invited into homes. She grabbed their arms, placing herself in between the two of them and laughing, marched them into the house.

Coffee was made and set out on the kitchen table with cream, sugar and hot cinnamon buns. Hustled into seats, a cup of coffee poured in front of each of them, Gene and Dog busied themselves spooning in sugar and stirring their added cream. Gene must have put five spoonsful of sugar into his cup; he just wanted to keep his hands busy and not have to look up. Doris broke their silence.

"I've been thinking about our conversation yesterday, Gene. Maybe I moved a little fast for you. I was just so excited at the possibility of seeing Nattie's baby. Well, of course we'll have to do blood tests to confirm things," she laid her hand on Gene's arm briefly, "I'm pretty convinced, just by your looks and your name. It was your great-grandfather's name," she finished with a smile.

"Now, Doug and I, we go back to high school," Doris caught the incredulous look on Gene's face. "No, we were not sweethearts, I was the one in high school and Doug was still in grade school when we met. I was his tutor. Anyways, Doug has often turned up on my doorstep through the years," she continued as she patted Dog's arm, "I think I'm the big sister he never had."

"He faithfully shows up every fall to cut firewood for me and eventually, before the snow flies, he settles in the old cabin behind the house for the winter. He's the only one left using it and every spring I let him know he can stay there as long as he wants however he likes the open road," she patted Dog's arm again. "I'm sure one of these years he'll settle down."

"Gents, here's my proposal to you. Doug, of course you have free use of the cabin. As I've told you before, it is yours. No one to my knowledge has been in it since you left. I've freshened it up and have all the bed sheets and blankets and towels in it, all ready for you."

"Gene, you are welcome to stay here, in the house for the winter. I expect you'll go to school. Where did you go last year and what grade are you in?

"Memorial High in Stony Plain. I finished Grade 10 last year," Gene muttered.

"Well, that is a good high school. Did you like it there?"

"Yes Ma'am."

"Well then, let's make sure you get to go back again this year. Now, it would seem to me that you are AWOL from some foster home. You and I will need to make a visit to the Child and Family Services and set things straight. They can arrange the blood test or let us know how to go about it. Now, Gene, for me, well, I am convinced. However, I am an old lady, living alone, and I have very protective nieces and nephews out there who will want proof that you belong to the clan. The blood test is for them."

Gene had a worried expression on his face. He was wondering what would happen if the blood test did not prove he was Natalie Dziuk's child, what then?

"I'm making a commitment of a school year to you, Gene. Regardless of how the blood test goes. There'll be rules and chores for you. You can stay here and go to school in Stony Plain as long as you comply. At the end of the school year, we can decide if you will stay here of if it will be better for you to move on somewhere else. Now how does that sound?"

Gene looked up at Doris and blinked. It sounded mighty fine to him, unbelievably fine. He was having a hard time believing it could be true. Gene tried to speak and barely croaked out a "yes ma'am." Dog and Doris laughed.

"I'll take that as a 'yes.' We have an accord," she sipped the last of her coffee and offered more around the table. No one took her up on her offer.

"Well, gentlemen, I think it is time for work. I'll call you when lunch is ready."

As soon as they were outside Gene teased Dog by constantly calling him Doug. Finally, he noticed the older man's face had gone white. He stopped and asked him if he was okay.

"Yas, I'm okay. I tole ya she was a lady. She calls me by ma Christian name but no one else does. Ever a one else calls me Dog. Ya too, ya great big baboon."

Gene suppressed his laughter and started splitting the wood as fast as he could. It was Dog's job to pick p the pieces and stack them.

Jim's mind came back to the present. The light in the room had changed. Looking out the window, he could see that the sun had begun its slow setting for the day; the field was now in shades of grey shadows. Jim stood up, his dog got to its feet and yawned noisily as it stretched out its lazy back. Jim ushered it out of doors and began making himself supper.

Later that night, after finishing his evening work-out and exercising the dog, he sat in his great room, a beer in hand while the TV blared the day's news at him. Jim found himself still brooding over Glenda McTavish and the Cardinal girl. Glenda was a TV news anchor and the Cardinal girl was just too plain nosy for her own good. Jim did not know her name and figured she was the Cardinal's daughter and that she lived in Stony Plain. She was a looker, shorter than Glenda, with an hour-glass figure and a very athletic body. Still, she was the only person ever to have almost stumbled across one of Jim's hidey-holes for a tramp that had become his plaything.

Hell, he should have known better than to date a local. Alice had reminded Jim an awful lot of Sheena, his first girlfriend and that was the only reason he had taken up with her on the sly, as he had with Sheena years ago.

When the Cardinal daughter came to check on her parents' property while they were vacationing, she had nearly stumbled on Alice Grant's almost dead body in Winston's work shed. He had stashed her in it under the workbench, having injected her with a tranquilizer that would keep her asleep and wrapping her up in an old tarp. That had been the one day that he had work to do at the pharmacy. After he dispatched with Alice's body, he had returned to the woodshed. Part of him wanted to take down that nosy bitch while his cautious side wanted to give her as wide a berth as possible. Once he spied the motion detector and camera, he left the property for good.

The few times he had followed the Cardinal girl, she had gone into Stony Plain and stopped either for groceries or a Tim's. He had never bothered waiting and following her past those points. There was no extra car at Glenda's place so how did that busy-body get there? He'd scout out the area and figure out if she lived nearby and not in Stony as he had believed.

He'd make that bitch pay. It would be so sweet, he would pay her back for that witch Tonya, who she looked like. He had never seen Marvin or Tonya again and he still remembered what he owed them. But not tonight. It was getting late and it was time for bed. Jim had a busy day planned for tomorrow; he was on duty at the pharmacy.

11 KHAKI

Gene learned how to play the Aunt Doris game very quickly. Aunt Doris approved of good manners, a proper deportment, an industrious attitude and a considerate disposition. So, Gene, the chameleon, became all those things. He appeared to be quite fond of Aunt Doris. He found himself defending her to his cousins at family get-togethers. They were constantly undermining her independence, inferring she should be placed in a home, pointing out small mistakes she would make on a person's name or some detail in the conversation as instances of her increasing dementia. All the nephews in particular were ever so polite to Aunt Doris in an annoyingly obsequious way. What Gene heard them say outside of her presence painted an altogether different picture.

The day after one of these family get-togethers, Aunt Doris, in a teasing manner, would call him her chivalrous knight, defending her honour and good name. She would reassure him that, if anything happened to her, he would be taken care of, that her personal directive named her lawyer as her Agent and that they had prepared documents together that covered just about any contingency the two of them could think up.

The reason the family were so anxious to control Aunt Doris's finances was that she lived on and owned the original family homestead and she retained mineral rights to the property. In Alberta these rights could only be passed down from one generation to the next, to descendants of the original homestead family. There was renewed interest in the area as fracking could squeeze out the remaining natural gas that was increasingly difficult to reach. Aunt Doris would not hear of any fracking happening on her land and was in a legal battle with a particular oil and gas exploration company that wanted to use adjacent land and horizontal drilling to approach a pocket of natural gas below the homestead property. So far, she was winning the battle. Gene tended to agree with Aunt Doris. Why wreck the watershed for a few measly bucks to go into the pockets of a bunch of oil barons?

Gene was a lot happier when the family left them alone, which was most of the time.

Over the next few years, Gene became quite comfortable at Aunt Doris's house. His blood test had come back positive. This elated Aunt Doris but did not win over the rest of the family. He sat with his Aunt and listened to her stories, learned to bake and cook all her family heirloom recipes, helped her in her garden and with chores around the property. Dog had finally accepted Aunt Doris's offer to live year-round in the cabin. He and Dog became pals and would often work side by side on the bigger farmstead jobs. Aunt Doris referred to them both as her boys.

The only thing Gene and Aunt Doris ever argued over was a part-time job for Gene. Gene knew he could easily make a wage of a dollar or two over minimum working after school, two or three times a week from five to midnight at the gas station where he had previously been employed. Aunt Doris said no to any part-time work for Gene during the school months. She was pleased that he wanted to work and earn his own money yet she would not allow it and insisted on giving him a two-hundred-dollar monthly allowance. She felt he could buy his school supplies, jeans and T-shirts with that as well as go to an occasional movie or school dance or take a girl out to dinner. Gene explained it wasn't the amount of money that mattered to him; it was the fact that he earned it. Aunt Doris craftily made up a list of all the things Gene did around the farmstead and put dollar signs to each. She ended up increasing his allowance to two hundred and fifty dollars a month. Gene gave up the argument but never his protestations that this went against his grain.

Gene was a good student. He kept mostly to himself and was not concerned that he did not have a gaggle of friends that he could call his own. He was polite, witty, clean-cut and well-liked by the teachers and his classmates, who often wanted him on their projects or study teams. Aunt Doris was pleased that he made honours and gave him a second-hand pickup truck as a present at the end of his first school year.

"Now I won't have to drive you to and from school every day, Gene," she said, "and you can use this for your summer job or to take a girl to a show and all," she added, her eyes twinkling.

That first summer living with Aunt Doris, Gene had applied for a position and was hired at the gas station where he had previously worked. Things were very much as they had been with the exception of one new hire. Stacy Dufault was a large, brash, self-assured woman who saw herself as everyone's boss, including Tony, who owned the gas station. She took an immediate dislike to Gene and made any shifts they shared as miserable for him as she could. Gene would ignore many of her orders to him, he had nothing to do with the shop and was not about to clean tools or the oil pit as she often tried to direct him to do. However, there was nothing he could do but comply when she demanded he clean the washrooms or wash down the pump areas and fetch clean water for the windshield cleaning stations or move ice from the back freezer to the smaller freezer just outside the store doors or fill up the coolers with pop and the shelves with stock. It wasn't that Gene minded the work, it was that she kept up a whole tirade while he was doing it on how he was going about it all wrong and kept making suggestions that in reality would make the job harder. Whenever he did not switch over to her prescribed method, she would berate him as stupid and lazy.

One Saturday, coming on shift, Gene was warned by a fellow employee that she was on the warpath.

"Her fat ass is just shaking with rage over every little thing. I got everything well stocked this morning. Good luck, man," he said to Gene on his way out.

Gene avoided going into the store. He stayed out by the gas pumps, ready to fill up tanks and clean windshields. He knew Stacy would not venture out into the blazing sun. She did open the door a few times and yell at him, demanding he come inside and do her bidding, calling him lazy and good-for-nothing. Gene went inside only when he needed to ring up gas sales for his customers.

The next day, when Gene and Aunt Doris returned from church, he received a phone call from Tony.

"What happened yesterday, Gene?" asked Tony.

"Not too much. Before Ryan left he told me everything was stocked and he warned me that Stacy was on the warpath so I occupied myself outside for my shift. I left everything well stocked and clean at the end of it. It was a pretty busy Saturday."

"That's not the story I got from Stacy. She said you were late, stoned and that you just sat outside in the sun all day."

"Well, you can ask Ryan about that, as we spoke together when I arrived, at the end of his shift. I was not late nor stoned, I never have been Tony. I don't go in for that stuff. Look at the till receipts, they'll have my number on them. You'll see that it was pretty steady all day. I just avoided going into the store to stay away from her constant criticism."

"You've got me in a tight spot, Gene. I don't like the fact that my employees are not getting along. Consider this a warning, if Stacy complains about you again, I'll be cutting your hours. It seems to me the first year you worked here that you did good at the beginning, then you slacked off. I talked to you about that when I hired you this summer. Make sure that doesn't happen again."

Gene was furious. Aunt Doris asked if anything was wrong and he answered no, smiling calmly to reassure her everything was okay. He would think about this and come up with his own solution.

That night after Aunt Doris went to bed, Gene got into his old pickup truck and let the brake and the clutch out. The truck rolled down the driveway towards the road. Gene turned on the engine, with the truck in second gear and switched on the headlights as he turned onto the road. He knew where Stacy lived, in a rusted old trailer at a boggy acreage subdivision.

Gene parked about a half a mile away from the subdivision in the closest unobtrusive spot he could find to stash his truck out of sight. He grabbed his rifle and cut through the bush to where her trailer sat.

Every light indoors and outdoors was on. Stacy was sitting in a little screened patio, eating potato chips and drinking pop. She was listening to the radio and reading trashy magazines. After quite a while, she got up and went inside. Gene climbed a tree behind the trailer. He was hoping to spot her through one of the high windows on its backside. A light came on and there was her head bobbing as she walked towards its window. Gene had it in the cross-hairs of his rifle. Just as he pulled the trigger, she ducked. He heard her scream, then her crashing through her trailer and out its front door, then he saw her running across a field towards a blue dilapidated trailer by some woods, to her nearest neighbour.

Gene skedaddled out of the tree, the glint of the casing in the moonlight caught his eye and he scooped it up before running through the woods back to his truck. He sat there for a moment wondering if it was wise to head home. What if a cop car came up the road and stopped everyone on it? He waited a half hour, sitting in his truck, all the windows closed tight with the whole inside slowly turning into a sauna from the moisture coming off his body. Not one police cruiser had shown up. Finally, he turned on the engine and the defroster and pulled out onto the road. Moving slowly, he opened his window and that helped clear his windshield. He smiled to himself as he drove away.

Gene was driving in the opposite direction from home. He had missed putting a bullet through Stacy Dufault's brainpan but he had scared her half to death. He laughed, remembering her screams as she ran across that field. Now he needed to make sure this did not come back on him in any way.

He pulled into the next subdivision along the road. It was past midnight and most of the houses were dark. One was quite brightly lit up. Gene parked a short way down the road and backtracked on foot to it. He crept up as close as he dared and aimed his rifle at that big picture window. Through his scope he could see an old couple watching TV. He aimed high and shot above their heads. There was the crack of his gun, then immediately the splintering of the glass and then the faint yells from the couple in the room. Gene found his spent casing and whistled as he walked back to his truck. He drove straight home. Tomorrow was a working day.

Gene got to work early and was locked out of the gas station. Neither Tony nor Stacy were there, the two key-holders. He went over to the corner of the building and used the pay phone to call Tony. Tony was pretty groggy on the phone. He said he'd be there in a minute.

Twenty minutes later Tony showed up, unshaven but dressed for work. He apologised to Gene and said he had a dentist appointment mid-morning and had slept in, thinking Stacy would be there to open the store. Once things were set up for the day, Gene overheard Tony phoning Stacy. He could hear the phone just ring and ring. Gene had a smile on his face as he went outside to serve a customer who had just pulled up to the gas pumps.

Tony never made it to his dentist appointment as Stacy did not show up to work until much later in the morning. She came in breathless.

"Oh my God Tony, you will not believe what happened to me. Last night, when I went to the bathroom before going to bed, to the bathroom, Tony, someone shot out my bathroom window. I thought they were trying to kill me. I ran all the way across the field to my neighbours. I was probably screaming the whole way. It took me hours to calm down. The RCMP didn't show up until way past one o'clock. And they told me there had been another shooting at a window about five miles north of where I live. They think it was teenagers or something. Oh my God, Tony, I was never so scared in my life."

Tony just looked at her blandly. He didn't believe a word of it, it was such an outlandish thing to happen in their corner of the world. He said, "you were supposed to open the store this morning and I was supposed to be at the dentist getting a root canal."

"Oh Tony, you don't want to have them do a root canal on you. My Uncle Alphonse did and it abscessed. He ended up in the hospital for a week and in the end, they pulled the tooth. Tony, how could you expect me to come in on time? The RCMP were at my place looking behind my trailer for clues for over an hour. It was probably three in the morning before they left. And I had no sleep ..."

Gene had been stacking pop into the cooler and heard the whole thing. The ding of the gas pumps sounded. Gene stood up, knocking his box cutter to the floor. Stacy jumped a mile at the noise. He looked over at her and winked as he went out the door to fill the gas tank for their new customer.

Gene realized he had been wise to pick up his spent casing. I'll keep that in mind, he thought as the gas guzzled through the hose held in his hand and into the car's tank.

The whole community was humming with theories over those shot-out windows. That very night Aunt Doris commented on it at dinner, asking Gene if indeed he thought Stacy Dufault was telling the truth or making the whole story up. With a straight face and a sombre tone Gene reported that she had come to work late, she was dishevelled, with no makeup or her hair done up as per usual and she jumped at every little noise all day long. Aunt Doris had made one of her famous peach pies for dessert. Finishing his dessert, Gene thanked Aunt Doris for supper and told her it was the best peach pie in the whole world. Gene thought he could not remember a more perfect day, Stacy finally taking a rap at work and his coming home to Aunt Doris' peach pie, or for that matter, a happier one.

This became the beginning of something Gene looked forward to and took great pleasure in. Around Aunt Doris and by day, he could appear to be the model, doting nephew. Once she was asleep, as long as the weather was not too cold or the snow a dead-giveaway to his wanderings, Gene would go out on dark nights and find a target. He did not necessarily have murder in mind, however, it wasn't past him either as it did give him a chance to settle old scores. And he did very much enjoy the uproar in the town that his shenanigans created.

12 FLAME

Gene returned to school in the fall. He was now in grade twelve, his senior year. There was a very popular girl in a few of his classes and somehow Gene was on her radar, front and centre. Sheena would loiter by his locker, ambush him outside a classroom door or in the constricted hallway at lunchtime. He did everything in his power to discourage her.

One Friday, on his way home, Gene scanned his rear-view mirror as he pulled off the highway. 'Unbelievable,' he thought. There was Sheena standing in the bed of his truck, her coat open, flashing her bare breasts at him.

Gene slammed on the brakes, the girl somersaulting forwards. He got out of the cab and marched to the back of the truck.

"What are you doing?" he demanded.

Coyly, she giggled as she righted herself, smiled at him and said, "anything you'd like."

"No, I mean, why are you in my truck? And do up your coat, aren't you cold?"

Again, she laughed at him and Gene could feel his face reddening. She fell to her knees in the truck bed, its tailgate between her and Gene and threw her scarf over his head and pulled him towards her. Off balance, Gene felt his head grabbed besides either ear as she pulled him even closer and kissed him, tongue extended, hard on the lips. She released him, tossed her head backwards and laughed at the sky.

"You need to cut loose a bit. Enjoy life," she said, looking at him.

Gene undid the tailgate. Sheena took this as a signal and pushing backwards, rose on her toes and pivoted her body backwards, her legs now outstretched in front of Gene as she sat on the box floor. She laughed, reaching for his hand.

Gene grabbed her harshly and pulled her out of the truck bed. He grabbed her by the coat to steady her on her feet then gave her a little push backwards.

"Do up your coat, you whore," he said in an angry tone. "Then get in the cab and I'll drive you home."

She looked abashed for a moment and did up her coat. Gene turned to get into his truck. She grabbed at his hand.

"Don't you want to have some fun? Don't you like girls?" she asked.

Gene put his face close to hers. Angrily, his eyes boring into her, he said, "I like girls. Statuesque white girls with long wavy hair. Blondes, brunettes, red-heads, I love them all. I have no truck with trashy Indian whores. Now I am willing to drive you home and you can go your way and I'll go mine."

Gene turned and got into his truck. Sheena stood in the road behind him, defiant. After a moment he started the engine. That was when, predictably, afraid of being marooned, she ran to the passenger door and got in.

She told Gene she lived on the reserve. He could let her off at its entrance. She began to cry. She blubbered, "I have such a crush on you. You're tall and handsome and muscular and smart. You got it all. What have I got?"

Gene interrupted, "a reputation."

She turned to him, her eyes bright, flashing anger and defiance.

"I have more than a reputation. I am smart and determined. I came to you first. Remember that. I'm going to make a better life for myself. I want all that you have, a good home, to be a good mother and have a good father for my kids and we'll have good jobs, nice clothes, plenty of food, everything," she yelled at him.

They drove in silence. Finally, Gene said, "why me? Why did you target me? You're popular at school; you can have just about any boy. Why go after me?"

"Gene, I'm in love with you," she said, giving him a searching look.

"No, you are not. You set me up back there. You hoped my teenage hormones would kick in. You were playing me."

After a beat, she responded, "alright. I studied you. You have money for whatever you want. You dress square but your clothes are good ones, not second hand or from cheap stores like Woolco. And you are all those things I said: smart, muscular, tall, sexy and you have a good sense of humour. What's not to like? We could be an item."

"I'm not looking for a girlfriend," he said.

"And you've made it abundantly clear that an Aboriginal girl could never be your girlfriend."

"That's right. I have no truck with Natives," he said, looking over at her.

"You know I could rip my clothes after you drop me off and tell everyone you lured me into your truck and tried to rape me," she screamed at him.

"It seems to me that your friends are in on this, that you would have told them of your little plan so that you can all have a laugh at my expense," he said stiffly.

"Huh, no. No one knows where I am. I told them I was cutting my last class. Everyone was in school when I hid in your truck."

They drove for a while with neither of them speaking.

"Hey, you just missed the turn off to the Reserve," Sheena noted, looking out the side window.

"Well," Gene said, smiling over at her, "maybe possibly there is a tiny spark there, let's just drive on a bit."

"Really," Sheena answered, brightening, "Wanna go to the Mall?"

"Naw," Gene said, "I think we should go somewhere private and see what comes up."

Sheena laughed harshly and gave him a poke in the ribs.

She reached into her coat pocket and pulled out mascara and a compact. She cleaned up her face with fresh makeup.

Gene turned off onto a secondary road. They drove around for a bit. Sheena had turned on the radio and switched through the stations until she found one she liked. Gene drove to a gravel pit. Rounding piles of gravel and sand, he drove on until he found a fairly secluded area. Now he turned to Sheena and asked, "So what do we do now?"

Sheena grabbed him and kissed him hard. She guided his hand to her breast, still bare under her coat. She was incredibly flexible and pushed herself onto his knee, right there in the front seat of his truck. Quickly she worked her clothing, then his clothing off, kissing him, nipping at his ear lobe, kissing his chest the whole while. Sheena did things that Gene could not believe. He came quickly and initiated two more sexual acts with her. They had stretched out on the front bench seat, Gene held Sheena down and roughly coupled with her, holding both her hands in one of his and using his larger body to keep her pinned. She did not resist, lifting her legs over his hip and gripping him to herself. Finally, with a laugh, she begged no more.

"I'm hungry, let's go get something to eat," she suggested, smiling.

"Okay," said Gene, turning the engine over and flipping on he defroster, "where would you like to go?"

"Let's go back to Spruce, to Jack's Drive In."

"No," said Gene, "there's something you need to understand. We can never be seen together by people who know us. You said earlier that you want what I have, a normal family life. Well I only have the vaguest memories of my mom and none of my dad. My aunt has taken me in and I have to live by her rules or I am out on the street. Do you understand? I can't be out on the street ever again. And my aunt does not want me to have a steady girlfriend because 'school is so important' so no one can know we are seeing each other. Ever."

"What? I don't understand, say it all again slower."

"Okay. But let's go and get something to eat. In Edmonton or in St. Albert where no one knows us," laughed Gene as moved the truck into drive and peered out the partially cleared windshield.

Gene explained the details of his life according to his big lie that his aunt would not hear of him having a girlfriend. They could not tell anyone they were dating. If she discovered it, she might turf Gene out. Gene made Sheena swear on her life that she would not tell anyone and agree that they would have to be very careful on how they would see each other going forward.

They found a Wendy's in St. Albert and ate and talked for quite a while. Afterwards, Gene drove Sheena as close to her home as possible. They shared one last kiss before she hopped out of the truck.

That night Gene had a heck of a time explaining to Aunt Doris why he was so late. It was after ten o'clock when he got in. He said he went to a school dance. But there was no school dance scheduled in Stony Plain. It was in Devin, he explained, and a bunch of kids in his study group were going and asked him to go along at the last minute. Gene could tell that Aunt Doris did not believe a word of it and he apologised profusely for not calling and for worrying her and thanked her over and over again for everything she did for him and promised it would never happen again. That was a promise Gene kept. From that day forward, he always phoned and had a backup story ready as to where he was when he was not home at expected times.

True to her word, Sheena never let on to anyone that it was Gene she was dating. She made up a story of having met a rich, handsome young man from Fort McMurray. Yeah, he was married, but he loved her and she could only see him on the sly. She called him Will. She explained to Gene that Will stood for wily, because they both had to be cunning to keep seeing each other.

The tryst lasted a year. Many a steamy night, Gene tied up Sheena in the cab of his truck, she was willing to let him do anything. He reciprocated by taking her shopping or out for dinner and movies, always in St Albert or the east side of Edmonton, where it was unlikely they would bump into anyone they might know.

Sheena's birthday was in October. She would be eighteen and wanted a big coming of age party. She kept pressuring Gene to be a man and own up to being her boyfriend so they could party together on her birthday. He kept resisting. As ever, Sheena resorted to sex to get her way.

Sheena had tied Gene, the way he often tied her, in the cab of his truck. She had excited him with little kisses from her warm mouth as she stripped him naked. She kept teasing him mercilessly. She laughed as she licked his torso or chewed his earlobe or ran a scarf seductively over his body. He kept lunging at his bindings to get at her, they held tight.

"I'll give you what you want, big boy," she whispered into his ear, "if you give me what I want."

Finally, Gene could take it no longer and said, "yes!"

With the sweet release of his bindings came Sheena's big, happy smile. Gene immediately grabbed her and rolling over, pinned her underneath himself. She giggled up at him as he tied her hands up the way she had tied him. He entered her roughly, she threw her head back, laughing.

"I love it when you do that. I'll always remember that about you," he said, looking down into her eyes. He reached over for another of the cloths they used to bind each other and quickly wrapped it around her neck, both hands holding onto an end. Her eyes went huge. Gene put his finger to his lips and made hushing noises. He pumped his hips, his excitement rising as she fought beneath him. He would have to time this carefully, soon she would be dead and at that moment he wanted to have climaxed and to whisper in her ear, 'I told you that you could never tell anyone about me."

Gene pushed her body onto the floor on the passenger side of the cab. She fit perfectly, she really was just a tiny thing. He wondered if he would miss her. Gene drove to the gravel pit where they had first coupled together. He dumped her body and her clothes there. He just sat in the front seat of his parked truck, looking down at her for the longest time. Suddenly a magpie flew in from nowhere and approached her body. Gene was aghast. He picked up a large stone and hit the bird hard. Gene ran to it and found it dead. He pulled out one of its tail feathers and placed it tenderly in Sheena's hair. Then he covered her with sand and as much rock as he could, almost moving a whole gravel pile.

There was a bit of a fuss over Sheena's disappearance. In the end though, most people figured that she had had enough of band life and now that she was practically eighteen, she left for a life of her own. Some of her friends thought she might have gone to California or to New York, or maybe it was Toronto or Vancouver, to pursue her dream of being a star and working in the movies. In the end, it was only her family that kept a vigil and periodically set up posters to search for her; feeble attempts at that, Gene thought. Most people's attention was now on a spate of drive-by shootings that seemed to be happening all over the place.

The time that Gene used to spend with Sheena, he now spent aimlessly driving around the countryside. Sometimes he would park and walk through the bush with his bow and arrows and sharp knife on his hip. He could hear coyotes on these lonely night treks. Once they had him surrounded and Gene shouted into the wind, daring them to attack. But that never happened, they would cower away.

Most times Gene had his rifle with him. He would drive down lonely country roads and spy on even lonelier farms. Sometimes he would see a tall grizzle of a man, balding, shaking a finger at his wife or standing and berating a child. Gene would linger. That son of a bitch reminded him of Mr. Doherty. If he could check that there was no one in a room behind the one he could see into and if he could squeeze off a shot that wouldn't actually hurt anyone else in the room, then he would. With a whoop he would find his spent casing and skedaddle out of there. He never even stayed long enough to check if he had killed the son of a bitch or not.

Winter set in and it got too cold to sit on a hill spying on old geezers or to chase ghosts through the woods. Gene kept indoors and focused on his studies. He was now in his last year of high school. Gene was fascinated by the chemistry of the human body. He thought he might go into medicine. He could not see himself as a family doctor and wondered if he should work towards something like brain surgery. He knew he would need top marks to be admitted to any university medical programs.

13 CLOUD

The next morning, after returning from their rounds at the track, Glenda reviewed all the notes on drive-by shootings. Taking a page from Helen, she created an Excel spreadsheet and entered the date of the incident, the type of shooting and its location. She then coloured the entries for road signs yellow, those for mailboxes green, the personal property entries blue and the commercial signs and properties entries orange. She had a comments box for each. In it she entered any extra information she had; if there was a newspaper article covering it with its date and other data like the weather. Out of curiosity she date graphed the information and compared it with some of Helen's graphs. What jumped out at her were the yellow and blue dots as they were more numerous before unsolved murders. Almost every murder had a yellow or a blue dot preceding it in the vicinity of the victim's home, some had multiple dots. Were they warning shots, sent across the bow, so to speak? It made Glenda think of Helen's granddaughter's playhouse. She decided to give Helen a call.

Once she reached Helen on the phone Glenda outlined her findings to her. Helen became very excited.

"My, that could be a missing link. This could be something that ties things together and it could help find this madman."

"Aimee and I are a bit frustrated at the lack of clues left at each scene. And of course, we don't have any access to anything the RCMP may have from their investigations."

"Yes, my dear that is an interesting point. I may be able to help you out somewhat. All on the QT, of course. As you know I was on staff with Roger Lafontaine. One of my duties was to act as staff photographer. I made contact sheets of everything I shot, plus anything else I thought might relate to this psychopath. Back then, I hoped someone would catch him and I held onto all this stuff for evidence. Give me a while to dig them out as I'm not sure where I put them when I moved in here. I'll give you a call when I find them. Now, this goes under our original agreement, my name and my family must never be discussed, except privately between you and your sleuthing friend."

"Of course, Helen, we will protect your privacy."

Glenda could not wait to update Aimee. She phoned her right away. There was no answer. Glenda figured her friend was in her garden. She packed Connor into his snuggli and headed through the woods, across the acreage subdivision, to the Brace's house.

Glenda came out of the woods by their backyard. No one was in sight and she noticed all the windows on the back of the house were closed tight. Most likely Aimee had gone for groceries or to her Mom and Dad's place. Glenda was just about to step out into the yard when she spied a white pickup truck parked on the acreage road, across from Aimee's house, mostly hidden by the bushes growing alongside the verge on this side. She caught her breath and stepped back into the woods. Barely breathing, Glenda watched the truck. Something glinted and caught the sunlight. She realized the person in the driver seat was using binoculars. Instinctively she ducked down, wondering how powerful were they and had she been spotted?

Watching for a while, it seemed the person was focussed on the house. Glenda cut back into the woods a little way, using the scrappy cover of the trees between the next lot and the Brace's, she carefully made her way to the road. The pickup truck was parked ahead of her and across the road. She was about ten feet behind it and about fifteen feet from the road, her hand on Connor's rump, jostling him a bit up and down absent-mindedly as she walked. She could make out that the driver was a man, with a hairy arm, wearing a large wrist-watch extended out the window, holding binoculars. Suddenly, the arm was withdrawn, Aimee could tell he was checking his watch for the time, and then he started his engine and drove off in a cloud of dust. She rushed out to the road, her hands protectively covering Connor's head. All she could make out were the first two letters of his license plate: SR.

She walked back to Aimee's house and left a stone by the patio door. Aimee would recognize it as a sign from her and give her a call when she returned.

Coming to the edge of the woods back on her side of the acreage development, Glenda looked both ways up and down the road before emerging. There were no pickups in sight and no raised dust signalling one had passed by. She had left the house unlocked and made a note to self to keep it locked from now on.

Glenda made lunch, nursed Connor, washed and changed him and set him down for his afternoon nap. She left the windows open in the house and locked the front door then, with the baby monitor in hand, she went out the back door to her garden. She would do a little weeding and mull over everything that had happened today.

14 CAMOUFLAGE

In his last year of high school, with Christmas approaching, Gene wanted to do something special for Aunt Doris. For the life of him, he could not come up with a super gift idea. Sure, she would put on a show for any gift, a new purse or scarf or gloves. These were banal gifts in Gene's opinion. Some people would love a trip to Las Vegas, or an all-inclusive holiday in Mexico or an Alaskan cruise. Aunt Doris would not. She loved to stay at home. Typical gifts bought for her by friends and family were specialty treats, coffees, teas, chocolates, bouquets of flowers, lavender sweaters or lavender soaps. Gene thought they were boring. He wanted to give her something better, something grander.

One night as he was chopping wood and Dog was stacking it, he mentioned this trouble. To his astonishment, Dog came up with an idea.

"S'pect she'd like another cat or a dog. Up 'till ya came here she always had a one in th' house. Could never tell which'n one she liked better, a calico cat or'n a little lap dog. Git her one a those and mind you clean up after 'em an I'm purty sure she'd be real happy."

"Well there you go," thought Gene, "that is very doable."

Gene cleverly worked pets into the odd conversation here and there with Aunt Doris to discover which animal she would really like. It turned out Aunt Doris thought young pets too much trouble, with training and all, and that was why she had not replaced her last dog when it died. Gene decided the calico cat was the way to go and began visiting animal shelters to find a cat, not a kitten, that was house-broken and might like to sit on an old lady's knee once or twice a day.

At the humane center in Edmonton, where he made weekly visits, Gene quickly became frustrated by hearing, "one came in the other day but it has already been adopted." Gene began chatting up all the volunteers.

A young volunteer named Allie befriended Gene. She suggested a plan that might help him find the perfect cat. She told him that he just needed to continually show up after school for an hour or two, two or three days a week and volunteer to pet and clean the cat cages. She archly pointed out that by being around the cats more often and getting to know them better, he'd have a better chance of finding exactly what he wanted. And once he wanted to adopt, they would most likely give him first preference on that particular cat. This led to his taking a volunteer position with the Edmonton Humane Society.

To cover the time that he would not be home straightaway after school, Gene told Aunt Doris that he was tutoring another student. Just in case she checked, he pulled aside a fellow in his chemistry class that was a bit of a nerd yet was not doing all that well in chemistry and tutored him during a spare twice a week, with the understanding that he would back up his story, should Aunt Doris ever check. Aaron was more than happy to lie for the extra help.

After a few weeks, Gene found the perfect cat. Tiger Lily was a two-year-old calico that loved people and sought their attention. She was gentle, even while being groomed; she complied without ever exposing claws or fangs. She was a loving cat, quiet, house-broken and very clean. Allie filled out the adoption papers for Gene and agreed to keep the cat at her place; there was still over a week to go before Christmas. Gene kept helping out at the shelter, albeit with less heart and would then give Allie a ride home and visit Tiger Lily. Allie shared with Gene that her original owners gave her up when they had a baby. She never hurt the baby, she explained, it was just that some people don't trust cats around newborns.

On Christmas eve, Gene brought Tiger Lily home, stopping in Stony Plain for cat food and cat toys. Dog had agreed to keep the cat for a night or two and Gene went to his cabin on his arrival home. He was surprised to see a cat tree there. Dog had built it and padded it with carpet; his contribution to Christmas for Aunt Doris. The two men hugged, wished each other a Happy Christmas and patted each other on the back as Gene left the cabin.

Christmas morning was always a beautiful time at Aunt Doris's house. Gene woke to the smell of frying back-bacon. He washed and dressed quickly and came into the kitchen. Aunt Doris was dressed, makeup and hair perfectly done, bejewelled and standing at the stove in her apron and oven mitts, ready to pull a casserole from the oven. As if on cue, there came a knock at the door as Dog entered the kitchen, stomping the winter cold from his feet.

Aunt Doris laughed. She wished both of them a Merry Christmas and shooed them to the table.

The kitchen table was arranged elegantly. Aunt Doris had set out her best china complete with its coffeepot, sugar and creamer and she had used a crystal pitcher for juice. With Christmas napkins and small gifts at each place-setting, it was very festive. Gene ran to his room to find the little boxes he had wrapped for Aunt Doris. He had signed them from your boys, Gene and Doug; Doug being the name she used for Dog.

Gene and Dog took their seats as Aunt Doris lay the egg and cheese casserole on the table and then the bacon and a fruit and sweets tray. Gene quickly got up and stood behind her chair and pushed it in gently as she sat down. Aunt Doris laughed and took up their hands. She bowed her head in prayer.

"Lord, keep my boys safe on this your special day and throughout the year. Thank you so much for both of them and all your bountiful blessings. Amen."

She smiled at both of them, "well go on, dig in!" she ordered, passing the spoon to the casserole dish towards them.

The breakfast was delicious. They ate her special Christmas Morning casserole with the bacon, drank coffee and juice and lingered over sweets and fruit. Dog talked about Christmases when he was a child; the gist of it that there never was a lot, hardly ever even a Christmas tree and that his mama made the best of whatever they had, making sure each child received one new toy, most often hand-made by one parent or the other. That made Aunt Doris laugh and point out the small gifts on the table.

"Well, I think it's time for us to open a small gift or two ourselves," she declared. "Doug why don't you go first? And Gene, please reach over and get my Christmas book for me."

Aunt Doris always recorded everyone's gifts in her Christmas book. When Gene had asked her about it on his first Christmas with her, she told him sometimes one is overwhelmed by life, or maybe Christmas itself, and can't remember who gave them what. Now that made thank you cards ever so difficult. With a Christmas book, you record each gift as it is opened and have a record that you can use to refer to as needed.

He had learned many lessons that first Christmas, about the holiday and about his family. He had made Aunt Doris a birdhouse and given it to her when the family was over at dinnertime and they opened their gifts together. They, well mostly his male cousins, had laughed and jeered at his birdhouse and on the next day, he discovered that they had tried to pry the roof off, succeeding in loosening it. He spent Boxing Day fixing it. He had noticed that no one gave him or Dog a present. Their presents to Aunt Doris were copies of movies, toiletries, candles, sweaters and scarves. If there was a new baby or a wedding or graduation, they gave her a photo album. The albums were her favorite gifts.

Aunt Doris gave each family a gift of a game, age appropriate to the children in their home. She gave him a gift of a game and Dog a gift of a puzzle. It was on Boxing Day that she gave them more personal gifts. So now, Gene did the same for her each year. This year he had bought her a puzzle with many cats and dogs in the picture. He had wrapped it in a warm lap throw she had admired at a church bazaar and signed it from your boys, Gene and Doug. Tomorrow she would have her real cat.

Every family brought something for the pot-luck dinner: buns, pickles, salad, coleslaw, buttered carrots or green beans. They left with platefuls of turkey and ham and Aunt Doris's baking.

Dog always sat in a corner, never really saying much, drinking only one beer all afternoon. Gene cottoned on, at the second Christmas, that he was watching out for any souvenir seekers. If a salt and pepper set made its way into someone's bag, later Dog would make sure it made its way out. If something went into a pocket and he could not retrieve it, then he'd let Aunt Doris know. Not always, but usually she would discover the lump, while giving them a hug goodbye and good naturedly have them return the purloined item. When Gene asked her about this, she answered that she had many of her parents' things and sometimes people just couldn't wait for her to leave this good earth to get their hands on them. Then she reminded him that her lawyer was the Executor of her will and she had given him a list so that he knew who was to get what.

At this year's Christmas breakfast table, Dog opened his gift first. It was a pocket-knife from Aunt Doris. Dog's knife was so old and the blade so thin that he had actually chipped off its tip earlier in the fall, attempting to pry open a candy tin's lid for Aunt Doris. The new knife was a beauty, made in France, it fit well in the hand and opened without a wobble. Gene whistled. He knew this would become Dog's favourite gift.

Gene opened the next gift. His was a small inexpensive camera. Gene held it up, realized there was film in it and snapped Aunt Doris and Dog's picture.

"Oh Gene, thank you!" exclaimed Aunt Doris. 'I was so hoping you would like it and take pictures for me. I don't think I have very many current ones of the three of us. Not even a school picture of you as you were sick again this year and didn't get one done, now that's two years in a row!"

"I love it," he responded, giving his Aunt a peck on the cheek, "and it'll be a pleasure to take pictures for you. Now it's your turn to open your gift. We got you one between the two of us. Hope that's okay."

Aunt Doris oohed and awed over their gift wrapping and very carefully undid the ribbon and tape. Inside the box lay a leather flowered brooch.

"A wild rose brooch! Oh, I just love it. Look at the color, pale by the stamens and darker on the edges. This is lovely boys. Thank you so much. Oh, I'm going to wear this today. And every time I wear it, it will remind me of your love." Aunt Doris leaned over and squeezed both their hands.

"Well, Merry Christmas Dory," guffawed Dog.

Gene got up and gave her a kiss on the cheek and a hug, "I love you Aunt Doris. I'm glad you like your gift. Thank you for mine."

Instead of sitting down again, he gathered up the dishes and headed to the sink and began filling it with hot soapy water.

"Now ya jus sit purdy," Dog said to Aunt Doris. "We's gonna do the washin up." Dog poured her more coffee and brought more plates to the kitchen counter.

Gene turned on the radio and tuned in a station playing Christmas music.

Once the dishes were done, Gene asked if it was time to put the turkey in the oven.

"Oh, it's already in there," replied Aunt Doris. "I set it in just as we sat down for breakfast."

"Well, Dog and I can peel potatoes and whatever else you need," said Gene.

"You can open the oven and baste my turkey. I made up scalloped potatoes and the ham is cooked, both just need to be warmed and we can do that once the bird comes out of the oven. I'm counting on everyone else to bring the rest. Oh, there's cranberry jelly already made in the fridge and a vegetable platter and dip ready to go. We can relax until they all get here, probably around two thirty or three."

"It's a purdy day out there. Wanna walk down ta tha lake ta see tha ducks?" asked Dog.

"That would be lovely. Let me change before we go."

"We can take my truck. I'll warm it up," Gene offered.

"Well, wait until after I get changed. The turkey should be browned by then. We can tent it with some aluminum foil before we go."

Gene and Dog played a game of crib while Aunt Doris changed. Then they helped take the turkey out of the oven, tent it with tinfoil and put it back in the oven for her.

Gene drove to Lake Wabamun.

They walked the short distance from the car park to the path leading down to the lake. Many ducks overwintered close to the power plant as its heat kept quite a large portion of the lake unfrozen. Dog was carrying a thawed bag of corn and as they approached, he used his new pocket knife to slice it open.

"Hoo-whee! See that. This knife's not only good lookin but man, it's sharp."

Gene and Aunt Doris laughed as they accepted corn from him.

Gene tossed his handful quite far to attract the ducks. They flew in, honking and squawking on his second toss. Dog tossed some halfway between Gene's toss and where they stood. While some lingered eating the corn from the first throw, others skipped closer. Aunt Doris tossed her handful; it landed about half-way between Dog's toss and where they stood.

Gene took pictures of the ducks feeding and of Dog and Aunt Doris tossing corn at them. They lingered watching the ducks and walking up and down the small beach for about an hour, then headed home. On their way, Gene tuned the radio to Christmas music and they sang along with it the whole trip back.

Once in the house, Aunt Doris asked Gene to fetch the cooler and fill it with ice she had waiting just outside the door. Gene and Dog readied the cooler with pop and beer while she changed. She bustled into the kitchen and checked her turkey, then set out her vegetable tray and dips with bowls of chips on the dining room table and filled up the candy dishes placed out in the living room.

"There. Everything is done. Let's sit and enjoy the Christmas music and the quiet until they get here," she announced.

Gene filled the kettle for tea and prepared the coffeemaker then sat down on the couch. Dog had taken up his spot in his corner chair. From there he could see the whole room and into the dining room and a bit into the kitchen. Gene knew he would stay there all day.

Margaret's clan was the first to show up. Margaret was five years older than Doris. They arrived in two cars. Her eldest daughter, Muriel and her husband Herman, and their two grandsons in one car and their son, Rob, and his wife, Debra in the second car with Margaret. They came in with flurries of cold, the bustle of food platters and wrapped gifts, all shouting out hellos and Christmas greetings.

Aunt Doris hugged each of them and handed Christmas parcels and food platters to Gene. Debra sought him out later and gave him a hug. Gene liked Debra, she was warm and funny and always made an attempt to include him in the clan.

While Aunt Margaret and Aunt Doris bustled about in the kitchen, Rob headed for the cooler and gave both children a pop and fished out a beer for himself. Gene asked his young cousins if they would like to play a game. They sat with him at the dining room table and played Jenga.

Boyce and Alice arrived next with their three boys, Beckett, Dean and Glendon, the eldest of all the cousins. These were the main trouble-makers, thought Gene. Boyce was loud and a bit of a drunk. His boys copied his belligerent example and made fun of Dog and Gene at every opportunity. Both men, graduates of the tough streets, knew how to take it without responding and kept things as quiet as possible for Aunt Doris's sake. Gene suggested they put away the Jenga game before the pieces ended up flying into the Christmas tree. His cousins, looking to the door, quickly agreed.

Paul and Evelyne came in next. Paul was the son of Darrell, Aunt Doris' youngest brother. Gene never met him, he had passed away many years ago. Paul and Evelyne had no children. He was an accountant, with a capital

A, Gene thought ruefully and she was a school principal. They were relatively well off, well dressed and groomed, widely travelled, and much more cosmopolitan and sophisticated than the rest of the clan. Paul opened a bottle of wine, gave his wife and both Aunts a glass, poured one for himself and walked into the living room. He would sit by Dog for most of the visit, the two sometimes engrossed in conversation, sometimes just sitting and watching the party unfold.

Eveline circled the kitchen, put on an apron, never found a spot to work at so she sat at the table and kept the conversation going with tidbits of gossip, anecdotes from their last trip to Hawaii and fashion updates.

MJ, with her three children were the last to arrive. She was harried, said they were late because she had forgotten the perogies and had to go back for them, but here they were.

Gene always thought he'd fit in best with MJ's children. They were the closest to his age, their mothers were sisters and none of them knew who their father was. But no, Norman, Luna and Peter were indifferent to him.

Dog told him Aunt Doris always made a big fuss over them when they were small. As they grew up though, they did not return the love. There was no contact from their end, no phone calls, no thank you cards for gifts, nothing. She still provided for them, she had a college fund set up for each of them and always remembered their birthdays. She stopped dropping in at their place with little gifts and stopped sending them Valentines and Easter cards with cash in them.

Dog said this had been going on for a year or two before Gene showed up but he became the reason they had been cut off, in their minds, they had been turned out for this Johnny-come-lately. They could not see that their self-centered behaviour was the cause.

Now that everyone had gathered, the ladies started filling the kitchen counter and tabletop with platters of food. People would serve themselves and then go sit at the dining table or into the living room to eat. Gene set up Aunt Doris's TV trays in front of the couch and chairs in the living room. Paul and Evelyne took charge of drinks, pouring wine or punch in stemware for everyone and handing it out as they left the kitchen with their plateful of food.

Most of the adults sat in the dining room while most of the young cousins sat in the living room. Dog was in his usual chair; he kept it through tradition. In the first few years he had joined Aunt Doris's clan at Christmastime, he left his jacket squished up along its back. This was a torn, raggedly, stained, smelly thing. No one chose to sit with it. Over the years, everyone had accepted this as Dog's chair and no one tried to oust him from it. He still had a piece of clothing staking out his claim; today it was a pullover sweater draped on the back of the chair.

Gene sat on the floor and used a footstool as a table top. Luna joined him on the other side. Luna was a quiet, shy thing and into grunge music. The grunge look that she adopted did not sit well on her, she was too tall, fair, and pretty to carry it off. She came across as unkempt with her greasy hair and torn clothing, as if she had just gotten up and thrown the closest things on and gone out the door. Gene talked to her about bands, both liking the music of Rough Trade, a Toronto grunge band.

After dinner, as per tradition, the grandchildren did the dishes while the adults sat around the table. Paul oversaw the kitchen chores while filling wine glasses or coffee cups for the adults. Gene gave Luna the job to go and collect the plates and cutlery while he filled the sink with hot soapy water and began washing. Paul corralled the laggards and found jobs for them, he had Glendon taking out the garbage, Norman wrapping up food for the fridge and Beckett filling a bag with empties. He gave Luna a damp, soapy cloth and asked her to wipe down the TV trays.

Once all the dishes were dried and put away, Aunt Doris, Aunt Muriel and Evelyne came into the kitchen and set up the dessert trays. These would be passed out after the gifts were opened.

Herman always played Father Christmas. He would don a Santa hat and shout out "Ho! Ho! Ho!" to get everyone's attention. The first gift always went to Aunt Doris and it was always from her sister, Margaret. This year it was a beautifully wrapped small box. Upon opening it, Aunt Doris found an exquisite chocolate yule log, its top lifted up to reveal a few beautiful delicate chocolates on the inside. Everyone oohed and awed over it.

Aunt Doris looked at her sister and said a heartfelt, "thank you."

"Well, I know you love chocolate," said Aunt Margaret. "It's Bernard Calebot chocolate so it should be good."

"He's the best chocolatier in town," informed Evelyne, "You know it will be exquisite."

Herman finally broke the chocolate spell with a "Ho! Ho! Ho!"

Gene busied himself with Aunt Doris's Christmas book. He knew he was the best person for the job as he would not be interrupted with opening gifts from the others. For Aunt Doris's sake, he had bought small gifts for all his cousins, travel games, ball caps, a cassette he had recorded himself for Luna. He was surprised to find there were three gifts for him, one each from Aunt Margaret, Aunt Doris and Rob, Debra and Children. The latter really surprised him. This was the first time any of the families acknowledge him with a gift. It was a small tool set, tied up in its cloth carry bag and perfect for carrying in his truck. Gene later found them alone in the kitchen and thanked them profusely for it. Debra ruffled his hair.

Once all the gifts were opened, Aunt Doris checked her Christmas book. Gene smiled over at her. He knew he had captured it completely.

Paul and Evelyne served coffee and tea and passed around the trays of Christmas cookies, squares, pies and cakes.

The youngest kids were opening up their boxed toys and setting them up. Boyce was repeating the same lame dirty joke around the room, guffawing loudly at his own punchline. Aunts Muriel, Margaret, Doris and Evelyne were gathered around the dining room table, discussing Aunt Margaret's latest medical checkup. Suddenly Gene noticed Dog motioning to him towards the hallway.

Gene headed down the hall. His cousins Beckett, Norman and Glendon were in his room. Gene walked in. Beckett was pulling books off his shelf, glancing at them, feathering them open, then tossing them onto his bed. Glendon was looking around, touching knick-knacks and flicking sports medals, Norman was at his closet going through his clothes. Gene stepped into the room and closed the door hard, gaining their attention.

"Can I help you gentlemen?' he asked.

"Naw," said Beckett, leering, looking to the others, then to Gene, "we're just checking out Aunt Doris's spare bedroom."

The other two laughed.

"This is my room and this is my stuff," said Gene. "I'd appreciate it if you left my stuff alone and left right now."

Beckett crossed the room in a lightning move and grabbed Gene by the throat, lifting him off his feet. "Who's gonna make us?" he asked. Gene was aware of Glendon laughing and Norman putting things back into the closet and saying, "oh, man, this is not cool."

Gene was in a choke hold. He grabbed Beckett's hands and knee-ed him hard between the legs then head-banged him. Beckett stumbled backwards. Gene opened the door.

"Out, gentlemen. I don't want to catch any of you in this room ever again."

Gene closed the door behind them. He started tidying up the mess they had made. He stifled his choking cough. He would not give them the satisfaction of hearing it. Once his anger was under control, he returned to the front room.

People were tidying up their gifts. Gene joined Aunt Doris in the kitchen. Alice and MJ were there. Aunt Doris was filling up each person's pan or plate with goodies to take home. She popped packages of wrapped Christmas desserts out of the freezer and small aluminum pans of turkey or ham, whichever they wanted from the fridge and another of scalloped potatoes for each family. All this she had prepared days before Christmas. She also sent MJ and Debra home with left-over salads and vegetables and buns.

Gene got out bags and helped her parcel it up. Everyone would be leaving soon. He put on his boots, coat and tuque and waited on the porch. They would need help loading up their cars.

When MJ left, herself and the three kids loaded down with goodies and gifts, Gene helped them pack up their car. Luna sheepishly approached him and gave him a big hug and wished him a Merry Christmas to her fave cousin. Norman was the last to get into the car. He turned to Gene and mumbled that he was sorry for being in his room. Gene felt he had won a small victory with both of them.

"Look out for those two. They'll want to get even," Norman warned, turning to Gene as he got into the car. Gene shook his hand. "Don't worry. I can take care of myself," he answered.

Boyce and Alice and the three boys were the last to leave. Boyce had thrown Gene his keys with a "boy, go fetch my car."

Gene brought it right to the door and popped the trunk open.

As he headed up the stairs, Boyce handed him a boxful of gifts. Gene took them to the car and put them in the trunk. He straightened up to find the three boys had surrounded him. They let fly a series of punches to his body. Gene, almost as tall as they were, pushed his way through them. Alice was hugging Aunt Doris goodbye at the door. Gene realized his aunt had seen the whole thing. He walked back to the house without a look back.

Once inside, Aunt Doris hugged him, "I'm so sorry for those boys' actions," she said.

"Don't worry about it," Gene answered. He smiled at her, "my coat is pretty thick. They didn't hurt me."

"You are my knight in shining armour," she replied.

That night, lying in bed, Gene thought, well this isn't the first volley from those boys. It is the first time Aunt Doris has witnessed something overtly though. And that is a good thing. He fell asleep happy.

The next morning while Aunt Doris cooked a breakfast of waffles and sausages, Gene wiped down the furniture in the living and dining room and vacuumed.

Dog came over with a huge box.

"My goodness, Doug. What in the world do you have in there?" asked Aunt Doris.

"Somethin fer ya from Gene an me. Well, go on, open it up," he grinned like a little boy at her.

Gene took the spatula from her hand and set the last of the waffles into the oven alongside the sausages to stay warm. He grabbed the box from Dog.

"Take your coat off. Let's go into the front room."

They had Aunt Doris sit in her favourite chair and placed the huge box in front of her. Exclaiming the whole time, she tore off the paper to find a rough homemade cardboard box that was jerry rigged from several supermarket boxes. Dog handed her his knife to cut it open, then seeing her struggle with it, he took it back and opened it himself.

Aunt Doris had to stand up to see inside the box. There was Dog's cat tree and at the very bottom, curled on the bottom tier was Lilly, purring and looking up at her with huge eyes.

"Oh my!" exclaimed Aunt Doris. "Will you look at that? A beautiful calico cat with big beautiful eyes."

Dog cut the box down its length and the cat scampered out. Aunt Doris sat down and the cat jumped up onto the arm of her chair, looking at her. Aunt Doris leaned closer and Tiger Lilly touched her forehead with her own.

"Looks like she likes yer," said Dog.

"Hello my beauty. And what is your name?" asked Aunt Doris, petting the cat, which had begun to purr once more.

"Her name is Tiger Lilly. She is two years old and she is perfectly house broken. She comes from a good home. They don't want her anymore because they just had a baby and are too busy," said Gene.

"An I made her this cat tree. See, she can climb up and there's places she can scratch an jest sit, maybe cat-nap," said Dog.

"Boys, this is the best Christmas present ever. We can set up the cat stand in the window once the tree comes down. Dog just put it to the side there for now."

"I got you some cat food and dishes too," said Gene, fishing them out of the bottom of the box. "I'm not sure where to set them up."

Aunt Doris laughed, "well, put them in the kitchen for now We'll figure it all out later." She petted the cat on her lap.

"Do you boys want to open your presents now or eat first?" she asked.

Simultaneously Gene called out presents and Dog called out eat. Aunt Doris laughed. Dog sheepishly gave in and said presents first.

Gene invited Dog to sit down and fetched two presents from under the tree for him to open. Aunt Doris had wrapped up a new coat for him. Dog got up and tried it on and exclaimed over every little feature on that coat.

"It's got an inside pocket right here, See Gene? An look, the outside pockets got zippers. Boy, is it warm. See how the collar fits, nice an tight at ma neck. It's got a hood too!"

"Enough on the coat," said Gene. "Open my gift to you."

Gene had bought Dog a crossbow, similar to the one Aunt Doris had given him on his birthday last summer. Dog always followed Gene when he did practice shooting and Gene would sometimes let him take a turn. Now he had his own bow and Gene would no longer feel he needed to share his bow with him.

"Wow! Gene ..., boy, this a cost ya a pretty penny. I cant take it."

Gene had to insist while Doug protested, trying to hand the bow back. It was only when he finally added, "I tell you what. After breakfast you and I can go out back and do some target practice. You can wear your new coat," that finally stopped Dog's yammering.

Aunt Doris pointed out two more gifts under the tree, both for Gene.

Her gift to Gene was also a coat, this one a leather jacket. The brown leather coat hung loosely to his hips, a sportscoat style with front and back yokes. Gene loved it and kept brushing the soft leather with his palm.

"Well, it won't keep you warm like Doug's coat. But you'll look sharp for the young ladies," teased Aunt Doris when he thanked her for it.

Dog had made Gene a wall plaque for Gene's sports medals. The top was peaked, like a roof and there was a small brass plate on it that had his name engraved on it. The medals hung inside, under the peaked part on brass hooks. Dog had used alder wood with a rich oak stain. He had outlined all the edges with his wood burner depicting sports equipment. It was a thing of beauty, showing real craftsmanship. Gene let him know this as he thanked him for it.

15 CHAMPAGNE

The morning of Dave's birthday party dawned cold, bleary, and wet. So much for an outdoor party, mused Glenda. She wondered if Dave and Kyle would still head out for their cycling tour as planned, giving her and Aimee the chance to set up for his party. She also wondered if he had cottoned on yet to the idea that they were organizing a party for him.

Glenda dressed Connor in a bright new play suit and sat him in the high chair. She placed a party hat on his bald head and was donning one herself when Dave came into the kitchen.

"Morning, Birthday Boy!" she greeted him, giving him a kiss.

"Mn," he said, grabbing her in his embrace, "will there be steak for supper, seeing as how it's my birthday?"

"Sure thing," she teased, "as long as you barbecue it in the rain."

"Oh, it's not that bad. Just a little drizzle." Dave let her go and bent down to give Connor a kiss. "Kyle and I are still going on our bike ride," he said.

"Well, you better give him a call to make sure."

"Oh, I've already texted him. I'm to pick him up in about forty minutes. But first, breakfast!"

Shortly after Dave left, Aimee came over with Trevor and a box full of the food the two mamas had prepared the day before. Connor had begun to crawl, so they set up both babies on a quilt with all of their toys in the sunless sunroom, just off the kitchen, and put a baby gate at its door.

Together the mamas wrote a to-do list. They began by making pies. Dave loved pies. Aimee made the dough for the crust while Glenda prepared the fillings. They had decided on a Saskatoon berry pie and a rhubarb-cherry pie, all the fruit having come from Glenda and Dave's garden.

'You know, Aimee, I keep pouring over all those statistics. Almost every

October, usually about mid month, there's something. At the least a very flashy rifle shot through a window," she sighed before continuing, "or worse." Glenda smiled over to her friend.

"Yep. I noticed that too. The other thing about it, it usually involves a woman and mostly they have been Native victims."

"I think you're right," Glenda went over to her laptop and looked it up." Yep. You are right. I hadn't noticed that."

"Pies are ready for their filling. Got them done?"

"Yeah, ready. I wonder why this guy targets Aboriginal women so much."

Aimee sighed, "well I have wondered about that ever since kindergarten. Why do some people just take a dislike to you because of your race? Are they afraid that somehow the Red Man is going to rise up, wage war, scalp all the white folk and reclaim our land? Don't get me going on it, because there is no end to the dialogue."

"I hear you, Girl-Friend. And I love and appreciate you," Glenda added, going over to Aimee and bumping hips with her.

"Hey, careful, I'm pouring Saskatoon berries into the pie shell here!"

They both laughed.

By the time Dave and Kyle came back from their bike rides, the pies, were baked, the babies put down for naps over at Aimee's house with a babysitter, the Ellis house decorated, guests accumulated, with all their cars parked over at Aimee and Kyle's place. The mamas had wisely hired a teenaged neighbourhood girl to babysit the babies, so all the adults could enjoy the party.

Dave came in the back door and headed for the shower in the back washroom. Glenda quickly realized he had no clue about the party and would, most likely, come out of the shower bare-naked and walk through the house, now full of their guests, to the bedroom, for dry clothes. Laughing she picked out some clothes for him and brought them into the washroom.

"Hey Birthday Boy, how was your bike ride? I've got some clean clothes here for you."

"It was awesome. We were on a dirt bike trail, up and down little hills. We got pretty muddy."

"Good, I'm glad you had fun. Okay, I'm going to check on Connor now," she fibbed, leaving the washroom.

The guests were twittering, impatiently waiting for Dave to finish his shower. Glenda stood just outside the bathroom door with a party hat and a beer ready for him.

Their shouts of 'Surprise! Happy Birthday!' really shocked him. Dave recovered quickly, took a swig of the offered beer and announced, "well, so much for a nap, hey?"

The mamas bustled around the dining room table and began taking the covers off the various dishes of food while Kyle set up his iPod filled with techno music.

The party was a huge success. Everyone busied themselves piling their plates with food while visiting and laughing. Dave was very pleased with his birthday pies.

Glenda had floated her ideas on featurettes about rural sign shootings and ubiquitous Albertan white pickup trucks to Dianne, her assignment editor. She wormed a reluctant go-ahead for both ideas from her, then asked if her favourite cameraman could be assigned to start collecting footage. Glenda was not due back to work until after the New Year and she did not want all the footage to include snow.

Later that week Glenda stopped in at the RCMP office in Stony Plain. She spoke with a public relations officer about her story on drive-by shootings. His first response was a low whistle.

"What kind of drive-by shootings are you talking about?" he asked.

"What kinds are there? Is there an ongoing investigation?" she asked.

"Well, I asked, first," he said with a smile, "so that means you get to answer my question first."

"But your question led to a new one from me that is way more intriguing than people shooting at stop signs and mailboxes."

"Fair enough. You have our cooperation on a story to do with drive-by shootings at road signs and mailboxes. We can contact you as they are reported. What's the best number to call?"

Glenda gave him her cellphone number and tried prying again for information on any ongoing investigations. Again, she was stonewalled and the officer excused himself to deal with other matters. Taking her leave, Glenda ruefully thought that, for a young recruit, he was pretty smooth at closing her down.

Glenda reported all of this to Dave that night over supper, as she informed him of her new project. Then she asked him if he would like to be the videographer on the project. He quickly agreed to take it on. Glenda let him know that she had already gotten Dianne's approval although she wasn't sure about a budget for scheduling hours for the project. Flashing a smile at her, Dave said he would make the time, shooting either before going into the television station, or leaving early and shooting on his way home.

Together the two of them reviewed once again Roger Lafontaine's file on night mischief. Dave could not make out a pattern, reaching the same conclusion as Glenda and Aimee.

"Well," Glenda said, "the calls will most likely come in at the strangest times. I'm not suggesting you run out at one o'clock in the morning and videotape anything. We don't really stand a snowball's chance in Hades to actually catch someone on tape shooting out a sign or a mailbox. What I'm after is clear, daytime pictures of a freshly shot sign or mail box."

"I'll video those on my way home or during down times at the station."

Glenda smiled at him. I'm so glad you're onboard with this."

"Let's put your phone on silent when we go to bed each night. It can go to a message if anyone calls late," he suggested. "In fact, let's do that now and pretend it is really late and go to bed early while Connor is still sleeping."

And with that, Dave grabbed up the dishes, dumped them into the sink, then grabbed Glenda and kissed her hard, walking her backwards towards the bedroom. He paused by the phone stand to silence her phone and put it on charge.

16 MIDNIGHT

Gene lived with his Aunt Doris just a few years before she died. Gene found her dead, one morning, in her bed. The coroner said she had suffered a heart attack in her sleep.

It was October, Gene remembered throwing on the leather coat she had given him that past Christmas, for the short walk to Dog's cabin. They came back to the house together. It was Dog who made the phone calls, first to the authorities then to the family. The RCMP and the paramedics showed up. Gene looked on, answered any questions posed to him monosyllabically. Then his three older male cousins showed up and accused him of killing her. Beckett had grabbed him by the scruff of his neck and pounded him in the face repeatedly. Gene did not defend himself, he just went limp. Dog pulled him off and took Gene indoors to clean him up, yelling at them to just leave.

To this day, he could not believe that he did not clock his cousin. It would have served him right. However, the RCMP officer who had witnessed the whole thing had given the three boys a stern talking to and they were told not to return to the property unless they were invited.

Aunt Doris had prepared for her own funeral and had taken care of the minutest details. The funeral home had a document, signed by her that outlined where she was to be buried, where the funeral would take place, the flowers, the caterers and suggestions on what to serve, guests to contact, right down to insisting Gene and Dog be seated alone in the first row in brand new suits, sitting ahead of her remaining relatives. She had left cash with the funeral home to take care of all of these details. The funeral staff was very attentive to every one of her wishes and carried them out as professionally as possible, over the family's many protestations.

The day after the funeral two carloads of family members showed up and asked Gene to move out of the house. They wished to enter it and take away what they wanted to remember Aunt Doris by. Gene held his ground and would not let them in. They called the RCMP. Gene thought for sure he would be kicked out on his ear; instead the RCMP took his side and told the family they were not to return to the property for any reason until the will was probated and that it gave them permission to do so. They also warned Gene and Dog that they could stay on the property until then, however, they were not to remove any effects, even their own, from the property until the will was settled.

Dog suggested to Gene that they hire some of the hobo brethren to set up camps on the property, as a way to guard and protect it from the family. Jim agreed and Dog arranged it. One group of three men camped in some woods by the road and another small group set up in the woods behind the house. If any incursions happened, Gene did not hear about them although he did see his one cousin, Dean, in the supermarket with a black eye. Gene grinned and bought extra groceries.

That evening he came out of the house with a whole bag of potatoes, each buttered and wrapped in tin foil, a large pot with a large bag of frozen corn in water and a warehouse pack of steaks. He built a huge bonfire and sent Dog to go collect everyone for dinner. They would eat like kings tonight.

Gene remained by the fire late into the night, staring into the dancing flames. From time to time he would get up and throw more wood onto it. The evening was perfect. Aunt Doris would have loved it. Everything was quiet. Looking up into the sky filled with a myriad of twinkling lights, Gene caught sight of a shooting star. He took this as a sign that yes, she was very pleased.

17 OXBLOOD

The first time Jim picked up a young, lone, female hitch-hiker on his way home from university was a week or so after Aunt Doris died. Things were in crisis mode and he let fall his usual self-discipline, giving in to his wild, dark impulses. Now that Aunt Doris was dead, he had no use for the Dzuik name and he was in the process of having his name changed to Jim Drucker. He had a temporary ID card and was waiting for the permanent one to come in the mail.

Jim realized that his truck could be a dead give-away to his identity. Because of the name change, his fingerprints were now on file and this worried him.

He knew of all kinds of dark, rarely used country roads and he planned to take his young hitchhiker to one. When she protested as they turned off the highway, he turned to her and gave her a charming smile. He could see her relax a bit as she looked at him and he quickly jabbed her hard with his fist between the eyes. Blood spurted from her nose, she screamed and grabbed her face with both hands. He quickly put his hand behind her head and grabbed a handful of hair. She turned slowly, looking in fear and bewilderment at him.

"Want more?" he growled at her. She shook her head no. "Then just sit there and be quiet," he commanded, slamming her head into the dashboard.

Jim parked the truck by some bushes on a rarely used side road, calmly got out, walked around to her side and opened the door.

"You're a fucking mess," he said to her. With a wide, happy smile, he added, "don't worry about it. No one is ever going to see you again.

Her eyes went huge in her face, her mouth opened to scream, and Jim stuffed an old rag into it, while grasping both her hands and yanking her out of the truck. He could hear her retching on the cloth and pulled the gag out of her mouth. She screamed. He slapped her and put it back in. She began hacking. He pulled the rag out. She screamed. He slapped her and put it back in. Standing back and laughing at her, listening to her struggle to breathe, Jim said, "darling, we can do this all night long if you want. Or just stop screaming. It is annoying and trust me, there is no one out here to hear it."

He pulled the gag out and she did not scream. He watched her for a beat.

"Why are you doing this?" she asked, choking and sobbing.

"Because I can and it is fun," he answered.

He grabbed her by the front of her jean jacket and threw her on the ground. She tried to get up. He kicked her. She stayed down, faced him, pulling her knees in front of her and holding her hands up in a whoa pose.

"Just let me go," she pleaded. "I won't tell anyone."

Jim leaned down to her face and said, "that's right. Because you will be dead." He quickly grabbed her hands and tied them with a bungee cord. He pulled her towards a barbed wire fence running through the scraggy bush and hooked the bungee cord onto it. She screamed the whole time and he brandished the rag, dangling it in front of her eyes. She continued to scream so he stuffed it in her mouth.

That girl fought Jim fiercely. He came away with many bruises, even a black eye where she head-banged him. He gave as good as he got. Then he used her clothing to slowly strangle her as he pumped his hips and came inside her. He lay on top of her, resting, and finally he felt her corpse slacken as the life subsided and ceased to exist in her feisty little body.

Jim got up and whistled a little tune. He looked down at her as he adjusted his clothing, noting blood on his jacket and shirt. He went through the pockets of her clothes, found nothing of interest and returned everything where he had found it. Then he went to the cab of his truck and grabbed her purse. He sat next to her dead body and started rifling though it. He found a packet of cigarettes and pulled one out and lit it. While smoking he finished going through her possessions, pocketing the few dollars and coins she had and leaving everything else alone.

"Well, party is over. I guess it's time to clean up," he said aloud. Jim got a tarp out of the back of his truck, put her body in the middle of it and gathered up all her clothes and belongings and threw them on top of her. He folded her legs up, then, holding them, he folded two sides of the tarp over her body then rolled the whole thing closed. He used two bungee cords to secure the package. He placed her in the back of his pickup and drove towards one of the many gravel pits in the vicinity.

Dog wondered at Jim's appearance when he came in and Jim sheepishly let it be known that he got into a scrap after school. Dog volunteered to make their supper as Jim showered and cleaned himself up.

That night, after Dog had left, Jim pulled his old cigar box out from his bottom drawer and, going to his coat, took a long black feather from his pocket and added it to his collection. 'Yes, sirree,' he thought, 'it has been a while but hoo-wee that was a good time.'

Lying in bed, staring up at the ceiling, Jim replayed the whole escapade with a wide smile on his face. Then he began to wonder what to do about the truck. It was like he needed two trucks, one for mischief and one for public use. They would have to be identical, excepting the license plate of course. And if he had two trucks, it might be a good idea to have a disguise in the second one, just in case. He'd have to figure out just how to pull all of this off. He fell asleep still puzzling it out.

18 UMBER

All was not going as smoothly as Jim would have liked. He had created a muddle of confusion for everyone by insisting on his name change and he was short of funds for the first time since moving in with Aunt Doris.

The will was not instantly probated, he was told it could take up to two years before it was finalised. Jim had saved money from his allowances and summer jobs and thought he could carry himself and Dog into summer.

As soon as he could, in the spring Jim took a job with a family friend in construction. A week later, Aunt Doris's friend let him go; he explained to him that his ties with her family were longer standing than his loyalty to a summer relief worker. Jim took odd jobs all over the county to keep himself and Dog in groceries.

One of these was with George Taylor, a bit of a drunkard, who managed to keep his renovations company operating, mostly by doing work for cottagers. George was hired to fix up some cabins at Lake Isle that had been trashed by some partying tourists.

First, they decided to tackle the plumbing problems, if only to make their own life more comfortable as they worked on the three cabins. Jim had snaked out all the toilets and George had called in the honey wagon to pump out the septic field. Jim had stood by the driver, watching as large bulges would come thunking up the hose to be deposited in the truck.

"I don't even want to know what those are and where you dump this shit, pardon the pun," he said, laughing.

George came up from behind and rapped Jim on the back of his head with his knuckles.

"I'm not paying you to stand by watching others work, boy."

"What's next?" asked Jim, rubbing his head.

"Dry-walling."

George went inside the first cabin, hollering over his shoulder for Jim to bring in the drywall sheets from his truck. Jim looked at them. George had obviously bought these at some discount place; their paper was ripped and corners were broken. There was no way by just picking them up that he could bring these in by himself. He fetched a wheelbarrow and laid a board across it and wheeled it to the back of the truck then gingerly slid one sheet of drywall onto it. The board was shorter than the drywall so he could not stack too many on each load. The whole time he was doing this, George stood in the doorway yelling at him to hurry up as he was waiting on him.

The grumbling lasted all day. Jim took too long to get the drywall, he took too long measuring and cutting it to fit instead of just eyeballing and sawing away. Jim complained that there were no drywall screws and did not want to use the nails George handed him. George finally sent him home early in the afternoon saying he would only pay him for half a day because he was useless and was holding up the job.

Jim went home in a foul mood. As a high school graduation present Aunt Doris had presented him with a compound bow and Dog had fashioned three new practice targets, hidden away in a back field. Jim grabbed a carton of juice and headed out to the field. He spent over an hour at target practice. When he came in, Dog had made a fry-supper of smokies, potatoes and onions.

Before Dog left for the evening, he said, "Jim, yore young. The world is against ya. It's against just about every young person. Don't be like me. Fight the good fight. You got high school, man. Yore smart. And ya know darn well once this will-thing is settled, it'll be in yore favour. Doris loved ya and she will have taken care of ya. She didn't have much truck with the rest of them Dzookers. Hang in there, man."

Jim smiled at the empty room. Dog was right. He just had to get through this spell and things would get better. Construction paid better than bagging groceries or pumping gas. He would look around for a better boss. Jim went to his room and counted up his stash. He didn't have a lot. There was eight hundred and forty-five dollars and some change. That could keep them in groceries for a while. He called George and quit. Tomorrow he would get a better job.

A week later, Jim started a new job with a large company that built new homes in Spruce Grove. He worked as a swamper and got on fine with all the men, watching as they worked and learning their trades.

However, this was not the end of his troubles. Two weeks later, Jim found his truck blocked in the parking lot of the grocery store as he came out carrying his purchases. He set them down on the truck bed and approached George Taylor's rusted out Chevy pickup. Arms akimbo, Jim hollered for George to clear out of his way. George laughed at him, called him a bastard and as Jim lunged closer, peeled his beater out of the parking lot, spraying him with loose gravel.

The following Saturday, a day off for Jim, he drove around Lake Isle and found George's beat up truck parked on a wooded road. Jim found a spot to pull off the road where he could leave his truck out of sight. He walked back through the woods to George's truck. George had obviously left his truck on the road because the cottage's driveway went down at a steep, curved angle. Jim walked through the bush all around the building. Being a good distance from the lake, this cottage sat alone in the woods. There weren't any outbuildings, sheds or garages around and there were no neighbouring houses either. It was quite secluded.

There were no other cars parked in the yard; it was hardly a yard, just the tiniest clearing barely able to hold two vehicles and with room for them to turn around. The trees totally hemmed in the little summer home. The tiny driveway was littered with George's tools. And it appeared to Jim that no one except George Taylor was on the property. Jim came out of the woods halfway up the driveway and whistled a cheery tune as he walked down its steep slope towards the house.

George finally spotted him and yelled down at him from the roof of the cottage.

"What the hell are you doing here?"

Jim smiled up at him, "I was upset at our last meeting. I came for an apology."

"Well you aint getting one from me," George hollered down. "You left me high and dry. I had a contract to fix up three cabins in one week and you up and quit on me."

"Oh, come on George. What did you expect the way you kept hollering and hitting me? Then you go and call me names at the grocery store."

"I got nothing to say to you," George said and turned back to the roof, resuming his hammering.

Jim climbed up a ladder, propped at the back of the house. He carried George's crowbar in his hand. Jim surprised George when he came over the peak and stood above him on the roof. Jim looked at the roof. George was working at its bottom, hammering in shingles. But the whole board he was hammering the shingles in shook with each blow; it was not properly anchored down. George was now hollering at him, swinging his hammer wildly, "Git out of here. I don't want no truck with you."

Those were his very last words because, before he could stand up, Jim had pried the loose board free with the crowbar, and it with George and his roofing hammer, shingles, nails, all slid off the top of that cottage, like a toboggan down a snowy hill.

Jim carefully climbed down the ladder. Back on the ground, he walked over to where George lay. He was moaning and cursing. One leg was caught under his body and jutted out by the other leg's hip. It would be broken, thought Jim. He bent down close to George's face and whispered, "well who is laughing at who now, heh?" Then, with one arm he raised him up by his hair, ignoring his pleas and screams, and with the other arm he pounded a pickaxe in the ground below where he had lain. Jim violently slammed George onto it. Jim stepped hard onto his chest until the axe penetrated his body more deeply. He sat on his haunches close to George's limp body. He wasn't dead yet, just passed out. But he would be dead soon.

Jim got up, whistled as he walked around the tiny yard then stood silently, his arm stretched out, his palm open to the air. After a small infinity a chickadee landed on his index finger. Jim quickly moved his thumb to trap it by its feet. Then he let it go, laughing. He had heard some magpies not far off and headed their way. Stopping at his truck, he pulled out a sling-shot. Going downhill towards the lake, he could spot the magpies. He aimed at the closest one and it fell, stunned by his stone. Jim did not kill it; he merely plucked a few feathers from its wing and sauntered back to where George lay. He tucked one of the feathers into the bib of his overall.

19 SHADOW

Fall came. Jim had registered at the University of Alberta. He had decided to major in pharmacy. This was his second year, things were really tight as he financed everything, the house expenses, his gas, the groceries for himself and Dog, plus his tuition with money from his summer jobs and part-time work while going to school.

It wasn't until his third year of university that Aunt Doris's will was probated and finally, he could breathe easier. Jim smiled to himself at the end of term; his grade average had gone up and he no longer needed to work part-time. He and Dog were even eating better at home.

There had been little time or opportunity for mischief. Jim had taken to abducting lone hitch-hikers, and only when there was no other traffic in sight. His opportunities were quite limited.

Jim was always careful when he picked up lone hitch-hikers. He still drove the old truck Aunt Doris had bought for him. There were a lot of similar trucks on the road, giving him some anonymity. He kept his truck mud-spattered so that it would be hard for anyone to read his license plate. He only picked up hitch-hikers on lonely stretches, where he could see ahead of him and behind him that the traffic was non-existent. He often passed up a tempting lone teen on the highway because of this policy.

Once Jim came into his inheritance, he bought two identical, used, white trucks at two different dealerships. The white truck was favoured by many in Alberta as the corporate truck of choice. No one remembered a white truck, they were everywhere. He named one Donald and the other Daisy. He bought both with cash. With Daisy, he gave the seller a false name and address. He found places to stash Daisy, moving her around the countryside, never too far from home.

Whenever Jim left home for school, church, or civic duties, he drove Donald. Otherwise, he drove to where Daisy was stashed and switched vehicles. Only Daisy could be traced to shenanigans. And Daisy could not be traced to him. He had never registered or insured the vehicle. He changed his clothing as soon as he got to the truck, donning coloured contact lenses and greasing his hair back. He put on a baseball cap and labourer's clothing, which he otherwise never wore. He carried fake ID and even wore different sunglasses. He replaced his Daisy clothes if they were blood-spattered, taking them home and burning them in his fireplace. Jim believed that no one would ever find forensic evidence on him or find his second truck.

That November, there was a woman that Jim picked up whose death did create quite a stir. Jim had come across her in a stalled car on the highway. He had passed her once and doubled back. She was still there. It was about nine-thirty on a Thursday night. He had stayed late at university, working on a project. He pulled up ahead of her, backed the truck close to her car, got out and spoke with her.

The woman reminded Jim of his foster mother, Mary. She was short, middle aged and a holy-roller. Her first words to Jim were, "thank God somebody stopped to help me out." Jim had smiled at her. He soon found out she was from Stony Plain and offered her a ride. Except he did not plan to take her to Stony Plain. Three different vehicles passed them while they spoke and before Jim had her hustled into his truck. He had driven her down a desolate country road and he had left her there, quite dead.

For some reason, this victim hit the local news. A local reporter, a lady by the name of Helen Majeau had written an article on her disappearance and had tracked down eyewitnesses who claimed to have seen a young man in a white pickup truck by her stalled vehicle. Jim had not disposed of this body in a gravel pit or by fire as he usually did, he had been cold and tired, he left her on that lonely secondary road, in a ditch. There was a second story in the local paper about a month later, just when Jim started to relax, about the discovery of her dead, raped and strangled body.

No one ever stopped Jim in his truck or questioned him about this death. He felt very lucky. He vowed he would never be so careless again.

20 STEEL

Helen Majeau sighed loudly, making sure that her boss heard her.

"I don't care, Helen, if you don't like it. Stories about dead Indians don't sell advertising. And as the paper is free, the advertising is what's paying our salaries. Forget it. Write me up a nice fluffy piece. What's coming up? How about something on spring prom, with pictures of young girls in dresses bought locally. Do ya think you can do that, Helen?"

Helen barely nodded, avoided eye contact with her boss, Roger Lafontaine, as she gathered up her notes, tapped her closed folder on the table's edge to settle its contents and turned on her heels to leave his office.

Before she reached the door, Roger hollered across the room, "and check with the RCMP on radar traps coming up and on any accidents. Might be something juicy there for the front page. Check what's coming up in court too."

Back in her own office, Helen sighed again as she settled into her swivel chair and rubbed her forehead with the fingers of her left hand. She grabbed the phone with the right. She checked for messages. There were none.

Turning away from her desk, Helen stared at her closed door. Through the interior window beside it she could see Roger on the phone in his office across the hall. She ran her fingers through her hair and spoke aloud to the empty room.

"Well, Helen, you know Roger can be fairly narrow-minded but he does pay you eighteen hundred and thirty dollars a month for work you can do in your sleep. If you really want to crack big stories, you are going to have to pack up and move your work to the big city and we both know you don't want to do that."

She chuckled at herself as she swivelled her chair back to her desk, grabbed the phone and called Brent, a young recruit she had befriended, at the RCMP office.

After lunch Helen left the office with her Nikon camera bag slung over her shoulder.

"'Bye, Roger. I'm heading out to get some shots over at Sandi's shop. She's expecting some high school girls to come in after school to try on prom dresses."

"Atta Girl, Helen, go get 'em Tiger," Roger called out to her back as she left the newspaper office.

About ten the next morning, Roger called Helen at home, on her day off.

"You still got that camera bag handy? A hunter's been shot over by old man Zelenko's property. Know where that is? I'm listening to the RCMP band, it's just been called in. Wanna go get some pictures, Helen? This could be a big story for us."

Driving her husband's pickup, Helen headed towards Highway 16 and took it west. By the turn off for Highway 43, she noticed an RCMP officer across the way had set up a speeding trap on the downside of the hill on Highway 16. She doubled back, thinking she could get a shot or two for Roger.

Pulling up behind the cruiser, Helen left the truck, carrying her camera and snapped a few pictures of the officer talking to a driver inside a vehicle. She made sure she did not catch the license plate in the picture nor a clear glimpse of the driver, yet she captured the officer in crisp focus, bathed in the light of the spring sun.

Helen had returned to her truck and was applying DEET. The mosquitoes were horrendous.

"Oh, so it's you, Helen," a voice she recognized as Officer Brent Turner said, approaching her.

"Hi Brent. I just got a great photo of you for your mom," she answered.

"Don't you mean for your boss at the paper?" he quipped.

"Yes. That too. Well, I'm off."

"Would you like a cup of coffee, first? I have my thermos in the car."

"Thank you, but no time. I have an appointment."

Brent chuckled, "where are you headed?" he asked.

"Oh. I'm going to look in on Gord's cousin, Darlene up at Alberta Beach. See you around," she fibbed, getting into the truck.

Helen smiled to herself driving away. Brent was younger than her, a bachelor. He hailed from Saint John, New Brunswick. On first meeting him and worming that information out of him, Helen had told him about her grandfather, who had been an RCMP officer and who had retired just outside of Saint John. She told him of spending many summers there at his cottage at Ragged Point. Brent knew the spot and had spent a few summers at a Boy Scout camp there. This common bond to a remote spot in the Atlantic provinces had cemented their friendship.

Helen headed north, past the turnoff for Alberta Beach and past Onoway to old man's Zelenko's property. Soon she spotted RCMP flashing car lights along the highway. Helen pulled over. A new recruit was manning the road.

"Keep moving please," he called out to Helen as she slowed down and wound down her window.

"Officer, I am with the Parkland Examiner. Can you tell me what happened here?" she asked as she braked to a halt.

"No comment, Ma'am," the young officer replied, tipping his hat to her, "no one is allowed to cross that yellow tape line over there and there's nothing to see from here."

"Thank you, young man," Helen said putting the truck into gear and moving away.

About a quarter mile up the road, Helen pulled onto a side road and parked. She got out of the truck and reached behind her seat for a lightweight hooded jacket. Putting it on, Helen raised the hood, tucked all her hair into it, grabbed her thin pair of leather gloves, slung her camera bag over her shoulder and headed down the road she had just driven. Dressed in dark colors, Helen knew she could walk fairly close to the police scene in the woods, undetected.

Once she was about four hundred yards away from the flashing lights, Helen slipped into the woods. She circled to the far side of the activity and found a bit of high ground to set up for photos. What Helen saw sent shivers up her spine in spite of feeling warm after her trek.

Two men were kneeling by a body, taking various swabs while officers stood by, smoking cigarettes and gesturing to each other in conversation. Helen was too far away to hear what they were saying.

Setting up her camera with a telephoto lens, Helen began taking pictures. She could see through the viewfinder that the hunter lying on the ground had been attacked fiercely. One eye dangled out of a deep gash on his face, the right arm hung at a wrong angle from his body. Helen slowly moved closer and shot as much detail in close-ups as she could, then snapped several wide shots, thus obscuring the gore so that one could recognize a police crime scene yet not the details inflicted on the victim.

An ambulance had arrived out on the highway and a stretcher was being brought in. The body was placed on a sheet lying on top of a body bag, its broken arm gingerly picked up and laid on top of it, then two more items were picked up and placed on it. Lastly the rifle, which Helen had missed up to now, as it had been on the far side of the body from her position, was bagged and added on top of the now zipped up body bag. Helen took a series of pictures while this unfolded, then boldly walked towards the highway, as noiselessly as she could, and took some shots of the cruisers and ambulance as the body was loaded. Helen then turned on her heels and made her way back quickly to her own vehicle.

She was feeling very nervous by now, trying to control her shaking, yet she kept to a steady pace. While taking photographs, she had heard something behind her, she had looked around and not seen anything. She dearly wanted to run to her truck yet controlled herself. Once at the truck, she unlocked the door, threw her bag across to the passenger seat, jumped in and immediately locked the doors. Trying to appear casual, Helen looked into the back seat to make sure it was empty while removing her jacket, satisfied, she then turned the engine over, made a U-turn and headed into town.

Helen drove directly to the newspaper office. Roger lived in the building on the second floor and Helen knew he would hear her enter regardless if he was upstairs or in the shop. However, Roger was not in the office. This made Helen feel angry and her anger surprised her. She realized she was not angry at Roger but at what she had just witnessed.

Helen went straight into the darkroom where she wound her film into a developing canister and began processing it. She was glad for the low light, the sense of security she felt in the tiny locked room, and even the headiness of the developing odours, which brought her back to her own body at this time and away from the memories of the crime scene. Once the negatives were hung up to dry, Helen rinsed everything off, dried her hands and unlocked the door.

Roger was sitting in the common area waiting for her. Roger had set out, on the table they used for lunch breaks and impromptu meetings, his black cast-iron tea pot, two mugs, two spoons, a small jug of milk and the sugar bowl. The tea Roger made was black, brewed strong and served very hot. He poured a mug for Helen as she sat down. Helen added two spoonsful of sugar and a liberal amount of milk and stirred her mug of tea. After she had taken a sip, Roger spoke.

"So how bad was it?" he said softly, his eyes searching her face.

"The worst. There's negatives of pretty young girls with stars in their eyes dressed to the nines next to the goriest scene I have ever witnessed, hanging up in there to dry," she answered, pointing with her spoon towards the darkroom. "Oh, and I got a few shots of Officer Brent manning a speed trap at the bottom of the hill by Highway 43 on the main highway," she added, with a shrug.

After a few sips of her tea, Helen opened up to Roger.

"The cops shooed me away so I parked further down the road then walked back to the scene. They don't know I took the pictures. You can sell them to the city papers," Helen looked at her watch, "it's past one o'clock, you'll need to call soon to make the evening edition."

After a beat she added, "there's quite a few close-ups so that we can see what happened – I wouldn't give them away, keep them in a file for now and see if the perpetrator gets caught. I didn't recognize the victim, he could be anybody. If this goes to court then the cops might want the close-ups – their photographer must have been there before me. I'm rambling. I don't want to have my name attached to this, you know the deal I have at home – stay low key. You can make up any story you want for Stan on how you got these shots. Just send him the wide shots though." Helen shook her head and chuckled, "Stan will love the story so charge him handsomely for my pictures."

Roger reached behind him and brought a cookie tin to the table and opened it. Helen chose one of the plain cookies, smiled and mumbled thanks and dunked it in her mug of tea.

"Nice to see a smile," Roger said, reaching across and patting her arm. Even in her fog Helen appreciated his kindness, a side of him she had seen many times and that he showed to so few people.

"Aren't you going to go and take a look?" she asked.

"After you finish your tea," he answered. She smiled across the table at him. They both ate another cookie and finished their tea in silence.

In the darkroom, Helen recounted her story, about stopping and speaking with the rookie cop who told her no one was allowed to cross the yellow tape line, and how she parked and hiked into the woods. Slyly she added that the yellow tape was only one-sided so technically she had not disobeyed the officer. Then she described the scene.

"There were two forensic officers examining the body. The way it lay, I'd say he had been shot in the chest and left undisturbed where he fell. But it wasn't a hunting accident – it plainly was murder, he had been tortured before he was killed. I bet if we could go right into the scene then we could find out more about that. It's not something I'd want to do though."

Helen paused and looked Roger in the eye. With the darkroom tongs, she pointed at her negatives.

"That's Jeannie Rutherford in a midnight blue dress. Isn't she a beauty? I bet old man Daniel Rutherford is really proud of her."

After a beat, she continued, "okay, back to business. See this lying a bit away from his head? It's not a rock, it's his right hand. See? Look closely – you can see a ring on his pinkie. The arm had been badly broken before he fell to land like that. And in this one, this is the closest shot I got of his face. His eye is dangling out to the side."

Helen covered her hand with her mouth. Roger took a moment to look closely at the negatives then indicated to her they were done and for her to turn around so they could exit the darkroom.

"Go on home Helen. Take tomorrow off and Friday we'll put the paper together. I'll call Stan now. And Helen, type up your notes. We'll put them with the negatives just in case."

Outside in the common area again, Roger helped Helen with her jacket.

"That is mighty fine reportage photography Helen. If you add your name to it you'll win a journalism prize."

"No Roger. I don't want any limelight. I'm a part-time country reporter, not a city-slicker one," she added, smiling as she left.

Helen did not go home. She drove to the city and pulled into a truck stop off the Yellowhead highway. There, in the brightly lit restaurant, she sat in a booth at the back where she could see everything that went on in the restaurant. She ordered tea and a grilled cheese sandwich. Helen pulled a booklet from her purse and tried to quiet her mind by focussing on her crossword puzzle.

Helen would look up and glance around the restaurant from time to time. She remained the only patron until about four o'clock. She used the public phone and called her husband and made up a story about being with his cousin. Once back at her table, the waitress came by and asked her if she was ready for her bill. Helen ordered more tea and a piece of apple pie.

About six o'clock, Helen finally paid her bill, left a decent tip and headed for home. She stopped at the Beach Corner store and bought a bag of frozen corn then drove to Hasse Lake. After parking, she walked to the beach and happily noticed quite a few ducks. She tore open her bag of corn and began feeding them.

It was about eight thirty when Helen got home. Both kids and her husband were watching a movie on TV. Normally they did not let the children watch television on a weeknight. Helen did not protest, she snuggled onto the couch with them. Later, after the children had gone to bed and her husband was reading a book, she put away her coat and camera bag and sat at the kitchen table. She made herself a pot of tea and sat with her crossword puzzle. Late into the night, she still sat there, weeping quietly in her quiet kitchen. Finally, about two in the morning, she went to bed.

Helen slept in the next morning. Her husband had somehow managed not to wake her or let the children wake her. There was a note on his side of the bed that read, 'hope you are feeling better, love, Gord.' Helen showered and dressed and went to the kitchen. Right away she noticed the phone off the hook; Gord must have taken it off that morning, before he left the house for work. She now replaced it, wondering if he had tried to call her. Looking in the fridge and then the freezer, Helen decided to make meat loaf, baked potatoes and an apple crumble for her family's dinner. This was the only task she gave herself to do that day.

As she was scrubbing potatoes, the kids came home from school. Her daughter, Lauren hugged her gingerly and said, "Mom, I hope your headache has gone away."

Helen smiled. So that was how Gord had covered her absence at breakfast.

"Much better," she said, smiling. "How was school?"

'Oh, you know, boring," answered her daughter as she grabbed a bag of potato chips and then some juice from the fridge.

"Share with your brother. And take some glasses for the juice. After your snack get to your homework. Dinner will be ready in about an hour and or so."

After dinner Helen asked to see the children's assignment notebooks. Then she checked on the progress of their work. Robbie, ten and in grade four, had only math homework and had done it all correctly. He skipped off to his bedroom to play with his Turtles fort and his Lego.

Lauren was halfway through a history essay. So far it had been written in only very general terms. Helen asked for her bibliography. Lauren answered with only her textbook. Helen then went to their bookcase, pulled down two volumes and handed them to her daughter.

"I'm sure your school library has more. Check tomorrow. If not then we'll go to the public library in town. Now go read and make notes from these."

Lauren, thirteen years old and already full of teenage angst, shot her mom a vile look while grabbing up the tomes. She sulked out of the room and stomped to her bedroom. The door slammed behind her.

Helen and Gordon exchanged a glance. Then Gordon got up from his easy-chair and came to the dining room table where Helen was sitting. Taking the chair next to her, he unfolded the city paper and tapped the front page. One of Helen's wide shots took up most of the top half of the page. It showed two forensic detectives hovering over the dead body with yellow police tape glowing in the background along with the flashing lights of the police cruisers.

Gordon looked to his wife.

"I sure hope this is not where you were yesterday," he said, searching her face.

"What happened?" Helen said, grabbing the paper and reading.

"Helen, please tell me this did not involve you," Gordon said.

Helen looked up into her husband's face and leaned over and gave him a hug.

"No, Gordo. I was with Officer Turner. Brent was manning a speed trap at the bottom of the hill on Highway 16 by the overpass to highway 43. My picture of that and a few cars he pulled over will be on the front page of the Examiner this weekend." She pulled away and smiled at him.

"Can I read this?" she asked.

"You spent all day with Brent Turner?" he asked, incredulous. "You know I don't like you being around him. He has designs, Helen," Gordon said, standing up.

"Well, of course I wasn't with him all day. Darlene came by, Brent pulled her over and she had been drinking. I drove her home and stayed with her. Remember, I called you.

Gordon sighed, "my cousin was drunk again? I thought she was going to AA. I can't understand her. She has everything. Her parents give her everything she wants, pay for trips anywhere she wants to go ... Well, thanks for looking after her. I suppose you talked Brent out of charging her?"

"No, I think he has a crush on her. He just gave her a warning," she smiled ruefully up at her husband.

"I doubt that. It is you, my beautiful Helen, that he lusts after."

"Oh really, Gord. You think every available man is after me," she laughed. "Go build me something in your shop while I read this article."

He kissed the top of her head and left the room.

Helen felt bad lying to her husband yet she did not want any connection to the gruesome story that she had uncovered last night to touch her family. She turned her attention to the paper and noticed right away that while the picture was huge on the page, the story was rather scant. The caption read, 'Hunter Comes to a Grisly Demise West of Edmonton.'

The story gave vague details. It said the RCMP responded to a call from a farmer on the discovery of a body on his property. Evidence at the scene suggested that this was more than a hunting accident. The RCMP are investigating further. The body had not been identified at the time of print and the identity of the victim was unknown at this time.

Helen noted that the farmer was not identified nor was the exact location of the murder scene. Tonight's news might have more details. Helen scanned the rest of the paper then went to the kitchen to clean up and make lunches for the next day.

Friday morning dawned dark and foggy. Robbie wanted to take a walk in the fog before catching the school bus and Helen joined him. From the back door they crossed the gardens and entered the woods. About two hundred meters in, there was a small micro climate. The older trees and much of the ground were covered with moss – even on sunny days it had the feel of a cool, stately cathedral. Robbie headed straight there. This had been his favourite escape space since he was a small boy. The fog was more of a mist here and Helen pulled her coat tightly around her neck. Robbie checked out rotten logs, climbed up a few easily accessible trees, came back down, then sat down on a fallen tree. Helen sat next to him.

"Timmy Wagner says going to Boy Scout camp at Skeleton Lake is for babies. What do you think Mom?"

"Hmm. I wonder why he thinks that? You two had a great time there last year. If I remember right," and here Helen ruffled his hair, "you cried when we came to pick you up."

"Yeah, it was fantastic. One of the leaders was Aboriginal and he taught us all kinds of things in the woods, how to survive a night by yourself if you got lost, how to find water, he was really neat," Robbie said smiling up in her face.

"Well, in life you make your own choices. You listen to what others have to say then you check with your own heart and decide what path to take." Looking at her son, Helen could see this was not the answer he was hoping for. "Tell you what. I'm going to give his Mom a call this weekend and see what's up."

"But do you think Boy Scouts is for babies, Mom?"

"No Robbie. However, there will come a point as you grow up when you will," she said this looking straight into his blue eyes with her grey ones. Then she added, "I don't think you and Timmy are there yet. Have fun. Enjoy just being a boy while you can. As you get older more things catch you, you have more things to worry about. Just stay a boy for now." She smiled at him. Robbie leaned over and hugged his mom fiercely.

"I love you Mom."

"And I you, now we'd best get going if you're going to catch the bus."

Entering work, Helen noticed that Roger was in a very heated discussion on the phone, in his office. Helen removed her coat, fixed a cup of tea and sauntered over to the layout for this week's edition. Roger's conversation continued and Helen could tell that he was not winning his case. She decided she better get to work.

Helen began by editing the columnists' columns. Just as she was finishing Roger's call ended and he came to her door.

"Helen, that was Stan. His lawyers insist I come into town, today, won't be put off till tomorrow when it's more convenient for me. The RCMP is busting their chops over those photos of yours. They made the story go public when they'd rather it didn't. I have to go make a deposition and they want to meet first to go over everything. Now here is my story. My story is there was a knock on the door and by the time I got it opened, no one was in sight and there was a package of negatives on my doorstep. I got Jonathan doing follow-up with the RCMP's press conference this morning, he should be back by noon. Dunno how long I'll be. Helen, I'm sorry, you can count on putting all this together on your own."

"Okay, Roger, I might make some changes though to your layout."

"Fine. I trust your judgement, just get with it. Help Jonathan with his writing, the two of you can share the by-line on it. I already told him it was supposed to be your story. And don't take any guff from him. I'm going now."

Before Roger left, he came up behind Helen at her typewriter, "you okay? Can you handle this?"

She waved him away, "I got it Roger. I'm okay. Go fight for freedom of the press," she said, smiling at him over her shoulder.

Once Roger left, Helen scribbled a schedule for herself. First, she would work on the columnists' pieces, her articles, Roger's editorial, his other pieces and the RCMP's speed trap. She'd aim to finish those pages by midday then have some lunch and work with Jonathan on his story. She checked Roger's office to see what stage his stories were in. At least his fishing and farmer's stories were completed. She was going to have to write the full editorial for him. She added a note to her schedule to recheck the table of contents before releasing everything to the printer.

Helen had finished with the columnists and began work on her stories about the prom dress shop and the graduating class. It was easiest to just tell the story with pictures so she began with pasting those in. Just past ten thirty, she finished and Jonathan came in. He was very excited over the homicide story and began filling in Helen on the press conference he had just attended.

Helen raised her hand.

"Stop right there Jonathan. Roger's been called into town to explain how he got the photographs and I am deputy editor until he returns. Set this story aside for a while. Before lunch I need your sports write-up and pictures. Lunch is at noon. You don't have much time. Get hopping."

Not giving him a chance to respond, she turned back to her own work. After barely audible grumblings with long pauses, Helen finally heard the darkroom door close and lock. She grinned to herself.

Just past noon, Helen brought out the two meat-loaf sandwiches she had made for lunch. She set two places at the common room table and boiled water for instant coffee or tea. Jonathan was clacking away on the receptionist's typewriter and seemed unaware of her actions.

"I've got an extra meat-loaf sandwich here if you want it," she announced, walking over and reading over his shoulder. "C'mon. Break. Eat. We'll get all this done soon enough."

Jonathan smiled up at her and turned away from the typewriter, went over to the sink and washed up.

"Thanks Helen. I'm famished. I haven't had anything to eat except the donuts and coffee at the RCMP office."

"How much longer do you think you need on sports? I'd like to start the homicide story as soon as possible."

"I'm almost done, Helen, it just needs a few finishing touches and a re-read."

Helen appreciated that about Jonathan. He seldom had a typo or syntax error in his writing and seemed to be able to work to deadlines, unlike most journalism students. His downfall however was how bull-headed he could be when his work was edited. Whether he felt Helen and Roger were just country bumpkins or whether this was just professional stubbornness on his part, she could not tell.

"Okay. Let's meet at one-fifteen to start our big story. But let's not talk about it while we eat. What are your plans for the weekend?" she asked, smiling across the table at the young man.

They ate their lunch quickly, tidied up and Jonathan returned to his work.

While Jonathan polished his sports updates, Helen went into Roger's office and found the copy of the homicide pictures they had shared with the newspaper. She selected a wide shot that the paper had not run to date, crossing her fingers they would not use it in any weekend editions, then she selected the shot of the body bag being loaded into the ambulance.

"Jonathan do you have any photos of the press conference from this morning?" she asked as she crossed the common area to where he was working.

"Yeah. I also need to print up a few shots on sports. The negatives are hanging up and ready to go. This is finished. Take a look and let me know how great it is," he said.

Jonathan stood up and went to the darkroom. Helen reviewed the sports article. Not bad, she thought. There were a few too many exclamation marks and it was hyped up a tad. She'd let him know what she thought and let him decide if he wanted to make any changes.

Helen went into the darkroom and gave him her verdict on his sports piece. Jonathon grinned. "Okay, I'll take another look. These are the shots I'm planning to use with it. Those over there are the ones from the press conference."

Together they moved to those negatives and Helen made her selection. She left the darkroom and heard the lock of its door click. Now she was waiting on Jonathon to print the photos they needed for the paper.

She went back to Roger's office to work on his editorial. There was one paragraph sitting on his typewriter. Roger juxtaposed a brave new world referring to the graduating class and to the new farm tractor with the putrid dark secret out in the woods, the grim murder of the hunter. Helen flushed out four paragraphs, one on the aspirations outlined by the graduating students, one on Brad Bilodeau, the high school football captain who had won a scholarship to play at the University of Alberta, one on the new tractor. She was struggling with the fourth paragraph when Jonathan called her to come look over the photos.

It was now past two and Helen could feel a headache forming behind her right eye. She left Roger's office and joined Jonathan.

The first thing Helen noticed was a shot of Brad Bilodeau in his football uniform, crouching down by an upright football with the goal posts in the background.

"Wow, Jonathan that is a good shot. I can see the detail in his eyes, the lighting is fantastic. Are you planning on using this for your sports piece?"

"Nope, the lighting caught my eye the other night when I went over and covered their practice so I posed some of the guys. I just thought they'd like these."

"Well, we can use a small one of Brad to go in with Roger's editorial. Now let's see what you have from this morning."

"I printed the standard talking heads at the podium. And I took some shots of their slideshow. Look at these."

Helen saw close-up photos of the crime scene that she had not taken. The cops did have a photographer out there before she arrived after all. She looked at the photos carefully. There were details of torture on the body, including a close-up of his left hand with burn marks and the little finger missing. The pictures were grainy, a result of shooting slide at the press conference, and given the circumstances, quite well done.

"Did the RCMP identify him yet?" she asked Jonathan.

"Yep. He is a local business man. He owns the drugstore his name was …"

"Ed Boyko!" said Helen with a gasp. Her hands flew up to her face and she sighed heavily. Then she got right back to business.

"Good work Jonathan. I'd like to use one of the shots of the RCMP officer at the podium. But before you print these, let's get the story written."

"I was hoping to use more – to show how badly mutilated the body was," Jonathan said.

Helen had already started to leave the dark room. She turned around abruptly and faced the intern.

"Jonathan, he was tortured. He was alive when all this was done to him. The mutilation is what the coroner will do to his dead body before it is released to his family. The RCMP have released his name. This is Ed Boyko. He was a pharmacist in Stony Plain. He had a family. A large extended family in the community. And lots of friends. Many people knew him either from the drugstore or church or other organizations in the community. He was loved and respected. We don't need to show this to them. If the city papers do, well, so be it. This is not what the Parkland Examiner is about."

Helen stalked out of the darkroom, poured herself a glass of water and found some aspirin. Jonathan followed her out and stood, dumbfounded.

"Sorry, Helen, I …"

She cut him off with a wave of her hand. After finishing her water, she said, "tell you what, you go start writing up the story from your notes on the press conference and what you know so far from the media and I'll go finish Roger's editorial."

"Okay, Helen, thanks," he smiled at her and headed towards his typewriter to write his report.

While Jonathan typed his story, Helen finished the editorial and loosely set up pages one and two then finalized the set-up on pages seven and eight. Roger had called and asked her to put the paper to bed. Meanly, she wondered if Roger and Stan were now in a bar together, commiserating over beers.

Hearing the silence from Jonathan's typewriter, Helen came over.

"It's done," said Jonathan.

Helen read over his story, suggested a few small changes which he, to her surprise, accepted without comment. Then she asked him, "can you add a paragraph on Ed? Pillar of society and all that, give funeral details too."

"I don't know what to write Helen," he said softly. "Tell you what, why don't you do that and I'll go print those two photos you wanted."

"Okay, I'll write your last paragraph for you," she smiled up at him, "you can then read it over and decide if it sounds like your voice and make any changes. And also read over Roger's editorial and make sure I nailed him there, too."

It was after five when Helen and Jonathan had the paper ready for the typesetter. Waving him out the door for a well-deserved weekend of fun, she phoned her husband.

"Hi Gordon. How was your day, Dear?"

"Oh, ho," he answered, "where is this going?"

She giggled into the receiver, "we've just finished getting the paper ready for the typesetter, only Roger's not here. I need to bring it into the city," she paused to give him a chance to comment.

"Helen, I hope you charge him extra for this. It's not part of your contract, you know."

"Well, Roger's not here to agree to anything so I guess we'll settle up next week. Gord, how about I pick up the kids and we meet you in town, then we all go into the city. I can drop this off at the typesetters and we can go out for supper and maybe a movie or we could go bowling. What do you say?"

"Okay I guess."

"That's great, Honey. I'll call the kids at home now and we'll be at your office in about forty minutes. See you then." She pushed the plunger down on the phone then let it up and called home right away.

Lauren and Robbie wanted to go to West Edmonton Mall and they ended up at Ed's Rec room for supper and bowling. After a few games, they wandered out and into the mall. The night was still young and Gordon surprised everyone by suggesting a movie.

Helen had shivers in the car on the way home; they had just experienced a fun and entertaining evening together, the quintessence of middle class family life. She felt happy and safe with her family. Yet she knew, out there, as she peered into the darkness beyond the windshield, lurked a monster.

Over the weekend and into the next week the whole town and

surrounding areas were abuzz with the story. Edward Boyko's funeral took place the following Friday and was very well attended. The RCMP had officers on site accompanied by a photographer. Helen noted that among the pictures he took were those of anyone brandishing a camera.

The town slowly returned to its normal routines. The RCMP never did get their man in this case. Eventually Ed Boyko's widow sold the pharmacy to a young pharmacist who had only recently graduated and had begun his career there. Apparently, he grew up in the area although young Jim Drucker was unknown to her. Helen did not know of any Drucker families in their community.

21 CRIMSON

"Oh, look one of the cops was over there puking his guts out," Jim chuckled to himself, revelling in the mess he had made. He had given them a good display. Jim was curious to see what the cops would do at the crime scene.

Ed Boyko had taken Jim under his wing when Jim first began work at the pharmacy in the spring after his graduation. During his interview, he told Jim that he was considering retiring and that he was looking for a bright young man to take over his business. Most of the summer Ed was absent from work. Jim learned he had a cottage in St Ives, British Columbia. It was on the Shuswap. Jim had never been there but heard it was a lovely summer destination.

In the fall, Ed became morose. Jim tried talking to him a few times, asking him if he was still thinking about retiring. Jim hinted he had the money in the bank. Ed could spend more time in the Shuswap or travel to the Caribbean in the winter. Ed turned sour on Jim, calling him just an average employee and let him know he would never make it as an owner of a drugstore, that he wasn't focused, had no business acumen and that he was a fool to think otherwise.

Jim was stunned by this outburst. Denny, the senior pharmacist, told Jim not to worry about it, that Ed was like this every fall. He likened Ed to a jock returning to school in the fall, sullen that the warm beach days were over and he was expected to work and perform for the next several months. Ed was quite a fleshy guy and this made Jim laugh. He made light of the whole episode.

Ed would not let go of Jim's ambition and presumption that he would just hand over his life's work to him. He would demand that Jim help the shop's clerks with cleaning and even assigned him to cashier duties scheduled on the worst shifts. He faulted Jim for petty things. Jim stayed positive and behaved like a model employee. He had set his sights on this pharmacy and by hook or by crook, he planned to have it.

Jim overheard Ed bragging to Denny about his hunting prowess. He was planning to go hunting during the week on a friend's farm and he named his friend. It was easy for Jim to find out where the farm was located and to set a trap for Ed.

Jim had enjoyed every minute of torturing Ed. He had even let him recuperate from time to time during the long night so he could prolong it. When Ed finally came to at dawn, he used Ed's gun to shoot him, aiming straight for the heart.

Jim snapped out of his reverie. Let's see what the boys with stripes up their pantlegs were doing.

At the moment everyone stood aside except for a photographer. He had an assistant with a special light that he shone wherever the camera pointed. He took an inordinate number of pictures, first from a distance, then a middle distance, circling the clearing then finally closeups of where the body lay and of the stuff strewn all about.

He nodded to his fellows, who had been putting tape around the trees about a yard away from the highway. The light revealed blood spatters and after they were photographed, another fellow then took samples. They examined every square inch of every surface and took more samples. Jim wondered about what they hoped to find? He thought they would find nothing on him. That fat slob could not get a punch in no matter how hard he tried. He was too fat, too slow, too stupid. And as for those clowns, well not one of them has noticed the feather he had planted after the fact on Ed's stinking body.

Jim next watched the reporter, Helen Majeau, sneak in from the back of the crime scene. This was the most gruesome death Jim had ever caused and not one that could possibly be construed as an accident. He hadn't tried to hide or dispose of the body in any way. Jim wanted everyone to know that Ed Boyko was dead.

Helen obviously did not want the cops to see her. She stayed cool, detached from the horror, stood behind it, looked all about and started taking pictures. Jim could tell some were close-ups and some were long shots. He was up in a tree. At one point, a branch snapped on him and Helen jumped, looking all about. Jim swore under his breath and moved to a better perch. She was looking in his direction through her viewfinder. She might have spotted him, except that was when the ambulance showed up and she wasted no time in turning about and photographing them. He did notice, with a chuckle, that she was nervous when she left, silently making her way through the bush, looking over her shoulder, presumably headed back to her vehicle.

Jim had recently started playing poker Wednesday nights with several businessmen in Stony Plain. One of them was Roger Lafontaine, Helen's boss. He would make sure to try to find out more about this steely lady from Roger.

22 AUBERGINE

With a crick in her back, muddy hands, and feeling very sweaty and hot, Glenda scrutinized the garden. Ruefully she thought only madmen and Englishmen gardened in the afternoon heat. Add to the list: new moms, she thought. She was satisfied with her work. A few little noises came over the baby monitor, soon Connor would awaken. She put away her tools and headed to the house for a quick shower. By the time she emerged from the washroom, Connor was bawling. She ran to his room and scooped him up, cuddling him in her terrycloth bathrobe. His cries swiftly subsided and he gave her a smile and wriggled to be free. Connor was not in a cuddly mood, awake now, he wanted to play. Glenda put him down on the middle of the bed while she changed. On their way back to the main part of the house, she noticed the light blinking on the phone; they had forgotten to put it back on ring in the morning.

There was a message from Lesley Lisiuk at the RCMP office in Stony Plain that came in at half past noon. The message was to inform Glenda that a shooting incident to a public road sign had occurred at approximately eleven thirty today at the junction of highway 43 and highway 16. For more information Glenda could call her back, and she left her phone number.

A second text message on her mobile was from Aimee and it had just been left. She was now home and found Glenda's rock. She was heading over to Glenda's and would talk to her soon.

Glenda looked out the front windows. There was Aimee sauntering up her driveway with Trevor in a snuggli. She ran out with Connor on her arm to greet them.

"We have a lot to talk about: it has been a very eventful day," she hollered to her friend.

"Hello to you, too," answered Aimee, smiling.

Once inside the house, the babies in the sunroom with all the screens opened, and baby gate in place, the mamas sat at the kitchen table. Glenda brought Aimee up to speed: Helen had some contact sheets of some of the crime scenes, that morning Glenda had spotted a white pickup lurking by Aimee's house, the RCMP had called as there had been a drive-by shooting of a road sign just before noon at the junction of highways 43 and 16.

"Wow!" Aimee said, "first things first, what exactly did you see? Describe the vehicle, the person, anything you can remember."

"Well, you know I am not good with kinds of vehicles. It was white, big, not new but not rusted or anything, boxy looking. He had his arm hanging out the window. It was muscular and hairy. I'd say that he's middle aged. He had on a large wrist-watch. The binoculars were black and fairly large, not overly so. I didn't get the full license number. They were covered in mud; the whole truck was dirty. I think the first two letters of the license plate were RS."

"Was he young or old? Wearing a hat? Could you see his clothes, or a logo on the truck?"

"I think he's middle aged. His arm was tanned and the hair was light. There was no logo on the vehicle and I couldn't say if he had on a shirt or a T-shirt. I wasn't close enough to see and the seat's headrest was in the way. He may have had on a cap, I can't tell you anything about his hair, it didn't stick up and I could not tell the colour from where I was."

"That's all good. So, we know someone was checking out my house in a white pickup, a male who wears a large wrist-watch and carries binoculars in his vehicle and that the plates maybe started with RS. We are assuming this guy then drove south and blew away a highway sign. Sounds like a real charmer."

As tense as all the information sounded, Glenda could not help but laugh and Aimee joined in with her.

"There's more, Aimee," said Glenda. "I went through the mischief at night file and made an Excel spreadsheet. Come take a look at it."

Glenda pulled up the Excel chart on her laptop. "Notice the red dots. They are shootings at properties that occur a week or so or just a few days before every murder. Look!" and Glenda pulled up the original Excel charts. "I was talking with Helen about this. We think he might actually send out warning shots, like he did with her grand-daughter's playhouse. But obviously not everyone picked up on them."

"Well, that is interesting," said Aimee.

"and ..." Glenda added, her eyebrows shooting way up on her forehead.

"Well, and what?" asked Aimee, impatient.

"Helen mentioned that when her grand-daughter's playhouse was shot at, the perpetrator was in a white truck."

"Wow!" Aimee paused and sat back in her chair.

"What if whoever was driving that truck by your house is the perpetrator. And he is the same guy, still driving a white truck? What if he was frustrated that you were not home, God knows why he was at your place anyways, but just go with this, he is frustrated and shoots out that sign on his way back to who knows where. And what if somehow, he knows we are on to him. have we, the hunters, become the hunted?"

Aimee looked at Glenda. "You do have a wild imagination however all of that is possible. We need to gear up on practicing our Tai Kwon Do."

"Aimee, we need more than Tai Kwon Do. If he knows who you are then he knows who your folks are."

"He could even be the person who was sleeping in their woodshed just after Alice Grant was murdered. Oh shit."

"Yep, it could all be the same person," said Glenda.

The friends were quiet for a few moments. Gurgles from the babies in the sunroom could be heard, breaking the silence. A robin trilled in the backyard as the aspens wheezed in the slight summer breeze. All of these normal sounds were very fragile to the mamas. They felt they were in deep, way over their heads.

"Why don't you call Kyle and have him come here after work and you guys stay for supper?" suggested Glenda. "We can go over all of this with the guys and get their point of view."

"Okay," agreed Aimee, "but they aren't going to want to hear any of this."

"Well, let's make them a super supper and that will soften the blow. I have some ground bison in the fridge, we could make up some taco bowls and have a sombrero salad."

"My asparagus is ready for harvesting. I can go back and get it."

"Okay, take my car; I'll get things started here."

While Aimee was gone, Glenda called Dave and let him know they had their first report of a sign that had been shot. She gave him Lesley Lisiuk's phone number for the details and she also let him know that Kyle and Aimee would be having dinner with them.

23 VERNAL GREEN

Jim was working in the pharmacy, of course, when old man Boyko 'passed away.' His wife had no idea of how to run the business. Jim kept the pharmacy going though, befriending the salesmen with their light banter and crude jokes, remembering the clientele and their litany of complaints along with the names of their children and even their grandchildren, managing his and the other pharmacist's schedule and the buying and displaying of supplies and wares. The rest of the store was another story.

One day, Jim came in and noticed more empty candy boxes than filled ones by the cash register at the door. He went up and down all the aisles. Dust bunnies were on full display in the many gaps between products for sale. One shelf had even fallen down and rested on the one below it. Whistling, he got to work in the pharmacy.

Later that day Vivian Boyko came in. Jim asked her if they could have a meeting.

A while later, Vivian came into the stockroom where Jim was receiving a new delivery. Right away she was on the defensive.

"I know you are working really hard, Jim, especially since Denny left. I could only afford to keep one of you and I am sorry I had to lay him off. But I have no money to give you a raise, if that is what you are after."

"Not at all," replied Jim. "How are you holding up?" he asked, touching her lightly on the forearm. "I noticed a lot of empty shelf space this morning when I came in. Is there anything I can help with? I don't have a lot of spare time but I am willing to help you out."

Vivian began to cry, "I don't think there's much you can help with," she sobbed, "the truth is I am not very good at this. Ed had a good business head on his shoulders. I don't. We never discussed the store. I am just making a mess of things."

Jim patted her hand, "there, there. I know it has been tough on you."

Vivian wiped at her tears, "I know Ed wanted to run this business for another five years or so, he could never make up his mind exactly when he would retire but I was looking forward to it happening. He was hoping one of the young pharmacists would buy him out."

"Really," said Jim. "That's an interesting thought."

Vivian brightened a bit, "Jim, do you think you might be interested? I heard you got a sizable inheritance from your Aunt, God rest her soul. Or maybe you know someone from school who wants to set up their own pharmacy?

"Tell you what," he said, patting her hand, "I'll think about it and get back to you."

Within six months Jim had bought the pharmacy outright. Vivian had believed his story that he had spent a lot of his inheritance on schooling and capitulated on the sell price very early in the negotiations. Her biggest sticking point had been over Jim's desire to rename the store from Boyko's Pharmacy to Drucker's Drugstore. They compromised. Jim promised to keep the name for two years, then rename it 'Drucker's Drugstore – formerly Boyko's Pharmacy' for another two years. Jim thought that could work to his advantage, with a rural client base, slow change was better than an overnight one.

When he had first taken over the pharmacy, he spent a lot of time there, managing the store and filling out prescriptions. He joined the town's Chamber of Commerce.

During those first few years, he lived like a monk and toiled like a serf. He did not allow himself any time off, when the drug store was open, he was there. Yeah, there were a few night excursions on the highways, searching for lone hitch-hikers; overall Jim led the perfect, clean, wholesome life. He had continued attendance at Aunt Doris's church and had been approached to be a trustee; years later he was practically the preacher's best friend and confidante. Remembering those first years made him smirk.

Jim soon realized the drugstore's profit margin was not that great. From discussions at the Chamber of Commerce meetings, he realized Stony Plain was transitioning from a rural hub for the environs to a suburban community for Edmonton. This was affecting a lot of the businesses, especially the smaller ones who could not buy their merchandise as cheaply as the big chains in the city could. Jim began dabbling in stocks and currency trading. He did quite well; in a few short years, Jim had repaid to his bank account, the monies he had used to complete his university degree, keep himself and Dog in food and supplies, and to purchase and renovate the pharmacy. It had been a gruelling time for him. He kept a smile on his face and acted as happy and friendly as he could to everyone. This was far from how he really felt and he knew he had to do something about it and soon.

Jim realized, even before he took over the drugstore that the staff, or what was left of them, were demoralized. They had lost their pride in their place of work, they just came in for the paycheck and gave very little back. He made plans on how to drag that country bumpkin drugstore into the approaching twenty-first century.

Once the store was his, Jim rolled out his program. First, he rehired Denny Swanson, the pharmacist Vivian Boyko had laid off. Jim paid him a dollar more an hour than what he had previously been paid. It was not much; it was a gesture of appreciation and a promise of more to come. Denny lived close by and, for a premium, would come in and fill prescriptions on an emergency basis. Jim really wanted this service to be in place. He could be in the middle of God knew what when a call could come in.

The next thing Jim did was clean out the office, purging old files and records and boxing up pertinent ones, taking them either to his accountant's or his own home office. He hauled the big, clunky furniture to the Goodwill, washed and painted the walls and replaced the dirty, thick carpet with linoleum. On a Sunday, when the store was closed, he turned it into a staff break room. There was a row of lockers and a clothes rack along one wall. The opposite wall, the one with the door in it, boasted a new fridge and counter. New dishes were housed in the counters above, next to a new shelf that housed a microwave. A rectangular table and chairs sat in the middle of the room. Just outside the office, there already existed a small counter with a sink and coffee maker. It had two washrooms behind it. Jim cleaned and repainted them. He brought in a better brand of coffee and a variety pack of premium tea.

Monday morning, as the staff came to work, they found Jim sitting in the new staff room. He invited them to hang up their coats and pick out a locker. They were welcome to bring a lock if they wanted and were free to decorate their lockers as they liked.

He had placed donuts and pastries by the coffee maker and they were invited to help themselves, a quick one now, he suggested, and to sit and enjoy a hot coffee or tea and another one at their break. As they left the room, he added, "you're welcome to put your lunches in the fridge. There's new dishes in the cupboard and cutlery in the drawer. Sorry, I could not afford at this time to add water to this room and get a dishwasher, so the dishes need to be done out by the coffee maker."

Most broke into big smiles and thanked Jim for the room. Previously everyone had hung their coats on pegs by the backdoor. They claimed a peg by leaving their staff aprons or lab coats on it when they left. The pegs were still there as were the boot trays below them. Jim had moved all the aprons and coats onto hangers in the new break room.

The staff were excited all day with these little changes that would make their break times more comfortable. Jim chuckled to himself. He could not tell if it was having their own lockers or having the fridge that was the biggest hit. Denny later confided to him that it was the chairs; the staff now had a place to sit inside while on break.

Jim wanted his staff to be happy. Personally, he couldn't care less about them however from a business point of view he knew that a happy staff meant everything would run smoother and that meant more profits. He had joined the Chamber of Commerce, he could care less how other businesses were doing, he joined to keep his finger on the pulse of the town and to keep his ears open to local gossip. At the meetings, he made a point of getting to know other business owners. He conferred with them, flattering their egos. Over the next year, Jim used the information he gleamed to make sure his staff were well compensated relative to other local businesses, another little tactic to keep them happy and loyal.

Jim knew that money was not everything. He made up the work schedule based on what the staff requested for hours and time off, giving preference to his senior staff. He hired students in the summer so that his regular staff could take extended weekends or vacations if they wished. It was important to him that new hires fit in with his staff and that everyone got along.

Especially in the beginning, Jim worked alongside his staff. he helped clean up the store, reset the shelving and made himself available to the staff and to the customers. He put in many sixty-hour work weeks.

For the first month, Jim curbed any impulse to reprimand the staff on how they spoke to a customer or carried out a duty. If something was truly amiss, he would step in and take over a customer's care or he would gently show the staff person an easier way to stock a shelf or count the floats in the cash registers. He had a little notebook in his back pocket and he would notate what he saw. Every night Jim made sure the dishes were done, coffee pot and counter cleaned, the bathrooms cleaned and the garbage dumped.

At the beginning of the second month, Jim polled the staff with three different timeslots for everyone to come in and meet outside of working hours. He chose the best time when most were available and he called a staff meeting, promising pizza. He took orders for everyone's favorite and arranged delivery for an individual pizza for each person accordingly. He stocked the fridge with pop, water and a fruit tray.

They started the meeting with a shared meal and small talk. Once the pizzas were finished and people were starting on the fruit, Jim set up an easel with a large presentation pad. He had already prepared many sheets of notes for the staff.

"Okay, folks, let's get down to business. I've been working a lot on the floor as you all know. I've gotten to know all of you better and you've gotten to know me. I like this little group of co-workers that we have developed and I hope you do too. I have some ideas to help all of us do our jobs better."

First, Jim polled the staff on where they felt that, as a team, they could improve. He wrote everything down on the top page of his pad, which he had left blank. Once everyone felt that everything had been recorded, Jim asked if they could focus on just three of the points for now. Everyone agreed. Jim underlined three of the points recorded: customer service, cash register and extra jobs. The points Jim had prepared ahead of time were on these exact three topics.

By the end of the meeting, Jim felt he had buy-in from the staff on a cash register protocol and he promised to laminate sheets that would be left at the cash registers with step b step instructions that would be easy for them to follow. They had role-played a few of the common sticky or embarrassing customer service situations. Jim felt the staff were comfortable enough to come to him or at least to confer with each other to better serve the customers. Jim agreed to look into hiring a beauty consultant to alleviate questions the staff were just not trained to answer. On a personal note, Jim was happy that the staff agreed they should all take turns with housekeeping tasks. Jim would add to the break schedule an extra duty roster. And, he warned them, he would police it.

They agreed to meet again in six weeks' time to talk about their challenges and maybe tackle three more of the points on their list. Everyone was excited. Jim took this moment to announce a big change he had planned; the store would begin to stay open on Sundays. He then softened the blow, sending everyone home with a chocolate bar and a pop, by way of a thank you for attending and participating. The staff left happy. Jim felt a weight lift off his shoulders. He had just developed a better staff and better working protocols for the store. Before he turned out the lights on his way out, Jim posted a new copy of the month's schedule with a new column besides the break schedules that was titled "Added Duty."

With these meetings, Jim developed buy-in from his staff and goals for the pharmacy, both of which improved its performance. He also formulated a great training manual, with a section devoted to each area that the staff identified at that first meeting and subsequent ones that he could use with new hires. More importantly, Jim had set into motion the steps he wanted in place to free himself from spending every open business hour of the week locked into being present at the store.

24 CROCODILE

If any local club came knocking on Jim's door for a hand-out, an item for a silent auction, a sponsorship of a kid's sport team, Jim happily helped out. He was quite surprised, attending one of the town's Chamber of Commerce's luncheons to find out that one of his employees had turned someone away. It seems the Calahoo Volunteer Fire Department were in desperate need of a new firetruck and were selling raffle tickets to help raise the money. Local businesses were being asked to showcase the tickets and sell them on the department's behalf. Jim sighed when he found out it was Randy who had turned them away.

Jim prided himself on hiring the kind of person that would fit into his team, who could get along with others, had the smarts to sell and offer good customer service and be happy working at the drugstore. Somehow, he had missed cues from Randy. Randy did not fit in. Worse, Randy took great pleasure is stirring up any whisper of discontent. Jim had received reports on Randy from many of the staff. He was nobody's best friend.

Jim wondered what it was that drove Randy to perform so poorly. The guy was older than Jim by about seven years. He had a lot of work experience. He had worked as a roofer, a car salesman, a general labourer, a waiter. The last five years he had worked in the city for the Brick Warehouse. Randy presented himself as outgoing, confident. He had a great smile, a firm handshake and he dressed well. Jim had questioned him during his interview on why he wanted to work in the pharmacy. He did not offer a commission and things would seem slow after the rush of selling cars or furniture. Shame-facedly, Randy said he had gotten involved with a co-worker, his wife had found out and insisted he quit and get a job locally. Alarm bells were sounding in the back of Jim's head but he decided to give the guy a break. After checking his references, he hired him.

Randy was a prankster with a mean streak. The first week he worked at the store, he discovered that Wanda, the cosmetician, was terrified of mice. He placed a rubber mouse just peeking out from under her counter not far from her chair. Wanda was in the middle of a customer consultation when she noticed it and screamed. A lot of commotion ensued. Jim was now thinking he should have fired the guy right then and there. He did see the humour in the situation, however, it had cost him a thirty-dollar gift certificate and an apology to the customer and he had spent an hour calming Wanda down and ensuring her that there were no mice in the store. Jim even showed her the blue cubes placed throughout the store that made sure mice could not survive there.

Other pranks ensued. A cashier was called away at lunchtime, when she returned her plate of dinner had been replaced by a plate of plastic barf. Jim had come down hard on Randy that time. He warned him that no more pranks would be tolerated.

Randy was often late for work. He ran into traffic snarls not experienced by other staff starting at the same time as him. He was constantly on his phone; once Jim eyed his screen and realized he was looking at porn on his mobile. He had been warned numerous times to keep the phone in his locker. And he just did not pull his weight. If he was on bathroom duty, the bathroom looked the same after he cleaned it as it did before he started. He was slow at restocking the shelves and often damaged stock by digging too deeply in the boxes with his boxcutter.

Jim had carved out an office for himself with dividers, in a corner by the back door. From it, he could see staff coming in and going out, he used it for interviews and private conversations, and it was used as the receiving desk. He called Randy in, the next day, at the beginning of his shift.

Looking Randy straight in the eye, he began, "I found out yesterday at the Chamber lunch that you told the Calahoo Volunteer Fire Department to bugger off when they came in here yesterday. They wanted us to sell raffle tickets for them."

"Yep," said Randy, sprawled in his chair, "we got enough to sell and there aint no profit in their raffle tickets," he added, with a leer.

"Randy, are you the manager of the store? Did you even think to come and ask me?"

"Well, no," said Randy, straightening up. "It just didn't make sense to me to spend time selling their stupid raffle tickets."

"Randy, I don't think you are trying very hard to fit in here. Everyone else gives the job their full attention. I've reprimanded you many times already about using your cellphone while not on break. I have to police your break times otherwise you stay in the lunchroom forever, even after another staff person has asked you to come out and help. You are constantly late and keep forgetting to do your extra duties."

Hey, you weren't even here to ask. And I just ...

"Randy, I don't want to hear any more excuses. You are on probation. You come to me with things from the public like these raffle tickets. If I am not here then you go to Denny, like everyone else. He is in charge when I am away. Not you. Now, I am going to give you three chances: if you are late, if you don't pull your weight during your shifts, if you are on your cellphone or take long breaks or give any of the staff grief, well, you get three chances. Then you are out. Do I make myself clear?"

Jim stared at Randy; Randy glared back then let his gaze fall to the floor.

"Okay, but ..."

"This is the end of the conversation, Randy," said Jim, rising and staring down at him, "now go get to work."

For quite some time, Jim had felt the store was ticking along quite well and he did not need to be there every moment it was open. He and Denny shared the pharmacy duties. Soon he hoped to hire a third pharmacist. When Denny was on, Jim might be in the back with paperwork or receiving new inventory. With those tasks accomplished, he felt confident he could leave, that the staff would take care of the store. However now, he intended to be there every moment the store was open and to ride Randy very hard. The guy either had to turn around or Jim would turn him out.

Jim grabbed an apron and headed for the front of the store. He couldn't see what Randy was up to from his office. He found him restocking shelves down the cold and flu and vitamin aisle. Jim grabbed some boxes for the next row over. He could not see the guy but he could hear him. Jim was filling the baby shelves and felt they would probably take the same amount of time to finish. So, let's see what happens, he thought.

Jim was called away for a phone call from one of his suppliers and later by a cashier, needing more change for the till. He still managed to finish first. He stood at the end of Randy's row with an empty box in his hand. Randy looked up and noticed him. Jim tapped his large wristwatch.

"Right," Randy answered, "it's my break time. I'm going for lunch right now."

Jim sighed and started filling up the rest of the aisle that Randy left. Randy never came back. Jim heard later that Randy had spent the afternoon in a bar. He had gotten quite drunk and bad-mouthed Jim and his drugstore to anyone who came in. Randy did not come in the next day for his shift, nor did he come in for his next scheduled shift. Jim redid the schedule, taking his name off. He put his help wanted sign in the window and phoned the paper to place an ad.

Randy showed up the following Friday and asked for his pay. Jim gave him a hard look.

"You abandoned your job. I owe you for three and a half days of work. However, by law, I only need to pay it ten days after proper notice of intent to terminate has lapsed. It will be ready in two weeks' time. Come back then."

Jim turned to leave. Randy grabbed his sleeve, turning him back to face him. Randy took a step closer, "I need my money now. Today."

Jim shook off his hold and shoved his face even closer to Randy's.

"Well, you aren't getting it today. I will let the accountant know to cut you a cheque next pay period." Jim turned to leave, then turned right back and added, "that's when it is due by law," he strode off.

Jim received a phone call that afternoon from Mrs. Sullivan, Randy's wife. She begged him to reconsider. Perhaps he could forgive Randy and give him his job back. They needed the money. She had no groceries for the kids and their rent was due.

Jim asked her point-blank, and how do you think you are going to pay for all of that, given that your husband only worked three and a half days in the past pay period and walked out on his job?

When Jim left the drugstore that night, he noticed that someone had keyed his car. A long, deep scratch traced along the driver's side, from the tail-gate to the front bumper.

"Well," said Jim to himself, "I know who did that and I know where he lives. He'll pay. Yessiree, he will pay."

25 CLARET

Glenda made up some light scones, formed them quite tiny and popped them in her toaster oven to bake. Aimee returned with her asparagus and began preparing it. She had brought along a bag of frozen salt and pepper chicken wings as a side to the Sombrero salad.

Glenda took out a package of taco shells from the freezer and set them on the counter to thaw.

She ran to the garden for some of her salad supplies. On her return, Aimee, who had finished with the asparagus, took the veggies from her and began by washing lettuce.

Glenda cut up purple onions, green and red peppers and tossed them with cherry tomatoes and a few sliced jalapenos. She mixed lime juice with avocado oil then added in chili and a pinch of salt and poured it over the veggies and placed them in the fridge to marinade. They would add this to the lettuce later.

The scones were ready; Aimee pulled them from the toaster oven while Glenda formed a taco shell into each of her two taco bowl molds and popped them into the toaster oven.

The boys began to fuss so Glenda lost Aimee's help in the kitchen as she went and grabbed both of them and sat in the rocker with both babies on her lap.

Glenda grabbed a fry-pan and browned the ground bison with a chopped onion, garlic, turmeric and chili. While it browned, she splashed a bit of oil in another pan, squeezed a half lemon, and sprinkled the asparagus with parmesan cheese, in preparation to cook it just before serving. She turned the heat off under the meat, covered the pan and leaving it on the burner, she joined her friend.

"Okay, I guess the kids get to eat first," she took Connor and sat in an easy chair and nursed him. Glenda reached over to the iPod control and switched on some music. Aimee nursed Trevor.

Once the babies were fed, changed, washed and put on a soft blanket on the floor, the women returned to the kitchen. Glenda formed two more taco bowls and set them in the toaster oven while Aimee set out the chicken wings on a pan to be cooked next.

Glenda found some blueberries in the fridge and partially filled four ice cream dishes with them. She set them aside for later.

"We're good. We've got the lettuce ready and the rest of the salad ingredients marinating in the fridge," said Glenda, looking around the kitchen.

"Yep, we just need to set the table. What do you have planned for the blueberries?"

"Oh. I'm planning on topping them with a biscuit, brushing it with a bit of Grand Marnier then sprinkling it with sugar and cinnamon and toasting them slightly to heat them up and then serve them with a scoop of ice cream. Sound good?"

"Yummy!"

Kyle came in first. He had stopped at home and brought over beer, Alley Kat Amber. Glenda smiled at him and thanked him, teasing that he knew full well Dave had Unibroue on hand and their Fin du Monde was an amber beer. Kyle just waved his hand and said he'd stick with the home team.

Dave came in and gave a report on the sign.

"Wow! The sign at the bottom of Highway 43 just before you get onto highway 16 is decimated! There must be five or six shots right through the middle of it. I'll hook up my camera to the TV and you can see it."

Glenda came over to him.

"Hi Babe, gotta smooch for me?"

Dave kissed her quickly then hooked up his gear. Kyle came over with an Alley Kat beer for him, which Dave accepted.

"We'll drink the good stuff with dinner," he teased his buddy.

They all sat down and watched the video, the guys scooping the boys from their blanket and sitting them on their knees.

Filling the screen in a huge close-up was the sign. Just off centre, the rifle shots bored a hole right through it, leaving bits of twisted metal at its edges. Dave's video shot stayed steady for quite a few seconds then zoomed out revealing a bit of its location. His following shots were from further away and from various angles.

"There was quite an aura of anger there," Dave reported. "Stepping away from it, the insects hummed, the sun shone, it's a glorious day. Yet right by the sign, it is quiet. Dead quiet. I suppose by tomorrow that will be gone."

"The insects stopped humming because you were there," teased Kyle,

"They were probably sizing you up, the mosquitoes anyways, to see how much blood they could get out of you."

"Ha, ha, very funny. Anyways, the mosquitoes don't bother me." Dave looked around. "It smells good in here, what's for dinner?" he asked, taking a swig of his beer.

Everyone enjoyed the feast of fresh asparagus, chicken wings and Sombrero salad. Before dessert, Glenda brought up their latest findings on their ongoing investigation.

"I went to visit Aimee today, cutting through the bush and I spotted a fellow in a white pickup truck, parked on the side of the road by the bushes. He had binoculars and he was looking at your house with them," she said, looking over to Kyle, "that was mid-morning."

"Our house?" Kyle asked. "Aimee did you see anything?"

"No, I wasn't home. I had gone into Stony for Trevor's checkup. There's more."

"I snuck up along the trees to get behind the truck. Before I actually got there, he looked at his watch and left in a big hurry. I could only read the first two letters of his license plate: RS; his truck was really muddy, I can't be sure those are right." Glenda looked around the table, even the babies had gone quiet. Everyone was staring back at her. She continued, "with what we've learned from Helen Majeau and what we can discern from the files on gunshot shootings, we think our suspect actually fires a shot across the bow, so to speak. Helen stopped her investigations when her grandchild's playhouse was fired upon. There's been shootings reported close to most of the murder victim's homes. You can see it on a spreadsheet I've created."

Dave added, "there was a white pickup truck on our road once before. Remember, before my birthday on a Friday night? When I came home you had just arrived from shopping in the city and Aimee was here?"

"Really?" Aimee said, "I remember you saying there was a maniac on the road and that a truck had almost hit you. You didn't say it was white."

Dave shrugged, "I don't remember if I mentioned the color but I do remember it was white and that a man was driving it."

"Wow, perhaps we are reading too much into all of this but we think whoever is behind it has somehow twigged that we are investigating," Glenda said, "we don't know how. We haven't really poked around except at Roger's place and our interviewing of Helen. We haven't talked to anyone about any of this except to you guys. Another interesting thing is the sign on Highway 43 today. That happened just after I saw the white pickup over at your house."

Aimee jumped in, "and I bet Dave, if you looked, you did not find any bullet casings around the sign. I doubt if the RCMP even sent a cruiser to look at it."

"Huh, I didn't look per se. But I stood on the road right by where I think the shot came from. If he fired from inside a truck, the casings could have fallen there."

The room filled with a sombre quiet. Kyle spoke next:

"Living in the country, we don't expect strange cars to park in front of our houses with guys carrying binoculars spying on us. Out of everything you said, that is the creepiest thing."

"We know this guy has a thing for Aboriginal women. I am worried for Aimee," Glenda squeezed her friend's hand.

"Bring it on. I can take care of myself. But I am worried about my folks. Remember someone was at their place just around the time Alice Grant was murdered."

Dave let out a big sigh, "maybe both of you should back off from all of this. We have two newborns here to think about."

"Dave, we fell into this investigation. It's not much different than a news story uncovering a scandal in a major corporation or in city politics. Except in this case, we didn't really do an investigation, only some background digging and very much on the QT. We are worried about our safety and the safety of the boys and yours and Kyle's safety and the safety of all those closest to us. That's why we are having this conversation. We need help in protecting ourselves and everyone else."

Aimee added, "this is what we think we know. We think the murders started in the1980's. The psychopath doing this isn't a typical serial killer in that the number of murders has not risen exponentially with time. There seems to be some kind of link between our suspect and those murdered although we don't see what could possibly link them together. We think the same person who killed Ed Boyko and committed the other murders is also responsible for raping and strangling a long list of Aboriginal women. Again, we can't find the connection between the two types of crimes, our gut just tells us they are linked. Glenda has poured over the data and correlated drive-by shootings in the areas close to where murders took place within a week or so later. Sometimes, these aren't shootings at signs and mailboxes; they are livestock or personal property, like cars."

"If the person in the pickup is involved," Glenda continued "and I say 'if,' then we know it is a white guy with hairy arms who wears a large wristwatch. Now to deduce further, Ed Boyko was killed in 1984. If our guy was in his twenties then, he's be in his late fifties today. Things have been going on for a long time so he has to be pretty smart not to have gotten caught. He is a local guy and he has a fair bit of free time."

"Why do you say that?" asked Kyle.

"Well, he's up in the night taking pot shots at people's windows. If he is the same person who was at Mom and Dad's, it looks like he was there mostly overnight. All the rape victims died late afternoon or evening. Yet if it is the same person who was at your house, he is not at work in the middle of the day. Who has that kind of work flexibility?"

"We have to keep you and the babies safe," Dave said, looking at both women at the table.

Aimee nodded and continued, "also, if he is the same guy that murdered and raped Alice Grant then he could be a local guy who graduated from high school in Stony Plain and who drives a pickup. That is what she told her friends about her new, secret boyfriend."

Everyone went quiet again. Glenda broke into their thoughts. With a sweet smile around the table, she asked, "anyone for coffee or tea? Let's have dessert and plan what comes next."

Both men exchanged a look and shook their heads. But they did stay at the table with the women and they talked into the night and made some plans.

Dave and Kyle would set up spy cameras around their properties and around everyone's parents properties that they could monitor on their cellphones. They would be more discreet than what they had set up at Kyle's in-law's place since they knew this was a savvy guy. They would lock their houses all the time and set up intrusion alerts that would feed to everyone's cellphones so there would be no chance of anyone coming home and being taken unaware. They would maintain more contact throughout the day on their cellphones. They would talk to all of their parents more frequently and set up intrusion alerts at their places as well.

The women would enroll in a self-defence class in the city, not in Spruce Grove or Stony Plain, just in case that triggered someone to know that they were on to them. They would also up their physical activity and Tai Kwon Do practice. The men would join them for lessons on the weekends and learn some moves themselves. They decided against arming themselves as none of them had much experience with guns and such and it appeared the serial killer had a lot of experience in that area. They would need to beat him with their wiles not their marksmanship. Kyle argued that they needed more help. They decided to bring in his two brothers, Ken and Nathan, and Aimee's cousin, Brock.

They also discussed at length if they were just being paranoid, reading more into unrelated bits of information than what was really there. In the end they decided to err on the side of caution and to put all their plans into effect.

26 METAL

Helen Majeau was becoming a problem.

After all the hoopla around Ed Boyko's death died down, things never returned to normal for her, as it did for all the town folk. Helen pestered the RCMP over every little thing. Jim had been driving around the countryside for years now, taking pot shots at old couples as they watched TV, sometimes just at road signs as a kind of target practice. He had broken into many cottages and deserted buildings, looking for likely places to bring women. These were never in the paper before. Now they were cropping up more and more. Worse yet, Helen would tie them to other drive-by shootings that had happened long ago. Why drag all that up, Jim wondered. He went further and further afield, hoping to escape her notice. Little, steely Helen, however, was his biggest fan and seemed to be able to sniff out almost all of his mischief, regardless how far he went.

Something had to be done.

Jim started watching Helen, timing things to be at the store or coffee shop when she was there. At the store, he overheard her talking about her grand-daughter to a friend one day. Another time, she was showing off pictures of the little darling over coffee. Jim stood up to leave and passed by their table. He glanced down at the picture as he walked by. He recognized the little girl. It was Chelsey Kusic. She was asthmatic and her mom frequented his drugstore. She often chose mojos as a treat and Jim sometimes would add a few to the bag holding her puffers.

"Well, well," he thought, "I got you now, Steely Majeau."

At home, doing bow practice with Dog, Jim pondered silently on how to get Helen to stop reporting on him. Later he went into the house and pulled down maps and the phone book.

Jim put the map up on his corkboard wall in his den. He started putting pins where Helen lived and where her grown kids lived. He decided he'd maybe hit a few mailboxes and road signs around them. Let's see what she reports on that, he thought.

Jim's plan back-fired a bit on him. Unbeknown to him, the mayor and some of the RCMP also lived close to where Helen and her family lived. The cops were out in full force, looking for gun casings, footprints, eye witnesses, anything to try and find the perpetrator. Jim laughed. As always, he was super cautious to not be seen and to not leave a trace of himself behind. He had used Daisy and had donned his disguise. Even if anyone had seen him, then good luck to them in identifying him.

Helen wrote her most scathing report and Roger, his good old buddy Roger, who he played poker with every Wednesday night, moved her article to the front page of the paper.

Two days later, Jim went and got Daisy. He made sure her back end was good and muddy and that her license plate could not be read. He put on his disguise, smudging his lower face with makeup to look like stubble, donning his hat and his contact lenses and his sunglasses. He parked down an alley from the Kusic home and watched the backyard easily, through their chain-link fence.

The house was on a corner. From where Jim was parked in the alley, he could clearly see down the one street and part of the intersecting road. There was no traffic.

Jim had been parked for about forty minutes. He could not tell if anyone was home or if little Chelsey Kusic was in the playhouse in the backyard. His intent was a warning shot, not a kill. Suddenly, a magpie flew in front of his truck, squawking. His hatred of magpies flared his boredom into anger. He decided to make a move.

Jim got his rifle ready, opened his window and started the motor. He planned to do this very quickly and to get the hell out of dodge.

As Jim's truck approached the Kusic property, he lifted his gun into position. He fired at the playhouse, aiming high, for the roof, just in case the little girl was inside it. As he fired, the backdoor opened with little Chelsey and her mom stepping out. Jim hit the accelerator, throwing the rifle onto the passenger seat and skedaddled out of there.

Later, Jim realized his timing could not have been better. Yes, they now knew he drove a white truck. So what? There were more white trucks on the roads than any other colour, most of them not logoed, just like his.

From the talk in town, Jim, who once again made a point of being where Helen Majeau would be, found out, over a nice cup of coffee at Tim Horton's, that the RCMP's investigation was completed. They had no suspects as to who, in broad daylight, had taken a pot shot at her grand-daughter's playhouse, destroying it and scaring the little girl half to death in the process. He watched as Helen shook her head and sighed. Later he overheard her say that she was getting too old for all of this.

Those words gladdened Jim's heart. He hoped she would decide to retire and leave his business the hell alone.

27 SAFFRON

The first day of the women's self-defence classes dawned. Josie and Winston had offered to babysit the boys. Later, in the afternoon Glenda was to meet Helen at her condo in St. Albert. Aimee was planning to return right after their class to her parent's place. She and Trevor would spend the afternoon with her folks, Trevor could keep Connor company.

Once at the Cardinal's, Winston suggested both girls stay in town for the day. The two women looked at each other. They were uneasy about leaving the boys without one of them being on site for a whole day. Just then Brock pulled up in his rusted truck. Winston informed them that Brock had agreed to help him with some roofing repairs on the garage. It would take them all day, he said. Brock had gotten on board straight away when the four of them had approached him with their fears. He had promised to patrol all the parents' homes as well as those of the Cardinal cousins and aunts and uncles in the area. The women accepted Winston's invitation and left both boys, happily playing in the front room with Josie, as they drove off in Glenda's car.

Before reaching the highway, Glenda pulled over and phoned Helen, letting her know that the two of them were planning on visiting after lunch.

Helen was delighted to meet Aimee. She served them tea and shortbread cookies. They did not stay long and thanked her profusely for her hospitality and for loaning them her pictures.

Glenda suggested they stop in at the station and see if Dave had any ideas on how best to look at the contact sheets. Once there, it felt strange for Glenda to sign herself in as a guest with Aimee. The temp receptionist phoned up to Dave's desk. It turned out that he was not in. She was in the process of informing Glenda and Aimee that they would not be able to enter if the person they wished to see was not there. Glenda was protesting, "but I work here!" when Dianne, her assignment editor crossed the lobby and intervened. Dianne ushered the women into a small conference room just off the newsroom.

She offered beverages and made a bit of small talk then suddenly asked, "what exactly are all of you up to anyways?"

Aimee looked at Glenda as Glenda instantly responded, "nothing, why do you think we're up to something?"

"Oh, I don't know. I see Dave talking more and more to the tech guys and I notice you are calling him or he is calling you more often and that the phone calls are very short and furtive."

Glenda shrugged. Aimee shrugged and looked at Dianne. Dianne said, "you aren't planning a move or anything? Are you making a demo tape for 60 Minutes or something?"

Glenda laughed out loud.

"Oh Dianne, I know your previous news anchor before I joined the station did that to you. No, we love it here. There have just been some shenanigans going on in the country. Dave wants to stay in contact throughout the day, just checking that our mailbox is still standing and that no one has shot out the tires or the windows of our car."

"Oh, is that why you want to do a story on sign shootings? Is there a connection? Should I assign more staff to it, I mean, not to take anything away from you, but you aren't back to work until the New Year."

"Oh, I think we're handling it okay. So far since Dave's birthday party there's only been one reporting of a sign that was shot at. And it's been almost a month since his party."

Glenda shrugged. Aimee shrugged too. Glenda added, "we're interested in sticking with the story. Who knows, maybe the perpetrator is on holidays or something."

"Well okay then, let's give your friend a tour of the station, shall we. Aimee come this way," invited Dianne, standing up and ushering them out of the room.

Once they left the station, Aimee could no longer hold her mirth.

"Miss Glenda, that was just pure fiction back there, no wonder you did so good in creative writing classes."

"Why thank you Miss Aimee. And I had no idea you knew so much about television make-up. Maybe that's why you did so well in art class."

They both giggled and laughed about the incident the whole way back to the Cardinal's place.

Glenda later called Dave and filled him in on their visit to the station. Dave said he would bring home a magnifier and they could use it to view the contact sheets. He explained that the magnifier was quite powerful. It was raised and would sit on the contact sheet, its bottom being perfectly smooth so you could move it across each thumbnail picture. You just had to hunch over it, putting your eye to the viewer to see an enlargement of each shot on the contact sheet.

Mid-afternoon the women practiced their Tai Kwon Do exercises in the Cardinal's backyard, then they collected the boys and headed home.

All day, they had all been distracted, wondering about Helen Majeau's pictures. What would they find on them? They headed back to Aimee and Kyle's place where Dave joined them after work. He set up the contact sheets with the magnifier.

The first sheet was of Ed Boyko's murder. The photos were extremely brutal, raw, gruesome in the extreme. Dave quickly switched it for the second sheet.

The second sheet was of the Crowchild twins. While it was a horrible crime, there was almost an art to the photographs, the two still bodies with drifts of snow along their silhouettes, lay in mirror image to each other on the ground, their hands touching, their heads slightly turned towards each other. Their vulnerability was so evident; it broke your heart to look at the photos.

The boys were fussy and everyone decided they had had enough for one night. Aimee suggested the Ellis's come back the following night for supper and they would investigate the photos further.

The next morning, on her own, Aimee looked at all the contact sheets. She pulled out the magnifier and peered intently at them. Other than taking breaks for Trevor and her own lunch, she spent the whole day inspecting Helen's pictures. In the afternoon, while Trevor slept, she once again found herself pouring over the well-lit table, shuffling through the photos.

She had gone back to the contact sheet of the Crowchild twins. Peering through the magnifier, she wondered about a person that would drug, brutally rape and strangle two young teenagers then artistically pose them and leave them exposed to be found. Their clothing had been cut and ripped from their bodies. Both sported bruises and split lips so they had put up quite a fight. The assailant must have had scratches probably to his face and arms or hands. Yet he was emboldened enough to just leave them there in the open to be easily discovered. No attempt had been made to hide the bodies. In a far corner of a disused gravel pit, he had draped their torn clothing partially over them; it had frozen to their bodies with their own blood and the blowing snow.

Aimee was peering intently at the clothing. Something very small stuck out of one twin's bosom. She focused the magnifier on it. Then she peered through it at the other twin, going up and down her body. There! Something similar was sticking out of this twin's hair. She would have to ask the others what they thought it could be.

When Trevor woke up from his afternoon nap, Aimee finally put everything aside and texted Glenda to come over and help her prepare supper. Twenty minutes later the two women were in the kitchen.

"What's on the menu?" asked Glenda.

"Dunno yet. Let's see what we got." Peering into her freezer Aimee called out, "salmon, a small ham, ground round – the real kind, no soya here – and salt and pepper chicken wings."

"We can make up a ham, new potatoes and beets from the garden," suggested Glenda, "or we can make tacos or chili with the ground round, or a meat loaf. Let's go with meat loaf, new potatoes, beets and whatever else you got going in your garden."

"Agreed," said Aimee. "Here's the ground round, can you put it in the sink in a bowl of water to start it thawing? I'll go to the garden."

Aimee came back with a basket containing some new potatoes, beets with their greens, chives, green beans and a large beefsteak tomato. Glenda took the vegetables and began washing and preparing them.

"Did you look at any of the pictures today?" she asked Aimee.

"Yep. I used the magnifier and went over them. I have something to show you guys later."

Glenda stopped and looked at her friend, "now you have my curiosity all stirred up. What did you find?"

"I don't know what it is; after we finish here I'll show you. It's something small tucked into the clothes and hair of the twins."

Aimee placed her meatloaf in the oven; on the stovetop, the beets were on a low boil, the potatoes and green beans in pots on their burners, ready to be turned on a bit later. Glenda was chopping up the beet greens with the chives. She put her knife down on the cutting board.

"Aimee, show me. I don't want to wait for the boys." Smiling, Aimee took her to the dining room table across from the kitchen. There was a huge raised deck just behind it, sunlight poured in through its large sliding glass doors. She found the right contact sheet and with a pen pointed out the two objects on the twin bodies. Glenda peered through the magnifier.

"Hmm," said Glenda," it almost looks like feathers. See, here where the top is uneven, like the ruffled top of a bird's feather."

"Could be," said Aimee "Let's see what the guys think." Glenda gave her a look. She went over to her bag and took out her cellphone. She snapped a picture. The two women sat on chairs next to each other and looked at the cellphone as Glenda used her fingers to make the picture larger. It pixelated but both of them agreed they were looking at feathers, the tip of one showing at one twin's breast and the tip of another peeking out of the hair, close to the ground on the second twin. They hooted and high-fived each other.

Aimee went back to the kitchen and Glenda went over to the boys and sat on the floor with them. She found them so much more interesting now that they could move about somewhat and that they made gibberish sounds as they explored their toys. Connor was crawling and Trevor was trying so hard to mimic his older friend. He could get onto all fours but still lacked the strength to move forward. He would rock back and forth, on his hands and knees, without moving forward one bit. Aimee came over and they both chuckled over his cuteness.

The men arrived home after their day's toil and happily tucked into the prepared dinner. Dave had stopped and picked up Haagen Dazs strawberry ice cream for their dessert.

As if by a predetermined agreement it was only after the last spoonful was eaten and the table cleared of dishes that the talk turned to the contact sheets. Aimee showed the men her findings. Dave said he would take a picture of the contact and blow it up and hopefully they would be able to see more detail. He pulled out his cellphone and took a picture of the thumbnail. He then emailed it to Kyle and together they went over to Kyle's Mac PC. Opening Photoshop, they enlarged it on the screen and manipulated it around to see the two objects. The image was pixilated but they both agreed that yes, it was indeed a feather on the one twin's clothing and stuck in the other twin's hair. A long, black non-descript feather, quite dark, blending in with the torn clothes and dark hair on the twins, but definitely a feather.

The four of them excitedly pulled out more contact sheets and with the magnifier, began hunting for more feathers. They found a feather planted on the body of every victim. This was a new clue.

Sitting in the living room, rocking their babies, they discussed the clues to date. Although no one understood the significance of the feathers, their presence tied all the murders together, the horrid gruesome ones and the violent rape and strangulations ones. They were looking at the handiwork of one person, over the span of thirty years.

28 GALL

The first thing Jim did, once Aunt Doris's will was probated and he deposited that huge chunk of money into his paltry Servus Credit Union Savings account, was to go out and buy and install a dishwasher. He had always respected his Aunt's denial for the need of one and had washed and dried many a dish and pot for her, especially in her last year. She was so tired all the time. Jim had even made Dog come in once a week and vacuum for her and told him he had to sweep or shovel the front porch and walkways every day. While Dog often acted like a big brother to Jim, Jim recognized that the man had a healthy respect of his anger. He just needed to take a slightly uptight stance and make a demand and Dog would comply with a, "sure buddy. Anythin ya need."

Once the new dishwasher was installed, Jim looked around the tiny kitchen and realized, for the first time, that it was fairly shabby. The finish had worn off the edges of the cupboards and at the most used spots on the counters. There was a stain that would not be bleached off the door under the sink and some of the cupboard doors no longer closed properly. The counter was chipped by the stove. The stove itself and the fridge were actually a ghastly gold colour that had been out of style for decades. Only the new shiny, white dishwasher looked up to date. "Well, all good things in their own time," he muttered to himself. "At least the dishes won't pile up."

Jim thought his next job was to run off the hobo town that had grown up in the woods by the road and driveway. He wanted to be fair about it; these guys had helped him out when he needed them. He thought Dog might be able to give him some advice. He called Dog over to the house under the pretence of showing off the new dishwasher.

"Wow, she's a beaut," Dog kept repeating as he opened and closed the door.

"Yep," Jim would reply and after about the tenth time, he added, "this'll take care of our breakfast dishes and our supper dishes and even our snack dishes. The lady that sold it to me said it will clean most pots and pans and casserole dishes."

Dog looked up happily. Jim recognized the look. Dog was unsure of his place in Jim's house. Before the will had been probated, they both still considered it Aunt Doris's house and Dog still felt entitled to coming in for meals and even cooking some himself. Jim had just let him know that that would still carry on.

"Dog, you and me, we now own this piece of land," said Jim. "Now I know on paper it's just me. But you are like a big brother to me and also out of respect to Aunt Doris; you know it was in her will that you are to stay in the cabin, remember? Well, I just want you to know it is now up to both of us to keep this property the way she would like it to be. Hell, you already do most of the gardening, mending fences and cutting the lawn and clearing the snow. And I don't mind helping out with that stuff. But I want you to know this is our land. Dog and Jim's. No one else's and it is up to us to keep it respectable the way Aunt Doris would have wanted it to be."

"Uh huh," said Dog. He had stopped playing with the dishwasher and Jim had guided him over to the table and set out the cribbage board. Jim handed Dog the cards, knowing that he always liked to start with the first cribbage hand in any new game.

Jim was letting Dog win, in fact, he had thrown away so many points that he was in danger of being skunked. Dog pegged the last point just after Jim barely crossed the skunk line.

"Hoo-hee!" exclaimed Dog, "I won."

'Yep, we need a rematch, little buddy," said Jim as he grabbed up all the cards and started shuffling them.

"Ya know," said Dog, "I've been thinking what you said about keepin tha place all tidy an proper tha way Dory would have liked it." He looked Jim in the eye, gauging his mood. "Well, it's up to ya an all but still, I was thinkin, Dory would hold no truck with havin the brethren sleepin in tha woods." Dog shot Jim another look, to see how he accepted this pronouncement.

Jim looked at Dog with a hurt look on his face, "wait a minute, Dog, they helped us out a lot."

"Yep, they did, but tha job is done now so theys should move on," said Dog emphatically.

Jim scratched his head. He got up from the table. "You hungry?" Jim rummaged in the cupboards for some crackers and brought out a slab of cheese and a package of baloney. Dog was helping himself before Jim had the plates on the table. "Hell, let's have a beer, too," said Jim, "I think there's two left from last weekend. Sorry, buddy, I didn't buy any this weekend, this little baby here," and Jim brushed his hand across the front of the dishwasher, "well, she has our beer money for this weekend."

"That's okay, Jim. But them hobos, well, ya know theys cleanin out the woodpile and they's cutting down good bush n trees. T'other night they's was howlin at the moon for Chrissakes."

"Yeah, I heard that. It woke me up and I was not too happy about it."

"Ya see, its time for them ta go," said Dog.

Jim scratched his chin this time. "Well, Dog, how in the hell am I supposed to let them know they are no longer welcome? It makes me feel like a schmuck to turn them out after all they did for me."

"They didn't really do much," said Dog, "Sure, they banged the heads o' those cousins o' yourn tagether in tha beginnin, but those boys have gotten used ta being written out o' Dory's will by now. S'pect they won't be back." Dog gave Jim a baleful look. "And the brethren, well, they's misbehavin! Thinking they's gonna stay here forever and get fed steak. By you," Dog pointed his whole arm at Jim and shook his finger at him, "an for what? They's stealin firewood. S'pect theys even got a still somewhere set up."

"What? They can't do that. We told them they couldn't do anything illegal when they came here."

"See, they's got to go," said Dog. "Wha'd ya s'pect from a bunch o' hobos, anyways?" He looked at Jim. "Ya gonna deal those cards? An aren't there chips left too?"

Jim sighed. He got up and fetched the chips and poured them into a bowl. Returning to the table, he grabbed the deck of cards and started dealing them out.

"I want them to know I appreciate what they did," he said to Dog with a pout.

"Sure, sure, but the job is done," Dog said gesturing up and down with both arms.

"So, how do we get rid of them?" Jim asked with a smile to his buddy.

"Have the cops come around," said Dog. "Youse in Stony Plain all tha time now. Let the cops there know they's built a still, ya don't know where but youse afraid its on ya property an ya don want no trouble. Cops pokin about, the brethren will pack up and leave."

He had obviously worked this part out while they were discussing things, thought Jim.

After playing for a while, Jim said, "Dog, I still feel I owe them more than that. I want to do something to let them know I appreciated their help."

Dog threw down his cards so hard, some fell to the floor. "Jim Drucker, or whatever tha hell ya want ta call yaself, youse nothin but a big softie like Dory was. What the hell ya think ya been doin all these years? Givin them a place ta stay, buyin em sleepin bags and feedin them steak! Why don cha throw em a big fare thee well party? Ya could have another big steak dinner for em. But no beans this time. That's jest a cliché that hobos likes beans." With his speech finished, Dog picked up his cards, unaware that Jim had seen half of them, and proceeded to lose the rest of the game.

Later, after they had watched the news together, as Dog was getting ready to leave, Jim said to him, "Okay. I'll do as you suggest. But you should warn the brethren. Let them know I've had complaints from the neighbours, God knows that is the truth, and that I want to thank them but that I don't need them here anymore. Tell them the neighbours told me they've seen and heard them drunk. That way, they'll think it was the neighbours that called the cops on them."

"Tell ya what," said Dog, conspiring, "I'll wait ta after the cops shows up ta say anything." He touched his finger to the side of his nose. "This is jest between ya and me. It'll be our secret." Dog yanked on his boots, bid goodnight and disappeared into the darkness towards his own cabin.

Eventually the cops came around to investigate, the homeless men became uneasy, the rumours about the neighbours and the still escalated. Some left as soon as the RCMP drove onto the property, melting away into the bush, then later, scrambling for their paltry possessions and scurrying away. Others hung on. Finally, Jim suggested to Dog that he let the brethren know it was time to move on, that Jim planned one last steak dinner for them on the full moon then it was time for them to go.

"Leave it ta me," said Dog. "I'se know 'xactly what ta do."

One lone hobo stayed on. Tony. Jim sighed every time he drove up the driveway and spied his orange tarp through the brush or a wisp of smoke from his fire wafting up through the trees. Both he and Dog had asked the fellow to leave several times. He kept promising to do so tomorrow.

Finally, Jim decided something had to be done. The temperatures were dropping. Jim wished the fellow would just freeze to death in his lean-to. He decided to make that happen.

Late one Friday night he crept to Tony's camp. The man was asleep in his sleeping bag; angrily Jim recognized it as one he had bought. Jim jabbed the fellow with a needle, rendering him unconscious. Jim dragged his body out of the sleeping bag, arranged it on top of it and used soft cloth to bind and gag the man. He planned to drug him a few more times over the weekend, leaving his body exposed. Now, all he had to do is make sure Dog did not stumble on him. Saturday, they would spend together target practicing and Jim had plenty of beer on hand to keep him indoors in the evening. Sunday, he would treat Dog to a day in town, get him a haircut and some new duds and maybe even take him out to dinner. Hopefully by Monday, things would have taken care of themselves and Dog could go discover the body.

Sunday night, waiting an hour after Dog had gone to his cabin, Jim went to inspect his handiwork. The guy was still breathing, his colour an awful grey. His fingertips, ears and nose had frostbite on them. Jim gave him one last dose, untied and ungagged him, doused him with Sterno and left him there. Let's see what happens next, he thought.

Returning from work on Monday, Jim passed an ambulance on his quiet country road. Dog ran up to his truck as Jim parked and killed the motor.

"Jim, Jim, ya won' believe wha happened!" he said excitedly and began explaining how he had found Tony, passed out from canned heat and half-frozen to death. He couldn't get him to wake up so finally he called the RCMP. They sent out a patrol car then they called for an ambulance and they took Tony away.

"An all through tha, he never once seemed to snap out a it," said Dog finishing his story.

Every now and then Dog would bring up the tale of Tony with a shake of his head. Whatever happened to Tony, after his ambulance ride, no one knew for certain. Some thought he was in the Charles Camsell Hospital and some in the General Hospital and some thought he was in jail. Jim hoped he was dead.

29 SPOTLIGHT

Glenda phoned Helen Majeau and asked if she and Aimee could visit, they had something to show her. They were invited to come over Monday next, in the afternoon.

Once again, the women recruited Winston and Josie to babysit for them and drove into town for the day. They went to their self defence lesson, loaded their coolers with newly bought groceries from Costco, ate their lunch and headed to St. Albert for their appointment.

Helen greeted them warmly and served them iced tea and blueberry scones.

The women carried in the magnifier and a folder with the contact sheets with them. All three chatted together at the dining table while enjoying their snack. Finally, Glenda said, "Helen, I think Aimee found something here that actually links all of these murder and rapes together. We are wondering if you are interested in seeing it."

"Yes, yes of course," said Helen. All of her body posture changed. She had sprung up taller in her chair, leaning forward excitedly. Her eyes had widened and her eyebrows had shot way up in her face.

Glenda opened the folder and set up the magnifier. She picked out the contact sheets of the Crowchild twins and placed the magnifier over them. She passed it across the table to Helen, who looked through the magnifier. She looked up at the women.

"I noticed something first on this one's chest. See, right here?" asked Aimee, sitting close to her and pointing to the small speck.

Helen nodded. Aimee continued, "There's another one here in the other twin's hair. Right here."

She checked to see if Helen was following her. Then she reached over for her folder and pulled out some blown-up photos.

"We had the guys enlarge both those parts of the contact sheets," said

Glenda.

Helen took the papers that Aimee extended to her an exclaimed, "why, those are feathers. Black feathers. Perhaps from a crow or a magpie."

Aimee and Glenda exchanged a glance and shook their heads 'yes.' Then Glenda exchanged the photo and said, "Take a look at this one."

Helen gasped. Her hands went up to her mouth and she felt weak all over.

"I'm okay," Helen said, looking up into their beautiful, young faces. "That's Ed Boyko and it is one of the photos I took. I knew Ed. He was a good man. It was just a shock to see that photo again."

Helen straightened her spine and pulled the photo towards herself and Aimee pointed out a small tuft on his chest. Glenda pulled another sheet from her folder that showed that part blown up larger.

"Oh my," said Helen, "another feather. It looks almost the same as the ones on those young girls. They were raped and strangled. Ed was tortured and killed with a shot to the chest. They all have a feather purposefully tucked on them. Is there more?"

"Yes," said Glenda, excitedly, "we found what we think is a feather on all the victims in the photos you sent us. All the murders and rapes are tied together. And there is more."

Glenda continued, "I went through all the records of drive-by shootings. Before each murder, a day to a week beforehand and sometimes longer, there have been drive-by shootings around that person's property. Like in the case of Ed Boyko. There was a drive-by shooting at the street sign to his street about six months before his murder. A stray dog was shot on the sidewalk just outside his house about a month before his death. Two months before that his storefront window was shot out but no robbery ensued." She looked Helen in the eye.

"Now I am not saying that all the drive-by shootings lead to deaths. I don't even think they are all done by one guy. However, our guy, we think, is definitely a local guy and part of his modus operandi is drive-by shootings. Besides the murders and rapes with strangulation, he is probably responsible for murders committed by drive-by shootings."

"Do you have any idea who this guy is?" asked Helen.

"No," Aimee answered. "We know he has been operating in the area at the time of Ed Boyko's murder. We know he targets young women, middle aged women, most of whom are Aboriginal. I suspect we don't have a full body count. There are more out there. Their bodies were not found or they've been written off as runaways. That is what they thought had happened to the Crowchild twins before their bodies were discovered at the abandoned gravel pit. And he targets older men, most of whom are known to have been cantankerous or difficult."

Aimee and Glenda exchanged a glance. Glenda said, "a little while ago, there was a drive-by shooting in our neck of the woods. That was the same morning that I had gone to Aimee's place the back way, through the bush. When I came out of it on her side, I could see a white pickup truck in front of her place. There was a guy in it with binoculars pointed at her house."

Helen gasped, "A white pickup truck is the description of the truck driving away when my granddaughter's playhouse was shot at."

"Exactly," said Glenda, leaning back in her chair.

30 FLESH

In the first two years after his purchase of the drugstore, every year around the anniversary of Aunt Doris's death, someone spray painted the front exterior of the store. Jim had a good idea who the someone was but could not confront his cousins without cause. The last time it had happened, his insurance agent said that if it repeated a third time, they would put a separate rider on his insurance and it would cost him a hefty premium, should he decide to purchase it.

Jim bought himself a pair of night goggles. He phoned the RCMP a few weeks before the anniversary, explaining the situation and asked for more patrol cars to drive-by during the week of the anniversary.

Every night Jim closed the store as per usual and appeared to drive home. In reality, he parked his truck away from the store, doubled back on foot, let himself in the back door and took up a post inside on a lawn chair set up by the window. Each night he would sneak over to the door and unlock it in the dark. Then he would sit down with his night goggles on and wait. By the third night it was getting hard to stave off sleep.

In fact, Jim felt he had fallen asleep and it was the sound of a car door being slammed shut that woke him. He bolted wide awake, looked out the front window, he recognized one of his cousins' trucks and saw a dark figure approaching the window with a can of spray paint in its hand. Jim quickly threw off the night goggles, dropping them onto his chair as he bolted out the door.

The driver was yelling "Holy Shit!" at the passenger door. The spray can painter, wearing a balaclava, turned to the truck to see what the matter was. He totally missed Jim's tackle, which came from his other side. The driver got out of the truck and was trying to pull Jim off. Suddenly a siren sounded, blue lights flashed and they all looked up to see RCMP Officer Brent Turner, running on the sidewalk towards them.

144

No charges were laid that night. However, the cousins were given stiff warnings by the RCMP, who had opened up a file on each of them. There had been other spray paintings on buildings in the downtown Stony Plain area and the RCMP told both brothers that they were now suspects for those. They were severely warned to cease and desist along these lines and that if there was ever any spray painting on the drugstore property or mischief of any kind on any of Jim Drucker's properties then they would be called in for questioning.

The brothers wanted to charge Jim with assault. Because Jim owned the property and the police were on hand immediately and had witnessed the second brother assaulting Jim, they would not write up the charges and suggested, in the interest of burying the hatchet, that neither party charge the other with assault or mischief and that they go their separate ways.

Dean was getting married in a month's time, a fact well known to everyone present. Two beefy RCMP officers towered over his chair, peering down at him and asked, in front of Jim, how it would look to his fiancée and her family if this little fiasco made the news. The biggest and meanest looking officer suggested that whatever family feud was being acted out here, they had better grow up and bury the hatchet.

Jim never had any trouble with his family again. As a way of a thank you, he invited Officer Brent Turner to the next Wednesday night poker game.

31 CINEROUS

It was Jim's third year of owning the drug store, in the dead of winter. He had repaid to himself all of the inheritance money from Aunt Doris. Jim had done so, not on the earnings from the drugstore, which were growing, but on his earnings playing the markets. Jim watched the stock market and would buy when prices dipped or started hedging upwards, then sell quickly once he felt they were about to peak. He followed international and business news on the internet and developed a good sense of how the stock prices would respond to what was reported. Sometimes Jim lost big, but mostly he gained significantly.

Jim realized he had not partied or cut loose in a very long time. It was the wrong season for shenanigans and this just made him all the more restless. He headed into Edmonton to find a casino.

Jim played the slots at the casino. A young waitress kept coming over to him, offering drinks. She bent so low, he could see quite a bit of her ample breasts. He had a few drinks and gave her a generous tip. Giggling, she came up to him, one last time, and announced that she was going off shift. Would he like to take her for a drink? Jim answered, "yes."

He met her outside by the front door and she suggested a bar that was not too far away. They had drinks, then Jim suggested they go for supper. He drove across town to Whyte Avenue and they dined at Chianti's restaurant. Later Jim drove her home. She invited him in and he stayed the night. In the morning, Jim left for home, happy.

That first night, Jim gave his name as John Schwartz. He found out that Sandy hailed from Truro, Nova Scotia. She still had family there, some aunties and uncles and cousins, but they were not close. She was an orphan. Jim, or John Schwartz, had added that he too, was an orphan but that he did not know of any family related to him. She had only recently moved to Edmonton and knew practically no one. She said she always had trouble making friends, especially girlfriends. She thought this was because she was a blonde and stacked and that they were just jealous. Jim soon discovered it was because she was so ditsy. He would phone her at work for a date, only to show up at her place to find her working on one of her paintings, or on the phone to one of those 'not close' aunties in Truro, and once she had not even been home. He began taking cellphone photos of her schedule and meeting her at the end of her workday, whenever he wanted to see her. He would phone and let her know he would be waiting outside at the end of her shift. Every time she came out the front doors she would give him a smile that would light up the night. "John, what a surprise!" she would declare happily. Before she could say more, Jim would outline the plans he had made for that night. She would smile and say something like, "well that sounds like fun. Let's do it!"

Jim now had a play-mate. He was ecstatic. She lived and worked a good distance away from him. He had given her a false name and he had bought a cellphone and given her its number. She was the sole person that had it. She was ditsy and self-centered. She didn't seem to be curious about what or where he was when he was not with her. Jim made sure he saw her two or three times each week so that she would not just wander away with some other patron of the casino.

Jim mostly used Donald to drive to town whenever he visited Sandy. Sometimes, when he did not have anything scheduled the next morning, he would drive Daisy. When he drove Daisy, after leaving her place, he would stop somewhere and change into Daisy clothes or sometimes he just drove to where he had left Donald, switched trucks and went home. After the first time, he never stayed overnight at Sandy's.

Once, on his way home, having already switched clothes, Jim realized he was hungry. He stopped at Denny's in the west end for a bite to eat.

When he was about to leave, there was a ruckus at the cashier station. A shabbily dressed couple were trying to dine and dash. The man managed to run out the door, however the waitress had caught the woman and was struggling to hold onto her as Jim approached the cash register. Jim grabbed the woman by the scruff of the neck and held her for the waitress. He asked what was going on.

While the woman screamed profanities at them, the waitress explained that they had not paid their bill. "Shh!" Jim said to the woman's face then asked the waitress, "how much does she owe you?" It was under forty dollars and Jim said he'd pay it and settle his own bill as well. The woman tried to run for the door as Jim loosened his grip on her to get his wallet. He grabbed her sharply by the arm, winked at her with a "now hang on there for a second, darling," and paid the waitress. He left her a fat tip.

Jim ushered the woman to his truck. He could see her partner hiding behind some parked cars. The man stepped out in front of Jim's truck as he came around in the parking lot. Jim gunned the engine and the man quickly jumped out of the way. Jim laughed. He turned to his passenger, now sitting quietly, her seat-belt done up, and winked. "Dunno what you see in that guy," he said to her, "he can't even buy you a sandwich."

"Well, you don't look so rich, yourself. You're just showing off, flashing money at that waitress," she replied, contemptuously.

Jim chuckled. He was enjoying this. The woman was about forty, maybe older. She was thin and Jim thought, tired of life. Yet, he felt she could be quite lively given the right incentive.

"Darling, just between you and me, I have three wallets in this truck. And none of them ever have less than two hundred dollars in them." He let a beat pass. They were headed west, out of the city. He asked her what her name was, she answered, "Rosie" and he told her his name was John.

"You live in Edmonton?"

She shook her head no, "I live on an acreage west of the city."

"You want to party? he asked her.

She considered. "What have you got in mind?" she asked.

"Hell, we could pick up some beer and head for my uncle's cabin. He won't be there this time of year. It's been years since I've been there. We can party all night."

She agreed as Jim knew she would. She would be considering how much booze it would take to get him to pass out. Then she would search his truck for his three wallets and beat a path out of there.

Jim stopped at one of the hotels just outside of the city, gave her two fifty-dollar bills and sent her in to buy some off-sales beer. She came back with a bottle of Jack Daniels and twelve beers, Pilsners, the cheapest ones they had. Jim laughed as they peeled away, his radio blaring rock music.

Jim drove to Lake Isle. He knew of a lot of lonely cottages out that way and randomly selected one. He pulled up the long, dark driveway and killed the motor.

"Wait here a second," he said, "I'll go around back and get the place unlocked."

Jim whistled as he walked away from the truck, towards the back of the cabin. There was a door there. Jim planned to bust a window or something to get in. He tried the door first. It opened a bit, there was a chain on it. Jim had snips on his toolbelt and used them to cut the chain. He walked through the house, getting a sense of its lay-out and opened the front door. He waved his new friend inside.

Jim walked out to meet her and took the beer from Rosie and carried it inside. Jim headed for the kitchen. He grabbed two beers. Jim found a glass, opened the beers, started pouring one into a glass after taking a swig of the other.

"Hey I don't need a glass," Rosie said, laughing, "save it for the Jack

Daniels. Got any ice?"

Jim opened the fridge. It was bare, the ice box was empty.

"Nope, the fridge is turned off. All that's in there is a box of baking soda."

Rosie made a face and moved to the next room. She found a stereo and tried finding a radio station. She finally settled on a country and western station. Jim watched her from the kitchen. Rosie noticed Jim looking at her and smiled at him. She took a quick tour of the cabin. She then returned to the kitchen and grabbed up her beer, taking a big swig.

Jim had poured himself some Jack Daniels, playing into her game. He picked up his glass and took a big sip. She clinked her beer to his glass and said, "cheers!" Jim obediently drank.

They drank and danced to the country and western music for a while, both still wearing their coats. It was as cold inside the cabin as the dark night outside. Jim had drunk two glassfuls of Jack Daniels, chased by beer. Rosie had two beers. Jim danced her down the short hallway towards the bedrooms. He backed her into one, saw bunk-beds there and turned her around to the other bedroom. It had a regular bed. Jim pushed Rosie onto the bed, falling on top of her. He began kissing her. She kissed back. Jim undid her coat part way and pulled it off her shoulders, half-way down her arms, effectively pinning her arms to her side.

"Hey, what gives?" she cried out.

"I thought you wanted to party," said Jim, while holding her down on the bed with his knee. He threw off his coat. He pulled the knife from his toolbelt and undoing the belt, he threw it onto his coat.

Still holding Rosie down with one knee, Jim tossed the knife from hand to hand. He laughed down at her. Rosie's eyes had gone wide and Jim could see the gears moving in her head. Finally, with a smile she said, "What have you got in mind, John?"

"How about if I tie you up to this bed?" he asked quietly.

"Okay," she smiled.

"Now, I am going to take my knee off your stomach. Then I want you to get naked."

"Okay," she said.

Jim rolled over, closed his knife and got comfy on the pillows. Rosie got up, looked at him, and slowly peeled off her clothes. It wasn't exactly a strip-tease but close.

"Were you a dancer?" asked Jim.

"Yes, I was," answered Rosie.

"Are you clean?" he asked her.

At this Rosie got mad. She made to put her clothes back on. Jim snapped his knife open.

"Don't do that," he said softly, "answer the question."

"Yes, I am clean," she said with a grimace.

Jim stood up, grabbed her arm and threw her on the bed. She lay there, waiting, her eyes on fire.

Jim slowly undressed and went to his toolbelt. He put on a condom, winking at her. He then grabbed some cable ties. Rosie did not object as Jim grabbed her wrists and secured them to the bedposts. Whistling, Jim left the room.

"Hey where are you going?" she yelled after him. Jim did not answer. "Hey, it's cold in here," she screamed.

Jim, naked, walked to his truck for bungee cords. He came back, gave Rosie a smile and a wink and tied each leg to the bedposts at the foot of the bed.

Jim grabbed his knife in his right hand and lay on top of Rosie, stretching his body spread-eagled along her lines. She thrust her hips at him. Jim laughed. He bent down and grabbed her breast into his mouth, working it harshly, then nipping at her nipples. She writhed and called out, "take it easy, John." Jim got up and found her socks. They were small and thin He bundled them up into her panties and got back on the bed. He knee-walked until he was straddling her again.

"Shh!" he said, giving her a wink. He lay the panties down next to her head. Jim then grabbed her hair with his left hand, tilting her head up to him and kissed her hard. He licked her down to her navel, moving his body away, knowing the cold room would feel like ice to her. She shivered. He laughed. "How about a blanket?" she asked.

"Nope, no blankets for you, not yet anyways, he said smiling down at her. And if you talk or make any more noises, well," and he held up her panties, "this will get shoved into your mouth." Looking down, his face inches away from her, he yelled, "Do you understand?"

Her eyes widened. She nodded her head yes. Jim grabbed her breast in his mouth and bit hard on her nipple. He could feel her body react, hear her whimper.

"You're nothing but a dirty bitch, you know that? He said to her ear, dragging the end of his knife down her face and along her body.

"You were planning on fucking me then robbing me, weren't you?" he demanded. She stayed still.

"Answer me," he said, holding her chin up with the tip of his knife, letting it cut through the skin and draw red droplets of blood.

"No, I wasn't," she stammered. Jim moved, putting both hands on the mattress besides her head, holding his face inches above hers.

"You wouldn't be telling lies, now would you?" he asked softly.

"No, John, no lies," she said.

Jim moved his weight to his left hand and slapped her hard.

"What kind of fool do you take me for? I know all your tricks," he snarled at her.

"No, no. You rescued me from that restaurant, remember? You gave me money and I went and bought booze like you asked. I could have cut then, I didn't. I wanted to party with you."

"Liar," snarled Jim, slapping her again. She began to cry loudly. Jim grabbed her panty bundle and shoved it into her mouth. Again, he held himself up with his arms while lying atop her, watching. He took the gag away.

"By the way, I noticed you did not give me my change back," he said calmly, looking down on her.

"I have it in my pocket. I must have forgotten. You can have it."

Jim punched her hard on the side of the head.

"Liar, you intended to keep it."

"No John, really. I got back into the car ..." Jim slashed his knife across her face, the blood spurted out, spraying him. He licked at it; she was screaming for him to stop. He stuffed the gag into her mouth.

Jim got up and came back with the woman's T-shirt. He kept twirling it and flinging it at her, watching her twitch in reaction to each hit. He laughed at her. Jim left the room again.

In the kitchen, Jim poured himself another Jack Daniels and went and sat on the couch. He listened to the music still playing through the stereo while he finished his drink. Once done, he returned to the bedroom.

Jim could see that Rosie had been struggling against her restraints; her wrists were chafed and red. Without a word, he threw himself on top of her, wrapped the shirt around her neck and entered her roughly. She writhed this way and that, trying to free herself and made a racket through her gag. Jim punched her in the face, yelling obscenities at her, she went slack. He moved his pelvis, slow at first, then quicker and quicker, holding the ends of the T-shirt, pulling the ends tauter and tauter, watching the fear rise in her eyes. Finally, he came. Exhausted, hell, it must be three in the morning, he thought, he lay on top of her for a good long while.

Jim went and took a cold shower in the cold bathroom. Whistling, he got dressed, washed and replaced the glass he had used, then packed up the beer, the bottle caps and the Jack Daniels into the truck. Jim looked around the house. Everything was as it was when they arrived. He went into the bedroom and cut Rosie's body loose from the bedposts. He threw all of her belongings on top of her with the towel from the bathroom. Jim wrapped everything up into a bundle in the bedspread and carried it outside, dumping it in the back of his truck. Jim went back to the bedroom and inspected the bed for any stains. He saw none. He took the top blanket just in case. He looked around one last time to make sure he had not left anything behind. Whistling, he threw the blanket onto the truck bed, closed the tail gate, got in the cab and turned the truck around, heading down the long driveway.

Jim drove to Pembina River Provincial Park and found a secluded campground He always carried firewood in Daisy and soon he had a huge, blazing fire going, on the site's gravel driveway. He unloaded his parcel, doused it with gasoline and watched it burn. He added more wood and gas to keep the fire very hot. Of course, not everything burned; Jim had a plan for the remains.

Jim drank the Jack Daniels sitting on the hood of his truck while the ashes cooled. He watched the sun come up. Then he grabbed one of the tarps from the bed of his truck, shovelled what he could onto it, rolled it up and tied it with a bungee cord. He put everything back onto the bed of the truck and closed it up. Jim then scuffed the gravel stones as best he could and drove off. He parked close to a hiking path along the river. Carrying the bundle, he hiked the path. He came to a place where he could access the river. No one was around for miles.

Jim opened his parcel into the river, letting the current carry its contents away. And wouldn't you know it, he mused, as a magpie scolded him from a treetop. Jim grabbed a stone and threw it at the bird. It toppled to the ground. Jim brought it to the water's edge, pulled out two feathers and let one of them go in the current. Then he grabbed a large rock and maneuvered it over the bird's body in the water. It began to flutter. Jim kept his weight on the rock in the icy cold water for a beat after the bird stopped its struggles. He splashed his way out of the river's edge and up the path. Soon he began to run. Both his feet were soaking and he was freezing Getting into his truck, Jim let out a big, happy yahoo, cowboy style, and he drove out of the park, the heater on full blast, headed for home.

32 CARMINE

Sandy liked it rough and 'John' was more than happy to comply. Once, early in their relationship, he went to her place, and she greeted him at the door, dressed as a dominatrix. He cautiously walked ahead of her down her long hallway, looking over his shoulder a couple of times. She followed, tapping her whip on the floor just behind his heels. He walked into the kitchen, saw an opened beer just waiting for him, grabbed it and walked towards the bedroom.

Once in the bedroom, he turned immediately and caught her up into an embrace just inside the door.

"No," Sandy squirmed, "Mommy is not happy with you," she angrily said, pushing him away.

"Well, Daddy is not happy with you," he said, pushing her onto the bed. Jim undid his buckle, pulled his belt loose, turned her over and began to spank her bottom.

"Hey, tonight is my turn to dominate," she shouted. Jim held her down, gave her a few more whacks then turned her over and laid on top of her, grabbing both her wrists in his hands.

"No darling, I am always in control," he said. Jim moved both her wrists over to his left hand and fumbled with her underwear. He meant to rip it off but it had an interesting slit. Jim fumbled with his own clothing, hurrying, he roughly entered her, holding both her wrists in his hands, keeping his torso high, elevated above her. He came quickly. It was only then that he realized Sandy was crying.

"Hey Babe, I'm sorry. Hey, hey," he said, stroking the side of her face. He rolled over, pulling her with him and snuggled her into his body. "Too rough, huh? Man, you just turned me on with this whole costume. And when I saw the panties, well, ..." Jim trailed off, stroking her hair, "let me make it up to you."

Jim began to slowly kiss her and gently fondle her body. It took only minutes for Sandy to respond. They coupled, in a much more vanilla manner, he brooded, and he rocked her gently with his hips until she came.

Later, after showers, he took her out for dinner to the Continental Treat Bistro on Whyte Avenue. Impressed with the surroundings but still upset, she pouted for a while.

"Tell you what, Babe," he said, after the wine had arrived and been poured for them, "I know you like it rough. Maybe I was a little too rough. I'm sorry. After dinner, lets go shopping and I'll buy you something pretty that you can pick out. I don't care what it costs. ... Well, you know, within reason," he finished, flashing her his most charming smile.

Sandy's eyes shone. She shook her head yes. He toasted them, "here's to us," they clinked their glasses together. Sandy began talking, her cute, bubbly body bouncing up and down with her hand movements as she relayed her gossip from work.

After dinner, Jim thought it would be a laugh to take Sandy to Sanctuary, getting there by cutting through Army Navy, so that she would think the destination was Army Navy. But he thought better of the idea as they strolled Whyte Avenue. They visited several shops before she found something that she loved. Jim shelled out the two hundred and thirty dollars at the cash register, with a wink at her via the mirror behind it.

John and Sandy dated for over two years. Jim figured eventually the relationship would come to an end and he kept the fires burning for as long as he could, even taking her for an extended weekend to Las Vegas for New Year's.

Jim had made the reservations on two separate flights; he had managed to secure a fake John Schwartz ID but thought it prudent not to fly with it. He had told her their dates, that they were both flying together on what was her itinerary. Jim planned to use his real identity to travel. At the last minute, he phoned her and said he had a crisis at work and could not leave. She was to take a cab to the airport, he would pay her back for it, and that he had changed his flight to a later one. When it came time to leave Las Vegas he planned to use the same excuse to change his flight to an earlier one home.

The trouble with his plan was that Sandy finally twigged that she knew very little about 'John.' She did not know where he lived or what he did for a living. All weekend in Las Vegas, she pestered him for details.

'John' explained that he played the stock markets. He lived out in the country with his ailing aunt. Because of her health issues, he had to stay by her side a lot of the time so he had found a way to make money at home, buying and selling stocks and currency over the internet. He hired a babysitter, one of the neighbours, to look in on her when he was with Sandy. He then tried to deflect her questions, with a "and you, my Babe, you get to enjoy a lot of my winnings. I love to wine and dine you and buy you nice things. Don't I?"

She agreed that John was generous with her but caught him in his lie about being an orphan and having no known relatives.

"So, I lied," he said, casually, "you'll never get to meet my aunt, she is pretty puritanical and would not approve of our relationship," he added.

Sandy was furious that he had lied to her and that he was judgemental of her, saying his aunt would disapprove. Jim realized, too late, that he had dug a bigger hole. He tried to deflect things onto her.

"Well, you said you are not close to your family back in Truro yet you are always on the phone with them."

"I am not close to them," she screamed at him, the tears starting to flow as she pummelled his chest. "Did I go home last Christmas or this Christmas? NOooo. I haven't been home since I came out here. They don't want me there and yeah, they want to know I am okay, but they are not interested in my life and they say my paintings are childish." The tears were really flowing now.

Jim agreed that her paintings were childish but he thought it wise not to say so.

"Okay, let's forget this," he said to the back of her head as he stroked her hair. Casting about the room, Jim just wanted this conversation ended and the fun to begin.

"We both have dysfunctional families. Let's leave it at that and let's go have some fun. I bet we could get into a show somewhere tonight. Wanna get dolled up and go out?"

For the remainder of their time in Las Vegas, Jim caught Sandy looking at him out of the corner of her eye. He suspected to hear more from her. However, except for the suspicious looks, she kept her peace.

It was once they had returned to Edmonton that trouble began. Jim was driving Daisy home from Sandy's place. Jim always checked his rear-view mirrors whenever he was driving. Leaving Sandy's place after one in the morning, with little traffic on the road, it was pretty easy to see that he was being followed.

Jim turned into a random subdivision. He passed an alleyway and turned down the next street without signalling. Jim quickly doused his lights and parked at the curb, waiting for his pursuer. He could see that this street was a cul-de-sac. Moments later the car came around the turn.

Jim boxed the car in by pulling his truck across the road. He saw that the driver knew he had been made and kept going down the street. There was an alley exit half-way down and the car quickly turned down it. Jim reversed his truck and turned back the way he came. He drove to the alley he had just passed, thinking the car might come out this way. Looking down the alley, he could see headlights approaching. He waited at the corner and at the last minute, he moved his truck to block the alley. With a screech of tires, the car stopped before hitting Jim's truck. Jim was out of the truck but before he got to the car, the driver had put it in reverse and was fish-tailing down the alley. Jim let him go.

"Dammit," he thought, "now I'll have to get new plates for Daisy."

Jim really liked Sandy. He had been thinking of coming clean with her, well, as far as his true identity was concerned, anyways. He entertained ideas of marrying her, moving her into Aunt Doris's house, maybe even having some kids with her. Of course, all of these daydreams ended with Jim wondering how in hell he'd sneak off for night mischief, or explain getting home late because he chanced upon a lone hitch-hiker, something that was becoming more and more infrequent as traffic between Stony Plain and the city became heavier, but just the same. There would be the odd bruise or scratch that a little wifey would notice, the absences; he could not see how it could work out.

His present problem was what to do with her now. Did he just walk away, throw away his phone, never go back to that casino and hope he never saw her again? What if he went to a different casino and she started working there? What if he took a different woman to dinner on Whyte Avenue and she saw them? No, he had to either break it off with her or get rid of her. He considered, he didn't have to make a decision right away.

When he had last seen her, because she had kept pestering him on where he lived and on his sickly aunt, he had told her that he had a business trip planned and would be away for two weeks. He had asked her sweetly if she would remain true to him while he was gone and wait for him to return. She demurely agreed and nodded her head yes. This gave him time to make his plans.

33 PEACH

Over the next two weeks, Jim gave a lot of thought on what to do with Sandy. He had played out a little wifey scenario so many times in his head over the years that he knew he couldn't ever go down that road. His appetites would be found out, he'd be required to do too much explaining of his whereabouts.

Sandy was an eight in his books, not really tall, yet statuesque, blonde, bubbly, great in bed and willing to try lots of new things. She just wasn't very bright. Jim wanted to end the relationship.

Jim had never had a girlfriend as far as anyone in his home or community knew. Aunt Doris and Dog had constantly encouraged him to find a girl. He had. Many girls, in fact. The special ones were lined up in various gravel pits. The rest, well, scattered to the winds.

Now that he was a 'successful' local business man, people in town and at functions were encouraging him to find a woman. He knew some people thought it creepy that he didn't have a woman. Maybe he was playing this all wrong. There were a thousand Sandy's out there. Why use Daisy and a false name when dating them? Why not let them know the truth about him, well part of the truth, that he was a pharmacist with his own business in a town close to the big city. He would end up with a slew of women and get a reputation as a playboy and that would be a public persona that he could live with and that could suit him very well.

Getting back to Sandy, Jim decided he would confront her on being followed. She would probably deny it. He would keep the argument alive with all of her snooping into his affairs. He would holler and thump his chest. He would tell her he was a very private person and that it was over. She would cry and cling to him. He would walk out like a cool glass of water. He'd actually go to a bar. Who knows? Maybe he would meet his new Sandy.

Jim visited many bars in Edmonton and many of the casinos as well. The new Sandys weren't always as much fun as the old one. But he did stay clean with them, giving them his real name and treating them half decently.

Then he met Nicole.

34 RUBY

It was the beginning of a cold winter, his fifth one as an owner of the drugstore. Jim had begun thinking about renovating the old house. With the bitter cold blowing so early this winter, he promised himself that he would redo the siding and add more insulation in the summer. He noticed Dog would come in for supper and spend a long time warming himself in the kitchen.

"Hey, how's it going in your shack, you got everything you need?" he asked.

"Yep, thank 'ee."

"Well, then how come you look so cold every night when you come over here?"

"Oh, it's not so bad. Me 'n ya, we cut lots o' wood. Mornings are damn cold though."

Jim came to a decision. He sure as hell could not live a winter in that old shack. There was a time when he would have thought it a great luxury to have a shack like Dog's, but that was a long time ago. Dog probably didn't have many years left in him. Aunt Doris wouldn't let him freeze in the old shack in his old age.

"Dog, why don't you move in here? We could fix up Aunt Doris's room for you. You won't have to worry about firewood anymore."

"No, no Jim. Ah couldn't a' do that. It's yore Aunt Dory's room. She was a grand lady. Ah couldn't sleep in th' same room as' n' her."

"Well, does that mean you'd be willing to move to the main house?"

"Huh. Let's a think on it," he said.

Jim let it go. He was still using the same bedroom assigned to him when he first arrived. He had taken over the third bedroom, a tiny thing, and was using it as his office. He had no qualms of taking over Aunt Doris's room and making it his own. Dog could have his. He would let him think on it and keep pestering him to just do it. He figured it would take two, maybe three days for Dog to give in.

Dog moved in on the weekend. Jim moved all his stuff out of his room and Dog moved in. That had been the easy part. Jim had never cleaned out Aunt Doris's room. He had invited all the women in the family to come and choose some jewelry and clothing after the funeral. Aunt Margaret had died before Aunt Doris and most of the clothes were still there; the younger women had not been interested in them. Jim boxed up the jewellery and stored it. He bagged up all the clothing and shoes and purses and dropped them off at the Goodwill in town. He then went into Edmonton and bought himself new pillows, sheets and duvets. He bought new towels while he was at it and he picked up a toothbrush and paste, deodorant and shaving stuff for Dog. He hadn't brought anything into the house of that nature. Jim did not want him using his stuff.

Life for the two bachelors settled into a routine. Jim made sure there was always a lot of food around, things that Dog could heat up and eat on his own for the nights he did not come home to cook for the two of them. Alternatively, he made sure there was never a lot of booze around so that the old geezer behaved himself.

Jim was seeing Nicole when Dog first moved into the house. Dog got used to his absences.

Nicole was a bad girl. Jim wondered how deep that streak ran in her. It turned him on that he had met someone just like himself. She was short, slender, dark haired and she had eyes that just flashed evil at you when you ticked her off. Sometimes Jim ticked her off on purpose just for the rush those eyes gave him.

Nicole would not ride in his truck.

"Oh, please," she had complained, when he first walked her to it. She opened her purse and tossed him a set of keys with a fob. "Let's take mine," then she stood there, waiting for him to figure out which vehicle was hers. Jim went up and down the street, pressing the fob, listening for the car to beep in echo. She stood there and laughed.

"C'mon, Cowboy," she called, "it's in a car park. It's not on the street. Follow me."

That first night, she let Jim drive her car, a sleek black Camaro. She directed him, sometimes asking for a left-hand turn right at an intersection. She laughed when he missed a turn. They drove for about forty minutes and ended up about two blocks from where they started.

"Let's get a drink in here," she cooed, pocketing the car keys.

Later she drove him home. To her home, a beautiful penthouse suite overlooking the river valley. Jim whistled when they walked in. He heard her famous "oh, please," in response, followed by her delicious laugh.

Jim headed to the bar to mix them drinks. He was tackled from behind, literally. Nicole had slipped off her shoes and used her leg to catch his foot, yanked, forcing him to slip towards her. She tumbled on top of him. It was a hard fall, broken only by the thick white shag rug. Jim kept trying to roll her over, to take control. She laughed at him and moaned in his ear, "just relax, Baby. I'm taking good care of you, relax."

Jim spent more and more time in the city with Nicole. Then she announced she had a business trip and that she would be away for a few weeks. Jim begged to go with her.

"Oh, please," she responded.

At home, in his own bed, Jim was awakened in the night by Dog's coughing. He actually got up at one point to check on him. Dog had assured him he was okay.

The next morning Jim was on duty to open the store. He called Denny and asked him to open for him.

He got Dog up and cleaned him up as much as he could and fed him some breakfast. Then he went out and warmed up the truck. He hustled Dog into the truck and took him to a medi-centre.

Dog had bronchitis. Jim drove to the pharmacy and got his prescriptions filled. Handing them to him, Denny had said he could stay and close for the night, if that was okay with Jim. Jim thanked him.

He took Dog home and set him up in an easy chair in front of the TV. He got him a blanket and found a sports channel for him to watch. Jim left the room and made him some chicken noodle soup.

Dog got better. And Nicole came home.

All that winter Jim and Nicole were an item. She had come out to Stony Plain for a Christmas party. Jim had taken a suite at the Ramada for the two of them. The next day they had gone back to Edmonton. Jim took her shopping for her Christmas presents. They spent New Year's at the Jasper Park Lodge. She taught Jim how to ski. And the sex was amazing. She was a creative vixen and brought out Jim's wild side, which he always kept in check with her.

After the holidays Nicole let Jim know she had another business trip. She would be back later in January.

Jim returned home. Dog was sick again. Jim bundled him up and took him back to the medi-centre. This time, they put him in the hospital. Dog was there for almost two weeks. When he was discharged, Jim thought he looked terrible. His skin was grey, his clothes were hanging on him, his arms were full of track marks from the staff either taking blood or attaching intravenous lines to him. He looked like a street person, coming off a drug binge.

Once home, Jim set him up with a blanket in his favorite chair, in front of the TV. He whistled, going into the kitchen, to fix him some lunch.

Jim hired a woman to come in and watch Dog in the daytime. He had her clean the house and make them meals. Jim stayed home every night so he could hear Dog, to be there for him.

Nicole came back. Dog was still sick. She wanted to see Jim. He explained that Dog was old and sick. She insisted he tell her where he lived, she would come there. Jim tried to explain to her that she would hate it. "Oh, please," she said. She arrived with fresh organic salmon doggie treats for Dog and laughed to find out Dog was a nickname for a man named Doug who had rescued Jim from the streets.

Jim could sense in Nicole that same dark empty streak he felt in himself. She stayed at his place, tip-toeing around the hired lady, keeping Dog company, making him laugh, giving him the will to get better. After a week, Dog was more his old self. It was Dog regaling Nicole with stories this time. She gave him a kiss on the top of his head when she left.

Dog continued to get better and Jim continued to see Nicole. He had the cleaning lady stay on, coming in three times a week and cooking for them.

It was now March. A warm spell in the weather had Dog, Nicole and Jim shooting targets in the back field. Jim was surprised at what a good shot she was. Dog was enjoying her camaraderie.

Jim cooked them Aunt Doris's famous crispy fried chicken for dinner, serving it with hand cut French fries and home-made coleslaw. They all squeezed onto the couch in the front room and watched a video. Dog wished them a good night with a twinkle in his eye as he headed down the hall to bed. And it was.

The next morning, Jim was the first one up. He started coffee then bacon for breakfast. Nicole appeared at the door. He put her to work toasting the bread. Dog had still not appeared. Jim went to wake him, he wanted to start the eggs.

"Shit!" Nicole heard loudly form the kitchen. She went down the hall.

Dog lay in the bed, one leg hanging over the side. He had passed in his sleep. Jim stood there dumb-founded. Nicole pulled him away, she took his hand and led him into the kitchen. She sat him in a chair and poured him a cup of coffee. She then called 911 and reported the death.

Nicole stayed with Jim at the house until after Dog's funeral. Dressed in black, statuesque, if petite, thought Jim, she looks like the beautiful Enchantress in a dark Victorian horror film, leading her army of the tattered and the ragged; the homeless brethren that attended Dog's final farewell.

Dog's death affected Jim as that of Aunt Doris had not. With his passing Jim grew sullen. They had both rescued him from a life on the street; Aunt Doris had the means to provide him security with a roof over his head, three square meals a day and an education, while it was Dog's quiet coaching, unbeknownst to the older hobo, that taught Jim how to hide his true nature and learn to blend in with the rest of society. When Jim first settled at the Dzuik homestead, Dog often coached him on how to behave in the lady's house, to remember his manners and to fit in so that he did not end up a hobo, as he had. Jim called this his chameleon skill. He perfected it, watching others as they reacted to happenings around them and later practicing their expressions in mirrors. This, his sense of humour and his physical prowess were what kept him alive and out of jail all of these years. Perversely, Jim realized his dark thoughts were caused by some emotional response to Dog's death yet that insight only made him more churlish.

After Nicole went back to her place, things were never the same between them. Jim was morose yet he wanted to be with her all the time. He did not want to go out. He wanted more sex. He craved the intimacy. Nicole hated his clinginess, his neediness. She felt the fun had gone out of their relationship.

They started arguing. Jim was surprised at how physical their fighting became. Often it turned into frenzied love-making. Bites drew blood. Fingernails trailing down a back or thigh left red droplets of plasma. The anger in both of them exploded.

Their last night together was in town, at Nicole's place. Jim had grabbed Nicole's wrists after she had slapped him, yelling at him to feel something.

He pulled her close to him, wrapped his arms tight around her, holding her so close. He looked down into her fiery eyes. "I'll feel you," he whispered. He carried her to the bedroom and threw her on the bed, ripped the clothes from his body. She watched with a wicked little smile upturning the corners of her mouth. He lunged onto the bed beside her and started undressing her. She grabbed either side of his face and kissed him hard. Jim had entered her, her body rising to meet his. He grabbed at her clothing and wrapped a piece around her neck, pummeling his hips faster and faster. She fought him, writhing, trying to flip him. Pain brought Jim back to awareness. Nicole had plunged a small knife into his side. He raised his torso, holding himself up by his arms. Nicole grabbed at her neck, found her breath.

"Steady there, Cowboy. I'm not ready to check out."

He leaned down and kissed her gently, whispering, "sorry, I got carried away."

Later, after showers and bandages, they took their dinner at the Continental Treat. They wandered Whyte Avenue for a while, stopping for drinks, then Nicole drove him back to his truck.

"I won't see you again, Jim," she said, standing in front of her sleek black car.

"Hey Babe, don't be like that. I ..."

"Cowboy, that wasn't your first rodeo," she said, getting into her car.

She opened her window.

"We were good, together, weren't we?" she asked, looking up at him while she started the engine.

Jim never saw her again. His precious dark jewel was lost forever. She did not answer his calls or messages. A few weeks passed and Jim found himself in town not far from the river. He drove to her building and let himself into the carpark with the pass card she had given him. He rode the elevator up to her floor. The knock on the door was not answered. Turning to leave, Jim passed a realtor leading a couple in the hallway. They were going to the penthouse. Her suite. He now knew she had left for good. Jim flipped the pass card out his window before leaving the garage.

Many, many years later, Jim came across a Black Widow story on an internet newsfeed. There was Nicole, as beautiful as ever. She held her head up, her eyes flashing anger at the camera. Jim smiled. His hand was caressing the monitor. Kindred spirits to the end, he thought.

35 TRUE BLUE

After Nicole left him, Jim began working on his renovations. This was during the best season for night mischief. Jim would not give into his wild desires, he knew they would get the better of him in his frame of mind. He needed time to brood alone, he had the break-up with Nicole and he needed to figure out where he was going from there. He did not want to follow his urges, he had always lived with self-restraint, from a position where he was in control. He knew that if he could not exercise his self-discipline then he might make mistakes that could get him caught. He immersed himself in the physical work of construction to right himself with the world once more.

Jim wanted a larger, brighter kitchen and a larger brighter living room. It was a small house and it had a solid foundation. Jim decided to build up. He contracted an architectural firm to draw his plans, followed most of the changes they suggested and got to work.

The first thing Jim did was clean out Dog's cabin. He threw just about everything out and moved in what he needed from the main house. He would sleep there while the renovations took place. Then he hired a St. Albert interior design firm to furnish his new home. This was the third company he had called, he chose it based on the fact that the woman who answered the phone was named Nicole. He hadn't liked any of the portfolios he had seen: he wanted modern, a lot of white, yet a definitely masculine look for his home.

His small, yellow, clapboard house was transformed. The east and south side boasted oversized windows framed with large white boards and dark stonework. A new porch ran along the west side. One came in through an inner porch, which still kept some of the old country charm of the original house then stepped into a gorgeous great room with a kitchen gleaming in stainless steel and marble countertops. Across the room was a fireplace faced with the same stones cladding the exterior of the house. A staircase wound its way to the second storey. It paused at the top, offering a railed view of the great room. The large master bedroom with a large ensuite took up the whole east wall, a guest room with a smaller ensuite and Jim's office filled the rest of the second storey. The basement was refurbished with a new furnace and hot water tank and a fully equipped gym with a sauna.

Jim would never again be ashamed to bring a woman home. Hell, he planned to have the guys over for poker some Wednesday nights.

36 COBALT

A few days later, Helen called Glenda.

"I've been invited to the Mueller's this Sunday for a barbecue at four o'clock. I am wondering if you and Aimee and your husbands and the babies, of course, would like to attend. Do you know the Mueller's?"

"Yes, of course, they have a booth at the Farmer's Market. He carves and builds things out of wood and she sells eggs, baking and vegetables."

"I have a friend that used to room with them. He is coming through, he needs to be in Edmonton on Monday, and I think he may want to hear what you two have discovered to date."

"Oh?"

"Yes," Helen continued, "he was a rookie RCMP officer at the time of Ed Boyko's murder. We became fast friends and we have kept in touch over the years."

"Okay. I'll talk to the clan and let you know if we can all make it."

37 ICE

It was a warm summer night with the stars twinkling in a midnight blue sky. Jim got into his pickup truck and drove away from home. He smiled at himself, seeing his transformed house looming, then shrinking, in his rear-view mirror. He had packed his rifle behind his seat along with his special backpack. He headed to his other truck, Daisy.

Be Prepared! He smiled to himself. He had no plan in mind. Jim quickly changed into workmen's clothing, donning a new ball cap. He moved the contents of his Donald backpack to his Daisy backpack then he filled the Donald backpack with his regular clothes and put it in his Donald truck. After going eastward for a while he turned north off the highway and after a while he turned east again. He began to follow the country roads. He would see what he could find. Maybe scare some kids out necking, he mused to himself, humming along to a tune on the radio. He recognized the Onoway dump as he passed it and he realized he was on his way to Devil's Lake. He wondered if the holy-rollers who had bought the place were around.

Everything was quiet at Devil's Lake. Jim realized it had been a while since he had seen any traffic so he killed his headlights and pressed onwards. Jim passed an upscale acreage right out here in the middle of the boonies and decided to investigate. Going beyond it, he found an inconspicuous place to park the truck, grabbed his gear and investigated on foot.

Jim plunged into the bush and set his rifle up on its tripod. He attached the rifle then folded in all the legs in and put the whole thing in a sling over his shoulder. Soon he came up close to the edge of the woods and could see houses. A few dogs barked. Jim double checked his belt. Yep, he had his pepper spray just in case any dog decided to chase him down. He could hear a backyard party going on. Jim could see the light of a fire through the trees and headed that way.

There was a huge bonfire roaring with many people sitting around it in lawn chairs and on a picnic table. Music was blaring, raucous laughter brayed, a few people danced, some men were throwing axes between each other's feet. The suburbanites are getting shit-faced, he thought.

Jim turned away, averting his eyes from the fire's blaze and circled past the Friday night revellers. The land sloped downhill and Jim found himself blocked by a slough. He circled it, frustrated by this barrier between him and the acreage houses. He knew from experience that it could only be so big so he persevered until he had gone all the way around it and could see the outline of one of the acreage houses. The first house he came to was dark. Not a flicker of light escaped through any of the doors or windows. Jim plunged back deeper into the woods and trudged onwards. The second house had a huge mown backyard. There was a huge play set in it very close to the woods. It had a little fort up high and swings and a slide. The whole backyard was dark.

Jim climbed up onto the fort. He looked around. Nothing. He pulled his night goggles out of his backpack. As far as he could scan, no one was there. Jim looked back to the house. All the windows were dark, except one. Under the large deck the blue flickering light of a television glowered into the night through what Jim thought must be sliding glass doors. Jim put away the night goggles and stripped the rifle from the tripod. Perched up on the kiddie's fort, his rifle resting on its balustrade, Jim put his eye to the scope and focused on that blue window. There! On the couch! Man! Were they ever going at it! Jim watched them intently for over twenty minutes. A couple was groping each other and humping under a huge blanket. He could barely hear the sounds of the TV, bits of music, angry sounding voices, nothing clear or definite; he tuned it out as had these two. They finally surfaced for air; a big blonde woman and a thin, dark-bearded and very white-skinned man, both about mid-thirties. The man sat up and poured wine into two glasses on the coffee table. The woman scooted over to sit next to him and wrap him back up in the blanket.

Aw, isn't that cute, there they are, sitting together, wrapped up in their blanket, drinking their wine. She does have lovely titties though, thought Jim, catching one in his cross-hairs. Suddenly she began stroking the man's face and they were necking again. She straddled him then wiggled down his body until she was on her knees, buck-naked, her large ass wiggling in the air, kneeling in front of her man. Jim could see her breasts stroke up and down his body; she grabbed his manhood and began stroking it. Hell, Jim was now stroking his own manhood. She plunged her head down into his lap, bobbed a few times then climbed onto his lap. They were rocking together, unaware of the presence of their third partner, Jim. He, with his hand down his pants, humped along with them. His other finger was still on the trigger of his rifle and when Jim came, jerking, the gun went off with the man. Jim raised his head and howled into the night. Then quickly, grabbing up his pants and his gear, jumped down from the fort and into the woods. He looked back. There was the man standing at the window, holding the blanket in front of himself and peering out into the darkness. "Thank you, Sir!" Jim shouted to him, then continued his circuit around the subdivision and back to his truck.

Jim had been driving around for quite a while. He came upon a hidey-hole that he knew, and found another vehicle parked there. The engine was still running with a couple inside the car.

Jim parked further down the road and crept back. Looking in the car, he recognized his ex-employee from many years back, Randy, who was making out with a woman that was definitely not his wife.

Jim went to the back of the car and stuffed a rag into the tailpipe. It would take a while for the car to fill up with noxious fumes and Jim stood, in full view, in front of the car and watched. The air in the car was definitely getting opaque. Finally, the couple noticed. They were coughing furiously and a window was opened. Jim went to it. There was Randy, lying on the backseat, eyes closed. His woman had opened the door across from Jim and was getting out of the car while getting dressed.

Jim switched on the flashlight mounted on his rifle, placing the barrel on the car roof over the open window by Randy's head and called out, "Run along now, darling." With one arm, Jim held Randy down. With his other, he aimed his rifle at the woman's head, across the top of the car. She screamed, running, looking back, trying to put on a shoe, all at the same time. It made Jim chuckle. Jim looked down into the backseat where Randy was squirming and trying to break the lock Jim had on his chest.

Jim leaned the rifle alongside the car, opened the door and pulled Randy off the backseat and out of it. He let him fall on the ground, his pants still down around his ankles.

"Interesting look, Randy," he commented, crossing his arms across his chest and leaning on the car. Randy scrambled to get up. Jim kicked him in his side. He pulled out his keys and began scratching Randy's car, from the back bumper all the way up to the front bumper.

Randy was screaming profanities at him, rolled onto his side and attempting to pull up his pants.

Jim jumped on him, snapping his knife open. Jim cut Randy's T-shirt open part-way and pulled it down his arms, effectively binding them to his body. at best, he had very limited use of his lower arms. Jim maneuvered him flat onto his back and brought one knee up onto his chest. With his knife, Jim drew a shallow line of blood from Randy's forehead, down the side of his face, avoided his neck, down his chest and moving himself backwards, down Randy' body, close to his penis and then down his legs.

Randy screamed and squirmed, landing a few punches on Jim. Jim stood up and looked at his handiwork. He casually kicked Randy in the head, "aw, stop your whining," he said, "we're just getting started."

Randy's demise did make the papers. Jim learned a few things he had not known. The victim was known to the police; the car did not belong to Randy. It belonged to the woman. The woman, at first, denied having been involved and it took several questionings from the RCMP and several days, before she admitted that she had been there. Jim noticed her in the pharmacy about a week later, her face sporting a huge purple bruise, her front lip split and swollen. It turns out, both she and Randy were married, to other people. While Randy's widow was playing the victim to the hilt, with collections being taken at all the banks in town to help her and the children, Connie was scorned, obviously beaten by her husband and had a keyed car. Jim's only regret was that he spent so much time with Randy that night that Connie was long-gone. Jim had driven up and down many likely roads that she could have taken, looking for her in vain.

"Oh well, there's always a next time," he thought, as he helped Denny fill prescriptions.

38 BRASS

Two carloads deposited the Ellis and Brace families into the Mueller's backyard just after four o'clock on a warm, August Sunday afternoon. It was a glorious day for a back-yard barbecue. The sun shone in a clear azure sky amidst small puffy clouds. There was a light breeze to keep away the mosquitoes and the gardens were still swollen and lush with their summer harvest, ready for the picking.

Mildred greeted them and shooed the men over towards her husband, Sam, who was sitting on the patio close to the house. She toured the women carrying their babies, proudly around her gardens. She knew the names of every variety growing in her gardens, the vegetable and fruit as well as the flowers and shrubs in her large flower beds, and even the names of the few weeds they discovered on their walk. Aimee noticed the beehives behind the gardens, on a small verge between the gardens and the woods.

"We have good honey and you'll get a taste of it tonight. I've used it to make my barbecue sauce," Mildred said, proudly.

Just then Mildred's son Joshua and his wife, Megan, pulled up in their Bronco. Mildred excused herself to welcome them and their children. Glenda and Aimee carried the babies over to their now seated husbands. The men had beers in their hands and were joshing with Sam, all laughing loudly. Glenda asked Dave if he had unloaded the van. Negative. Exasperated, both women dropped the babies onto their husband's laps and went to their vehicles. They added a salad and a plateful of cookies to the long banquet table set up on the far side of the barbecue, then went back for their extra chairs and blankets for the babies.

As they returned, the men got up and placed the boys on the blanket, offered their wives their seats and set up the extra chairs close by, then found drinks for their wives. From where Glenda was sitting, she could see the landscape of the whole backyard. She sighed happily.

"Sam, it is so lovely here," she said to their host. He beamed appreciably.

"Thank you. And you'll get to taste some of produce with dinner."

Just then Helen came across the back lawn towards them A tall, husky, well-dressed man followed her.

"There you are! I'd like to introduce Brent Turner to you. Brent is with the RCMP and has come to Edmonton on business. We've known each other for years. When he was a young recruit, he boarded with the Mueller's."

As the introductions were made, Glenda could see two more pickups drive into the yard. She wondered who else had been invited. Just then Sam stood up, obscuring her view as he pounded Brent on the back.

"This fellow helped me out a lot. We fenced together and pulled out stumps. Guess I finally managed to put some muscle on that skinny frame of yours, eh Brent? Well, looksee here. I invited some of your poker buddies to come on out. Looks like Roger Lafontaine and that fellow that owns the drugstore, Drucker something, well it looks like them now."

More introductions ensued as the rest of the Mueller clan and the newly arrived guests all converged on the patio. Chairs and drinks were found and Mildred passed around bowls of chips. Small conversations buzzed. The baby boys were introduced to the Mueller grandchildren, a new baby, Mia, and her older brother, Logan, who was three. A second blanket was set up at the adults' feet to accommodate the children and their toys.

Brent was in conversation with Roger and Jim, catching up with each other since they had last been together, over ten years ago. Roger and Jim invited Brent to come fishing with them sometime. He whipped out his cellphone and pulled up his calendar, but no dates could be agreed upon then and there.

Brent caught Helen's eye across the crowd and excused himself to speak with her. He grabbed another beer and moved across the patio to her. Helen had already maneuvered the Brace and Ellis clan to a picnic table across the yard, set in a little clearing by one of the vegetable gardens. She had Sam and Mildred promise to keep an eye on the boys. Helen now led Brent across the yard.

"Wonder what's going on over there?" muttered Roger.

"Dunno. But there's only one way to find out," said Jim as he started to rise from his chair. Just then Megan sat in the chair across from both men.

"Gents, what a surprise to see you here. I wonder if I can go over some of the changes we would like to propose for this year's Labour Day Festival?"

Megan was referring to the event sponsored by the Stony Plain Chamber of Commerce. Both Jim and Roger were on its Executive Committee. Jim swore under his breath as he sat back down. Megan was as tenacious as she was vivacious. It would be a while before they would be finished with this discussion.

Over in the clearing at the picnic table, Aimee and Glenda were bringing Brent up to date with their findings. They had explained how they first got involved in this grisly business, how they found Helen's newspaper articles and met her, how they analysed her data and how Aimee discovered something left behind at each scene by the killer, even the recent one of Alice Grant. Aimee had pulled out several sheets with photographs of the crime scenes and with close-ups of the feather stuck onto each victim's body.

Brent told them that this was indeed new material however it did not bring them any closer to who the perpetrator was; he reassured them this was an important discovery, that they needed to keep a lid on it to keep themselves safe. Everyone nodded yes as Aimee started gathering up the photos. She had the whole pile together and was just about to tamp it down when they heard someone approach. Reaching for her folder as she turned to look over her shoulder, Aimee could see Roger and Jim approaching their table.

"I've been a newsman for twenty years, and my Spidey sense is tingling. What the hell are you guys discussing way over here?"

Brent laughed, "Roger, we are in fact talking about news. Dave here is a videographer and Glenda is an anchor at CFRN and Kyle is a techie. We've been talking about how technology is used more and more in solving crimes. Sorry we didn't include you in the conversation. But as I recall, Helen had the dickens of a time to get you to invest in personal computers way back when."

They all laughed. Dave said, "it's getting on. I bet Sam could use a hand barbecuing."

They all agreed and headed back towards the main patio to join the rest of the party.

39 SANDSTORM

Jim was the first person to leave the party. He had gotten one shock after another since arriving. This was supposed to be a get-together for Brent's old buddies. What the hell were Glenda McTavish and that Cardinal girl doing there with their husbands? Something was definitely amiss and that Cardinal woman was right in the centre of it. How the hell did she ever meet Helen Majeau? Helen and Brent were close when he worked out of Stony Plain, who knew they would stay in touch over the years. Were they a menace to him now? They must be, but none of them acted strange to him. Those busy-body mamas somehow connected with Helen and they probably discovered something. He thought he had caught a glimpse of a closeup of a mashed-up feather in that bunch of photos the Indian was shuffling together. What the hell?

Jim drove to Daisy, changed into camouflage clothing and headed back towards the Mueller's. He passed their son's bronco, going the opposite way than Jim. He pulled over just past the bend after the Mueller driveway and left Daisy on the side of the road. Jim jumped over the Mueller's fence and crossed the farmland towards the house. He took up a position where he could see all the vehicles parked together. Those busy-body mamas were packing up the babies into the Indian's truck. Kisses to their men, who stood aside as they drove off. Sam was calling to the men; he had a fresh beer in each hand. Jim noted that Helen's small car and Brent's rental were missing. They had already left.

Jim headed back to Daisy. He did not take the same way back. Instead he followed the road away from the Mueller's. He knew the dirt roads in this area. They were really rough and poorly travelled. But, with luck, he could get ahead of those two bitches and make them pay.

40 JUNGLE

BOOOM! Aimee fought for control of her truck. As she hit the brakes, it fishtailed on the road and then ended up on the very edge of the meagre shoulder, almost in the ditch.

"Get out, get out!" Aimee screamed to Glenda.

Aimee and Glenda exited the vehicle, both using the front passenger seat. They left the front passenger door open and pushed the seat forward to get the babies out. They set the boys, still in their carseats, down on the ground. Aimee signalled to Glenda to stay where she was, to stay with the boys. Then she quickly darted noiselessly across the road and into the woods. Her face twisted into a grotesque angry mask, Aimee promised herself she would find this person who had shot at her pickup truck, smashing the window in on her and Glenda in a shower of glass shards, terrifying the boys and to top it all off, grazing her shoulder. She ran downhill then quickly uphill through the trees in the direction from where the shot had come. Cresting the hill, she stopped suddenly and looked around. Aimee swept the woods with her eyes in a full circle. The bush was silent. Not a breeze stirred; all was still. She could make out the break in the trees where the road lay and caught a glimpse of the truck's roof reflecting the setting sun. That placed Glenda and the babies over by that stand of trembling aspens. She looked again at the bush all around her. There! A slight movement in the undergrowth – a bird flew up unexpectedly into the dark sky – their shooter had circled around in front of the truck and was heading toward Glenda and the boys.

Aimee snapped a sapling and as she ran back towards the road, her hands stripped its thin branches and leaves. The shooter was ahead of her, crouched behind brambles, peering at the downed truck. Pausing, Aimee quickly unlocked her pocket knife and slashed at the thin end of the sapling, setting a point. Then, deftly she set out for his hiding place from the rear.

176

Only a small hill lay between the two of them.

Aimee came up behind Jim, whistled to get his attention and flung her spear at him as he turned. Jim jumped, the sapling caught him on the leg, above his boot. Jim swore, he looked up at Aimee with murder in his eyes. Aimee ran straight for him and gave him a Tae Kwon do chop. Jim staggered, quickly regained his feet and jumped at her. They wrestled until Jim managed to pin her on the ground. He forced her into to a sitting position and used a bungee cord to bind her arms to her torso. He head-banged her. Aimee passed out. Jim stuffed her mouth with a gag and secured her to a tree.

41 MAIZE

Glenda stood on the passenger side of the truck, a carseat on either side of her feet, and took stock of her position. She thought the shooter was either moving towards the truck or skedaddling out of the area as fast as he could go. Either way, this spot, this side of the road, with the smashed truck, this was not the safest place to be. She unhooked both boys from their carseats and held them in her arms. Using the truck as a shield, she half-crouched while half-walking and half-running straight down into the ditch on this side of the road. It was a deep ditch, engineered to catch the spring run-off and channel it away from the hay field just beyond that fringe of trees, to keep it from flooding. She ran along the ditch in the direction of the Mueller farm. It would be faster to go cross-country, however, she did not know the area well enough to trust her ability to find their farmhouse at dusk, carrying two babies and going through fields and woods. She would follow the ditch along the road.

Suddenly she stopped, turned back towards the truck and crouched. She thought she had heard something. The thought of Aimee out in the woods with the serial killer, for that is who she believed had attacked them, paralysed her. She could neither stomach the thought of leaving the boys alone or the ▮ of her friend out there in the woods, unarmed, against a serial killer. And this particular serial killer targeted First Nations women and was armed with a rifle.

She needed a moment to think. Remembering a news story, she had covered years earlier, about army maneuvers, she began fumbling in her pockets. When faced with a hard decision, the soldiers always reached for one of their special gumdrop candies. The sugar rush to their brains would give them more clarity of thought. Glenda found the nub of a roll of Life Savers and popped them into her mouth. Chewing them quickly she swallowed and looked around her.

If the killer was following her then she would be an easy prey to track, loaded down with the two babies. Connor slept, however Tyler was awake and jabbering away in his small sing-song voice. If the killer was nearby he could surely hear him. She needed a place where she could stash the babies and set up an ambush. She did not have Aimee's gift of feeling at home in the woods; Aimee always knew exactly where she was and had an uncanny sense of direction. She did have other skills though.

Growing up she had watched her dad, who was a natural tinkerer. Glenda had spent many hours with him in his shop or working on cars. She knew the truck was a treasure-trove that held many useful things. Perhaps she should go back. She looked behind her. The road above was straight, she hadn't yet made it to the curve, the ditch behind her was just as straight. A straight narrow path through the tall grass marked her route back to the truck, edged on one side of the ditch by a thin strip of aspens and on the other by the road. She could easily make out the clear markings in the tall grass of her trek through them; she realized anyone following her would have an easy trail to follow.

Glenda scaled to the top of the steep ditch and peered down the road towards the truck. Further along, past the truck, a man wearing night goggles and carrying a rifle was walking on the far side of the road towards the truck. She ducked down quickly. She ran in the ditch back towards the truck. The thought crossed her mind that he was walking along the opposite side of the road, a foot or so from its edge; if he crossed to this side, he would spot her in the ditch. Just then headlights swept around the curve beyond her and reflected off the fringe of trees above the ditch along the hay field. She ran as fast as she could up the bank and onto the road. She waved wildly, jumping up and down, while still holding the babies and she watched as the car swerved to miss her, heard the driver swear then the angry blasting of the horn as it sped past the downed truck. The one thing she had not seen was the man with the rifle.

Glenda ran full tilt towards the truck, willing herself onward. She ran to the open passenger side. Setting the crying babies down on the seat, she tore open the glove box, her hands searching for the mag light she knew Aimee carried there. Glenda felt a rough grab; the killer spun her about. Surprised, she had not heard him come, she quickly clicked on the flashlight and flashed it in his face, while kicking one of the baby carseats into his legs. He let her go as he reached up to his night goggles. Glenda kneed him hard and shoved him away.

She was aware of many things in that instant. The boys were wailing unconsolably, more headlights were approaching, would this car stop? The killer had dropped his rifle and curled into a ball, rolling away from her. She grabbed for the rifle. When she looked up the killer had disappeared into the aspens. She flashed the light all around. Nothing. The car on the road came to a screeching stop behind the downed truck. Glenda ran towards it, still carrying the rifle and flashing the mag light ahead of her.

42 FOG

Dave and Kyle had stayed to help clean up at the Mueller farm, allowing their wives a head-start home. They now sat with Sam around the bonfire for one last quick beer.

"I can remember you two playing football over at Onoway High," started up Sam, setting both of them laughing. In fact, neither of them had grown up in the area, nor had they ever heard of the Town of Onoway until they had dated their future wives. They had met each other only through their dates. They had heard this ramble from Sam Mueller many a time and knew there was no way on earth to convince the old man of the folly of this tale.

"Yes, indeedy," went on Sam. "You!" he said, pointing to Dave, "were the quarterback. Skinniest quarterback I ever saw, but man! Could you run."

Both men guffawed, Kyle pointing to Dave. They no longer tried to dissuade Sam that they were not in fact the legendary football players he remembered. They had long ago acquiesced to Sam's wild tales of football glory and now reminisced with him gleefully, occasionally taking a humble bow after a play well described and generally just laughing the whole thing off.

Mildred came out of the house just then.

"Sam forget that nonsense," she bellowed as she crossed the dark yard to the bright flames of the dying fire. These two boys did not go to Onoway High School and you well know that. No, never you mind, Sam Mueller, it's time you got into the house and let these two boys go on home. Now you two, I expect your wives are waiting for you; go get a move on. You drive safely now and go straight home, you hear?"

"Yes Ma'am," Dave and Kyle chorused, wondering at the brave soul that would contradict any edict given by this forceful woman. They got up, folded the lawn chairs and carried them over to the house where they

181

leaned them up against the back deck. Turning back, they could see Sam was still arguing with Mildred so they waved a goodbye in their direction and headed towards Dave's van.

The men had barely driven five kilometers when they came upon Aimee's empty truck, deserted, with its windshield blown out by what appeared to be a rifle shot.

Dave and Kyle were shouting in the van as they approached and stopped behind Aimee's truck. Outside there was someone running towards them with a bright light aimed at their eyes, then Kyle shouted gun.

Glenda reached Dave's van and banged the rifle and flashlight onto the hood, staring at both men through the windshield. Both men got out of the vehicle. Glenda stood rooted to the spot. Behind her the two boys were wailing in the front seat of Aimee's truck. The men rushed towards her, shouting questions at her. Dave wrapped her in his arms, Kyle took the rifle from her hand and put his hand on her shoulder. Both men were asking "are you alright?" She nodded yes and was embarrassed as she realized that she was almost crying. She walked them hurriedly to the side of the pickup. Kyle bent down and picked up Trevor and Glenda scooped up Connor and took him into her arms.

Staring over Connor's head up at Kyle she said, "I don't know where Aimee is, she ran into the woods after the person that shot at the truck. Her shoulder was bleeding but she said she was okay."

Kyle looked at her, "but he must have come back here, how did you get the gun?"

"He did. He grabbed me from behind when I was trying to find Aimee's mag light. He had on night goggles. I turned the light on and I kneed him and pushed him away. That was just before you guys showed up."

"He'll be long gone by now," said Dave. Did you get a good look at him?"

Glenda shook her head no. "He had on night goggles and was wearing camouflage," she said, discouraged.

Kyle faced the woods and began hollering Aimee's name. Dave pulled out his cellphone.

"We're in a dead zone here. Kyle, I couldn't get through on my phone. Let's pile into my van. I'll drive down the road a bit and call for help." With his eyes he indicated the rifle, now leaning against the pickup. Kyle understood. He handed it to Dave, who put it in the back of the van while Kyle and Glenda secured the babies in their carseats in the backseat. Dave got in the driver's seat and signalled for Kyle to get in the van. Kyle refused to go. He fetched the rifle out of the back of the van and, as Dave Glenda and the boys drove off, Kyle crossed the road and silently headed towards the hill Glenda had pointed out to him, as the route Aimee had taken.

43 HUNTER GREEN

Aimee came to with a hell of a headache. She tried spitting out the gag and could not. She wriggled and twisted, trying to get loose, in total frustration. But, she had seen the attacker, it was Jim Drucker, the pharmacist, who had just been at the Mueller's barbecue with them. She was still shocked by that fact. Aimee realized a bungee cord was holding her. It had the slightest bit of give. Her knife was on her belt by her right hip. Her hands were tied at the back. Slowly, painfully, she worked her hands, with only that tiny bit of give in the bungee cord, over to her right side. She managed to get to her knife and finally cut through the bungee cord. She stood up, removed the gag, stretched, checked that she was okay. She did not know how long she had been tied up.

Cresting the hill, Aimee fell into a low crouch and searched the landscape below. She could not find the shooter. She kicked off into a run back towards the pickup. All her senses were on high alert. Crouching low she speedily crossed the road to the truck and moved to its passenger side. Glenda and the boys were gone.

Jim was within earshot of the vehicles. As he had tumbled down the ditch from the road, blinded and in pain, he realized how badly things had gone for him. He hid in the aspens to spy on them. He heard them calling out Aimee's name. "Where was that bitch anyways?" he thought. As his head cleared, the pain ebbing away and his vision returning, Jim put on his night goggles and looked about him. Nothing.

He watched as Dave, Glenda and the babies drove away and he watched Kyle cross the road, heading towards the hill, with his rifle. Then he saw, as Kyle disappeared into the bush, Aimee come running towards the truck.

Aimee heard Kyle calling her name. She crouched by the pickup, hands on her knees. They were safe. The men had found Glenda and the babies. She felt relief. She wanted to call to Kyle, to let him know where she was. She would do it in a minute, once she caught her breath. She had no way to know that the killer was now creeping up behind her, stalking her by the downed truck.

When Jim had spotted Aimee return to the truck, he was on the verge of giving up, thinking of getting the heck out of there to go plan his next move. He was wondering if he could be traced by that old rifle. It was not registered to him; it had belonged to Aunt Doris and he had taken to 'borrowing' it as a boy. But he had used it to go hunting with Roger Lafontaine. He would puzzle this problem later.

Jim waited until Aimee passed in front of his hiding place then crept up behind her. Grabbing her around the neck and placing his gloved hand over her mouth, he used his teeth to uncap a needle he had ready in the other hand. He injected her with a tranquilizer just as she spun around on him, full of fury. Her eyes had burned with anger before his needle quickly took effect. He smiled to himself as he replaced the syringe on his belt.

Jim slung her body over his shoulders and headed for Daisy.

44 NAVY BLUE

Dave drove away, he and Glenda both constantly hitting redial on their phones; Dave was furious that there was no signal. He sped along like a madman for over fifteen minutes before he got a signal. His call to the RCMP went through and Dave reported the car-jacking, the frightened women, crying babies and that one of the women was still missing. He was assured that an officer would be sent out to the scene immediately. He shouted at the phone, "we need more than one officer, the killer is still out there and we need a search party for the missing woman." "Sir, a dispatch has been sent," was the only reply he could get back.

Dave returned to the truck. He called out to Kyle to come back to the road. Dave helped Glenda into the backseat of their van with the two carseats on either side of her. Dave got into the driver's seat. Kyle moved to the front of the van and continued his shouting out of Aimee's name. He kept the rifle with him, the barrel pointed at the sky. They were waiting for the cops.

Ten minutes later an RCMP cruiser came speeding towards them, its blue and red lights flashing. As the cruiser was about to pull up, Dave called to Kyle to get into the car. Kyle kept the rifle in his hands. "Dude, point that at the floor or the cops will freak out." Then Dave said to everyone, "stay in the car, I'll do the talking."

Two officers exited the cruiser and walked up from behind on either side to the front passenger doors of Dave's van. The officer on the passenger side took up a position about two feet from the vehicle. Dave had opened his window and greeted the officer with a hello. Kyle opened his window and nodded to the officer on his side. Both officers had flashlights in their hands and it was hard to actually see them from inside the van. The officer on Dave's side poked in closer then backed off tersely shouting "gun." Both officers drew their weapons and aimed them at the doors. Dave and Kyle threw up their hands. "Officer it's not our gun, it's the shooter's gun," said Dave. It took a bit of time and a lot of shouting before the officer on Kyle's side reached in and grabbed the rifle from between his legs. Both men were asked to step out of the car and frisked. Only then were the officers calm enough to ask what the heck was going on.

Eventually they were able to explain that the women had left the Mueller's earlier than the men, that their truck's windshield had been blown out by a rifle shot and that by the time the men arrived one woman was in the woods, they did not know where, or if she had been harmed by the shooter and that the other woman had managed to wrestle the rifle from the shooter who ran into the woods.

Within twenty minutes two more cruisers had arrived and the city's police department's helicopter was sweeping the woods with its searchlight. The first RCMP cruiser sped off with Dave following close behind, with Glenda, Kyle and the babies aboard. They were going to the Stony Plain detachment office to give their statements.

Kyle was on his phone, calling the clan. He felt bad waking Winston and Josie with the news that Aimee was missing. Brock was ready for action right away. He suggested Kyle rendezvous with him at the Cardinal's acreage. He would take care of things until he got there. A short while later, everyone's phone messaged that their houses had been breached. Kyle smiled at everyone and reassured them that it was Brock's men, protecting their homes.

There was a slight light in the eastern sky when Glenda, Dave and Kyle were released from the RCMP office. Finally, the search party would have light to see by as they combed the woods for Aimee, thought Glenda.

45 BURNT ORANGE

Jim had been very busy. He had stashed Aimee at a gravel pit, shackling her to a fence at its darkest, most deserted point. He was already imagining the fun they would have together. He headed for their homes. Jim guessed they would go to Glenda's house and he wanted to have a whole party prepared for them. First, he would have to disable their intruder alert monitors. "Phhht," he thought, "mere child's play." He allowed himself a smile. Glenda's place had better visibility from the road and the house had only two doors, without any patio slide-outs like the Brace's house. It was also more secluded from its neighbouring houses, another plus.

Unfortunately for Jim, he guessed wrong.

Kyle insisted they go to the Cardinal's acreage as soon as they were released by the RCMP. Dave drove them there. Kyle phoned Brock while on their way and Brock filled him in on the plans made so far.

Before going to the Carpenter's place, Brock had phoned others to meet him there. The men conferred together and made plans. Kyle's two brothers, Nathan and Ken, would stay with Brock at Josie and Winston's place. Brock's brother, Gabriel, volunteered to put together two posses of his buddies to go and sit in the Ellis and Brace homes. Winston had given him keys to both of them, with instructions on their alarm systems.

Brock then called up his old gang. Bull, its leader, had assured him choppers would be dispatched to check out gravel pits, the open and the closed ones, that lay throughout the county, looking for Aimee.

Once Kyle, Dave, Glenda and the babies arrived at the Cardinal's acreage, they were ushered into the kitchen, sat at the table and asked to tell the story to everyone present. Josie cried when she heard Aimee was wounded and again when she heard they could not find her. Winston hugged his wife.

"Josie, Josie, look at me," he said to her, "she has a scratch, don't cry.

She is a tough, resilient girl. She'll kick his butt."

Josie smiled at that, wiped her tears and asked who was hungry. She busied herself making breakfast for everyone. Once they had eaten, Dave helped her with the dishes.

Brock suggested that he, Dave and Kyle, Glenda, the babes, all stay at the Cardinal's. The men could keep a sharp eye out and protect the Cardinal's property and the babies. For now, he suggested, Nathan and Ken could go home. They both refused.

Josie led Glenda to the guest room, Aimee's old bedroom to lie down and rest. She kept the boys in the front room. Taking care of the boys would help her worry less about her daughter.

46 NEON

Aimee came to in a gravel pit. Her hands and feet were bound and there was a gag in her mouth. She had jolted awake and, attempting to sit up, she quickly realized her state. Cold, thirsty, her shoulder aching, holding panic at bay, she looked around. She had the intuition that she was alone. Aimee looked around a second time, this time more carefully. The place looked eerily familiar. She put that thought away and was searching for something sharp to use to cut off her bindings. From a sitting position, she scooted across the rough ground as best she could to a sharply angled rock she had spied. She couldn't quite reach it, something noisy jerked her back. Aimee realized her waist was tied with a chain linked to another one between two very secure-looking posts. Shit. She threw her feet ahead of her to see if they could reach the rock. They could. She sawed the cord binding her feet along the rock for an age. Finally, it broke free. Aimee worked her way to standing. It was still quite dark, not yet dawn, she thought. She seemed to be deep in a huge gravel pit and she thought she would need to hike a good mile to get out of there.

The feeling that she knew this place kept nagging at her. Finally, she got it. This reminded her of the photos of the murdered Crowchild twins. She shivered. She needed to free her hands and get this gag out of her mouth. She started walking as far as her chain would let her, scuffing at the gravel to see what was under it. She just about tripped at one point and looking down, she found a jagged rock buried in the gravel. She set to work freeing her hands then ripped off the tape holding the gag. She rubbed her wrists and gingerly touched her face. She would be okay. Aimee checked her pockets. Her knife was gone. She pulled at the chain around her waist and angrily yanked it about in frustration. The recoil almost knocked her off her feet. Aimee knew she needed to break that miserable chain so she set around looking for heavy rocks to use as a base and as a hammer. It took her an age but eventually she freed herself, still wearing a belt of chain however. She got to her feet and headed west, towards home. She noted a sparse lightening in the eastern sky behind her.

Aimee could see the road beyond the chain link fence. The fence that was bound and locked, she noted. She was thinking of climbing over it when she heard the roar of motorcycles coming up the road towards her. Aimee fell to the ground behind a small pile of gravel.

Four bikes came into view. They stopped at the gate. Two men got off their bikes and went to the lock. A few minutes later they had it opened. They held the gate while their brethren drove in and then mounted their bikes and followed. Once they passed, Aimee scooted out from her hiding place and continued on her way out of the gravel pit towards home.

Aimee followed the road south to the main highway. Dishevelled, bloody, tired and dirty and with a chain dangling from her waist, she knew she was not very presentable. She toyed with the idea of going to a business and asking to use the phone. Chances were that they would run her off with a stream of obscenities, calling her racist names. She would walk to Spruce Grove, to the RCMP Detachment there. Aimee clung to the side of the road, ready to run into the ditch at any moment. Her pace increased with her determination the further that she walked.

Aimee could see the highway. She was almost there. Then she heard the motorcycles again. She ran for the ditch. There was a small fringe of trees with a barbed wire fence running through them and a farmer's field beyond. The motorcyclists had spotted her. One cyclist came after her down one side of the ditch and up the other. She could hear others dismounting. Men were running into the bush, calling her name. Aimee made herself as small as possible in some bramble at the base of two thin aspens, her head tucked down to her chest, her arms wrapped around her crouched legs. But they were calling her name, she thought, were they friends or foe? She could not decide. She was shivering, she felt total confusion.

The lead motorcyclist let his hog fall to the ground. He pointed with his hands to his fellows, towards the ditch and beyond. The woman had run into the bush. The men called her name as they searched through the trees. One had stepped past her. A glint from the chain caught his eye. He looked back and saw Aimee, so small and defenceless, her back against a tree. He signalled to the others and stepped back silently, placing both his feet squarely in front of her. She did not move. He reached down and gently but firmly grabbed her by the arms, shushing her as he pulled her up.

Aimee felt her arms jerked up. "Got her," she heard someone close by say. She was just about to kick out. The shushing was so reassuring, it had made her pause.

"Aimee, Brock sent us to find you," the fellow who had pulled her up said, pulling her in tight and hugging her to him. "My name is Axel. You are safe now. C'mon. Let's get you to a hospital."

Aimee could feel her legs go weak. She was safe. But what about everyone else?

"Trevor and Connor and Glenda?" she managed to croak, looking up into a bearded face.

"All safe at your folks' place."

Finding her determination, she said fiercely, "then take me there. I don't want to go to the hospital." Her words came out almost a whisper, her voice cracking

The bearded face broke into a smile, "will do, little lady. The cops can come to you. They'll have a million questions for you, I am sure. I'm going to carry you now over to my bike and we'll go straight there."

Axel put Aimee down by the bikes and all the fellows crowded around her, gawking. One found a bottle of water and gave it to her. She drank thankfully. Her throat felt so choky.

Another phoned Brock to let everyone know at the house that they had found Aimee, she was okay and that they were bringing her to the Cardinal's place, as she asked. He then sent pictures he had taken to Brock's phone, of Aimee crouched in the bush, being carried by Axel, standing with the men by the bikes, drinking water.

When Glenda saw the pictures, she argued that they needed to call the RCMP. This was evidence, the way her best friend looked and they needed to collect it to put that sicko in jail for the rest of his life. Josie cried. She argued. Aimee would not want anyone to see her like that. She kept wailing, "my poor baby." Glenda went out of doors and made the call.

Aimee hung onto Axel, resting her head on his back the whole way to the Cardinal's acreage. The bikers kept close to Axel, surrounding him, flanking his bike with theirs, protecting Aimee. Aimee fought to stay awake She wasn't sure, once in her parents' familiar yard, if she had succeeded.

Everyone ran out of the house to meet them. Kyle was at Axel's bike first, ahead of everyone. He helped his wife from the bike and held her tightly to him, sobbing.

"I was afraid I had lost you," he said over and over again.

Josie had caught up to him and hugged both of them, "are you okay? Let me have a look at you."

A loud noise was building and drowning everyone out. Josie and Kyle broke off their hug, both had an arm around Aimee and they all faced the driveway. Two RCMP cars were racing up its hill, with their sirens and lights flashing.

"Damn Glenda!" said Josie, shooting the newswoman a dirty look, "let's get you inside, honey." She led Aimee away from the crowd. "Winston, go get something to cut this chain off her," she yelled.

Glenda thought it best to stay outside until Josie had cooled off. She hung back and watched.

Kyle was talking to the first officer from the first squad car. As an officer from the second cruiser approached them, the first sent him back to his car to call off the search for Aimee. The first officer then directed his partner to go into the house to interview the victim. Kyle made to go with him, the officer called him back. Dave tried to step in for Kyle. The officer told him he would get to his statement later. He kept asking Kyle questions that Kyle was answering mostly with, "I don't know." The timber of his voice was rising as his and the officer's frustration were mounting.

The fourth officer was taking statements from two of the motorcycle gang members. The other two had turned their backs on the arriving police and moved their bikes away a piece. They were over by the woods, looking a bit shifty. When they saw the officer questioning the other bikers, they peeled off with their bikes into the woods. Glenda knew the path they were on led to an old, no longer in use, outhouse. She wondered where they would go from there. Apparently through the woods towards the road. Later she heard their bikes start up and as they left the area.

The officer that was sent back to his car to call off the search for Aimee was still there, on his radio, most likely being asked questions he could not answer.

Dave was on his phone to his and Glenda's parents to let them know Aimee had been found. He walked over to Glenda. "I called everyone I could think of. But I didn't get a hold of Gabriel. It just keeps going to voice mail."

Glenda shrugged her shoulders. Gabriel would be either at their house or at Aimee and Kyle's. Nothing much ever happened in their quiet neighbourhood.

Josie led Aimee into the house and had her sit down on a kitchen chair. "You're home now. You're safe," she kept saying over and over, stroking her hair off her face. Aimee croaked that she wanted to see Trevor.

"He's sleeping, Baby," replied her mother, "come, we'll tiptoe in so you can see." They went to the master bedroom. Both boys were sound asleep amongst a pillow fort on the big bed in the centre of the room. They tip-toed out and Josie closed the door softly. She led her daughter back to the kitchen. Winston came in with a set of bolt cutters. He knelt to cut the chain off his daughter's waist. Josie pulled out a wash basin from under the sink and began to fill it. Just as Winston was about to snip the chain, an RCMP officer came into the house.

"Sir, step away. Don't cut that chain." Everyone looked at him dumb-founded. "It is evidence," he added, by way of explanation. They all stared at him as if he was crazy.

The officer held up his hand, "we'd like to take some photos and see if we can get any forensic evidence from the chain. A crew will be here shortly."

Winston stepped away, the bolt cutters dangling lamely by his pantleg. The officer crossed the room and squatted in front of Aimee. He said to her, "Ma'am, I know you have been through a lot. Can you tell us what happened?"

Aimee nodded. She began to speak. Her voice broke. Josie rushed over with a glass of water. Aimee took a sip.

"We were at the Mueller's place. My husband and I and the baby and Glenda and Dave and their baby. Glenda and I left early with the babies. The men were going to follow a bit later. Suddenly, someone shot at us. I kind of sensed it coming and hollered for Glenda to get down. I hunched over the steering wheel. But my shoulder was grazed," Aimee showed the officer the gash.

"The windshield was shattered and we were headed for the ditch at this point. I told Glenda to stay with the babies and took off into the woods to whoop the ass of the idiot who had shot at my truck.

Aimee's eyes flared, remembering the anger. Then she teared up.

"Oh, Aimee," said Josie, rushing to her, hugging her tight. Aimee straightened up, took another sip of water and continued, "I didn't find him right away. Then I saw a bird fly up and figured out where he was. He was sneaking towards the truck. I went to him. It was Jim Drucker."

"Jim Drucker, the pharmacist, did this?" sputtered Winston. The RCMP officer signalled him quiet with his hand, "go on."

"We fought and he knocked me out. I came to, alone and headed back towards the road. I was back at the truck. It was deserted. I heard Kyle call my name. Then something happened. It's really fuzzy. I think I was grabbed from the back, I was in a choke hold. And then I woke up hours later in a gravel pit. My hands and feet were tied, I was gagged and chained up to another chain along a fence. I got myself loose and started heading home. A bunch of motorcyclists found me and brought me here."

A team of men came into the house, one carrying a camera, the others were paramedics.

The paramedics did a quick assessment then nodded to the camera man. He gently asked if he could take pictures. Aimee nodded yes. And he snapped her sitting in the chair, close-ups of her hands and feet, her neck and face and the chain around her waist. The paramedics had brought in a gurney and assisted Aimee onto it, amidst her many protests.

Kyle, Dave and Glenda came into the kitchen, followed by the first RCMP officer. They found out Aimee would be taken to the hospital in Stony Plain. Aimee made a grab at Glenda, they clenched their hands together for a beat as Aimee was being placed on the gurney. Glenda reached down and gave her a quick hug. Aimee whispered to her, "it was Jim Drucker. The cops don't believe me, I can tell by the look in his eye.

But I saw him. I threw a spear at him and hit him on the leg." Glenda gasped. The paramedics whisked Aimee away. The second patrol car followed them towards town.

The first RCMP officer stayed behind to question Glenda, Kyle and Dave. Josie and Winston drove to the hospital to be with Aimee. Kyle texted Brock, who was still outside. He wanted to make sure there was muscle at the hospital. He had no confidence that the RCMP had a clue of what was really going on.

Dave made a pot of coffee while the two RCMP officers conferred. They all sat around the kitchen table, with their coffee and answered more questions. Dave could see the pieces coming together for the officers and their incredulity at the story they were hearing. Glenda told everyone that Aimee had identified Jim Drucker. The officers said they would take it under advisement. Before Glenda could argue further, a baby cried. Then both began crying. Angrily she left the room, "I'll get them," she said.

The officers were conferring again, reading over their notes. One made a call. They wanted to contact Axel and verify exactly where they had found Aimee to investigate the gravel pit where the kidnapper had stashed her. They would send out a forensic team to investigate.

Glenda was in the room with the babies for a while. They could hear her murmuring to them and the babies chatting back. She was changing their diapers before returning to the kitchen. She came back, carrying both boys. Trevor reached out for his father once she reached the table. Glenda handed Connor over to Dave. She went to prepare something for them to eat. Both babies sat in their father's laps and stared at the RCMP officers, looking from one of them to the other and back to their father. They were obviously awed by these new, big men.

47 VERMILION

Jim drove to Aimee's and Glenda's acreage development. It was set up in a figure eight. They both lived on the first loop of the eight, but on opposite sides of it. He parked on the top half of the eight and walked to its bottom half, cutting into the bush on his approach to Glenda's house. As he neared it, he took out a Grim Reaper Halloween balaclava from a pocket on his toolbelt and pulled it down over his face.

Everything was dark. Jim thought they would have been here by now. He had seen them driving back to the truck as he was lugging his find to Daisy. Jim wondered what was keeping them? The police sirens he had heard coming to their rescue, perhaps?

Jim approached the house slowly. There was no window to the garage and its back door was locked. He could not tell if a vehicle was in it or not. He decided not to try busting the lock; if they were home, they might hear him. The back of the house faced north and all its windows were small and high up. Jim noted they were all closed and their curtains were drawn. He moved to the east side of the house, passing the back door. These windows were of a good height for him to see in. They were all closed but their curtains were open. Jim could see the room within was long and narrow and had one door leading from it to the house. It was a closed-in porch. The inner door was open.

Jim returned to the back door and tried the handle. As soon as he touched it a light came on over the door. Jim ran for the woods, about thirty feet behind the house. Nothing happened. No lights came on. Nobody came to check the door. Jim went back. When the light came on, he moved to the side of the house. He waited a really long time. Nothing happened. Jim went back, stayed this time when the light came on and he shimmied the door.

Once he had the door opened, he left it slightly ajar. He stood on the outside of the house, listening. Nothing. Finally, he stepped through it to the inner door. Bracing his arms on the door frame, he poked his head into the kitchen and waited. Nothing. There was a little light on in the washroom to his right and various clock faces gave off a blue light in the kitchen. The rest of the house was in shadow. He could hear crickets, nothing else.

Jim walked through the house. There was no alarm on either the back or the front door. It really was very modest. He wondered about these white picket fence people. A door to a bedroom down the hall was open. The others were all closed. Jim went to it and peered in very carefully. It was obviously the master bedroom and it was empty. Jim walked back, nonchalantly opening up the other two bedrooms doors. They were all empty.

He had guessed wrong. They did not return to the Ellis home. He would have to make his way to the Brace's house. As Jim was passing through the living room, he saw headlights coming up the driveway. Shit. They were only now getting home. Jim looked for a place to hide. He decided to stand along the wall by the china cabinet in the dining room. He was on the side by the window, the furthest side as you entered the room.

But it wasn't Glenda and Dave with little baby Connor who came in. Jim could hear voices, all male. They were in the kitchen. He could not make out what they were saying. There was tension in their voices. What were they doing here, he wondered?

About a half hour had gone by. Jim heard the coffeemaker burbling. They had made a pot of coffee. Hell, it was the bloody middle of the night, they must be planning on staying till morning. They wanted some caffeine to help them stay awake while they sat in the kitchen of someone else's house. Why? he wondered. Jim was thinking about leaving his hidey hole to go peek into the kitchen when someone came walking into his room. He was talking over his shoulder as he came in and missed seeing Jim duck back into his corner.

"I'll check for some booze. If I remember right, they stash it in the dining room," he heard the wanderer saying.

Jim could see a credenza across the room. The table and chairs were between him and it. This fellow was making a beeline for it. Jim crept up behind him, put one hand over his mouth and jabbed his spare syringe into his neck. He would sleep for a good four hours.

Jim dragged the guy over to the table and sat him in a chair. He chose a chair close to the entrance so if anyone looked in, they would see his back. He placed a bottle of booze on the table by his resting head. Jim returned to his corner.

After quite a while, one of the other fellows came in the room to check on his buddy.

"Shit. He's sat himself down and drunk till he's passed out," he hollered over his shoulder, while slapping and shaking his buddy, trying to wake him up.

By the voices Jim estimated there were only two still-standing men. He had an agenda tonight but surely, he could take a bit of time for some fun. He was enjoying this.

The fellow returned to the kitchen, Jim creeping quietly behind him. He let the fellow join his mate and peeked into the room. Yes, there was only one other man at the table.

Across from Jim was the doorway to the porch. To its right was the stove and there was a cast iron frying pan sitting on it. Jim wanted that pan. He wanted to walk like a ghost past these two country bumpkins and get that frying pan. He waited and watched. Finally, the fellow facing him got up and went to the counter. Jim moved. He grabbed the frying pan with barely a noise and stepped into the porch. Jim stepped close to the wall by the door frame, the fry-pan poised for a good smack, should they follow him.

"Hey, who just went by the door?" said the man who was now standing by the sink. Jim heard the scrape of a chair. Here comes hombre number one. SMACK! Jim hit him right in the face, probably breaking his nose. As he fell forward, Jim hit him on the back of the head. Nighty night.

The second guy was now at the door yelling "Holy Shit!" Jim pulled his knife, threw it at him and watched him fall backward. Jim stepped over the first guy and squatted in the kitchen over the second, who had fallen and was leaning against a wall. He scored a lung. He could hear the man's belabored breathing as his lung filled with blood. He would most likely drown in his own blood. Jim pulled out his knife and watched the fountain of blood that ensued. He wiped his knife on the fellow's shirt. Putting his hand on his chest, Jim pushed him back onto the floor. Jim put the fingers of his other hand up to his lips. "Shush. Shh, shush," he said, watching the man's eyes. All hope had left him. Yet this one did not have fear. Interesting.

Usually Jim stayed until the person checked out. He felt an urgency to get to the Brace's house. He stood up and looked around the room. He dragged the bleeding guy into the washroom and locked him in there. Jim put a chair on an angle up against the door, its back resting under the doorknob and left.

Robert heard the intruder leave. He rolled over on his side so that the wound was almost under him. He could get some air. His breathing was torturous, the pain unbelievable. Robert fumbled in his jeans pocket for his cellphone. It took an eternity. He finally managed to hold it and dial 9-1-1. He managed to say, "Ambulance. Dying. Sunset Acreage off highway 43. Lot 5."

He waited, his breathing laboured. He tried not to pass out. He dialed his girlfriend and left a message, "I love you." He dialed his folks. His dad answered after several rings.

"I love you and mom," he said weakly.

"Where are you?" asked his dad.

"Inside washroom at Dave and Glenda Ellis house. Knifed," he sniffed, "Dad ,I think I'm dying."

"Hold on son. I am going to get help. You talk to your mother."

Robert Senior called his wife. Robert could hear them talking then his mom came on the phone.

"Robbie, baby, hold on okay? Dad is calling 9-1-1 on his cell then he is going there. They live off highway 43, right?"

There was a long pause then Robert answered, 'yeah. Hurry, Mom."

"Okay, he has already left. Hang on Son."

"k"

You know you promised to come over for dinner tomorrow night. You are coming right?"

There was no response. She yelled into the phone, "Robert Joseph McConnelly, wake up!"

After a pause, she heard, "here, mom."

"You stay awake, you hear. Dad is on his way; an ambulance is on its way. You are not allowed to die on me. Who is going to help me out when I really need it. No sir, you stay awake."

After a long pause, "K, mom."

Finally, she could hear the ambulance in the background. Then noise in the room. Then her husband's voice.

"Robbie, it's Dad. Let's try sitting you up a bit."

Then more noise in the house. Then her husband shouting, "in here." Then the phone went dead. Mrs. McConnelly ran to change her clothes then grabbed her car keys and raced to the hospital.

48 SCARLET

Jim walked on the road to the Brace's house. At this hour, no one was around to see the lone figure making his way around the acreage development. As he approached, he noticed there were several vehicles in the driveway. He figured they were more vigilantes. He laughed to himself. He did not know if he should be excited with the prospect of taking them on or disappointed that the Ellis clan was not here.

Jim crept to the house, sticking to the shadows, taking advantage of any cover offered by the lone trees and bushes on the front lawn. He circled around the house and came right up to it on its darkest side. There were no windows. Jim slowly made his way around to the back of the house and carefully peeked into the windows there. He could tell lights were on and people were in the house but he could not get a peek at them. There was a deck on the back of the house with a sliding glass door. He crept noiselessly onto it and made his way to the furthest side of the window and peeked in.

Two guys were sitting around a table just feet away from Jim. A third was in the adjacent kitchen. Jim thought the obvious: Glenda and those two yapping babies were not there. Where the hell could they be? I bet these dudes know. He smiled, wondering what it would take to get them to tell him.

Jim crept off the deck and went to the furthest basement window. He found one that opened. Using his knife, he worked at the window, attempting to lift it slightly and pull it from its frame. Finally, he got some leverage and managed to yank the window out with a minimum of noise. Jim lowered himself into the basement. Something crunched under his feet. Jim looked. On the floor were a bunch of little toys, spiky dinosaurs in little pointy corrals. Good thing he had his boots on or that could have hurt. Jim moved across the room. He opened the door. A metal garbage can came crashing down on him, full of odd sized metal bits and BB pellets. An alarm sounded and blue lights flashed. Dazed, Jim brushed the metal bits off himself. He could hear the guys upstairs reacting. They would be down here pretty soon. Jim opened the door across the hall. A second garbage can fell, this one full of firewood and red lights flashed. Quickly Jim moved down the small hall and opened another door. A different alarm sounded and white lights flashed. But nothing fell on his head this time. Jim entered and closed the door and waited in the room. He could hear the men entering the basement.

Jim waited for them. He looked around, he was in a bedroom. There was a bed, next to it was a night table with a lamp and a book on it and across the room there was a closed closet. Jim decided to grab the lamp. He could throw it at someone or use it over their head. He got an electrical shock as soon as he touched it. "What the hell?" he thought, "these people must be big fans of 'Home Alone'. He moved to the closet. Jim hesitated before opening the door. He decided against it and went back by the bedroom door. He pulled out his mag light from his toolbelt. He would use it to give the first guy that came into the room a good crack over the head.

Gabriel, Mike and Steve were engrossed in conversation when they heard a ruckus in the basement. They grabbed their baseball bats and headed for the stairs. Gabriel stopped them at the bottom. "My cousin's husband is a computer nerd," he explained to his buddies. "He went through all his little surprises down here with me and Brock. Don't touch anything and stay behind me. Blue and white lights are for the two bedrooms on the left. The red flashing light is for the bedroom on the right." Gabriel found a remote control and clicked a few buttons. The alarms and flashing lights went out.

"I hear something," said Mike.

"Your heart beating so quickly from fear," teased Steve.

"No. Listen."

All three men stood still. Faintly at first, then building, they could make out a siren. Gabriel signalled them to back up. Further away from the bedrooms, he conferred with his buddies.

I don't think that Kyle set up a call to the cops," Gabriel said, "let's see what we have here before we call them. Steve, why don't you go check on the others. Drive your truck around. Check out the other house. If there are any cops, flag them down and bring them back here." Steve nodded. As Steve headed back up the stairs, Gabriel grabbed a different remote and turned on the television. He found a movie with a car chase and turned up the volume.

Jim noticed when the alarms were shut off. Then nothing. He was wondering what those dudes were doing. "Sweet Jesus they were taking their time, most likely shitting themselves," he thought. Then all of a sudden, he heard the TV. "Mother of God! Are they sitting down to watch a movie?" he wondered. Jim relaxed a bit and scratched his head.

Gabriel and Mike faced the short hallway with the bedrooms. Gabriel pointed out the debris on the floor. He whispered, "The metal came from the bedroom on this side. The wood is from the bedroom on that side. I think he is in the third bedroom, on this side. He'll be standing by the door, ready to knock someone on the head or knife them most likely. So here is what we are going to do. I am going to open the door and rush in, but I'll roll as I go. You swing that bat and get the sucker." Mike nodded that he understood.

Gabriel opened the door.

Jim, who was scratching his head, automatically swung his hand down with the mag light, intent on braining him. Instead, he landed a punch on Gabriel's back. Jim swung the arm with the mag light up as he realized a second person was there and managed to deflect the hard blow from the baseball bat with it. His left hand was pulling out his knife from his toolbelt. Jim blindly swung at the fallen Gabriel with his right hand, the one holding the mag light, he landed a blow, not sure where. With his left hand, he waved the knife at Mike, then lunged at him. Mike was fast. Jim missed his slash to Mike's chest and moved his hand quickly enough to draw blood from his leg. Gabriel, was rolling, getting to his feet, Jim jumped on him and sunk the knife into his back, slashing downward. This gave Mike a clear shot at Jim, smacking him across his back with his baseball bat. Jim sprung up and turned around. A second swing hit him in the shins, he buckled instantly, then straightened right back up. He slashed at Mike with his knife and swung his mag light, hitting him on the side of the head. Mike fell. Jim grabbed the baseball bat and hammered Mike a few blows with it. He hammered Gabriel a few blows, hollering obscenities at both of them. Then he marched through the room, ignoring the blood gushing from the cut Aimee had inflicted on his leg, now opened, thanks to Mike's blow to his shins. He wanted the third guy.

Marching upstairs, Jim hollered, "come out, come out, wherever you are." He quickly searched the house and came up empty. Jim headed out the front door and looked down the driveway. One vehicle was missing.

Shit, the little bugger has gone to call the posse, he surmised, deciding to get out of there. Jim walked out the front door, down the driveway and on the road to the second circle, to Daisy.

Jim got into his truck. He removed his Halloween balaclava. What was going on, he wondered. They had a welcome party at both houses. Why? Had the Cardinal girl managed to get loose and call the cops? He finally turned the engine over and drove towards the gravel pit. Driving the outside road forming the eight, Jim drove by the deserted, dark Ellis house without so much as a glance towards it.

49 FERRARI

Steve drove over to the Ellis's home. An SUV and an ambulance were parked on the front lawn. He pulled his truck up behind the SUV. As he got out a paramedic came to the ambulance, rifled inside and rushed back into the house. Steve could hear more sirens approaching. He walked to the door and stepped in. He recognized Robbie's father.

"Mr. McConnelly. What happened?" he asked.

Robert Senior looked over at Steve suspiciously, "what are you doing here?"

"I was guarding the Brace house; these bros were guarding this one. Jesus, what's going on?"

An RCMP cruiser had arrived and two officers were piling into the house. Soon there was a whirling noise growing in the night sky. The paramedics had called in a STARS helicopter. They had placed Robbie onto a gurney and hustled him out of doors. The police were flashing lights, letting the chopper know where to land. It barely touched the ground and the paramedics lifted Robbie in. The chopper left right away.

The paramedics went back to see to Hunter and Phil. They efficiently placed both men onto gurneys and hustled them into the ambulance.

Meanwhile the RCMP were questioning Robert Senior and Steve. Robert Senior asked to make a phone call and called his wife to let her know that their son was still alive and that STARS were flying him to a hospital in the city, he did not know which one.

Steve threw up his hands.

"I don't know what happened here. I think the guy who did this is over at the Brace's house. And I just left my two buddies with him."

The RCMP officers looked at each other and back to Steve.

"You can ask me whatever questions you want. Just go and check that out first."

One officer nodded to the other. They let Robert Senior go, after capturing his contact information in the event they had more questions for him later.

The two RCMP officers walked Steve out to their vehicle and put him in the back seat. They got in the front seats and Steve directed them to the Brace's house.

"Mother of God!" exclaimed the driver as he pulled into the driveway. Steve craned to see out the front windshield. The front door of the house was wide open.

The officers parked and both opened their doors to leave the vehicle.

"Hey, let me out too," hollered Steve.

The officer on the passenger side of the car opened Steve's door and barked at Steve to hold out his hands. He had handcuffs at the ready and snapped them onto Steve.

"You sit here."

Steve fumed as he watched the two RCMP officers approach the house. He noted that they had both unsnapped their gun holsters.

As he sat there, it dawned on Steve that perhaps the officers thought he was the perpetrator. But if he was, why would he have gone to the Ellis's house and then brought them to this one? It just did not make sense to him.

After what Steve thought was a hell of a wait, one officer came back to the car. The officer opened the driver's door and turned on the car's flashing lights. He then walked around the car, opened the back-passenger door and ordered Steve out. Once standing, Steve held out his hands, expecting the officer to remove his handcuffs. Instead the officer gave him a shove and told him to enter the house. Steve walked to the house with the officer following close behind him.

"Down the stairs," barked the officer as he closed the front door behind them. Steve noted he did not turn his back to do it. He was now worried for Mike and Gabriel but thought better to say anything to the officer.

As he got to the bottom of the stairs, Mike looked up from where he was sitting on the couch and said, "Steve, thank God you are alright. Good man, finding the cops and bringing them here."

Steve turned and gave the officer a hard look. "Mike what happened? Did he get away? Where's Gabriel? Is he okay? Did you see who it was?"

The RCMP officer now came in front of Steve and undid his handcuffs. He asked to see his ID and wrote it down in his notebook, as well as taking a photo of it with his phone.

"We'll ask the questions. Your other friend did not fare as well. There's an ambulance on the way." He left a pause, sighed, then said, "this has been the busiest night ever. Tell me what you know."

Mike was holding his head and signalled for Steve to answer.

"Well, Gabriel is the cousin of Aimee Cardinal. She is married to Kyle Brace. This is their house. She was abducted on her way home from a barbecue. That happened earlier tonight. Gabriel asked all of us, me, Mike and the guys at the other house, to guard these two houses. That's all I really know for certain, the rest is conjecture."

"You stay here." The officer went to check with the second officer, who was attending to Gabriel. Steve could hear them conferring, but he could not make out any of their words. Then the officer came back.

"I'm going to move the squad car to the road to make it easier for the ambulance driver to find this place. You stay put." He gave Steve a stern look as he turned to leave on his errand.

"What the hell happened Mike? Did you get a look at the guy?"

Mike shook his head no then held it again.

"Okay buddy, just take it easy. That ambulance should be here soon." He sat closer to Mike and put his arm across his shoulders. Mike looked really bad, he thought. Finally, he held his head up and looked at Steve.

"We let her down, Steve," He hung his head again in despair.

Commotion at the door let Steve know that the ambulance had arrived. He had not heard any sirens. These guys obviously weren't as badly hurt as the ones at the other house. Before the paramedics got to the basement, he said to Mike, "No, Buddy, we didn't. Listen to me, the other house, well, things went much worse there. They took Robbie to hospital by STARS ambulance. We did what we could. We were up against a madman, an animal. And I am damn proud of you for standing up to him."

Mike flashed him a wan smile. Steve gave him a thumbs-up gesture with both hands. The paramedics had arrived and Steve moved out of the way so they could treat Mike. He pulled out his cellphone and dialed Brock to give him an update.

Brock listened to Steve, disbelieving what he was hearing. Six solid dudes had just had their asses handed to them by one lone, sick psychopath. One was hanging on for dear life, his brother was seriously wounded and three others were banged up. He told Steve to come out to the Carpenter's place. Then he called Kyle into the room and gave him the update.

50 CADMIUM

Highway 16 is a four-lane divided highway. Just before reaching Stony Plain as he drove east, Jim noted an ambulance across the median going the other way, its lights flashing as it sped by. "The clean-up crew," he said aloud to himself and smiled, "hell, I could use some cleaning up myself." He decided the Cardinal daughter could wait. He'd get some shut-eye before dealing with her. Jim turned around to head west at the first opportunity that presented itself.

Jim drove Daisy to Donald, changed, put all the clothing he had worn, excepting his belt, into his Daisy packsack, placed that into a black garbage bag and stowed it in Donald. He added in the two spent syringes and the mag light he had used to brain Gabriel. He made a mental note to bring replacements for those items when he returned to Daisy.

Jim went home. He dumped the contents of the garbage bag into his burn barrel, doused it with gasoline and set it afire. Jim went into the house, stripped, put all his clothes into a laundry hamper and took a shower. He cleaned and taped up the gash on his leg then slept for a few hours.

It was past dawn when Jim woke up. He made himself a huge breakfast of eggs and ham, then he made coffee and brought it to his second-floor bedroom. Whistling, he found new Daisy clothes, an old pair of brown twill pants, a brown plaid shirt and a grey windbreaker. His 'new' Daisy ball cap originally had been navy blue. It was old, worn, faded and sported the words "Edmonton Cracker Cats."

Before leaving the house, Jim packed some regular clothes into his Donald packsack and grabbed some granola bars. He drove to Daisy, left his parcel in Donald, locked it and drove off in his second truck. He figured it was time to make a visit to that bitch, the Carpenter girl. He smiled and whistled a jaunty tune.

Past Spruce Grove, Jim left the highway and turned north. He was wondering if Aimee had regained consciousness, surely, she would have by now, and what was going through her little pea-brain. This road had a few turns and blind hills. Cresting one close to the turn-off for the entrance to the gravel pit, Jim became a little concerned. He could see flashing red and blue lights inside the gravel pit. Jim opened his glove box and took out a baseball cap with a fringe of wild, oily, brown hair and put it on, tossing the Cracker Cat cap into the glove box. He opened a compartment by his seat and grabbed a flask of whiskey. Twisting the cap off, he splashed it on his face and collar. "Man, that stung on the cuts," he grinned to himself. If the cops stopped him, he intended to be a quiet, bumbling drunk on his way home to sleep it off.

The RCMP had a cruiser parked just inside the entrance to the gravel pit. An officer was recording the license plates of any passing vehicles. The officer did not make out Daisy's plates and swore to himself, "Damn Red-necks!" then went back to his reverie of the last night he had spent at his girlfriend's place.

Jim drove past him and found a place to stash Daisy. He would go cross-country to where he had chained up the Cardinal woman. As he closed in on the right spot, he slipped his box-cutters out of his trusty belt. Jim received his second surprise of the morning. Right by where he had left his prize, there was a whole forensic team with huge lights set up, looking for God knew what. Where the hell had she gone? How the hell had she gotten loose? Jim could remember several women he had left out here, once he had left one for almost three days before returning. Not one of them had ever disappeared on him. And no one came to get rock from here. What the hell?' he wondered. Jim tracked back and forth on the dark side of the fence like a ninja. He was puzzling over what the cops were up to and what his next move should be. He had his knife out in his right hand. Suddenly, he heard, "hey, what is that over there?" Someone had spotted him.

Jim dropped to the ground. The huge light was flashed back and forth all around him. He was a bit far, just on the periphery of its focussed brightness. Nevertheless, he heard footsteps approaching. Jim looked up, there were two officers with bright mag lights sweeping the terrain as they approached. Jim scrambled to his feet and ran for the bush.

"Halt! Halt or I'll shoot," they shouted at him. Jim dove into the underbrush, then scrambled to his feet and took off running for the woods. Shots actually whizzed past him. Jim was a bit shocked that an RCMP officer actually fired his pistol at him. Damn, one grazed his left arm above the elbow. Jim ducked his head down and ran as fast as he could. At last he stopped. He turned. No lights were coming this way. He found a place to hide. He caught his breath. He stayed still for a very long time. He could neither hear nor see any activity. He guessed they gave up chasing him.

Slowly, quietly, stealthily, he backed-tracked out of there and cut through the woods to where he had parked Daisy.

Jim made his way north to Highway 16A then headed west. He was brooding on last evening's events. His world had turned upside down and he wasn't sure how. "Shit, I better not go home. Who knows how much they have figured out," he said aloud. He drove to Lake Isle and broke into a secluded cottage.

After building a huge, warming fire, Jim rummaged through the kitchen and found instant coffee, crackers and peanut butter. He sat by the fire and ate, thinking things through.

There was the party at the Mueller farm for Brent Turner. Those two busy-body bitches and their husbands had chatted him up. And Helen Majeau was with them. At one time all of them were sitting at a picnic table together with Helen and Brent. Glenda had a laptop and was showing them something in it. She was across the table and he could not get a glimpse at it. The Cardinal bitch had a folder and he believed he had seen a closeup of a ruffled feather before she hid everything away when he and Roger approached the picnic table.

Jim got up and made himself a second cup of instant coffee. He inhaled its warmth deeply into his lungs. And that is when he started to worry. Helen had been on his trail years ago. Brent Turner was just a young, fresh-faced, newly graduated RCMP Officer. Sure, he and Roger played poker with him. Jim had wormed his way into Roger's life. What better way to stay on top of the local news and gossip mill than to befriend the newspaper editor?

He had invited officer Brent Turner to the poker nights after that mischief with his cousins. He, unwittingly, often tipped his hand on the status of ongoing investigations. As Roger's old cronies dropped out of poker night, Jim filled their places with other people he wanted to keep tabs on, always including a new RCMP recruit, if he found them promising.

Jim sat with his coffee, his hands wrapped around the warm mug. In his mind he travelled backwards in time. Officer Brent Turner. Loved his coffee. He was either at Tim Hortons or he had a cup of coffee at his desk and there was always a thermos of coffee in his cruiser. Well shit.

And he was sweet on that Helen Majeau, the nosy reporter. Jim could remember seeing the two of them together in the coffee shop, their heads leaning close to each other, discussing God knew what, oblivious to everything around them.

Closing his eyes, Jim strained his memory. He was in a booth at Tim Hortons. He was finishing up his bagel BELT. Along came Helen Majeau, who chose a nearby table. Then along came Officer Turner, who joined her. He remembers she brought up some night mischief. He listened intently to what they had to say. Huh, nothing much came to him. it seemed the good

Officer Brent Turner was talking psycho-babble and saying something like murders were usually crimes of passion. Shootings at mailboxes were usually teenagers blowing off steam or really frustrated, really angry people getting back at society.

Jim opened his eyes and laughed. He remembers chuckling back then. He very rarely murdered out of passion. Revenge, yes, but not passion. And he shot at windows mostly. Sometimes, if he could not take the shot he wanted, he shot at mailboxes and signs. But hell, it was all for fun. He wasn't angry. Or frustrated. There were plenty of runaway teenagers to deal with his frustrations then as there are now. Besides, this was about the time he was dating Sandy. And once he figured out what type of woman to date to feed his appetites, he almost totally laid off the hitch-hikers. Hell, Donald had more miles on it than Daisy did.

Jim concluded that, just like Helen Majeau, these two snoopy bitches were trying to tie things together and talking to any RCMP officers who would listen. Brent probably told them a bunch of psycho-babble and that was that.

But.

Back in the day, Officer Brent Turner had a nose for shenanigans. He was the guy who pulled over a car for a burnt-out brake light and discovered illicit drugs. And there was the time he drove his little thermos of coffee down the back alleys of downtown Stony Plain for a little cuppa and came across a break-in at the jewelry store.

Shit.

Jim used to keep a CB radio in his truck, Daisy, all the time. He constantly monitored the police channels, while hunting for young hitch-hikers or other night mischief. He had given it up years ago. Hell, those clowns were so far in the dark where he was concerned. Jim was confident they just didn't see him, he was invisible, he was invincible, and he gave the CB up. It was sitting in Dog's empty cabin, keeping the mice company.

Jim got up, threw the remains of his coffee on the fire, washed up his dishes and put everything away as he had found it. He wanted to hear the chatter on that radio.

Even though Jim did not take the time to change clothes, it still took a while to stash Daisy and drive home in Donald. He had a hidden back lane into his property which he used. He parked Donald about twenty feet away from the clearing around the house and walked towards the edge of the bush. Jim used his binoculars to examine the house and driveway to make sure he had no visitors.

Once Jim felt safe, he went to Dog's cabin and ransacked it to find the CB radio, which he carried into the house. He needed to clean it and change its batteries to get it working. Jim had it set up on his kitchen counter. He was sitting on a stool, the radio in front of him and a can of cold beans open with a fork sticking out of it. His lunch. He tuned the knobs and began to listen to the radio.

There was little chatter on it. Then codes were being called out. Jim no longer knew all the codes but obviously something was happening. He listened intently. Someone was giving a coordinate. They must still be at the gravel pit. They must have been there all morning, poking around, and by now they had probably discovered someone's little pinkie, sticking up through the gravel. Shit.

But that did not mean they were on to him. Many of his bodies had been discovered over the years and none had led to him. He was still safe.

Nevertheless, Jim decided to go lock his gate. Years ago, he had set up a sophisticated system to keep his fortress impenetrable. A motion activated voice would warn trespassers to back off and an alarm would sound in his house. He could see what was happening at his front gate on his laptop. Well, his old laptop. He had never set it up on his new one. He would have to settle for the alarm, which he could switch on when he returned to the house. If needed, he could take the back-way out of the property. He hadn't really used it in years. He had parked his truck under the trees, if they sent helicopters they would not be able to see it.

Jim listened all day to the radio. He got an update on the medical condition of his victims from last night. He learned Aimee had gotten free and had joined Glenda out at the Cardinal's acreage. Mid-afternoon he heard he was a person of interest.

Jim packed his bags and stash of cash. He packed a knapsack with snacks, coffee and water. He planned to leave the country, using a false ID. But first he had some business to attend to; a midnight visit to the Cardinal household. And no one would come out of there alive, he vowed.

51 ARMY GREEN

Noon was approaching and Kyle and Dave were counting heads, wondering what they could feed everyone that had showed up at the Carpenter acreage. Kyle checked Josie's freezer. He found a few packages of moose meatballs and he knew Josie still had canning jars full of tomato sauce from last summer. They decided on spaghetti and salad.

Kyle enlisted the men to help out. He set his brother Nathan to making salad and his other brother Ken to grating cheese, while he cooked. Dave and Steve moved the table to the next room, extended it, and found chairs for everyone, while Brock brewed fresh coffee.

Kyle hustled the food to the table and Glenda hustled everyone into chairs. Dave passed around a water jug and poured coffee.

Once everyone had eaten, the phone rang. Winston was calling from the hospital to let them know Aimee had been released and they were on their way home. He also told them that Mike and Hunter would be released soon. Both had concussions and were advised to go home and rest. Phil seemed to be fine, he was released earlier in the morning. Robbie and Gabriel were in the intensive care unit at the University hospital. They had both undergone operations. Robbie was in critical condition. Gabriel however, was reported to be in fair condition.

Everyone reacted to the news and were speaking at once. Steve stood and raised his hands, gaining their attention, "from what Aimee said, there is only one man who has done all of this." Slowly, intently, he looked around the room at everyone. "This fellow is an animal. Like a crazed grizzly bear. He is wild and he is hurt and he is hunting. Don't for a minute let down your guard."

Brock nodded, "well spoken, Steve. We need to make a plan. He will figure out that we have what he wants here and he will attack. Let us think like him. What would you do, one man, well trained obviously, but one man, up against six men?"

Glenda got up and taking both boys, left the room. Passing through the kitchen, she was surprised to see that Kyle was drying dishes. She took the boys to the main bedroom, straightened out the bed and set them down in the middle of a pillow fort for their afternoon nap.

A car pulled up. Winston and Josie were bringing Aimee home. Kyle grabbed her and hugged her, swinging her off her feet. She smiled and gave him a kiss.

Kyle asked if they were hungry, there was spaghetti with moose meatballs if they were interested. Everyone nodded yes. Josie put the kettle on for tea while Kyle reheated the left-over spaghetti.

"I'm so sorry Aimee," said Glenda, coming into the kitchen.

Aimee smiled at her best friend, "you should see the other guy."

They both laughed. Josie looked over and smiled at them. Winston was right when he said 'resilient,' she thought, that is the word that describes those two.

While they were eating, Glenda filled Aimee and her parents in on what had happened at their homes last night and that the cops were soft on the idea that Jim Drucker was their suspect. Everyone agreed that he might try something at the Carpenter's and that they should at least set themselves up to guard the house that night.

Kyle's brother, Ken, sketched a diagram of the house and the yards. The second brother, Nathan, sat next to him, making suggestions. Kyle was at his computer, looking something up. Brock stood over his shoulder. Dave and Steve sat across the room from the big table.

Aimee said, "I threw a spear I made in the woods at Jim Drucker and caught him on the lower leg. He was wounded but he did not stop. Glenda blinded him and kneed him. He fell to the ground but he did not run away. He hid and caught me a second time. He is a formidable foe. You're thinking about defending this house. I think we need to expand on that, try to stop him or wound him at least before he gets into the house."

"Great idea, Aimee. If we post guards with walkie-talkies, as soon as they see him they can let everyone know and we can call the RCMP," said Kyle.

"I timed how long it took the RCMP to get here when I phoned to let them know Aimee had been found in chains this morning," said Glenda, "and they took over fifteen minutes. Axel had called Brock to let us know they found her," she continued, looking around the room, "and they were on the far side of Spruce Grove, about twenty minutes from here. They showed up with Aimee before the RCMP. A lot happened last night in less than that amount of time. We need to create some obstacles to slow him down before he gets to the house, to give the police enough time to get here."

"Glenda is right," croaked Aimee. "Ken, can you draw the whole property, with the road and what's around it on your diagram?"

Ken agreed, asking Josie for scotch tape so he could expand his diagram with more paper. Nathan told Ken he would go outside and take photos on his phone to help him.

"I can set up some electronic flashes and more electrified doorknobs," volunteered Kyle.

"I can call the motorcycle gang and see if they'll help out," offered Brock.

"Well, that's a start," said Glenda, "let's get this project rolling."

They all looked at Ken's diagram and everyone began brainstorming on what kinds of traps they could set up. Aimee wanted a decoy of some kind with a net over it. She hoped to catch the psycho outright. Kyle came up with a clever idea.

Once they finalized their plan, Kyle made out a list of things he needed. Handing it over to his brother, Nathan, who had volunteered to do the shopping, he was worried if they would be able to find it all. Aimee asked him why he just didn't go and get it himself.

"Aimee, my place is here, with you. To make sure you are safe."

"Oh, I'll be fine. Look at all these people. Go."

"And if you're going by a store, you can pick up a few things for me," chimed in Josie.

"And we need a few things for the boys," Glenda added, sweetly.

Kyle and his brothers headed into town, with three shopping lists. Once they were gone, Winston suggested that Brock and Steve might like to catch a few zees as they had been up most of the night. He suggested they go out to the camper, it would be quieter than the house. Brock agreed on condition that they call him on his phone if anything suspicious happened and to wake him once Kyle returned.

52 ALIZARIN

It was past the supper hour when Jim arrived at the Cardinal's acreage. He had a full knapsack as well as his belt of tools, his rifle and his bow with him. He approached the acreage from the back, by where he had tied up that squaw on that big old stump and used her for target practice. The dumb bitch had almost died of a heart attack. Jim had made sure not to shoot her, he just wanted to scare her. "Huh, well I guess I did a good job of that," he chuckled to himself.

Across the yard, not far from the house, Jim could see a compact car. There were two people in the front seat, probably RCMP officers under cover, he thought. They were talking to each other by how much they were moving around. For now, Jim wasn't worried by them. Between him and the house was Winston's toolshed, the large vegetable garden and Winston's camper. There was a huge pile of straw sitting by the garden. Mid garden stood a scarecrow. On the other side of the yard, there was a sitting area. It had a fire pit with a picnic table close by.

Jim made a wide circle around the property. Nothing else was unusual, he noted. Driving in, he had seen a bunch of bikers with a big bonfire, drinking beer, playing loud music over in a field, across from the Cardinal property. One of them probably lived in the old shack over there. Jim gave them a wide berth. Nothing else was amiss, he believed.

Jim returned to the back of the property, by the old tree. He pulled out his binoculars and swept them over the house. It looked like they were getting ready for dinner. Oh, there was the statuesque Glenda, hoisting her brat on her hip. Jim planned to pin her up against this tree and have her watch him burn that damn house down, with everyone in it. She would probably cry, he thought.

Jim swept the binoculars over to the cruiser. Huh. Both of those dumb-fucks were looking down. Were they reading books in there? Jim got out his parabolic microphone from his backpack and pointed it at the cruiser. Nothing. Just crickets and the rustling of the aspens behind them. He listened longer. A crackle on the radio could be heard; he could not make out what was said. One of the officers lifted his head and looked outside. The other kept reading. The driver went back to his book. Jim packed up his microphone. He had a wait ahead of him; a wait for darkness.

Jim brooded while he waited. He did not want to end up like Nicole. No way would they cage him up. Everyone in the house would probably stay in the house. An hour or so after dark, he would take care of the cruiser. Then he would lob a smoke bomb into the house. He would enter, with his gas mask on and slash anyone in his way. He would knock them out or take them out. Except the babies. He wanted to drag Glenda into the backyard and have her watch as he burned that house to the ground with her babies inside. He was looking forward to that moment.

Jim was a bit stiff and decided to take another perimeter walk. It was just past dusk, nine ten by his watch. He went further into the bush, did a full circle then came closer and did a second perimeter check. Nothing to note. Those two guys in the car will be really easy to knock off, he thought, they hadn't even left the car for a pee. But it was still too early to act.

As Jim headed back to his viewpoint by the old tree, something glinted from the garden. Jim gave it a wide sweep with his binoculars. There was a huge pile of straw bales on its edge and a scarecrow in its centre. The scarecrow had holographic tape on it. That was probably what I spied, thought Jim. He did another perimeter walk around the whole backyard, just in case. There was a crackle coming from the squad car that Jim heard as he walked silently by, not ten feet away from it. Its windows were done up tight. He could not hear what was said. He did notice that neither cops moved, engrossed in their books or girlie magazines. Those two have got to be the dumbest rookies on the force, he thought.

The twilight was advanced enough now to walk into the open. Jim cut across the top part of the yard to Winston's shed. He had been carrying a club in his hand. He put it away on his belt and tried the door. Jim got an electric shock. He jumped back, swearing. More of the son-in-law's wily tricks, he thought. He was looking forward to slashing that guy's throat. Jim thought twice about moving into the shed to wait for another hour or so to pass. He went back to his dead tree stump, sat, leaning against it, pulled out a granola bar and a thermos of coffee.

53 CARROT

Josie had cooked hamburgers and French fries for everyone for supper. She had made a big salad and had Jello and cookies for dessert. She sat at the table, now back in the kitchen, with Winston, her daughter, Kyle, Glenda, Dave and the two babes. Conversation was quiet. Everyone was nervous. Kyle had his computer open at the table and flicked through screens on it while eating. Josie could hear her backyard noises through its speaker. There was also a walkie-talkie on the table. She wondered what Brock and the other boys were eating. Glenda had helped her earlier to make sandwiches for them while Aimee and the babies slept. She was thinking they were grown men, they probably ate those sandwiches around five, when everything was ready and they had all been in their hiding places for a while. It would be a long night. She sighed. Later, she would cook up something else for them.

Once the meal was over, Winston, Aimee with Trevor, and Dave with Connor moved to the front room. Kyle stayed at the table with his computer. Glenda helped Josie clean up and start a new meal.

Kyle chuckled as he heard shuffling sounds over his speaker. He knew Jim had been on the move. Brock, in Winston's shed, with night vision goggles on, had spotted him and texted Kyle. Jim was over by the cruiser, Kyle signalled Aimee. She used a walkie-talkie to alert the fellows over there. Jim would think it was the cruiser's radio squawking. Kyle hit some buttons on his computer. He was checking the GoPro camera feeds Dave and his brothers had set up earlier. A beat went by. Then they heard Jim swear. He had just tried the door of the woodshed. Glenda looked over at Kyle, who was pumping his arm up and down, exclaiming a loud 'Yes!' of victory. Kyle replayed the video for everyone to watch.

Once the hoopla was over, Glenda and Aimee prepared the babies for bed. Tonight, they would start their sleep on the floor of Winston and

Josie's bedroom closet. They were both given a dose of Advil Pediatric drops in the hopes that it would induce a deeper sleep for them.

Returning to the kitchen, both women looked over Kyle's shoulder at his computer monitor. They saw Jim, limping ever so slightly, walk boldly through the backyard, towards the cruiser. A beat later, they saw Brock and Axel leave Winston's shed behind him. Kyle changed the view on his computer and began inputting a series of keystrokes.

54 VIOLET

Jim stood up, stretched, checked his belt, rummaged through his backpack, slung his bow across his shoulder with its quiver of arrows. He walked diagonally across the backyard. He cut into the woods about twenty feet in front of the cruiser, confident that those fools would never see him.

Jim circled behind the cruiser. In a crouch, he approached the driver's door and yanked it open. Jim grabbed the closest officer to yank him out of the car and got a surprise. Everything happened all at once. A huge cargo net was falling to the ground over the car. Jim realized the cops were animated dummies sitting in the vehicle. He was about to be trapped. He rolled away. Bikers were charging the net. He was on its edge, trapped under it. Someone jumped on top of him. Jim twisted. His knife was already in his hand. He punched up with it. He caught the guy in the gut. As he was rolling him off, Jim was grabbing the edge of the net to get out from under it. He was aware that he had lost his bow and shrugged off the quiver of arrows. Two more bikers were closing in on him from either side. At the last second, Jim moved back; their baseball swings landed on each other. Through the net Jim lunged at both, knocking them off balance. He lifted the net over his head. The bikers charged him again. Jim turned sideways to catch one blow on his shoulder and back and stepped towards the other, slashing with his knife. Jim fell forward. His feet were still tangled in that blasted net. Jim turned, his knife facing upwards as a biker threw himself onto him. The knife got him on the side, Jim kneed him away. The other biker had his club held high, preparing his swing. Jim threw the knife at him and scrambled out of the netting.

Jim was aware of three more men charging towards him. He made a grab at his belt for his second knife. He was smacked over the neck and shoulders for the second time by a baseball bat. Jim turned around quickly and stood up, ramrod straight. He looked his assailant in the eyes and flicked his knife the short distance between them. The fellow fell over backwards. The last two bikers were now on either side of him. One swung low catching Jim on his calves, making him buckle to his knees. The other swung, hitting Jim across his back. Jim reached up and grabbed the baseball bat out of his hands, sprung to his feet and swung towards him. Then he swung at the other, hitting him in the groin. The man rolled on the ground in agony. The last biker ran away, down the driveway. Jim let him go. He took the baseball bat and bashed every fallen man until he was satisfied that they were either dead or unconscious.

Jim recovered his bow and arrows and cleaned his knives on the nearest body. He rubbed his hand over his neck and back. Jim stood up and stretched. He grabbed a walkie-talkie off one of the bodies and said into it, "quite the welcome party. Very nice appetizers. I can't wait for the main course."

Jim strolled over to the picnic table and sat down. Let them stew on that for a while, he thought. He kept looking at the driveway, half-expecting a wild horde of bikers to come charging up it. He let five minutes go by. No hordes. No bikers. He spoke into the walkie-talkie once again.

"Well, it looks like that last guy, who ran off by the way, while I killed all his buddies, well, it looks like he didn't go get help for you. Nope. It's all quiet out here. Just me and a lone cricket. I'm coming for you now, you hear? I'm coming for you and your babies."

When Jim first started his attack on the decoy car, Glenda had called the RCMP. She now speed-dialled them again, her voice much more agitated than on the first call. This was not going as planned.

Jim got up, shifted his gear and began walking purposefully towards the house. Movement in the garden caught his eye, some of the straw bales were tumbling. All of a sudden, Jim was being hit by rocks, a whole barrage of rocks. Jim withdrew a few steps, grabbed his bow and one of his special arrows that he had previously prepared with kerosene. Jim took the plastic off the arrow's tip, lit it, and fired it at that wall of straw. It caught fire, huge flames and dark smoke rose to the sky. The rocks stopped flying. Jim saw two guys run from the straw bales towards the camper. His next target.

As Jim slowly walked towards the camper, he used the walkie-talkie again.

"Very funny. What was that? A bunch of your girlfriends throwing rocks at me? Well, they've run off now. I huffed and I puffed and I set their straw house on fire. The tin Lizzy is next. Then the house you are in. I'm going to burn it to the ground and guess what? Your babies, who I won't touch, will still be in it," Jim laughed then clicked off.

Jim circled the trailer twice. All of the curtains were shuttered and he could not even see a light on inside it. He wondered what the two dudes were up to?

Jim grabbed the handle with his coat just in case it was electrified. As he swung the door open, he was blinded by a super bright strobe light. Jim tumbled backwards as two men tackled him. Brock straddled his body, pinning him and trying to get the knife from him. Axel straddled his legs. Jim fought with Brock, eventually he head-banged him, knocking him almost unconscious and he managed to get him off himself. Axel had his back to Jim. He was tying his ankles with a bungee cord. Jim plunged his knife into Axel's back, stabbing him three times. Axel, growling, fell off Jim. Jim was cutting the bungee cord from his ankles when suddenly the whole light came crashing down on him as two more men came rushing out of the camper. They were swinging at Jim with baseball bats and caught him a good few blows. Jim threw the light off himself towards Nathan and sprung up to face Ken. Ken was a huge guy, the youngest and the biggest of the Brace boys. He swung his bat at Jim's legs and knocked him off balance. He stood over Jim, waiting to see if Jim would stay down. Brock and Nathan were just regaining their feet.

"Big mistake pausing, buddy," said Jim. He threw his knife at Ken, who, amazingly, twisted his body away. The knife caught in his shoulder. He impassively removed it with his left hand and threw it at Jim, catching him in the upper thigh.

"Another huge mistake, buddy," Jim said, "thanks for returning me my knife."

As Jim pulled the knife out of his leg, he reached for his second knife. He quickly threw one at Nathan, catching him in the upper chest and one at Brock, catching him in the leg. He got to his feet.

Jim ran towards Ken, bending over, hitting him in the stomach with his head. They were both rolling on the ground. Jim had pulled his tazer from his belt while charging at the big guy. He plunged it into his chest. Somehow Ken managed to kick with his foot and push him aside. Jim quickly scrambled to his feet, Ken was rolled up in a ball. Jim used the tazer on his back and watched him go slack.

Nathan was moaning. Jim pulled his knife out of him. It had landed mid-chest and Jim figured him for a goner. Brock had gotten to his feet and held Jim's second knife in his hand. They were about three feet apart, on either side of the downed men. Simultaneously they threw their knife at the other. Jim's knife caught Brock on his side as he turned, Brock's knife would have pierced Jim's heart had he not moved so quickly, anticipating the throw.

Jim could hear sirens. Shit. That biker did go call the posse. The sirens were still a long way off. Jim kicked Brock and left him there, conscious and impotent. Jim, using a bungee cord, tied up his new leg wound and headed for the house. He lobbed his smoke bombs through the kitchen and a bedroom window. He donned his gas mask.

Jim ran for the door, smashing it open. He expected the give and managed to stay on his feet. What he did not expect was Winston, pointing a loaded gun at him.

"Well, shit, you got me," he said through his gas mask. Standing up straight, loose, putting his hands up over his head, Jim let the knife fall to the floor. Winston watched it fall. Jim had waited for that moment and took advantage of it. He kicked up with his good leg, catching Winston in the groin. He rushed him and knocked him down, aware that the gun had gone off. Jim punched him hard on the side of the head, just as Glenda brought a cast iron fry pan down on his head. Staggering, Jim got to his feet and grabbed her. He had his second knife out and he held her tight to him, facing outwards. He held the knife to her throat.

"Shut up. Everyone shut up. Your little games are over. Open up that trap door under the kitchen table and get down into it. NOW! MOVE!" he shouted at them, "or by God I will spill her precious blood."

Coughing and gasping for air, Josie helped Winston up from the floor then down the steps, followed by Aimee who looked daggers at Jim, then Dave, then Kyle. Kyle had his laptop with him. Jim kicked it out of his hands and slammed the trap door shut, turning its bolt. Glenda used this moment of distraction and kicked hard on his lower leg, the one that Aimee had speared the night before, and wrestled herself free. She had a gash on her chin where his knife had caught her. She touched it, looked at him. Jim licked the knife. Glenda turned and ran to the bedroom, slamming the door behind her.

Jim ran to the door. He paused, wondering if this one was electrified. He felt something in his ribs.

"Fun is over. Drop your weapon and spread them."

Once again Jim went loose. He stood straight, putting his hands in the air, letting the knife fall to the floor. Steve, who had been the puppeteer, manipulating the two 'bodies' in the car, had followed Jim into the house. He did not fall for Jim's ruse of being compliant. He grabbed one of Jim's hands and pulling it down, he wrapped a cord around it to tie it. Jim used that moment to turn. He swung up with his right fist and caught Steve under the chin. Jim saw a tooth fly as he went down. He shouldered the bedroom door open.

Glenda was sitting on the bed. As Jim approached she retreated backwards towards the head of the bed. She was making herself into a small ball. Jim began walking on his knees on the bed towards her, his second knife in his right hand, Steve's rope dangling from his left hand.

Glenda had a small remote in her hand. She pressed a button. A second cargo net fell over the bed, on top of Jim. Still coughing from the smoke-bomb, Glenda scrambled off the bed to the window. She was frantically trying to get it open. Jim was struggling with the netting. Glenda left the window, coughing, and ran from the room, grabbed the fry pan, came back with it and kept whacking at Jim through the netting. A squad car had arrived. RCMP Officers were rushing into the house. One gently grabbed Glenda from behind, disarmed her and half carried her outside. The second officer stood by the bed, his gun aimed at Jim.

"Cellar," Glenda said, passing through the kitchen, "family in cellar." The officer holding her continued outside with her, ordering her to stay there. He went back and unlocked the cellar door and began helping people out. Aimee fought off the officer as he was trying to guide her outside. She ran to her parent's bedroom for the babies. There was smoke in this room, not as thick as in the rest of the house, but it was smoky. She came out carrying both boys, bundled in blankets. The officer followed dragging Steve towards them. He had everyone wait together at the picnic table.

Jim was still partially pinned under the netting and had a gun pointed at him. The second officer came into the room, manhandled him and handcuffed him behind his back. Both officers were coughing as they led Jim out of the house. They placed Jim in the backseat of their cruiser, removing his gas mask and doing up his seatbelt. One officer moved to the front seat and radioed in for an update on the fire truck, for ambulances and for backup. Sirens could be heard halfway through his conversation. They were on the way.

Pandemonium reigned in the yard. A second RCMP squad car pulled into the driveway. Two officers rushed out of the vehicle, an officer from the first squad car came over and conferred with them. They told them the family was safe but there were a lot of wounded and that they had called for ambulances and the fire department. While one officer stayed with Jim, the others began to check out the fallen men.

More sirens sounded. The volunteer fire department had arrived. They drove their truck over the front lawn around the house and around the trailer, squeezing between it and the woods beyond to get to the backyard. They parked on the garden, their siren still sounding as they began to put out the fire. An RCMP officer went over to them and asked them to shut it off.

Two ambulances pulled up behind the second police cruiser. Two paramedics began attending to the bikers. Two more came to attend the family. They passed out space blankets, one put Winston on oxygen and began bandaging him up while the other looked at Steve, who had come to. Dave interrupted them, "there are others, on the far side of the house, by the trailer," he told him. The younger attendant nodded, excused himself and walked towards the decoy car to let the other paramedics know there were more people to tend to, then he moved towards the trailer as the others radioed for more help.

Axel gritted his teeth as the paramedic approached where he lay. He

knew he was growling while the medic looked at him.
"Easy, easy there, fella. You've been knifed."
"No shit," said Axel and he passed out.

55 FOREST

Jim was hauled out of the first cruiser and frog marched to the second one. Two new RCMP officers looked him over. One ordered the other to frisk him. He was patted down and relieved of his tool belt, which they locked into the trunk. They roughly helped him into the backseat and strapped him in. Once the doors slammed, the cruiser took off, bouncing on the uneven grass beside the driveway to avoid the ambulances. Jim looked around and felt proud. Look at the huge mess I have made, he smiled to himself and laughed out loud. The officer in the passenger seat turned and looked at him, then turned back to his partner. Jim could not hear what he said. He didn't care. He put his face down on his chest, he looked like he was nodding off. The officer turned again to look at him. When he turned back to his partner, he said, "what a cold son-of-a-bitch. He's taking a nap."

In reality, Jim was using his teeth to pull at the button he had on his front chest pocket. He had a surprise, something he had sewn on before leaving his house. It was sure to leave him with a nasty burn, but it would get him out of this cruiser. Suddenly a smoke bomb went off in the back seat, aimed at the front windshield. The officer driving pulled the car over to the side of the road, both officers jumped out of the vehicle, coughing profusely. The officer on the passenger side opened up the passenger door and yanked Jim out. Once on his feet, Jim butted into the officer, head first, knocking him to the ground. They rolled down the shoulder embankment together. This effectively put out the small smoke bomb that Jim was wearing. Jim kicked at the officer, shoved him down and ran for the woods. The second officer had run around the patrol car. He had a mag light and shone it into the ditch. He saw his partner lying down, coughing, struggling to get up. His partner pointed into the trees. The mag light swept up into the bush and wavered as the officer ran towards them.

Jim needed the officers to follow him, they had the key to his handcuffs, the handcuffs that were behind his back. It would be a lot easier to have his hands free to get back to Daisy, considering his leg injuries. He found a spot he liked. Jim stood, silhouetted between two larger trees. The officers spotted him and headed towards him. Jim turned to run as the first officer was almost on him. He did not run though, merely stepped behind the tree and stuck out his foot, tripping the officer, who then rolled down the hillock on the far side of the trees. The second officer was right behind him. Jim crashed into him, bumping him off his feet. Jim head-banged him, knocking him out. Jim turned and fumbled into the officer's pockets for his set of keys, found them and ran off towards the road. Looking both ways first, to make sure no other vehicles were coming, Jim ran across the road and into the thin copse of woods on its far side. He walked over to a farmer's fence post, turned and placed the keys on top of it. He turned to face the post. There were a lot of keys on that ring. Not one of them was small and slender. Jim's luck had run out. He did not have the key that would unlock the handcuffs.

Jim raised his head and howled like a coyote into the night. He was furious. He leaned against the fence post and rested for a minute. Then, resigned, he continued through the thicket of wood. For a moment he entertained the idea of trying to open the trunk of the squad car to retrieve his belt. He had a handcuff key in it, which they had confiscated when they removed the belt from his waist. He was afraid of being seen by either more cop cars or ambulances coming or going on the road. He did have another key safely stowed in Daisy. He only had to walk a mile or two, staying out of sight, then he could disappear forever.

Jim followed the thin border of woods along the road back towards the Cardinal acreage. He debated crossing the road to avoid the motorcycle gang in the lot across from them. An ambulance went by on the road. More would be coming. They would see the cop car and raise the alarm. Jim tried to hurry, hampered by the handcuffs behind his back and his twice-injured leg.

When he came to the clearing where the motorcycle gang had their big bonfire, Jim followed the fringe of trees around to the back of the lot. He saw, in the bush, facing towards the road, several men on their choppers. He stopped abruptly. What were they doing? He figured they were wary of all the cop cars and had prepared for a dash, should the RCMP cross the road towards them. Hell, they had enough of a mess over there to keep them busy all night, he thought. Now he had to make his circle even deeper into the woods. He came up against another farmer's barbed wire fence. Jim was only about a dozen feet away from the bikers. He could make out their talk, hear them light their cigarettes. He needed to be very stealthy and quiet to get past them. He had almost succeeded when suddenly he was grabbed on the shoulder from behind.

"Hey, who are you?" a voice boomed in his ear. Jim was whisked around. He could hear others crashing through the bush to their spot. Jim was pushed and dragged from the woods into the clearing by the bonfire.

"He's the guy!" someone shouted. "The whacko that was attacking them, that did all that!" the fellow finished, waving his arms across the road.

"Why you…" someone punched Jim in the stomach. Then the blows came from all directions. Jim fell to the ground and was kicked viciously by several men. Then he heard a gunshot and the punching and kicking ceased.

56 MUSHROOM

Brent Turner had had a taxing day. He was a key witness in a trial being held in Edmonton and had undergone a gruelling cross-examination in the afternoon. He still loved his coffee and had taken too many cups to keep himself sharp. At the end of the day, he was not excused; however, the crown attorney assured him he probably would not be called upon to testify again. They had enjoyed a nice dinner together at the Bistro Praha. He was surprised, when he returned to his room and checked his phone, which he had forgotten there in the morning, that he had a couple of messages from Kyle Brace and Glenda McTavish, the young people Helen had introduced him to at the barbecue the previous evening.

The gist of their messages, sent at various times during the day, reported that Aimee had been kidnapped, Aimee had freed herself and named Jim Drucker as her assailant; and later that they were under attack by Jim Drucker. Brent tried to call them back; they did not answer their phones.

Cursing, Brent grabbed his gear and headed for his car, stashed in the hotel's underground lot. He made calls to the Stony Plain office, got an update and was given the Cardinal's address. He headed west, out of Edmonton.

Brent kept trying both Kyle's and Glenda's cellphones. Passing Highway 43, he finally connected with Glenda. She reported that Jim had been captured, there were a lot of wounded, the backyard had been set on fire, and two men were dead. The ambulances were being loaded and the volunteer firemen had almost put out the fire in the garden. The family were told that soon they would be allowed to return to the house. Brent assured her he was on his way and would be there shortly.

As he drove, Brent reviewed everything he knew about Jim Drucker. The guy was a pillar of the community, he successfully ran a small-town business, he supported the little league baseball teams, the hockey teams, all kinds of sport teams and community events. He was a member of the Chamber of Commerce, on their executive as something or other. He attended church. He, with Jim and Roger Lafontaine, had gone fishing and hunting together, they had played poker together every Wednesday night. Jim would have been a good catch for any of the young local ladies, he was a bit of a playboy though, and dated mostly city girls. The only negative thing that Brent could recall about Jim was that he hated magpies. Brent had caught him on a fishing trip with a newly killed magpie that he was cutting up for bait. The two of them had laughed it off. Now that memory, and that of the photos of feathers that Aimee had shown him, had the hairs on the back of his neck standing up.

Brent saw an RCMP cruiser on the side of the road. He pulled over. As he got out of his car, he saw across the road, two officers, one helping the other to walk, come out of the bush. Brent ran to them and got an update from the standing officer. Their prisoner had escaped. They surmised he had a vehicle stashed somewhere in the environs of the Cardinal acreage. The second officer had taken a tumble and hurt his ankle. He had a large bleeding gash on his head. Brent suggested they call in their position, then drive to the hospital. He would scout out dark turnouts for Jim's vehicle.

Brent got back into his car as one, then two ambulances drove past him. He started his engine and drove slowly, casting his eyes along both sides of the road. He was even with the Cardinal's driveway and could spy a big bonfire jut past it on the other side of the road. He decided to investigate it.

Brent parked his car across the bottom of the driveway and walked towards the bonfire. He could hear loud cursing and he realized someone was being beaten by a small group of bikers. He un-holstered his revolver as he approached and he fired it into the air. Everyone stopped what they were doing and looked at him. Brent was not in uniform. He had his wallet pulled out and held up his ID. He called out, "RCMP. Step away and put your hands up."

The bikers looked at each other and began walking backwards. Some broke off and ran into the woods. Brent bent down to see who was being beaten and recognized Jim Drucker. He let the bikers go. Jim opened his eyes and said, "hiya Brent." Several motorbikes came charging out of the woods past them towards the road.

Brent helped Jim up to a sitting position. He was squatting across from him. Jim did not look good, he had taken several blows to his head, there was blood on his shoulder and on one of his legs; he had obviously gotten a good workover from the bikers. There was still an RCMP cruiser over at the Cardinal's place across the road, Brent intended to walk Jim there. The officers present could take him in. Brent holstered his gun and put away his ID. Standing, he reached towards Jim, intending to grab him under the arms and haul him to his feet.

As Brent approached, Jim bent his legs under himself and pushed up from the ground with his toes. He propelled himself upward and into Brent, knocking him off balance. Jim, now on his feet turned his head. He saw Brent looking up at him and he threw the handful of dirt he had gathered while sitting, into Brent's face. Jim began running across the field to the far side. Daisy was not far now.

Brent caught a direct hit from the dirt in his face, he had grit in his eyes, which he blinked out and a lot in his mouth, which he spat out. He could see Jim close to the edge of the field, heading towards some trees. He hollered for him to stop and began chasing after him, un-holstering his revolver once more.

As soon as Jim was in the woods, he headed towards the road. Daisy was just a little bit further along. Brent could not see or hear anything in the woods and kept going in a straight line. After a while he came up to a barbed wire fence. Brent followed it in the direction of the road. He looked both ways, up and down the road. Nothing was moving. He headed further along the road, away from the Cardinal's house.

Jim had reached Daisy. He opened the passenger door and the glove box, turned around and felt inside it. There, he could touch his handcuff key, in a little plastic pouch. Jim scrabbled with his fingers, finally got hold of it, got the key out and undid his handcuffs. He slammed the door shut, went to the back of the truck and ran his hand under the bumper. Finally, he found his key safe. He ran around to the driver's door, got in and started up the engine. He just had to get by the Cardinal's place and he would be safe. He decided to leave his lights off until after he passed it.

Brent heard the vehicle start up before coming upon it. He moved to the centre of the road and held up his revolver. A white truck was growing larger and larger in front of him. Funny thing, he found himself thinking, Jim always drove a white truck. He hollered out for Jim to stop or he would shoot. He could tell the vehicle was not slowing down and began shooting at the windshield in front of the driver as he quickly moved to the side of the road. He shot again, this time at the driver's window as it passed him. The truck drove into the ditch and stopped there. Brent ran up to it, his revolver held firmly in front of him. Jim was slumped over the steering wheel, bleeding anew from his head. He was unconscious or dead. Brent yanked open the door and stood back. Jim did not move. Brent reached in and felt along his neck for a pulse. There was one. Jim slowly came to. Eventually he opened the eye that Brent could see, but he did not move. Brent said, "hiya Jim."

"Kill me now," pleaded Jim, "shoot me."

"You know I can't do that," answered Brent. "You sit tight. I'm calling for backup."

Brent stepped away from the door and pulled out his cellphone. He called the RCMP detachment in Stony Plain. As he spoke to them, he could hear Jim moaning, however, he saw that he had not moved. Speaking into the phone, he looked down and turned slightly away. Jim reached under his seat. He had a pistol there. When Brent looked back up, Jim's head still rested on the steering wheel and in his hand, he held a revolver. He called out, "shoot me Officer Brent Turner or by God, I'll shoot you."

Brent dropped the phone, let his revolver fall to the ground, and held up both his hands.

"Jim, we've been through a lot together. Don't shoot."

Jim attempted to laugh, "you think we're friends, huh?" He waved the gun and his eyes went cold. "Pick up your gun or I will mow you down."

"No Jim. Listen. They're going to send an ambulance. We'll get you all fixed up."

"You're a dumb-fuck if you think I'm going with you. That," Jim said as he waved the gun slightly to indicate the Cardinal's home, "is nothing. I will not sit and rot in a small cell while you and your posse comb through the countryside looking for forensic evidence."

"Jim, listen to me," said Brent. A change came over in Jim's eyes, they looked into the middle distance with no expression. Before Brent could finish his thought, Jim moved the gun to his mouth and pulled the trigger.

57 SUNSHINE

The day was warm for November. It was a month before Christmas. Josie and Winston were at the Onoway Community Hall, welcoming their family and friends as they arrived. Josie was bustling about the kitchen surrounded by aunties, sisters and cousins. She accepted dishes of food as they came in, stopped to stir the gravy, gave directions to Glenda and Aimee and the aunties as to what was to go where. Winston was greeting everyone at the door, taking coats and hanging them up as people came in.

He was quite nervous. He had a speech to deliver and he had never given a speech in his life. Josie had helped him write and practice it. He had no confidence in her words that he would do fine.

Everyone was out of the hospital. Two funerals had been held. This gathering of these precious people was to thank them for what they did for his family, for what they gave up for them.

Winston noted the RCMP sat along the furthest wall, facing the door and the kitchen. The bikers chose the opposite wall and were filling up the long banquet tables set up there. That left the centre of the room for family. He smiled to himself. He knew Brock and Gabriel would choose to sit at the very back of the room, backs to the wall, where they could watch both groups and keep watch over their family. Gabriel was one of the people he would bless tonight. He had lost a kidney. He would also bless Brock, who had never given up and ultimately gave them a few more precious moments they needed for the RCMP to arrive. He was a fine warrior and had rallied so many to help them out. He had new scars attesting to his bravery.

The round tables in the centre of the room were filling up. He and Josie, with Aimee and Kyle, would sit at the one in the very front that was closest to the RCMP. Glenda's parents arrived and he watched as Dave led them to the other front table. Dave, Glenda and Helen Majeau would sit there with them.

Winston smiled at everyone once they were seated. His nervousness had left him. He realized it really didn't matter what he said to this group. They were now a tribe, he smiled, looking at Aileen and Owen McTavish with their son-in-law, realizing they would label it a clan. Each of them had bonded to the other through what they had experienced, what they had defended and what they had beaten.

The headlines had read: "Two Hot Mamas on the Trail of a Serial Killer." He was so proud of those two women. Glenda had been invited to give many interviews. She always insisted Aimee accompany her and gave Aimee the credit for finding the last clue that lead to the identity of the serial killer and for thinking up the netting trap that had snared Jim Drucker over the bed in the guest room.

Dave had taken all the footage captured on the Go-pros and had worked it with other footage into a special news feature. Winston heard that he might win a fancy award for it. And Kyle had been interviewed by one of his computer magazines for his ingenuity that helped capture the serial killer. They had showcased all his traps and gizmos and had paid him handsomely for the interview.

Winston rehearsed the opening lines of his speech.

"Tonight, is a night of celebration, giving thanks for good people, for their gifts of intelligence, of perseverance and bravery, and of their devotion and love for each other."

58 SINOPIA

A year had passed since Alice Grant's death. Friends and family held a vigil in her memory in Stony Plain on a Sunday afternoon. Both Glenda and Aimee attended. Later that evening, they held a private smudging ceremony with Josie, Winston and a few others, around the old dead tree and Winston's toolshed.

The next evening, when Glenda pulled into Aimee's driveway, to pick Connor up after work, her friend invited her to stay for supper. Both husbands were out of town, they planned a girl's night together. After dinner, they moved to the lower level of the house, to the family room for tea and cookies. The boys played at one end of the room while the women lounged on the sofa. They were both in reflective moods.

They discussed Jim Drucker. The details of his life had come out in follow-up news stories, as did the details of his death. Families of missing persons were contacting the authorities to find their loved ones. Conversely, the police had calls out to the public to identify still nameless victims.

The media circus went on for months. First, there was the story of the attack on the Brace and Ellis families, followed by his capture and his grisly death by suicide, and of the attack on his lifeless corpse by a murder of magpies, that took place when Officer Turner walked a hundred meters away, to get help from the two remaining RCMP officers at the Cardinal's home. A second gruesome detail emerged when Jim Drucker's home was searched and a cache of magpie feathers was found. The RCMP confiscated Helen Majeau's contact sheets and reviewed their own photographic files, searching for evidence of feathers planted on victims. They came up with more memento feathers than victims, leading them to suspect there were more bodies out there. Next came profiles of many of the victims, both male and female. Then the media turned the spotlight on Jim Drucker's childhood, discovering his name change from Gene Dzuik to Jim Drucker, and investigating his care with Child and Family Services.

Jim Drucker's truck, the one he called Daisy, yielded an inordinate amount of DNA material that was still being processed. DNA samples taken from his second, almost identical truck all belonged to him. When it was found, a few weeks after his death, it still contained his packed bag, counterfeit passport, a large sum of money and, incongruously, a last will and testament. He had left his drugstore to long-time employees and all his other worldly possessions to his cousin, Luna.

Aimee, who had had a rough childhood, felt that his treatment as a child was no excuse for how Jim Drucker had turned out. Glenda, who had done a lot of research on psychopaths, reminded her of the different brain wiring they had from the majority of society; that they did not feel the emotions most people feel and that they do not discern right from wrong. The whole personae of Jim Drucker, the friendly druggist who willingly helped anyone, had been a mask to enable him to survive in society.

They both felt for the victims and their families. Because so many had no voice, their murders had never been fully investigated. It was heartbreaking to know some of his victims were never missed and as devastating to know that people were searching for missing loved ones. Even to find out their sister, daughter, mother, wife or friend had died brutally was more closure than not knowing what had become of them.

Glenda felt the whole experience had made her more reserved, she felt herself keeping co-workers and new people at a distance. She laughed ruefully, this was the quality in her mother that she hated the most.

"What gift did you gain from the experience?" asked Aimee.

"I am much more confident that I can take care of myself and Connor," replied Glenda. "I may not have your physical prowess, but I learned I have other skills at my disposal. I am resourceful and I think fast on my feet and I can talk a good story, if need be. I mean, there is definitely evil in the world, in psychopaths like Jim Drucker. God help their victims. I hope I never meet another one. I find myself studying people more, searching for sincerity to make sure they aren't like him."

"There you go," said Aimee, "you are nothing like your mother, who, by the way, is a snob. She keeps her distance and silence around those that she thinks aren't up there in her class. You are just being less open and more careful of whom you let into your life."

"Of whom," laughed Glenda, "listen to you. You'll be drinking tea with Mother any day now."

Aimee joined in the laughter. "No, I'll stick to my own tea and the cookies I raid from my mom's freezer." They laughed some more.

"Okay, seriously, what did you learn from all of this, Aimee?"

"Well, I already knew I could whip anybody's butt, but I do still have the odd nightmare of being choked by that monster. I am so glad that he is dead." Aimee paused for a moment, then continued, "being physically fit is even more important to me, now. And I am more willing to ask for help with things than before. At first, I thought I was being weak. Then one time, Kyle said to me that it isn't weakness to ask for help, it was strength. Strength in knowing one's limitations and strength of conviction that you can expect help, that you are worthy of help from others. I have taken those words to heart. My community means more to me than ever before and I don't ever want to take someone for granted or the next day for granted. They are gifts to be treasured."

"Hmm," said Glenda, "I need more of that in my life." She took in a deep breath and let out a long sigh. They smiled at each other. "I guess the experience has tempered both of us, made us stronger, yet wiser." She reached over and took Aimee's hand for a moment, "we treasure those closest to us more than ever and we cast a wary eye on anyone trying to enter our circle."

Aimee chuckled, "remember Dad's speech, he tried to use every different word for clan, family, tribe, circle that he could think of?"

"He was ahead of us on this life's lesson."

"Yes, and he calls them life's gifts, not lessons," said Aimee. Then she changed the subject, "how are things going with your cook book?" she asked.

"Good, our viewers keep ordering more and more copies. The Journal did a spread on it just before Mother's Day and that brought in a lot of sales. The competition, Global TV, has asked me for an interview. That prompted my station to pre-empt them. This'll all happen next week. I am sure CBC will then want a piece for both radio and television. All of that will push sales till next Christmas," she answered. Then she added, "I'm being asked to consider a volume two."

"Glenda, that is so exciting, you'll have a whole new project on the go," exclaimed Aimee.

"Yep, time to accept the gifts of life and move on to new adventures," she answered her friend.

ABOUT THE AUTHOR

For over 30 years Jan Piers has called Edmonton, Alberta home, having moved there to follow a career path, recording and mixing sound for television and independent film productions. Very artistic, Jan's hobbies include photography, hiking, camping, gardening and concentrate mostly on art and writing. Published works include sound for film and television, publications in anthologies, local newspapers and "Chicken Soup for the Soul: Christmas in Canada." "Eye of the Magpie" is her first novel; Jan has already begun writing a second novel that also deals with strong women characters and has a third novel hazily forming at the back of her mind.

You can follow Jan at http://authorjanpiers.blog or on Instagram @ authorjanpiers or contact her at authorjanpiers@gmail.com.

The cover artwork is by Joelle Johnson. Joelle is a very talented tattoo artist from Saskatoon, Saskatchewan, she has loved art her whole life. Joelle enjoys working in everything from paints to pencils. She did the artwork for the cover of the "Eye of the Magpie" in watercolours. You can see more of her work @joelletattoo on Instagram.

Made in the USA
San Bernardino, CA
01 August 2018